Praise for Wesley
by
George

"Before I read *by George*, I was terrified of ventriloquist dummies. After reading this hilarious, loving, and strange novel, I am still scared of dummies, but that fear is now mixed with equal parts wonder. How does a ventriloquist dummy become a hero? How does any human become a hero? How can I learn how to write as well as Wesley Stace? Buy this novel now."
> — Sherman Alexie, author of the National Book
> Award–winning *The Absolutely True*
> *Diary of a Part-Time Indian*

"Stace reprises his mesmerizing, whimsical, neo-Dickensian story-telling, revealing himself to be one of the freshest fictional voices at work today. Indeed, *by George* delivers two fresh fictional voices for the price of one. . . . Stace both investigates and celebrates the art of ventriloquism while simultaneously lampooning every storyteller's dilemma: finding just the right voice in which to tell a story. . . . *By George* enthralls from its first page, with fanciful characters in oddball situations."
> — Skye K. Moody, *Seattle Times*

"A wonderfully witty and imaginative family saga. Stace weaves a compelling and highly readable tale with strongly realized main characters who are deeply sympathetic. It's the characters who pull the story along, and Stace's obvious affection for them makes them come to life on the page."
> — Natalie A. Luhrs, *Romantic Times*

"Compelling. . . . Wesley Stace nonchalantly mixes genres, voices, and prose styles from several centuries. . . . His vivid set pieces of life on the stage [are] convincing and enjoyable."
> — Wendy Smith, *Los Angeles Times*

"*By George* is one of those rare works of fiction with an essential triple helix — it's funny, it's clever, and it's perfectly woven together with story. If writing is how we imagine not being lonely, as Wesley Stace suggests, then his conjuring trick as a writer is that he brings a large crowd along with him."

— Colum McCann, author of *Zoli* and *Dancer*

"Don't call Wesley Stace a dummy. Every novel is a ventriloquist act. . . . In some books you can see the author's lips move; in others the actual speaker seems to vanish altogether. . . . Stace occasionally alerts the reader to his presence. . . . But these intrusions don't sour the spectacle. Some illusions delight even when you know how they're performed. . . . Stace is using [his] power for good; very good, in fact."

— Alexis Soloski, *Village Voice*

"An entertaining and daring work in which wooden dolls can bleed and break hearts. . . . An original and moving coming-of-age story." — Graham Joyce, *Washington Times*

"Mr. Stace, you are ruining my marriage. All week Lisa has not paid a whit of attention to her charming husband or her mewling toddler. I've cooked marvelous things and she has not noticed. I've mixed perfect martinis and she merely sips them absently. . . . Clearly you are an astonishing writer — we all knew this already — but did you have to bewitch my spouse? She finished it this morning and I was going to ask her to read something of mine, but that's just suicide after *by George,* so I'm suggesting that she read *War and Peace* so she can finally forget you. With bitter awe . . ." — Daniel Handler, author of *A Series of Unfortunate Events* by Lemony Snicket

"A rich Dickensian tale. . . . The reader is left both happy and moved." — Jonathan Ames, *New York Post*

by
George

ALSO BY WESLEY STACE

Misfortune

by George

A Novel

Wesley Stace

BACK BAY BOOKS
LITTLE, BROWN AND COMPANY
New York   Boston   London

Back Bay Books / Little, Brown and Company
Hachette Book Group USA
237 Park Avenue, New York, NY 10017
Visit our Web site at www.HachetteBookGroupUSA.com

Originally published in hardcover by Little, Brown and Company, August 2007
First Back Bay paperback edition, August 2008

Back Bay Books is an imprint of Little, Brown and Company. The Back Bay Books
name and logo are trademarks of Hachette Book Group USA, Inc.

Library of Congress Cataloging-in-Publication Data
Stace, Wesley.
  by George : a novel / Wesley Stace. — 1st ed.
    p. cm.
  ISBN 978-0-316-83032-4 (hc) / 978-0-316-01868-5 (pb)
  1. Boys — England — Fiction.   2. Ventriloquists — Fiction.   3. Mannequins
(Figures) — Fiction.   4. Family secrets — Fiction.   5. Diaries — Fiction.
6. England — Fiction.   I. Title.
  PR6119.T33B92 2007
  823'.92 — dc22   2006038194
                  10 9 8 7 6 5 4 3 2 1

RRD-IN

Printed in the United States of America

For Abbey

Imaginations, fantasies, illusions,
In which the things that cannot be take shape,
And seem to be, and for the moment are.

Henry Wadsworth Longfellow, from *Michael Angelo*

Ernie Wise: But I can see your lips moving!
Eric Morecambe: Well, of course you can, you fool.
   Because it's *me* who's doing it for *him*. He can't do it on
   his own: he's wood! That's my hand in there, you know!
Ernie: You're not supposed to move your lips. Ventrilo-
   quists don't move their lips. When the dummy talks, you
   keep your mouth shut.
Eric: Hello, Charlie. How are you? *(Dummy's mouth
   moves, but nothing emerges.)*
Ernie: He's not saying anything.
Eric: You told me to keep my mouth shut!
Ernie: You keep your mouth shut, but you still talk!
Eric: *(in disbelief)* How can you do that? *(to the audience)*
   He lives in a little dream world of his own!

Morecambe and Wise, from their stage show

Prologue

Ad Lib Till Ready

Half an hour later, George was on his knees in his bedroom, the door locked.

In front of him lay his second victim of the day, facedown, naked but for his trousers. The rest of the uniform — cap, white shirt, striped tie, forest green blazer — was scattered across the floor.

George had found him in the attic wrapped in a tartan blanket, just as Queenie had said, hidden in a turquoise valise beneath a tower of forgotten suitcases. Despite the pungent smell of camphor, frail silken threads clung to his blazer, the cuffs and the lapel of which were partly eaten away.

This boy weighed less than the other. George turned him over.

"Speak to me."

The tattooed date was where he expected, and there were tiny silver welts around the boy's heart: on closer inspection, pieces of embedded shot. George pulled the trousers down slowly. Whereas the other boy's legs had been entirely wood, elegantly hinged, these were different. Beneath each knee, a metal tube was attached with wire to the wooden thigh above and the shoe below.

"Sorry," George said as he took his pliers to the wire beneath the right knee. A leather shoe dangled from the bottom of the *newly amputated metal shin. He put the tube to his eye, telescope-style, but found his view blocked by something he couldn't shake from its hiding place. He coaxed the contents towards the opening with his little finger until he was able to pinch their top edge and pull them out. It was a rolled document, tied with string. George performed the same surgery on the left leg to find a matching manuscript, rolled tighter.*

At first, he simply stared. Then he undid the string on the first, expecting the pages to spring forth in celebration of their new freedom, but the brittle paper had been too long in confinement.

He unrolled the scroll from the right leg. On the first page was written "The Memoirs of George Fisher."

Discovered On

Finally, our number is up.

"Starting places, please! Number eighteen. Joe Fisher and George!"

The orchestra's crescendo becomes a climactic round of adoring applause as the Can Can Cadets high-kick past us into the wings. Their accompaniment drowned out, they stage-whisper through clenched smiles, "And a one, and a *two!* And a three . . ." Though long out of the sight lines, still they high-kick, the dopes, and I duck beneath a trailing leg, narrowly avoiding a splintered chin as I pretend to peek up a Cadet's skirt: no one notices.

The curtains sweep together; the stage is safe and the Can Can Cadets a distant memory, already walloping their way across town, sequined storm troopers bound for a late turn at the Alhambra.

We walk centre stage, as businesslike as it is possible for a man and his dummy to be. Props runs by with a chair; he positions the legs precisely upon the chalk crosses.

Our mark.

I love it when our number is up and the curtain is down. The stage is our world then, and everything works in harmony towards the beginning of the act. Hands scurry about, snatching up cardboard Tour Eiffel and Arc de Triomphe, gathering a stray ostrich feather here, a spangled jewel there, until all that lingers of the Cadets is the faint whiff of cheap perfume. A broom whisks away tinsel, sawdust, and the sweeper's own fag ash.

Then there is no scenery at all. The stage has never been emptier: just the two of us and, close by, a table with decanter, glass, and ashtray.

Am I ready? A cigarette! There isn't time.

Last-minute adjustments — the smoothing of my fringe, the primping of his bow tie, a moment's look of mutual admiration — as I hear, from the other side of the curtain, the chairman's introduction. We've sat here ten minutes in the past and listened to him stall, bullying the punters into ordering more, but tonight — and thank God, for I am in no mood for delay — there is the almost immediate bang of his gavel and whoosh of satin runners: "You want them! You deserve them! Joe Fisher and Gorgeous, Garrulous Geeeeeeeeee-orge!"

The curtains part. We are discovered on.

There is a hush in the stalls.

The moment is here. The moment when I come alive.

An audience knows that there is nothing better than a good ventriloquist show. To see a man and his dummy working in perfect synchronicity . . . yes, sir, that really is something. It makes adults of children and children of adults. That ventriloquist is not just an entertainer. He is breathing life into an inanimate object. He is making that inanimate object think and breathe and feel, and he is making people believe that the figure lives. The great ventriloquist is more than an illusionist; he is a creator, a dream maker, a kind of god.

And I should know: I'm his dummy.

Part One

Ventriloquism for Dummies

1

I Am Built

I shall now do a little ventriloquism of my own.

Whether I shall turn out to be the hero of my own life, or whether that station will be held by anybody else, these pages must show. To begin my life with the beginning of my life, I record that I was built (as I have been informed and believe) at Romando Theatrical Properties of Henley on Friday, the fifth of September, 1930.

That, at least, is the date tattooed on the inside of my chest in the specific form V/IX/30. I was made over a period of time: what was so special about the fifth of September? Was it when I was ordered, when the great artiste first conceived me, or when his minions started to mix my papier-mâché? Was it perhaps the moment I was taken from the mould, or even the date of the final stroke of his paintbrush on my flushed cheek? I don't precisely know.

One thing is certain: there was always something special about me. Whereas many of my Romando brothers were bought off the peg (for example, from Henridge's Magic Emporium on the Strand), I was different: I was *bespoke*. Ever since negotiations had commenced, I had been marked out, for I was commissioned by a star as great as my father was an artiste: the most famous ventriloquiste of the Golden Age — your own, your *very* own, Echo Endor.

Echo Endor and Narcissus — names to conjure with! Echo, whose famous scena "The Ocean Deep — A Vaudeville Fantasy" played all over the Continent, and Narcissus, Naughty Narcissus, the boy who captured the hearts of all: "Do you love me? You *know* you do!" No one had seen a boy partnered by a *woman:* only men had dared say such cheeky things.

Yet when Echo first swept into Romando Theatrical Properties, there was no Narcissus to place her. In person, she looked somewhat smaller and older than her public might have imagined. She never made any reference to her age, nor had since her thirty-ninth birthday, but she was fifty-one and had never been busier. If well prepared, she could pass, through opera glasses (which is how she was often seen), for twenty-five. (She readily gave Narcissus's age as thirteen, although he was thirty if he was a day, and shabby to prove it.)

Despite dramatic eyes, always emphasized by garish makeup, she was in many respects an average-looking woman: her voice alone announced the presence of a true star. She spoke with astonishing vigour and clarity of tone, a lip-reader's dream, sidling up to C's, attacking T's, caressing S's, rolling R's, and exploding P's. The clear voice was a family trait. Her father, Vox Knight, the beloved polyphonist, had employed the same ringing tone: the louder and more clearly *you* spoke, the more your voice was differentiated from the *other* voice, the voice that came from elsewhere, from up on the roof, from your boy's mouth. The greater the distinction, the better the illusion.

"I have come . . . ," she proclaimed, "for a Romando boy." She set about his name with an aggressive purr, a cat toying with a defeated mouse.

Even from the depths of his workshop, the great artiste recognized her voice immediately. Drying his hands on a towel, he untied his apron and, to the great surprise of his business manager (and lady wife), Nellie, popped his head into the reception room. Nothing ever distracted him from his work, but here he was, drawn by that siren sound.

"Miss Endor," he said. She was pleased to be recognized, but hardly surprised. "Romando, Joseph, at your service."

I was the boy she had come for — better call me *boy* than *doll* (a little girlish), *figure* (too formal), or *dummy* (for obvious reasons); *mannequin*, though preferable for its manliness, is archaic — so you can understand why perhaps I do not flatter myself in the assumption that especial care was taken in my creation. Deposit down — Nellie hardly thought one necessary, but Echo insisted — I was built.

The prime architect, the great artiste, was my father, the legendary Joseph Romando. There were great craftsmen before and many will follow, but to be a Romando boy is something special. Compare the dull and emotionless faces of my predecessors, Narcissus and his acned ilk, with mine, my fine soft skin tones, my stylish side parting, not to mention the flexible chamois leather that I call lips — tell me I wasn't sired by a kinder, cleverer man. My father made superior sons in every way. He sent his boys to the best schools — witness the splendid crests and mottoes on our forest green blazers — and gave us the most magnificent mops of hair, often worn beneath impishly tipped school caps. His brushes were more delicate, his sculpture more sensitive, and his mechanisms more innovative. But greater than any of this: he gave us each a personality. It was as though we had character before we met our partners: in some cases, sadly, more.

An account of my manufacture, however interesting, would unfortunately prove rather too technical: my genesis in paper regressed to its primordial state of pulp and ooze, my moulding and drying, my subsequent attachment to my spine (or "control stick"), and so forth. Much of this labour was entrusted to subordinates, but it was the maestro himself who, with his improbably skeletal and impossibly expressive fingers, pressed the papier-mâché mix (his own recipe) into the plaster mould, persuading it patiently into every nook and cranny, and then (fortified by one of Nellie's enormous breakfasts) prepared me in makeup. Given his painstaking methods, I wasn't able to leave the chair for the entire working day. Or the next day. But on the third, I was ready for my close-up.

Brandished by my spine, I was scrutinized in natural and institutional light. My kindly maker knew when to leave well enough alone, and as I sat drying in what I can only describe as a flowerpot, he gazed at me with an unearthly love. His eyes seemed to say: you are my perfect creation.

The day of my delivery was upon us.

I was placed on the ottoman that the great artiste regularly used to display his boys on first presentation. Only rarely did a customer feel the need to make any changes to the natural design. "His socks don't match," someone once said, pointing out what he considered an oversight. "No," replied the great artiste. "He has another pair just like it at home."

So there I sat, with my clashing socks and my beautiful mouth, lifeless yet brimming with potential. My father wrung his cap like a sponge; mine perched proudly atop my newly combed hair.

Nellie walked in behind Echo, who, barely a moment later, proclaimed: "Yes. Yes. Yes! I knew it." There was silence. "I knew it. The great Romando! A miracle child!" She loomed over me. "May I?"

"Miss Endor, of course," said my father. "Consider him yours now."

She picked me up, letting her finger fall across my lips, slipping her hand quickly into my back, feeling her way in the darkness. I was about to speak for the very first time.

And now . . .

And now . . .

But nothing.

She laid me back on the ottoman without particular care.

"The very boy I was looking for! Mr. Romando, to you I say," and she rather intoned, "many, many thanks." My father picked me up again, patting the back of my head. He was saying good-bye.

All three went back to the office, me in the arms of my maker, to sighs of mutual appreciation and nervous coughs that presaged the exchange of money.

"A delight!" said Echo. "Can you . . . ?" She waved her hands about.

"Of course, madam," said Nellie. "Romando prides itself on the best presentation box at no extra cost to the customer."

From behind the counter, my father lifted a plain but durable black box, with simple metal handle and engraved brass plate, an extra granted only to ventriloquial royalty. Upon it was written, *For Echo Endor*. And beneath this in the most florid of all scripts, *Romando Theatrical Properties of Henley*.

"I see," sang Echo. "How thoughtful."

"We can put the name you intend for him, but we weren't sure . . . ," said Nellie.

"No, quite, quite." Echo drummed her fingers next to the banknotes she had unfolded on the glass counter. "I'm afraid it's not for me at all. . . ."

"Not for you?" Disappointment sighed over Nellie's question. She had pictured an official endorsement on their new print advertisements: *Makers for Echo Endor*, the ventriloquial equivalent of *By Royal Appointment*. "We thought . . ."

Echo regarded her blankly. "For me? But I have Narcissus. You surely didn't think . . ." She laughed politely, more at the thought itself than at any presumption of Nellie's. "Our public wouldn't stand for it. For Echo Endor, there can be only one boy, for all time."

My father looked down at me, full of pride, as he massaged his beard. I was my own reward. He busied himself with the box, which didn't look big enough. He undid the two catches and lifted the hinged lid back, revealing the abyss within. *Don't put me in the box*, I thought, not for the last time.

"No, no," Echo continued. "This is a birthday present. For my son."

My father scooped my legs up beneath me and, bending me double, put them level with my ears, one foot on each shoulder.

Then, taking me by the middle, he placed me carefully in the opulently lined case, so that my hips were on the bottom of the box and the soles of my black leather shoes faced up. He swivelled my head to the left to avoid any damage to my nose and closed the lid. A key turned in the lock. Their voices were muffled.

"Your son?" said my father. "Does he dream of following in the magnificent footsteps of his grandfather and mother?"

"He will," said the ventriloquiste, "if I say so."

"Well, *this* boy has a name," said my father, handing her the key. "We name all our creations."

"Oh," said Echo without curiosity.

"Yes, they're all very much part of the family. This one we call . . ." I heard him quite clearly as he turned around to christen me. "George."

George. What a name! How manly! How noble! How *royal!* How easy to say without moving one's lips!

"Oh, no no no no, I think not," said Echo, to whom disagreement came easily. "We'll need something cheekier, something more suited to little children. I rather like . . ."

Whatever she said remained a mystery, for she spoke as my presentation box, hoisted by the handle, lurched upwards with a seasickening heave. Presently, I began to swing to and fro more agreeably. A small bright light shone in on me, illuminating a precise green keyhole on my blazer.

I was outside Romando's Theatrical Properties for the first time.

My journey had begun.

Fisher Goes to School

When he was eleven, George Fisher was sent away to school. It was September 1973.

The Fishers had not previously been great believers in a general education. The unusual step was forced upon them by the death of George's stepfather, Desmond Mitchell.

George had attended classes before, often with other backstage children, when itinerant teachers visited the theatre; there had been a casual relationship with a local day school, and two happy summer terms spent at a village school outside Bournemouth, where one of the two schoolmistresses taxied him into town for the evening performance. But he had never actually felt like a schoolboy, just a guest.

His mother, Frankie, was in constant work, and George could no longer tag along as he had when he was younger. He wasn't old enough to join the chorus, let alone to work on the piers, or young enough to play soldiers in the dressing room. With no Des around to ferry him to and from the lodgings, and since he could no longer live with Queenie and his great-grandma (who had taken a turn for the worse), there was nothing else for it: Upside School for Boys.

*   *   *

His mother, who had also to take the train to open three weeks as Peter Pan in Brighton, deposited him with his trunk at Charing Cross on a wet Tuesday morning. She was beside herself with happiness.

"All boys together — how exciting!" She was only slightly taller than he, and their bodies had roughly the same proportions. She surveyed the platforms for any sign of his travelling companions, who were identified, on the forecourt outside the station pub, by the forest green blazers that matched George's. "There they are! I know it'll be strange at first, Georgie, but soon it'll be midnight feasts with the first eleven and you won't even remember to write home at all!"

George was unconvinced by this rosy image.

"All on your own?" she asked briskly of the five matching boys, introducing herself, insisting they call her Frankie. It was the same voice she used when she asked the audience volunteers what they'd got for Christmas, and the boys were able to rustle up more than the mumbles with which they greeted the tired conversational gambits of other people's parents. Her blond hair was cropped short like theirs, as if to school regulation, and she shared the same toothy smile and freckles.

"Mr. Potter will be back any moment," said the tallest politely, indicating the pub over his shoulder where the Latin master was anaesthetizing himself against the coming term. George stood in the background, watching the train arrivals board click over, and wondered about the location of the announcer whose voice rattled through the station. He pictured a drab office and a grey employee who leaned forward at his desk to broadcast throughout his kingdom, cleared his throat before he turned on the microphone, and regretted to inform his subjects of the late running of the 11:42 to Orpington.

A bedraggled Mr. Potter emerged, sucking froth from the corners of a ginger moustache. He counted his charges with a cocked little finger. "Ah, you must be George Fisher and . . . ," as though she couldn't possibly be mature enough for motherhood, "*Mrs.* Fisher?" She was thirty-seven.

"Frankie Fisher, sir," she said, saluting confidently, *schoolboy* with a dash of *bonny lad at sea.*

"I say . . . ," said Mr. Potter, wondering whether the name rang a bell. "Well, we certainly hope to see a lot of you at Upside." Frankie secretly squeezed George's hand, to let him know that she was doing her utmost on his behalf. It was as if George could hear her thinking out loud, broadcasting like the station announcer: *I know it's going to be a success, I just know it!*

"Be brave, Georgie," she said, and then, turning to the assembled company: "You all be nice to him, mind, especially you, Mr. Potter. I'm holding you responsible."

"Keith," he said with an intimate smile, and then, waking from his dream, "Oh, my lord, look at the time! Campbell, get a porter. Come along, George." As he was shepherded to the train, George was determined not to look over his shoulder. Good-byes were best dealt with swiftly. "She's waving, Fisher!" said Mr. Potter as they boarded. George didn't turn around, thinking it better for both of them, particularly for her, so he didn't know — though he might have guessed — that she was singing softly, "Wish me luck as you wave me good-bye." They could have swapped places quite happily.

"Wave, boy!" said Mr. Potter, amused at George's reticence, assuming it was stiff upper lip that kept him from turning back, and expecting tears when he did. There were none. "That's better."

As the train sped from the station, George stared through the rain-streaked window. The dirty backs of the houses reminded him of the back of his teeth, never quite as well cleaned as the front, and he traced his tongue along his gums. With the flicker of film, these houses washed into drab towns and then rolling countryside. He knew the name of every station, every one en route to somewhere Frankie had played.

George had liked the idea of school ever since it had first been mooted. By the time of its initial tentative dangling, however, and unbeknownst to him, it was a fait accompli, so his enthusiasm had merely made things easier for his family. He had imagined that, an unknown new boy at school, he could become whoever he wanted, in the same way that Dick Whittington became mayor of London. Just like Frankie, he would take a trip to wardrobe, emerge with something fantastic in green, and charm his way to the top. His chosen costume box had been John Lewis; his chosen outfit, schoolboy. Unlike Dick Whittington, however, he was leaving London behind.

The other boys paraded new acquisitions. They more or less ignored the stranger, and George was quite content to look at the patterns of the rain on the window, twiddle his thumbs, and explore the inside of his mouth. The atmosphere changed only when Mr. Potter disappeared to the restaurant car with a telling "Well, I think I might . . . ," as though he had to excuse himself. Campbell, who had been left in charge, sniggered and made a mime of drinking, while his friend supplied the sound effect, before they burst out laughing. George looked up, and they stopped.

"George Fisher?" asked Campbell, the tallest, before checking pointedly: *"George?"* It was rather an old-fashioned name, attached only to the occasional grandfather or the author of an unread volume on a family bookshelf. A few footballers still flew the flag — Best, Armstrong — but these meant nothing to George. At Upside, he would find democratic Jonathans (Jontys), Nicks, Richards, and Edwards, but no other Hanoverian Georges.

"How old are you?" asked the smallest through his upturned nose.

"Eleven." He had to break his silence at some time.

"Where were you before?" asked Campbell.

"I wasn't."

"You weren't? You have to go to school," said a third.

"Yes, it's against the law not to!" said the piggy one officiously.

"I had teachers," said George defensively.

"Homeschooled!" scorned Campbell.

"What does your father do?" demanded George's other interrogator.

"Probably does the teaching," sniggered Campbell.

"I don't have a father."

This bizarre answer brought the cross-examination to a shuddering standstill, as though George had pulled the emergency chain. Finally, without alternative and in apology, Campbell was decent enough to enquire, "Is he dead?"

"Yes." George declined to say more. Sometimes he'd lie, claiming his father was alive, an astronaut, a politician, an explorer, whatever suited. But on this occasion, he just wanted to shut them up. They wanted to know how his father had died but couldn't ask.

"Well, your mum's all right," said Campbell, by way of conciliation, but the death had been an icy slap in the face of their fun, and they left the fatherless child alone for the rest of the journey.

This suited George. A tunnel squeezed the air against the train like the roar of applause.

"Say your prayers," the matron said unaffectionately as she switched off the light. The Fishers had never been keen Jesusists. They distrusted men generally, finding them unreliable and accident-prone: by and large, a weak lot. Jesus and His Father were no exceptions.

The dormitory felt like a hospital ward — the only place George had come across a matron before — and the association made him queasy. As he lay between rough sheets in that dark, thin dungeon of whining bedsprings, grumbling mattresses, foreign creaks, coughs, and groans, there was no hope of sleep. Gradually, Pope dormitory became contentedly quiet, a peace punctuated only by the rasp of floorboards in the corridor.

He tested himself with thoughts of home.

Des's death had left George the only male. There were plenty of women, however: his mother, Frankie, of course, as busy as she ever had been, and grandma, Queenie, always in charge. Even George's great-grandmother lingered on, though, at ninety-four, for how much longer nobody knew.

Evie, they all called her: she couldn't bear to be called *Great,* except in praise, and wasn't fond of *Grand.* She could no longer leave her bed, but despite her dilapidation, there was no doubt who was in control of the household. The strictness of her schedule was legendary. George knew exactly what she'd be doing at any given moment: when napping, when playing patience, when organizing her scrapbooks, when doing crosswords (always general knowledge), when playing a cantankerous game of Scrabble with Queenie, and when watching television. She didn't like *Coronation Street*, complained about it constantly, and never missed an episode.

Evie was inordinately proud of her first great-grandchild, allowing George, from the moment he had first twanged up and down in the baby bouncer set in her door frame, an inordinate amount of time in her bedroom. When he was old enough, she paid him the tribute of teaching him games as she had been taught: without mercy. If he put cards down and then changed his mind, it was too late — they stayed. If he had only one card, forgot to knock, and then won, the game was declared invalid: "There you are, then; that'll teach you, Georgie, losing to an old woman!"

Her hands had never been big enough to shuffle the two decks required for canasta, although she claimed to have been master of all the magical shuffles for one pack, numbering (according to her) seventeen. "It helps to be slight of hand," she had said many times. Such dexterity was now a memory — crippled by arthritis, she could barely hold the cards at all, although she was too vain to admit it. For her so-called silent shuffle, she used a specific table with a raised edge, called "the card table" (though this was the one thing it was specifically designed not to be), on which she spread the entire deck facedown. Then she simply muddled the cards with a flamboyant stirring before gathering them once more and strenuously battering them back into a pack. "The most honest shuffle of all," she proclaimed. "You can tell I'm not cheating." Who had mentioned cheating? And who would, unless they were considering it? He followed one card suspiciously as she spread the deck across the tabletop, and he saw the many opportunities. "Look, it's raining!" she remarked, but he didn't.

He lost to her at everything, not only canasta: pelmanism, Scrabble (she used outlandish words like *xu* and *qat*), and even, on one memorable occasion, darts. How had that happened? It had been his idea to set the board up at the bottom of the bed, and hers to play competitively. His only chance was Monopoly, a game she declared to be based entirely on luck and of no interest at all.

"I can't beat you at anything," he moaned.

"You'll beat me at life," she said, once more spreading the cards thinly over the oval mahogany table.

And as he lay in bed, he realized that his moment of victory might be upon him before too long. Perhaps that was why he was away at school. At half-term — a concept he already cherished — he would listen closer when she complained about *Coronation Street*.

In truth, George had inherited his love of Evie from his mother, for, although it was never mentioned in the family, between Queenie and her mother-in-law there was a simmering discontent. The matriarch ruled from her bed — there was still a Victorian bellpull, which rang imperiously to the kitchen — and Queenie fetched and carried with good grace, taking in trays, filling in crosswords, and changing the channel. Appreciation, however, was not given as freely as it might have been (dependence caused resentment), and though no unkind words were ever spoken, the strain sometimes showed. Frankie laughed it off with typical lack of concern — "Those two!" — but George worried that Evie would one day scratch too deep. He had seen Queenie in tears of frustration, tears she blamed on her blessed hay fever.

But this was a rare moment of vulnerability. Queenie (or "Mum," as almost everyone called her — as though they were addressing the Queen Mum herself) was solid. She had married into the Fisher family, survived her husband (who had died in his thirties in the last year of the war), and brought up their two daughters, Frankie and Sylvia, on her own. She was a large jolly woman, as unlike the female Fishers as a human could be engineered, with a plentiful bust (always entirely covered) and a stack of unmanageable chins. "They broke the mould when they made that one," said Evie, never short of a joke at anyone's expense. "Or *she* broke it trying to get out."

Whereas her mother-in-law and her daughters had dedicated their entire professional lives to show business, Queenie was no more than a talented amateur who found herself most comfortable entertaining at children's parties. She carried on the modest family business she had started with her husband in their corner of London. Children loved their Auntie Queenie. There was something daunting and matronly about her appearance and manner, but this made their joy even greater when the silliness began. She didn't need a script: she'd simply ask a child what he had for breakfast and she was off and running.

"Always in work, that one," Evie admitted with grudging admiration. The old woman paid for the big expenses, but it was these parties (including some rather poor magic tricks, no better than they needed to be) and the war pension that kept Queenie in pin money.

It was she who had taken George to John Lewis to buy the Upside uniform. This kind of errand always fell to her, for of all the Fisher women, she alone could be considered capable. On this expedition, George had the honour of brandishing the official checklist: one black overcoat *compulsory,* two *optional.*

"You already have a dark blue overcoat, Georgie. That will be good enough, I'm sure."

"I thought *compulsory* meant . . ."

"How many hankies?"

"Fifteen."

"Eh? Fifteen?" she asked in the tone of someone who is being overcharged for a pint of beer. "What does fifteen mean?"

"Fifteen means fifteen," interrupted a shop attendant, who peered down his nose through half glasses and brandished his tape measure. "Upside, is it? They're *notorious.* When they say fifteen, he'd better have fifteen. Nor am I sure that dark blue will be quite *good enough* at all."

Like all the Fisher women, Queenie had little sympathy for males over the age of eleven, and from time to time even George had started to wonder whether his grace period was drawing to a close. She could show terrific forbearance to the birthday boy who spilt ice cream on her lap, but not to a supercilious busybody masquerading as a haberdasher (her words).

"Madam!" said the John Lewis employee as he retreated behind the safety of his counter.

The new black trunk, on which George's name was emblazoned in black on sloping gold parallelograms, gradually filled to bursting. He closed it with some satisfaction and sat on it.

Completing the collection of Fisher females were George's mother and aunt. Evie's great favourite was Frankie: she treated her more as daughter than granddaughter, assuming rights that might have been presumed Queenie's, and because she could no longer support Frankie in person, she demanded firsthand news of every show — the size of the house, its reaction, Frankie's appraisal of her own performance — and these details she filed away with the reviews in her scrapbooks. Frankie was the family's great hope, and George had always been taught that nothing was to get in the way of his mother's career, including himself.

George was born to Frankie Fisher on November 6, 1961. Despite their surname, she had given him the middle name Jeremy, which reminded her of her father's voice, reading her to sleep. She idolized him, this man who, though a civilian, had died a war hero. He was gone when she was eight, and even then she hadn't seen him since she was five. She remembered his face only from photographs, but she could summon his voice whenever she wanted: "Once upon a time there was a frog called Mr. Jeremy Fisher; he lived in a little damp house amongst the buttercups at the edge of a pond. . . ."

Frankie never revealed the identity of George's real father. Queenie honoured her daughter's silence, partly because his identity was no great secret (and speaking his name aloud wasn't going to change anything) and partly because she felt the pregnancy her own fault. It was she who had introduced Frankie to the charming theatrical entrepreneur when he had taken such a special interest in her career. And then he was long gone, the damage done, and Frankie too proud to say anything. Frankie received the subsequent news of his death (a car-racing accident at Silverstone that made the front page of *The Express*) with indifference and never mentioned his name from that moment on. There was no criticism of her in the Fisher family, for such behaviour was hardly considered scandalous: Queenie had herself enjoyed a hastily arranged wedding on Frankie's account.

The Fisher women made sure that George had never felt himself lacking a father, so it was easy for him to proclaim the man dead, or alive and in any profession he fancied: there was something dashing in the Father of a Thousand Faces. He had pestered Queenie, of course — What was he like? What did he look like? How did Frankie and he meet? — questions she bore with good grace, since she knew Frankie would not want to be asked. It was the one thing George could never talk to his mother about. Only she could bring it up, and she never did. Queenie, the sole source of information, was as forthcoming as she could be: he had been a handsome man, a charming man, a married man. Finally, George managed to winkle his name out. He did some research in the library, where, thinking he was requesting another obituary, he found himself confronted with the front page of *The Express*, the grainy picture of a twisted wreck knotted in barrier rope, surrounded by oil drums and straw bales at the Abbey Curve. There was no sign of a human, as though the driver had vanished on impact. His father was long gone. George left the library immediately and told no one.

He would have happily considered Des a father, or stepfather, or even a father figure, but this was not encouraged — Des was simply Des: chauffeur, chaperone, and champion of all things Fisher. Frankie's longtime agent, he had bounded to her side when scandal became inevitable. They accepted him as the exception that proved the rule, a necessary evil. His had been a kindness, and for this Frankie thanked him with affection — his name was never heard without the prefixes Good and Old — but without passion. Des was Queenie's contemporary and could only manage avuncularity with Frankie. He patted her bottom, complimented her on her hair, and gave her pocket money to buy records. It wasn't unlike how he treated George. But now Good Old Des was gone: the family had lost their friendly chauffeur, and George was packed off to Upside.

This just left his aunt, Frankie's sister, Sylvia, six years her junior. With her long brown hair, her ruby red lips, and her deep, throaty laugh, she was as unlike Frankie as a sister could be, at home where Frankie seemed most out of place. She had had similar aspirations but never the same success. Evie hadn't offered this granddaughter an equal share of her support. Her reason? It didn't come so naturally to the girl. At Queenie's pleading, Evie had reluctantly agreed to make funds available for Sylvia to attend the Franca DeLay stage school, where Frankie had begun her career. It was something Sylvia laughed about years later. She had walked into the audition to find herself surrounded by framed lobby cards from films in which her sister, spotted in her first term at Franca DeLay's, had starred as a child. "And," said Sylvia, without a hint of malice, "they took one look at me next to this blond vision of innocence and said, 'You're *her* sister?' And it was all downhill from there, particularly when one of my tap shoes flew off." Evie had felt vindicated when the bad news landed on the doormat.

And Sylvia was sent instead to the Ashburton Drama School, where she was not spotted. In the years since, after some time on the fringe doing shows to which George was not invited and about which no great boasts were made over the dinner table, her crowning moment had been her casting as the girl in an instant-coffee commercial that was never shown and was subsequently remade with another woman in the same part. But Sylvia could always laugh at herself, and there was rarely a cup of coffee brewed in their house without reference to the catchphrase-that-never-was: "This is real, *right?*" (accompanied by a saucy wink at the camera). Frankie's career, meanwhile, went from strength to strength.

And then, three years ago, George and Frankie had been in Edinburgh, the year of her greatest pantomime triumph, and when they'd returned to Cadogan Grove, there was no Sylvia, just an empty kitchen. No reasons were given to George and nothing explained beyond the fact that there had been an argument. (Evie's "Must have been hard for her playing second fiddle" was the closest he ever got.) Sylvia's name came up every now and then and was quickly discarded, like a black three in canasta.

"Where's Auntie Sylvia?" he once asked Frankie.

"She has her own life now. Far away from us."

He got the message. He theorized that Sylvia could no longer stand the rivalry with his mother, and for this reason, he thought slightly less of her, for anyone in competition with his mother was destined to lose. But there was nothing he would like more than to be with his aunt right now, to hear her smoky laugh, to see her smile, however far away she lived: the farther the better.

He pictured the women of his family one by one: his mother, nearing the end of her night's performance; Evie, in bed, snoring in front of *The Good Old Days;* Queenie, clearing up the front room, perhaps recently returned from one of her parties; Sylvia, far away. By the time he thought of Des, wherever *he* was, George's thoughts were muddled. Dreams took over.

2

Love at First Sound

Although I can't say precisely when I was born, I can be most specific about the date I spoke for the first time: May 12, 1931.

I passed through at least two pairs of hands before my journey from Romando's was over. And when I landed, I waited and I waited, gestating in that dark wooden womb.

Nothing at all happened. Time passed. A clock chimed every thirty minutes. For months.

Finally, finally, tension began to build, as though an orchestra were tuning up. Then I distinctly heard *that voice:* "No, no, I say no! The guest of honour *must* sit here, oh, and I shall put the Romando . . ." My box was swooped through the air, a baby in an eagle's mouth. ". . . behind here." The best silver was laid under Echo's direction, as the hushed whispers of wary servants scurried above me. Just as it seemed that one more U-turn on the settings would drive them to murder her in cold blood, all was done, and Echo spoke with a new serenity. "There we are, thank you, thank you. Quite charming. The guests will start arriving any . . ."

With the chime of a doorbell, the party began: I was to be the main event. I was soon surrounded by merriment and spillage, by drinking, toasting, arguing, smoking, and throat clearing. A big moment was upon us. Crockery and cutlery clinked from my path as I was placed on the table. It was time.

I heard a woman's voice: "Hey, let me out of this box!" There was laughter. "Let me out of here! Give me to Joe!" Joe! Her son was called Joe! What a rum coincidence: my father Joseph, my partner Joe. It surely boded well.

"Echo, you'll give it away!" came a solitary complaint. "Let him see for himself!"

"Yes," sighed Echo. "They put the wrong name, *my* name, on the box. I believe they actually thought that I was going to replace Narcissus — ridiculous! We'll have that redone. Your name instead, Joey. Go on, then. Open it!"

Light poured in.

"Whatever is it, Joe? A treadle fretsaw?" some wag asked.

Joe said nothing. My feet tumbled beneath me as he lifted me by the shoulders and sat me on the edge of the box, the rest of the party behind me. Here he was — my partner, my ventriloquist; the straight man who would set me up for a million punch lines, repeat my jokes purely so people at the back could hear. I looked at him. He looked at me, but coldly, analytically, as though he had never wanted a boy to call his own. Shouldn't he have cracked a smile by now?

"Well?" asked Echo, somewhat impatiently. Still Joe held me in scrutiny. He was twenty or twenty-one but appeared older. His was an awfully good face, I told myself. That strong chin, that gleaming head of perfectly ploughed hair, those deep sad brown eyes! "Only the best, Joe," Echo continued, supplying the enthusiasm lacking in her son. "It's a Romando. They're the very finest, and Signore Romando was so honoured. I'm sure Ogilvy won't mind. Good lord, I've brought him enough business over the years. If I'd had a boy that good when I began . . ." She thought better of it. "Well, happy birthday."

"Say something, Joe," beseeched an earnest relative, mindful of Echo's moods.

In a lightning movement, Joe stood, put one foot on the chair, and picked me up, sitting me on his knee. He slipped one hand into my back and with the other gripped the lapel of his dinner jacket. What was he going to say? What was I going to say?

I surveyed our audience. It was as though someone had opened a tin, a party assortment of hard- and soft-centred guests, and scattered them about the room: a dependably jolly vicar, a trembling leaf of an old woman with perpetually quivering chin, a middle-aged impresario in bright yellow waistcoat, sucking the life out of a cigar, and, sitting at Echo's side, a dashingly handsome young male lead, not many years older than Joe. Rather than her son's friends, Echo had invited her own. All eyes were upon us.

The silence was broken by my first-ever words.

"Thank you for buying me for him, Mrs. Endor," I said, looking at her and nodding at Joe. "He's exactly what I've always wanted." This bon mot was met with laughter and applause. My top right lip sneered, and out popped a small white wooden cheroot. More applause. I smiled and raised my eyebrows. So far, so good.

"Res ipsa loquitur!" declared the vicar.

"I thought magic was his forte, Echo," said the yellow waistcoat with a guffaw. "Watch out! He'll be as good as you!"

Echo managed a smile. "Now, a *name!*" she said. The excitement of naming me raised eyebrows around the table.

"George," I said without hesitation. There was no doubt about it. A general cooing of approval confirmed the choice.

"*George?*" His mother grimaced. "That was what Romando named him. How did you know that? No one wants a schoolboy called George."

"George! That's my name," I said, winking at the assembled crowd, who took up my cause in a moment, claiming that such coincidences could not be easily dismissed, that I was every inch a George, and that it was still a very popular name.

"No." Echo pouted. "Take it from me. George is wrong. I was right about Narcissus and I'm right about this. You should call him . . ." She had the name ready. "Pip Squeak."

Pip Squeak? Pip bloody Squeak? It wasn't even a real name. Pip might conceivably be Dickensian for Philip, but Squeak? *Squeak?* I didn't sound like a mouse.

"Oh, that's too much," the vicar appealed to Echo. "Let the poor boy call him what he will."

The matinée idol to Echo's right began to repeat "George . . . George . . . George . . . George . . . ," a tribal chant taken up around the table until Echo begged them, pleaded with them to stop.

"No more! Derek, please! Please!" She covered her ears and sighed in an unsaintly display of martyrdom. "George it is . . . but don't blame me."

"Well done, child." The vicar beamed, a proud father congratulating an eight-year-old for offering the last boiled sweet to a guest. "A glimmer of charity remains despite the heathen name." Echo groaned at this obligatory jovialism.

"Heathen?" enquired Derek earnestly. "Echo?"

"No, no. *Endor,*" said the vicar, delighted to be asked, installing himself for a sermon. "Ventriloquism began, one might even say *found its voice,* in the biblical story of the Witch of Endor: 1 Samuel 28. 'And his servants said to Saul, Behold . . .'"

Echo yawned. "Cake!" she exclaimed. And in the cake was wheeled. Iced in large letters upon its vivid mint frosting was the unfortunate wish: "Happy 21st Birthday, to Joe and his new friend Pip Squeak."

"George," he said later that same evening, reflecting on the small victory with satisfaction as he placed me on his knee in front of the mirror in his bedroom.

It didn't seem the room of a young man about town, more a dark and dusty theatrical museum. Show posters, some tattered and some brand-new, papered every square inch of the walls not covered by bookshelves. Outcrops of books made little islands in the sea of blue carpet.

"Hello, Joe," I said. "Happy birthday."

"You're a handsome devil, aren't you?" I hadn't heard him use his own voice downstairs; he had spoken only through me. His seemed a little frail for his strong chin and evidently flexible vocal cords. Perhaps he needed me as much as, more than, I needed him.

"Why, thank you," I replied. "You're not too bad yourself." As I'd suspected, his technique was breathtaking: you couldn't tell. That aside, my voice was a marvel. The limitations of a mediocre ventriloquist dictate that he will, quite sensibly, choose as his partner either a drunken toff (because slurring is easier than enunciating) or a schoolboy with a high-pitched voice (because good voice production is daunting). But my voice was rich in tone: it was cheeky, yes, charming too (if I say so myself), and quite, quite clear. "Introductions, then. I'm George, as you know. How *did* you know my name was George?"

"How did I know your name was George?"

"Yes, how did you know my name was George?" Best to play along. This crackling rapid-fire dialogue, our two voices so perfectly distinct, was spellbinding.

"Receipt on the inside of the case." There it was. *George, sold to Echo Endor* with the date (and the price, of course — a snip too). "You're George; I'm Joe Fisher. I'm twenty-one today, and you're my present."

"My father was called Joseph," I said, keen to reignite the banter.

"I'm just Joe. I'm named after one of your forebears. The most famous of all."

I thought about this for a second before the penny dropped: "You're named after Coster Joe?" He nodded. "Your mother is Echo Endor and she named you after a ventriloquist dummy?"

Fred Russell and Coster Joe. I could see them as clear as day: Joe in his pearly gear with a voice that could cut glass, and Fred Russell, softly spoken, clean shaven, and immaculate in evening dress. The world had not seen their like when they walked onstage together at the Palace in 1886. Fred was the father of modern ventriloquism; their act was the Original. But still, you shouldn't name your son after a . . . dummy. "Well, look on the bright side: at least she didn't call you Naughty Narcissus."

At the mention of the name, his fingers slackened inside me.

"George, I have bad news." My head moved around slowly so I was facing him. "I don't want you." He didn't *what?* If it was a joke, he wasn't smiling. His eyes never left mine. "I don't want you," he repeated.

"But . . . but . . . ," I spluttered. "But you could be the greatest ventriloquist in the world. The technique, the lips, the manipulation: you've got it all."

We were interrupted by two loud knocks on the door, which (without invitation) opened to reveal Echo in oriental nightdress of tangerine and plum. She lifted her arms above her head, twirling like a human flame, before she came to rest, one hand on each side of the door. Joe snapped to attention, caught red-handed.

"Darling, you're already hard at work. What a wonderful, wonderful present. But I will say: don't be foolhardy. I always warn of the hazards of premature laryngeal overexertion." She floated in and kissed him, depositing an outsize aubergine smudge on his forehead, which she then rubbed distractedly with the heel of her right hand as she considered the furnishings. "Let's decorate!" she proclaimed, and with a final birthday wish, made her exit. The room breathed a sigh of relief.

"Is *that* why you don't want to be a ventriloquist?" I asked when the coast was clear.

"Who said I didn't want to be a ventriloquist? I'm going to be the greatest of all time."

At last! This was more like it. This was what we wanted.

"So you were only joking. You do want me."

"No, I don't."

"But if you want to be a ventriloquist, you need me. You need a boy. I'm the focal point. Everyone thinks the voice is coming from me. It's genius! Fred Russell and Coster Joe . . . Coram and Jerry Fisher . . ."

"Echo Endor and Nauseating Narcissus. I know."

"So what do you want if you don't want *me?*" Surely not a girl or some species of animal assistant. It was too perverse to contemplate. The audience would never stand for it.

"I don't want anything, George. You're a nice boy, but . . ." He paused. "The dummy is the death of ventriloquism." He was a good ventriloquist, and no mistake, but evidently something of a crackpot.

"The dummy *is* ventriloquism!" I snorted in disbelief.

"You might be forgiven for thinking that, George. Have you ever heard of my grandfather?"

"Vox Knight?"

"Yes."

"No. Never heard of him."

"Vox Knight didn't need a boy. He only needed a voice."

"A voice?"

"A lone voice. Oh!" Joe interrupted himself. "There's someone at the door."

As he pointed, I turned around. There was a little knock, followed by a muffled voice that I took to be Echo's, telling us to be quiet: "Practice tomorrow, darling. Bedtime for Jojo!"

"Shut up!" yelled Joe.

"Shh! Don't say that to your mother!" I begged, secretly impressed by his spunk.

"Mind your own business! Go back to Narcissus and Derek," said Joe, getting up and going towards the door. I accompanied him unwillingly, closing my eyes like the child who thinks no one can see him. As he threw the door open, I winced in the face of the impending confrontation. Nothing. Nobody was there.

"Where is she?" I said. He popped my head out, and I looked left and right down the hall.

"She was never there," he said, and smiled before announcing, "I'm going to be the greatest ventriloquist in the world."

"How did you do that?" I asked, narrowing my eyes as I checked the hall one final time.

"Distant-voice ventriloquism. I threw my voice."

"Out there?"

"Yes."

"From back there?"

"Yes."

I thought about it as he closed the door.

"It's good," I said, impressed. "What an act!" Then I remembered that the act excluded me. "So you're taking me back to Romando's?"

"I can't. You were a gift."

"I'm staying?" He nodded. "Can I stay out? Watch you practise? No need to put me back in the box, is there? Perhaps there's a way," I continued. "I mean, with the distant voice, and you, and me. If you . . ."

But there was no time to finish the thought. He had set me down on a burgundy armchair next to a pile of books. At eye level was *The Memoirs and Adventures of Mr Love the Celebrated Ventriloquist,* above it a hefty green volume called *The Adventures of Valentine Vox the Ventriloquist.*

Curiouser and curiouser.

I was Alice through the looking glass.

Fisher and the Secret Compartment

When he woke, surprised he had ever fallen asleep, George saw the extent to which he had been wedged into the other boys' lives. His blue cotton bedspread was like all the others, but only now did he notice how the bed itself was shoehorned into its space, jutting out under an eave at an angle, an embarrassment among all the parallel lines.

Matron was on the prowl, sniffing out any residual holiday behaviour, the legacy of lenient parents. She did not spare the new boy her litany of petty complaint, taking one look at the dark blue overcoat that lay at the top of his trunk and shaking her head. "Oh no, no, no. Oh dear, no. No. You're not getting away with that, my lad. It'll be a mighty cold winter without a coat."

He joined the herd on its way to the trough. The previous evening had been a disorientating blur, but now he was able to map the route downstairs; past the other dormitories (Shakespeare, Chaucer, Spenser, Dryden), through a hallway converted into a public changing room, past a library and a colourless corridor that could only lead to classrooms, down a flight of stairs, past an array of hanging roller skates (he had none), the room where everyone (except for him) kept his tuck box, and the board where the day's teams were displayed, the names of the chosen handwritten on disks dangling on hooks in formation. Many of those ahead of him were unable to resist the urge to finger these disks as they passed. George did not. Then down the corridor, newly painted boy-proof neutral, that led to the arch of the dining hall, past dressing rooms that returned a promising echo; on the left, the kitchens, from which wafted the unappetizing smell of burned fat (to the soundtrack of staccato bickering in an indistinguishable language); and as they drew nearer, official notice boards, drawing pins, gold letters, a display of crests, a list of scholarships, a billiard table. George was about to submit to breakfast with some relief when the line turned sharply right and snaked outside through a door flanked by two iron griffins.

"Griffins," said a pudgy oracle, who had been shadowing him. "Lion with the head of an eagle. Are you new?" Gravel crunched underneath George's shoes. The leaves had not quite started to fall. "I'm Nick. We're in the same class. . . . Morning walk," he added by way of explanation, looking as though he needed to exhale. He was simmering with this kind of helpful information and had to let off steam regularly. "Every morning. Down the driveway, past the building site for the new assembly hall, down to the conker trees, and back. Unless it's raining." Today there was only light drizzle. "Then you do a lap of the Green Court and say good morning to the headmaster."

This moment assumed ever-increasing importance after the turn at the trees. George practised in his head, hoping to chance upon the perfect tone. Nick, sensing this nervous rehearsal, was happy to play the old hand. "Just don't say 'Good morning, Swish!' That's his nickname, Swish. It's the sound of . . ." Nick took great pleasure from a deft flick of his wrist. Canes had loomed large in George's vision of Upside. Aside from Frankie's quaint visions, he had gleaned his entire knowledge of such schools from books (*Tom Brown's Schooldays* and Dotheboys Hall in *Nicholas Nickleby*) and television (*Billy Bunter and Whack-O!*). "But it's his initials too," continued the talking almanac. "Stewart W. S. Hartley. You see? Swish." He repeated his sadistic mime. "You don't *say* much, do you?" The group ahead of them extended satirically enthusiastic greetings to Hartley, who, framed by an oak portico beneath a Tudor arch, rocked back and forth on his heels and banged a pipe against his palm.

"Morning, sir," chirped Nick.

The head nodded, regarding the clouds suspiciously. He was a large bear of a man with well-padded hands and a scarcely controlled black and grey beard that he stroked as he inspected the heavens. Though thinner than Giant Haystacks, the wrestler, and more urbane than Grizzly Adams, he had something of the wild man about him. George felt himself about to speak, but he found himself lost in his options, and nothing emerged.

"Mr. Fisher, I presume," boomed Hartley.

"Yes," George said, taken aback, and stopped, conscious of the obstacle he presented to the group behind.

"Just walk around," said the head impatiently. He seemed about to pass judgement either on George, the weather, the school, or life in general. "Fisher, it's time to sample the delights of your first Upside breakfast. It could be kedgeree, a kipper, porridge. Will you rise to the challenge?" He was unexpectedly jolly, almost a bearded pantomime dame.

"What's kedgeree?"

"That, Fisher, is the six-million-dollar question. In you go." The interview at an end, Hartley transferred his attentions to those behind. "Good morning . . . Good morning . . . Tuck your shirt in . . . Morning . . . Haircut . . ."

The dining room, overseen by the stern, knowing eyes of ancestral headmasters, echoed to shuffling feet and screeching chairs. A moment's silence was replaced by an unenthusiastic mumbling, culminating in a reverberant Amen, which in turn became the clanking of plates and the chatter of the breakfast table.

At the top of George's table sat a large naval type, whom someone made the grave error of addressing as Mr. Poole. This impertinence was corrected: *Commander* Poole. The main event was a charred sausage accompanied by either a golden piece of fried bread, happy entire or in small crumbs, or pre-buttered toast. George imagined the cursory swipes of a knife that eked out one portion of butter over ten slices of toast, leaving the last few dry. At home, butter was spread as extravagantly as conversation: only thick enough when accurate dental records could be taken from the impression of your incisors. Every last inch of surface area was covered, to save having to butter the crusts separately.

According to Captain Bird's Eye, who littered his speech with cryptic nautical jargon, whatever anyone did at the table was wrong. Tentative attempts at conversation were constantly interrupted; the offender had taken too much or too little, taken it with the wrong implement, or with the right implement but in the wrong way; he was swinging in his chair, leaning in his chair, not sitting with his back straight, or sitting with his back too straight in a way that mocked the previous command; he poured the tea either too quickly ("It's splashing"), too slowly ("Don't make a meal of it"), or too carelessly ("It's going everywhere!"); most grievously, if he managed to start eating, he was talking with his mouth full, and no one wanted to know what he was having for breakfast. It was impossible to predict what would be right and what wrong. The tea was hot: was it best to leave it till it cooled ("Don't let it get cold, boy") or drink it while it was hot ("Be careful, you'll scald yourself")? The drinking was equally fraught with hazard; they were lectured if they slurped, sipped, or swilled, for which offences they were variously threatened with the plank, swabbing the decks, or, most vituperatively, the cat.

This onslaught was unlike any communication George had experienced between human beings in the real world. Frankie never told George off; she never told anyone off for anything. This task sometimes fell to Queenie, who offered rebuke in such a kindly way that it seemed only a heedless repetition of the offence would constitute a true sin. George had been ordered out of the way by brusque stage managers, but backstage was their world, all their tuttings in the greater service of the show. His mother had represented school as a paradise for boys, a playground for equals, for so it was in her dreams; by the end of the meal, George had realized that school was a Neverland for teachers only. Grace came as a relief.

"For what we have just received," muttered the boy next to him, "may the Lord be truly grateful. Amen." That didn't seem right.

There was a second shock that morning: his name had been changed. The Fishers had been mystified by the suffix "mi" on the name labels that his mother, whiling hours away in various shades of green room, had shown surprising willingness in sewing onto every item of clothing bound for the large black trunk. This job, which would once have fallen to Sylvia, should have been Queenie's, but Frankie, who had bought a thimble especially, insisted. "Mi? A name I call myself?" was as far as Frankie got. At roll call before morning assembly, George understood. He had a namesake at Upside, older, more experienced, bigger. He was no longer George Fisher, he was Fisher Minor. "Yes, sir," said George, reluctantly acknowledging the diminutive.

In his beginning-of-term address, the headmaster expatiated on the school motto, *Vincit Veritas*. "'Honesty is the best policy'? 'The truth will out'? No. These are attractive but loose translations which Mr. Cope," he nodded towards a chalky gown, "would rightly deplore. 'Truth Conquers.' Truth is the beginning of every good to the gods and of every good to man." He then regaled the shuffling assembly with an anecdote about Plato, before the introduction of the school song: "There'll Always Be an Upside."

George said nothing during the first two classes. His arrival threw things out for the school photo at break: there wasn't room in the back row with his contemporaries, and he had to sit cross-legged at the front with the other newcomers, most of whom were four years younger, teachers breathing down his neck from the row behind.

That night George dashed off a quick postcard to his mother c/o The Stage Door, Palace Theatre, Brighton. "It's quite strange here, but I'll get used to it." He didn't want her to worry. "They changed my name to Fisher Minor. Love, Georgie." A week later, his name was called after lunch: he had a letter. It was a faded, crinkle-edged postcard of the West Pier in all its dated, shabby splendour. "Dear Fisher Minor, I am so happy for you. I wish someone would call me that, but then we'd get muddled. With love from your always loving Frankie (Fisher Mater)."

School was a new world with unimagined customs and codes, where maps had no keys, rituals no explanations. A few of the natives reluctantly offered help, but most paraded the exclusivism of their fellowship, its in-jokes and its private language, and laughed at George's pidgin attempts to be accepted. They had all learned together, three years previously, and they weren't going to make it easy for any Johnny-come-lately. Anyone overeager to offer himself as Man Friday obviously had his own reasons for doing so: Nick was unpopular — the physical attributes of a griffin weren't all he didn't know you knew. Even when you thought you'd got rid of him, he lingered, like something you'd stepped in.

For the first few days, lessons proved a relief from the harder work of fitting in. What had the others learned until the age of eleven? Only an ability to read and write was taken for granted. Basic general knowledge allowed George to participate in most subjects: from History, which dawned with Henry VII; and Geography, mainly concerning clouds; to the irrelevancies of Scripture; and Latin's dark, incomprehensible code (apparently pointless beyond its illumination of well-known words and phrases: *Et tu, Brute?*, *Quo Vadis?*, *Per diem*, *Status Quo*, and *Exeunt*). Of equations and chemical formulae he knew nothing, but these they seemed to be learning together for the first time.

George had imagined that his many skills would be useful. He spoke a little French, knew a theatre outside and in, had a comprehensive knowledge of lighting gels, loved to read (anything), could catnap at the drop of a hat in almost any position, was an accomplished maker of all kinds of beverages (hot brews for the throat, cold cocktails for the after-show), and could busk unselfconsciously on the piano and recite any number of the monologues that were common Fisher currency; but none of these were on the Upside timetable or uppermost in the minds of its pupils. George knew nothing of anything that was, neither *Top of the Pops* nor the in-swinging corner, and liked neither the look nor smell of compulsory games. To everyone else, the midafternoon was a joyful respite from the rest of the day, but to George it was a miserable trudge in a damp shirt. His classmates treated him with suspicion: they did not like a boy happy in his own company, and they let George know this in many predictable ways, all apparently quite acceptable in the eyes of the staff.

One thing was clear: there was no room at Upside for pleasure. Of those things he considered luxurious (sweets, comics, television), none was allowed. The one pleasure that remained was reading, but even this was discouraged. The school did not advocate use of the library, at least not to read a book; it was the venue for detention — this summed up the general attitude to literature. An imported novel had to be vetted by the headmaster, who (after an agonizing day or two — he was in no particular rush) returned it outside his office with his initials scrawled inside the front cover. George, whose family had encouraged an early graduation to grown-up fiction, was in the grip of *The Ministry of Fear* by Graham Greene. The English teacher, Mr. Burgh, a petite yet pugnacious northerner who, despite his drowsy mole-like features, was always spoiling for a fight, proclaimed it too grown-up and recommended the works of Arthur Ransome, Frank Richards, and Captain W. E. Johns.

Sundays were particularly unusual. Despite the absence of God and His relations from the Fisher pantheon, the sabbath remained sacred: a late rising, a long lunch, the full works cooked by Queenie, always followed by the washing up (from which Des excused himself, absconding to the bathroom with the newspaper); then a lazy afternoon, the centrepiece a matinée, as dictated by the BBC schedule. *The League of Gentlemen, The Court Jester, The Last of the Mohicans, Roman Scandals,* any number of Sherlock Holmes — he loved them all, sat next to Evie, whose job it was, *Radio Times* and magnifying glass at hand, to alert him to the identity of every actor, outline his previous experience, and then rack her fading memory to recall where she had seen him most recently, while George struggled to pay attention to the movie and humour her in equal measure.

He had known he wouldn't be going home on Sundays, but not that everybody else would. Only the most foreign, the strangest, did not spend Sundays with their own families. Homegoers could take pity on the forlorn and offer an invitation — but term was too young for such generosity, besides which George did not yet register on the meter of popularity.

He watched from Pope as matching parents in a vast range of Rovers reunited with their spawn. He surveyed the Barbour-jacketed fathers, all identical, and the mothers, in whom there was allowed slightly more (but very little) variation. George couldn't produce anyone like this to pick him up, nor could his family have produced anything to pick him up in — only Des had owned a car: no Fisher could drive. The tardiest of the parents arrived, and the last of their sons disappeared; peace reigned in the driveway, and the long Sunday ground remorselessly on.

George's day was spent with a motley assortment of his fellow deserted, which included a Lebanese boy who could barely speak English, an Indian whose parents must have been uncommonly generous benefactors to Upside, for their son was all but retarded, and younger English twins whose widowed father lived in America. Mr. Potter let it be known that their resentment at having to stay at Upside was nothing compared to his own. The weather was considerately mediocre, prohibiting sports, so they spent most of the day inside, playing games and, miraculously, watching television, which showed nothing but religious and farming programmes until the matinée finally began. In sympathy, food and sweets were handed out to these orphans with a freer hand. The day trudged on.

"Can I go to the library, sir?" asked George wearily.

"Why?"

"To look at the books."

"Take the twins with you."

George could locate none of his recent favourites — no Greene, no Ambler, no MacLean — not that anything was in order, the shelves bowed by books with grimly coloured spines, each with a little picture below the title. Tatty how-to books harkened to a bygone time when schoolboys habitually boasted a healthy interest in genealogy, knots, and the avid collection of postage stamps or birds' eggs. The extant novels were similarly dated and unpromising, tales of child detectives, adventurous airmen, courageous pets, and fat, unwilling schoolboy skivers. There was a vast preponderance of heavily abridged versions of the classics (ruined for children), volume upon volume of bowdlerized Greek myth, and nothing at all to interest Tweedledum and Tweedledee.

"Hadn't we better be getting back?" said one.

"Yes, hadn't we?" agreed the other.

It was still only early afternoon.

At 6:30 those who had enjoyed shore leave returned in time for evening chapel, full of boasts, happy and spoilt. Many had done no more than watch television, like the abandoned, but they had done it in their homes, with their pets, with their parents, surrounded by their toys, eating their homemade fudge.

George stood in line and waited for roll call.

"Fisher Minor?"

"Yes, sir."

Another Sunday with the lepers was best avoided. But his family certainly wasn't coming to pick him up. Queenie getting Evie out of bed and into a train, and pushing her wheelchair down the drive, furs flapping round their necks — it didn't seem likely. George knew to avoid becoming too friendly with the Sunday colony, in case he too came to wear their mark. But what was the alternative?

He spent the next few days in a conscious effort to make himself available for somebody else's family, a would-be evacuee standing on tiptoe, looking his smartest; but he was ignored. It was time to be noticed — what did he know that they didn't?

On Thursday evening, lights-out was, as usual, the signal for dutiful noise. The participants called themselves the Blackout Society, the name of which, supposedly handed down through generations of insomniac Papists, styled its members outlaws, though its rules were as unprogressive as a St. James club. George, whose preferred illicit pleasure had been to read under the covers by the light of a key-ring torch, had by no means yet put himself forward, let alone found a sponsor.

This evening, the members of the Blackout Society were reduced to telling the most frightening stories they knew. George had heard these tired tales from countless stagehands. It was time to up the ante.

"I've got one," he piped up. There was a giggle.

"Is that you, Fisher? Are you a member of the Blackout Society?" Campbell was the secretary, a job he was pleased to take quite seriously. "Your initiation is to tell a ghost story. Do you have one?"

George cleared his throat. "It's called 'The Green Eye of the Little Yellow God.'"

"Little? Yellow?" Someone sniffed.

"Shh!" said Campbell, encouraging a fair trial. There was silence. Recitation was one of the many ways that George and Queenie passed the time when it was just the two of them. Every Fisher knew "The Green Eye" by heart, and each gave it her own twist. George leaned up on his elbow and intoned, "'The Green Eye of the Little Yellow God.'"

"Get on with it, then."

And George began: "'There's a one-eyed yellow idol to the north of Khatmandu, / There's a little marble cross below the town; / There's a broken-hearted woman tends the grave . . .'" He took it slowly, seriously, mysteriously, his voice assuming a slightly metallic tone in imitation of Evie, the source of all monologues.

"Boring!" said someone.

"Shh!"

"'There's a broken-hearted woman tends the grave of Mad Carew, / And the yellow god forever gazes down.'"

"Was he a Chink?" squeaked a voice, but hecklers were nothing to the Fishers. As he continued, the dormitory slowly surrendered. Initially, they were enthralled rather by the medium than the tale — the urgency in George's voice, the gathering pace, the dramatic pause, the relished word that darted at them from the shadows. By the time Carew "returned before the dawn, with his shirt and tunic torn, / And a gash across his temple dripping red," there was a deathly hush. To maximize the drama, George crept from his bed and stole around the room, so his voice seemed to float in the darkness. As he brought the story to its chilling conclusion, he could hold himself back no longer: "'His door was open wide with silver moonlight shining through; / The place was wet and slipp'ry where she trod —'"

He was on the point of a thunderous climax when, accompanied by a roar of anger, the room was suddenly flooded with harsh light. A dormitory of blinking eyes focused on Commander Poole. Everyone was in bed except George, poised midstab over an imaginary corpse.

"Fisher? What the *hell* do you think you're doing?" Swearing was rare, serious.

"Telling a story, sir."

"He was, sir," agreed those who dared.

"I don't care if you were stealing the Crown bloody Jewels. Get back in your hammock or I'll have you keelhauled." He left, then returned with his verdict: "And you can finish the story in detention tomorrow afternoon."

George got back into bed, happier about the punishment than he should have been. When it was certain that the commander had returned to his cabin, a timid voice whispered, "Fisher . . . Fisher . . ."

"Shh! He'll hear" came another.

"Fisher. What happens?" asked Campbell.

George didn't answer. He'd had them in the palm of his hand.

The next morning, the commander was spotted in conference with the headmaster. George, who had until now been unable to see a downside, was instantly struck by the fear that his *performance* was the subject of their conversation. The headmaster looked directly at him, and George's stomach fluttered. He couldn't even speak to Pigling and Campbell, who were more interested in George's point of view than at any time since his arrival ten days ago. His worst fears were confirmed at the end of assembly: "Fisher Minor. At break. My office."

Classes went by too quickly and too slowly at the same time. Someone whispered "Good luck"; this made him feel even worse than Nick's reprise of his flicking wrist mime, now with added relish. Legend had it that one boy had been thrashed severely and then charged for the resulting broken cane. Whack-O.

"Come!" thundered Hartley from the depths of his cave. George entered the book-lined room, a campfire of tobacco smoke, and speculated as to the fearful chair.

"Fisher! Delightful." It was as if the headmaster enjoyed meting out punishment. "News, Fisher, news!" He brandished a letter. "An unexpected visitor!" He looked through thick-rimmed glasses. George didn't answer. "Your grandmother has asked permission to visit you tomorrow, Saturday, bringing with her a tuck box and an overcoat. And I am inclined to grant that permission."

"Thank you." George felt blissful, if a little faint; it was the headiness of the fumes and the news combined. Queenie. No thrashing.

"This will *unfortunately* spare you games. Well? Be off with you, then! Oh, one more thing . . . 'The Green Eye of the Little Yellow God'?" George didn't commit himself. "Wonderful stuff! 'An ugly knife lay buried in the heart of Mad Carew.' And how about 'They speak of a dead man's vengeance'?"

" 'The Pigtail of Li-Fang-Fu.' "

"Wonderful. Wonderful." It seemed as if they were just about to head off on a picnic together when the head's mood abruptly changed: "But not after lights-out. Best do your detention and recite 'The Green Eye' at Talent Night."

"Sorry, sir." Queenie was coming!

"And one more thing," said his unlikely champion. "Only you and I know what has passed in this room. Sometimes boys have pretended to be caned to gain the respect of their peers."

"Oh, I would never . . ."

"Feel free, Fisher, feel free. Have you ever tried public speaking, oratory, debate? Just a thought. Bear it in mind. Away." The headmaster returned to a volume of Robert Benchley. As George reached the main corridor, he felt light as air. He slowed down, however, mindful to move a little less freely.

Of the many shocks that school had offered, the greatest were the lack of privacy (some of the toilets were doorless) and the overabundance of masculinity. As far as he could tell, there were more women in his immediate family than there were on the entire school grounds. From the row of chestnuts that separated them from whatever civilization lay beyond, to the metal fence at the bottom of the great lawn, on which boys perched crowlike, gazing wistfully at nothing in particular, they were almost exclusively male. The thin-lipped, flat-chested matron, Mrs. True, who derived pleasure only from wielding her scalpel on verrucas and cutting toenails too close to the skin, offered as little mothering as she could manage. Her junior assistant, Miss Hutchinson, could show no evidence of humanity in front of her superior. Of the rest, the music teacher was full of smiles but rarely seen, for Upside attached no particular importance to the activity, and the headmaster's wife was not ideally suited to being around small children, for fear that she would crush them. There was a rumour that the Spanish who ran the kitchens had a daughter, but this was unsubstantiated.

So when Queenie came the next day, driven in an old grey Bentley by a man George recognized and knew as Reg (clearly costumed, rather than uniformed, as a chauffeur), it wasn't the generosity of her affection that made George cry, or the gifts she had brought, or the fact that her visit spared him the daily competitive mud bath: it was being so close to a woman. When she pressed his head into her cavernous cleavage, he couldn't stop himself. He pretended he wasn't crying, as did she.

George was unaware that the headmaster had recently written to the Fishers, suggesting that this unorthodox visit might be beneficial for the recent arrival, who was not mixing with the other boys as hoped, nor making his presence felt in the classroom, nor speaking much at all. The letter had also advocated a black overcoat, which might help the boy's integration, and the purchase of a tuck box: privacy built confidence.

Reg walked around the motor. George considered him from the bench on the grass ridge where he sat with Queenie. He had previously wondered why this perenially unoccupied bench was there at all. Now he knew it had been waiting for him.

"You know Reg," she said to George, tutting with amusement at her chauffeur's humming of the *Billy Bunter* theme. "Don't know what I'd have done without the lift. He made it quite the outing." She gave him the latest on Fisher matters: Evie sent her love but wasn't doing well, Frankie was sold out every night, and the Variety Club had moved to name a Children's Awayday van after Des. Everything made George sad.

They watched a mess of dots running around in a distant haze to the ghostly echo of whistles and yells.

"Look at them playing rugby," said Queenie.

"It's football."

"How can you tell?"

"They're not picking it up."

"Which reminds me . . ." From her handbag, Queenie took out a stack of flat items (postcards, notes, cut-out shopping coupons, unfinished crosswords) secured with a rubber band, which she put around her wrist for safekeeping, and flicked through until she found what she was looking for. "She listened to the radio and wrote in all the football scores for you as they came through." George unfolded the newspaper cutting, where Evie had filled in the goals, when she could quite easily have cut out the official version the next day. And why did she suddenly think he wanted football results? Had she forgotten him in a week? Then he saw the trouble she had taken. Every number, every goal scored by every team, was the labour of her spindly arthritic hand; he remembered the way the Bic biro perched awkwardly, how it hurt her to press hard on the page. When he cried this time, he couldn't pretend he wasn't. So Queenie held him close, a dead fox's glass eye poking into his cheek.

"Shall we go out for tea?" she asked.

"I don't think we can."

"Think again," she said. "Queenie's here."

She got up, made a comment as she passed Reg, and marched through the front door with the confidence of the school chairman. Reg bowed and clicked his heels rather unnecessarily, before huffing his breath on the Bentley emblem, polishing it with a rag, and smiling mischievously at George as though they were both in on a big joke.

While they waited, Reg continued his charade of chauffeury, which involved taking the tyres' pulse. George hadn't been overjoyed to see him. For some reason, this apparently benevolent but slightly comical man, whose wide mouth, inappropriately small nose, and somewhat protruding eyes had always brought to mind a Muppet, was a controversial figure among the Fishers.

Reg was a driver by trade, no mystery there — although not generally in uniform or with this sort of motor at his disposal. George knew (though he didn't know whether he was supposed to) that Reg sometimes drove Queenie to and from her parties, but she never had him pick her up at the front door, nor was the lift referred to again. George would gloss over the unexpected cameo in his next letter home, where the mere mention of Reg's name spelled trouble, a frosty silence, once even a harsh snort of "That criminal!" Evie *never wanted to hear his name again,* Frankie thought him *not so bad really,* and Queenie simply didn't mention him.

"Evie? Oh, he's not her favourite," she once said with a shrug, after patiently explaining that it was best not to mention that they'd bumped into him at the market. George and Reg had never actually been introduced, though Queenie always casually said, "Oh, you know Reg," as though introductions weren't, had never been, necessary.

When Frankie teased Queenie — "I know who you were out with today, and wouldn't *she* like to?" — Queenie threw her a look and said pertly, "That's not funny. I was out with Georgie, wasn't I, Georgie?" George nodded but widened his eyes. He didn't like to lie to his mother.

Foot on the back fender, the chauffeur had momentarily fallen out of character. He'd removed his cap, revealing greasy black hair that looked a relic of the rock 'n' roll years, and was exploring his gums with a toothpick. When the Muppet saw Queenie emerge from the portico, he snapped to attention, flicking the toothpick into a hedge.

"I have, in my hands, a piece of paper," proclaimed Queenie grandly as she strode towards them. In fact, there were two. One was a chit allowing them to go for tea, the other directions to Mrs. Cakebread's Tea Shop.

"You call 'em out," said Reg, "and I'll do me best."

George would ideally have done without Reg, who came in and ate with them, but could allow nothing to dampen the festivity of the occasion. The only bad thing was that it would soon be over. To compensate, George ate with a hysterical appetite, cramming down scones and flapjacks. Queenie laughed. "Don't they feed you there?"

"The food's not bad, actually." He was in a mood to be generous to Upside, to make his family feel better.

Before it was time to leave, he and Queenie sat on the bench again while Reg kept a self-consciously low profile. A stream of shivering boys passed them on their way to the showers.

"He looks a nice lad," she said, randomly waving at a muddy straggler. "Have you made any friends?"

"Not really."

"Are you talking much to the others?" He shook his head. "It's hard at first, George. But it gets better. Oh, we have a present for you." He smiled without feeling like smiling, creasing each side of his mouth outwards while the rest of his face frowned.

"Reg!" she called. He carried up a wooden tuck box with George's name painted on it like the credits on an old adventure movie.

"Jimmy Props made it," said Queenie, "and there's a treat too. Open it." Within, there was a dense mass of dark material. "Oh, don't worry about that. You have to have that. It's a black overcoat. There's something else. Look." Overcoat removed, the box was empty except for a shelf on the right with two smaller compartments. "Something special from Frankie and Evie."

"I can't see anything."

"Let me put it this way: you're allowed to have a tuck box, but you aren't allowed to lock it."

"Somebody brought back a tortoise and it died."

"But we didn't think that was terribly private. So if you look closely, you'll find there's somewhere else in there, to keep things."

"A secret drawer?"

"I'll say no more."

"What if I can't find it?"

"Write and I'll give you a clue."

Reg, Queenie, and George walked the tuck box into the school, right through the front door, and into the tuck box room, where he had previously had no reason to go. All the other boxes were shop-bought, in dark blues and greens like the endpapers of old books. His stood out, in a good way: handmade, unpainted, new.

As they walked back to the car, Queenie commanded Reg brusquely, "Open the door, then."

"Ooh, sorry, ma'am!" said Reg and winked at George. Regally, Queenie flicked the fox once more around her neck, and then reconsidered. "Oh, I'll drive. You cringe."

"I'm giving her lessons," said Reg. "She's a natural."

Queenie hugged George again. "If you want to run away, run away. But write to me first, and I'll have Reg wait at the bottom of the drive."

"Psst!" said Reg, as she got in. "If they push you around, go for the goolies. Don't think twice. Just . . ." He lifted his knee in unambiguous demonstration. "That's the last you'll hear of them."

"Thanks, Reg," said George thoughtfully. He'd never been given advice by a man before.

"Don't forget your medicine!" Queenie shouted out of the window in classic style. The car grumbled and lurched as she dithered between forward gears. George stood waving.

Halfway through dinner, the tray of preserves arrived at his table. When the others had removed theirs, one remained. A large jar of Mrs. Cakebread's strawberry preserve made its way towards George. On the top was written in black marker pen: "FISHER MI — from Queenie. Take once a day as prescribed. Refills available."

In the dormitory that night, they asked him if he knew another story. He thought about giving them "The Pigtail," but his mind was absorbed with the tuck box and its secrets.

"Tomorrow," he said. By then they would have returned from their day at home and the mystery would be solved.

The next morning, he watched with impatience as the school emptied until it echoed with pleasure. He spent as much of the day as he could alone in the tuck box room. Sundays were ideal for this kind of privacy. The bottom of the box seemed solid, and this he confirmed with a ruler. If it wasn't a false bottom, it must be the side obscured by the overhang of the shelf. X marked the spot, but how to get to the treasure? He felt under the shelf for a button, and finally, as he pushed in a particular spot, the right wall came down with a ping, pivoting elegantly at its base. From behind, there fell a rather tatty green book with a golden design stamped on the cover. He took it out and clicked the now empty compartment closed again.

This ornately designed, Victorian-looking book was called *The Life and Adventures of Valentine Vox the Ventriloquist,* by Henry Cockton. He opened the front cover. In it was scratched: "For My Georgie, Impress your friends! See you at half-term. Love, Evie (Sep '73)." Above this, in the faded ink of a fountain pen: "For Joe, Practice makes perfect — I know! Echo (April '27)."

A piece of paper fluttered from the book: a show bill for a national tour to benefit the Sunshine Club, with "Peter Pan" in bright bulbous green lettering, decorated with shooting stars and fireworks exploding spectacularly upon a sea of deep blue. There was a list of the cast members, Frankie's name slightly larger than everyone else's, against the sand of a desert island on which stood one lone palm. On the back, a list of dates, venues, and ticket prices was presented more conservatively. One stop in particular was circled. His heart beat faster. She was coming! She'd be in Whitley in four weeks' time, just before half-term: "Fisher Minor. Bring some friends, and don't forget to think happy thoughts! See you there! Frankie xx."

By the time his mother came to Whitley, George had come to understand all he ever would of the mysteries of Upside. His popularity as a monologuist was short-lived, and the suspicion in which he was originally held, on account of his late arrival, curious breeding, and offhand attitude to teamwork, never ebbed away.

He had made one friend: Mr. Morris's son, Patrick (also generally considered a mixed blessing), a shy child with a face blotted with freckles, who bore the burden of being related to a teacher with good grace and had been the first to extend a Sunday invitation. That night, George had returned with a glimpse of life beyond the chestnut trees. He began to feel a nudging sympathy for even those teachers he detested. Didn't they have a wife, a fire, a TV? His greatest weapon against their hectoring was his sympathy. Who wouldn't rather be at home? They didn't want to be at Upside any more than he did, so best to play out the farce as perfectly as possible: they'd do their bit and he'd do his.

Lessons came and went. It was easy: the teachers just turned up on cue. You sat there and produced the appropriate textbook. George found his mind wandering as each period went on: he tried to make his telling contributions early, so the teachers, satisfied with his preparation, turned their radar elsewhere. Even games, the low point of the day, came to present themselves as an enjoyable conundrum. He had already worked out how to avoid any physical contact at all (yet give the impression of trying his hardest); next, he would try to hatch a plot to rid himself of the inconvenience entirely.

There were unexpected kindnesses. Campbell had proved that George was one of his twelve best friends by giving him a slice of birthday cake. And the headmaster had taken him aside at evening prayers one day, inviting him to his study at 7:00 p.m. on the dot, hastening to add, "Nothing wrong." On George's arrival in this nicotine den, the headmaster asked, "Well, boy. When did you last see your mother?" and pointed to the television, where at that very moment the compere of *Variety's the Spice of Life* was announcing, "Now touring in *Peter Pan,* please welcome Frankie Fisher!" George sat down cross-legged, rather self-consciously, and watched Frankie sweep onstage to the cheering of the studio audience. Frankie disdained television but watched it a lot, and he knew how much her rare appearances meant to her. He didn't check whether Hartley, behind him, was paying attention. Who wouldn't?

"*Peter Pan* at the Clark Street Theatre," said the headmaster, puffing a bonfire of Balkan Sobranie after her plucky bow. "The redoubtable *Queenie* . . ." (he put it in affectionate inverted commas: although it couldn't possibly be her name, he would play along) "has asked permission for you to go. *She* can't take you. But *I* think I can send someone in loco parentis. Perhaps you would like to invite Patrick Morris and Mr. Morris?" George nodded. "OK!" Hartley had a way of saying OK as if it were a very cool word, *with it.*

It was the general consensus that if George clicked his fingers, four large buses would appear to ferry the entire school to *Peter Pan,* where there would be concession stands at which the boys' money was no good; further, that George chose to deny this for selfish reasons of his own. He came to be seen, by everyone except Patrick, as the withholder of this invitation to paradise. Campbell even alluded to his birthday cake, as though the two were comparable.

"You can have some of *my* birthday cake," said George in mitigation.

"Oh, *thanks*," said Campbell. Birthday cake suddenly meant nothing.

There was less than a week till half-term, but that didn't dampen his enthusiasm or diminish anyone else's pique. Every text he read seemed to contain some cryptic reference to the impending excursion. He loved to see Frankie in her element; never did he love her more. The moment she materialized on-stage, a lump came to his throat: a physical muscular spasm that left him seconds away from tears and subsided only of its own accord, a combination of his love for her and his fierce pride. He would buy her a box of After Eight mints — he always did: a poor symbol for what he felt, dignified by the mock surprise with which she received them, as if they summed everything up. It was their secret joke.

They left frustratingly late. Mr. Morris's car was short of petrol, so they had to make a detour, which coincidentally took them past the Duke of Athole, where Morris had to drop something off. George and Patrick waited impatiently in the back for Morris to down the swift half that would doubtless accompany the possibly fictional delivery. They arrived at the theatre much later than expected. George impatiently watched Morris make a hash of picking up the tickets at the box office, as though the man had never been on a house list before, and then took over himself, charming them from behind the glass in a matter of seconds. They found their seats only moments before the lights dimmed.

It was clear that Frankie knew not only that he was there but precisely where he was sitting. Her eyes sparkled in George's direction, and she delivered a couple of her lines with extra verve, lines that had a special meaning. When she spoke to the children, she spoke to the child in every person; when she flew, she soared above them; and when she told them to make a wish, it was a certainty that it would come true. Unhappy thoughts were impossible. There was the lump in his throat, as usual, but this evening, it spared him tears in front of the Morrises, who applauded enthusiastically as the lights came up for the interval.

All around him, there was a buzz about Frankie and the production: how wonderful to get the real quality in Whitley, how lush the costumes, how adorable Peter Pan, how evil Captain Hook. Morris was just about to get choc ices all round, when an usher called from the end of the row, gesticulating towards George, "Just time to pop backstage, if you'd like to see Miss Fisher!" George, obeying a far greater power than Morris, danced down the aisle without bothering to ask permission. He followed the burgundy uniform that led him through the pass door and into the backstage maze, where all was breathless activity. They passed Nana, the large Saint Bernard, as she pulled off her head to reveal the face of the sweaty actor beneath. "This costume smells fucking awful," he moaned.

Frankie was in her room, in her bra, pulling on a new top for the second half. They shouldn't have kissed, because of her makeup, but Frankie couldn't resist, leaving two lips' worth on his cheek, which she pointed out to him in the mirror and he removed.

"It's going well, isn't it? How's school? What does your teacher think? Could you dress up my coffee?"

There wasn't time for answers, but this was normal. Elsewhere, in other dressing rooms, things would be more serene. George remembered the two ugly sisters in Edinburgh, who had been so relaxed at the interval, with their chatter and casual nibbling, that you might well have thought they'd been written out of the second half. With Frankie, though, you were always in the eye of the hurricane. There was the familiar wreath of good-luck cards around the mirror, George's front and central.

Frankie sat down, talking as she reapplied her makeup, stretching her lips as taut as possible, barely pausing for breath: the other boys, his best friend, her missed note — had he noticed? She quoted a joke from one of his cards back at him, and they laughed. George fiddled with the flex as the tan plastic electric kettle, decorated with a chain of pink and purple daisies, came to a boil and turned itself off. A spoon of instant coffee was waiting in a cracked brown mug; he added two spoonfuls of sugar and some Carnation milk.

"Ooh, the glamour, eh?" She laughed, displaying her teeth to the mirror and picking off stray lipstick with the nail of her index finger. "No one makes it like you."

"Beginners, Part Two, Peter; Beginners, Captain Hook," a deep voice echoed down the hall.

"Thank you, Glyn. Go! See you at the end, darling. And don't forget to make a wish."

He made his way to his seat to find the Morrises agog that he'd been able to flit back so easily, as though he had the run of the place. The second half managed even to transcend the first. Although George had initially been put out that various members of the Upside common room were in attendance, as if they were all spying on Frankie, he realized how proud he was for them to see her in her splendid, shining glory. And when it came time to make a wish, George wished that he could get out of sports. After the bows and bouquets, George looked around for the same usher, but he was nowhere to be seen.

"Shall we perhaps go to see your mother at the backstage door?" asked Morris. George didn't want anyone else to see his mother at all, but things could play themselves out no other way. A rather harassed stage manager materialized as they were finally vacating the auditorium.

"George Fisher? Yes. Oh." He dabbed at his brow with a handkerchief. "Could you go to the upstairs bar, please?"

"Rather," said Morris, counting his blessings, though George thought this request odd. Perhaps Frankie wanted to meet them anywhere apart from the cramped backstage to make a better impression; somewhere away from the cracked mugs, purple daisies, foul-mouthed Saint Bernards, bottles of medicinal gin, and damp bras dangling from ironing boards.

Amidst greetings and congratulations, their group picked up hangers-on as it made its way through the foyer, until by the time they reached the mezzanine, they seemed, to George's distress, to consist of most of the Upside common room and its other half. The bar was unmistakably closed, the upside-down bottles safe behind silver bars.

The last person George expected to see was Reg, who emerged through an anonymous side door, and he knew it meant trouble. He wasn't dressed as a chauffeur anymore. His hair was spivved back with grease, a small quiff at the front.

"Hello, George," he said, as the teachers milled around, anxious for the coming attraction and the subsequent pub.

"Reg? Is Queenie here? Where's Frankie?" George resented Reg's presence, the way it implied that Reg was somehow in control.

"She's coming, George, she's coming. Don't worry."

It was then he started to worry.

Seconds later, Queenie shepherded Frankie through the same door. Instantly, as Morris and the group burst into a chorus of congratulations, George knew what had happened. He ran to Queenie — he wouldn't be able to get any sense out of Frankie — and she hugged him.

"Yesterday, George. In her sleep. Very peaceful. Just as she would have wanted."

Yesterday? he thought. *Yesterday?* But what about tonight? The show? What about the interval? Frankie must have only just found out. He could hear her talking to Mr. Morris about the wonderful night, what a marvellous audience they had been.

"Queenie . . . ," he cried. He hated himself for not having started reading the tatty green book Evie had given him. He hated himself for not having run away and seen her one last time before half-term.

"I know, darling, I know."

"When did Frankie know?"

"Yesterday, of course." And then, as if she could read his mind, "But the show must go on. It's what she would have wanted."

And on the show went behind George, as Commander Poole invited Frankie out for a drink, and she asked his party humourously pointed questions about her favourite boy's progress at Upside.

"Look at you all! Now, whatever is the collective noun for teachers? A school, is it? A rule of teachers?" she teased to the laughter of all. "This is early for me, you know, though you're probably all tucked up in your beds by now, aren't you, children?"

She turned around to George, who felt a box of After Eights planted firmly in his hand by Queenie. He disentangled himself from the various layers of material that covered Queenie's chest. As he handed his mother the After Eights, it was clear to all that he had been crying. In their excitement at Frankie's arrival, they hadn't noticed George's beeline for Queenie, pleased only that he wasn't delaying the star.

"Come on, bosun," said Commander Poole in an unusually kindly manner. "Pull yourself together. For your mother."

"No," said Frankie. "I'm afraid we've had a death in the family — his great-grandma; and if a boy can't cry in front of his mother, when can he?"

Approval for this laudable sentiment whispered among the troops, and a drink seemed less pressing.

"Well, perhaps we'll . . . ," said one.

"Yes, and it might be time for us to . . . ," said another.

"Can we take George out for a quick bite?" asked Queenie.

"Well, we really ought to be getting back to Upside, George," said Morris, who planned for the boys to be sitting in the back of the car with a bag of ready-salted while he caught last orders. "I think it's bedtime after a wonderful evening."

Queenie said firmly, "We need to talk to George. If you'd like to wait downstairs, we'll bring him in a moment."

"Absolutely," said Morris, who had met his match.

Congratulations mingled cheerfully with good-byes; commiserations were tastefully murmured.

The four of them — Queenie, Frankie, George, and Reg — sat around a table that hadn't yet been cleaned after the interval.

"A wonder she lasted as long as she did," said Queenie. "But she clung on." It was as though the news had just hit her for the first time.

"Grand old lady," said Reg dutifully, but his mind was elsewhere. "I wish I could just slip my hand through there and have a nice drop of scotch and steal one of them packets of crisps. Send her off, like."

"Scotch'd do the trick," said Queenie. "Scotch and milk, her favourite."

"A bottle of Teacher's: maybe that's the collective noun," said Frankie. "Go backstage and get a drop."

George couldn't get over the fact that she hadn't said anything during the interval.

"Back in a tick," said Reg.

The three of them considered the oversize Red Barrel ashtray that occupied most of the table.

"George, one more thing. And you're going to have to be very brave," said Queenie. He had never seen her so awkward. "You can't come home for half-term. Frankie's everywhere from Plymouth to Morecambe, and I have to sort out a god-awful mess. Reg'll drive me up to see you one day, but we can't manage it at home."

"But I can't stay at school for half-term," he said in astonishment. "They don't let you. There's no one there." He had visions of his roaming the playing fields, foraging for nuts and berries, and running through the corridors to the kitchen, where, on a huge range that cooked for two hundred, he would fry the single egg he managed to pilfer from the local farm.

"We'll sort something out, darling. We'll sort something out. And we'll have the best Christmas of all. I promise."

"Any good?" asked Reg, waving a bottle of gin. He had three mugs with him and one paper cup. He poured a tipple into each, waving away George's concerns: "Drink up. Don't breathe on Mr. Morris is all. If he can smell it through his own, that is." He chuckled and lifted his glass, remembering that he should make some kind of toast. "Well, God rest her soul. She never liked me much, but here's to her."

"Shh!" said Queenie. They bowed their heads. "A grand old lady."

"My great-grandmother," said George.

"No *Grand*. No *Great*," said Frankie. "She hated them both." She looked up with a sly wink. "Do you love me?"

"You *know* you do!" they chorused, and downed their gin.

In the car on the way back to school, George was still considering the horrors of a half-term at Upside. However, he had become self-conscious about his thought processes, a new feeling that amused him. In fact, he was slightly drunk. Patrick had fallen asleep on the backseat while they waited for George, who had been rather longer than Morris had expected, so George was sitting in the passenger seat. He hadn't wanted to breathe too near Mr. Morris, but he couldn't resist the lure of the front.

"Terrible news about your bereavement," said Mr. Morris, magnanimously overcoming his tetchiness at missing last orders.

"We called her Evie, short for Evangeline, but that wasn't the name she was known by. Oh, no." Words weren't coming out of George's mouth quite as he expected.

"What was her name?"

"She was known as Echo. Echo Endor."

"Echo Endor? That rings a bell. Wasn't she a ventriloquist?"

"*Ventriloquiste*," said George pointedly. "Yes. She was the greatest ventriloquiste who ever lived. Bar none."

3

The House That Echo Built

Over the next month, I made a thorough analysis of Joe's life from my resting place on the deep burgundy cushions. It wasn't hard. He rarely ventured outside his room, preferring to sit surrounded by books in a pool of artificial light, writing in inky black and burgundy accounts ledgers, scribbling on cards that he filed in a mahogany cabinet. It was all part of a magnum opus, which already ran to volumes, on magical technique — it was to be his life's work. He had mastered the various sleights of hand early; now he was deeply involved in the realms of "pure magic," speculating on illusions that were possible only in theory, that yet-to-be-invented technology might allow. He had also delved back into the history of the dark arts for clues to the way forwards — this had led him to dust off distant voice.

When he wasn't rapt in secret studies, I watched him watching himself at his dressing table, scrutinizing his reflections in the angled mirrors for any sign of extraneous movement. These exercises were thorough and tedious. He was after perfection all right, but where was the practical application of his genius? Rather than pick me up afterwards, he went back to his books. No one was invited to Prospero's inner sanctum. His magic kept the world at bay.

Most of the world.

*   *   *

Echo was unconstrained by a closed door, and Joe lived in constant fear of her next invasion. She came often and unexpectedly, for the slightest of reasons, never failing to raise an authoritative finger in my direction and declare loudly that practice made perfect. Once, as he paid her no attention, she said: "And don't forget, it's good to move your lips just a *little*. That way they know it's *you* doing all the work. Put that in your little magic books! Back late!"

He dismissed her with a wave of the hand and returned to his book.

Things improved when she was in the provinces. Joe emerged like an animal newly out of hibernation to range through the wider spaces of the house. He left his door open, lingering downstairs rather than scurrying back to the safety of his den. It was during one of these safe periods that, on a whim, he took me for company on an excursion.

Number 34, Cadogan Grove was a draughty town house of four floors, unmistakably the home of a diva. The colours were rich and earthy, like glazed pottery, the furniture draped in coverings of different lace, shawls she could snatch up at a moment's notice. As we descended, her perfume, a distinctive fragrance she had sent up from Brighton, grew more and more overwhelming; in the parlour, the bloodred velvet curtains, trimmed and sashed in gold, were so extravagant that they might have been exacted from a West End theatre in lieu of payment.

Every available surface, horizontal or vertical, was crowded with photographs in frames of varying size and magnificence, jostling for position, commuters elbowing their way onto the escalator at rush hour. On any given table, only the faces in the front row could be seen: behind those, nothing more than a selection of hairstyles. If one frame fell, the rest would topple like dominoes. And this happened often, for Echo loved to shuffle them — she called it *dusting*, and it was all the housework she managed — bringing new ones to prominence, depending upon which stories were at the forefront of her mind, flattered which guest, or suited which suitor. Yet, despite the quantity of pictures, few showed any two members of the Fisher family together. Most were not of family at all but admiring associates: "Darling Echo, Speak through me. Your greatest fan, L. H. Curzon."

There they were, she and her favourite boy, stage left or right, before curtains closed or raised, standing in front of radio microphones of all heights and descriptions. Some of these pictures flattered their subjects, retouched to smooth away the crevices in Narcissus's and perhaps Echo's face too.

Nor did the collection gloss over the many Memorable Moments of their career. In these more candid pictures, the smiles were less clenched, the figures smaller, the crannies deeper. Here they were presented to the king, who shook Narcissus's hand with regal forbearance; there, with none other than crown prince of funny men Pick Eurone. Other pictures were taken in army camps and hospitals, where even the mummified patient, though little more than a human hammock suspended from the ceiling, smiled gratefully.

Wandering through the exhibition, Joe took particular care to introduce me to his father, a few pictures of whom were scattered among the frozen smiles. Joe remembered little more than a presence: some pinstripe trousers, a waft of thick cigar smoke, and a fur collar, which tickled Joe's nose when his father hoisted him into his arms in the hallway upon his return from work.

There were two photos of Joe: one as a baby, his mother holding him up, not unlike the way she held Narcissus but without the same intimacy, and another of an early foray into conjuring — there he was, aged six, beneath an oversize top hat; in front of him, a table on which were two packs of playing cards, an eggcup, some sugar cubes, and two matchboxes. In his right hand, he held a wand, which, at that split second, he brandished towards the heavens in mid-abracadabra. The trick was going to work: you could see it in his eyes, fixed on eternity somewhere behind us, far beyond the lens of the camera.

There were pictures of another baby too: his brother, Clifford, who died, aged two, in the whooping cough epidemic. And a sickly little thing he was, barely strong enough for his image to register on the film.

We had yet to see half the wonders of the house when we were climbing the stairs once more, as if we had been on a day trip to the seaside, and when the sun finally came out midafternoon, Father insisted that we head home before the traffic got too bad.

Back in Joe's room, nothing changed. All dedicated to closeness and the bettering of his mind, he thought of me so rarely. It was my added misfortune to be a gift from his mother. And what is worse than being an unwanted gift?

I was marooned, gathering dust, nothing more.

And one day, there she was again at the door, in full primary orientalia. Joe did not feel he owed her the favour of acknowledging her presence, and continued reading. She let her head fall to one side in mourning.

"Darling, darling, *darling*, darling, darling, *darling*, darling, darling, *darling*, darling, darling, *darling*." It would be impossible to describe the unleashing of this torrent of love and pity, but by the end of her apostrophe, she was croaking through tears. "Whatever should your father have said, darling Jojo?" She swept in, her own chorus line. "Curtain *up!*" she exclaimed, features obscure as the harsh light flooded in. "You can't sit up here all day, reading and writing. You can't breathe. Let the world in!" She opened a very small window and asked in defeat, "What are we to do with you, Joe?"

"Mother . . ."

"I can't hear! I am deaf!" She froze. She searched the room with the desperate eyes of a silent actress. "Soft! Soft! Is this a voice I hear?"

"Echo," he obliged. He couldn't even call her Mother.

"Joe." Her manner softened. She smiled her charming smile and sat on the windowsill, hugging her legs to her chest.

"I'm working" was his gentle plea.

"Working, working, working, Joe, yes. But playing, playing, playing. Where is life, where pleasure, where friends?"

"I don't have friends."

"And what of me?" she asked in high dudgeon. "What of Derek? Narcissus? Polly? The vicar?" As evidence to the contrary, she had managed only to name herself, her young male companion, a ventriloquist's dummy, a serving maid, and a man of God whom even she didn't like. Joe could only shrug. He was too shy, too happy in his own world to be anything but lonely.

"I'm *busy.*"

"Oh, Joe," she said at this shameful confession. "Whatever are we to do?" She turned around and fixed a tragic gaze beyond. Five seconds later, with an abrupt change of mood, she chirped airily, "I tried!"

Under normal circumstances, this would clearly have signalled the conclusion of the conversation ritual, Echo's own cue to glide out. But, in the silence, her eyes alighted upon me. I was to be her final roll of the dice.

"And how are you getting on with your new friend . . . *George?*" She put great emphasis on my name, to eradicate any thought that I might have been called Pip Squeak; in her mind, this was an act of selfless generosity bound to win Joe over, but it served merely as a reminder. Despite this, the question caught him off guard, and he had no immediate answer, since he wasn't *getting on* with me at all. "We have a famous family name, you know. It *precedes* us. You don't remember your grandfather, but he too was a great star in his day."

Joe finally put his book aside. She had managed to pique his interest. "I'm interested in Grandfather. I've been reading about him."

"If," she said, ignoring him, "you'll only show me that you're ready, I'll . . ." She stopped. Her double take involved a repetition of the whole sentence, then: "I beg your pardon?"

"I've been reading about Vox Knight."

"Darling, tell *Mother.*"

"I have been working on something."

"Your book?" She tried not to sound critical.

"An . . . act." He had been working up to this, and it was going to take all his determination.

"An act?"

"An *original* act."

She gasped and clapped her hands together. "What are you saying, Joe? Oh, this is the best early birthday present I could ever have. This is marvellous! I knew it!" I wondered whether she did. Perhaps he was lying, playing for time. "With George? Joe and George?" Her own vision immediately subsumed his, and her mind was clearly brimming with narratives: how she would build his career, help him through the early heartbreak as he paid his dues, give him a leg up, of course (but never one that would earn him the resentment of his peers), pass on the benefit of her years of experience, yes, but never reveal the real secrets: that was for his own good. He would learn for himself, make his own mistakes, and be all the better for it. She was delighted, absolutely delighted.

"The act is more like Grandfather's, like Vox's."

"What do you mean, Joe?"

"I intend to reintroduce the most skilful of the vocal arts, that of polyphony."

"But, darling . . ." Joe missed the note of caution in her voice as he warmed to his theme. She yielded the floor because it appeared from his somewhat oratorical stance that her son was readying to hold forth, to give her a unique insight into his mind. What he delivered was a speech, rather in the manner of a theatrical prologue.

"I will make voices appear from nowhere, from out of the air and under the stage, the balcony and stalls, working without the aid of puppet to deceive the eye or beard to conceal the movement of my lips. Like Vattemare of old, who at the age of eleven entertained the emperor Napoleon himself, my act shall be comic, vocalic, mimetic, multiformical, and maniloquious. I shall work with only the gifts that God Himself intended for me." Echo was laughing in a self-consciously generous way. She tried once more to punctuate his address with whatever caveat she had for him but failed. "Voices will appear in each corner of the theatre, in persons so distinct from my own that the audience will not believe that the entire spectacle is the work of one man. Like William Edward Love and the unsurpassed vocalion 'Vox' Knight, who entertained kings and queens with his polyphonic . . ."

"But darling. Darling!" She had to shout to be heard, unable to restrain herself any longer. "It's a wonderful idea, darling. Wonderful." She clearly thought it anything but. "How can I put this? That business went out with the *ark*."

"Perhaps . . ." He had finally been ready to prove himself, to show off, to make her proud, but whatever confidence the speech had conjured vanished with her interruption.

"No *perhaps* about it. No one wants it, darling. It's gone the way of the dodo. When Father died, he couldn't even get on a stage."

Joe slumped on the floor among his books. He'd known she would do this; he'd foreseen the torture she would inflict for daring to impress her. All his work: useless.

"Listen to me, Jojo. I don't know everything, but I can tell you about this. Look at me." He wouldn't, so she got down on her hands and knees, a gaudy scarlet tent of dragons and flowers, and took him in her arms, where he hung limply, an animal on her gibbet.

"I love you, darling." Silence. "Joe, please, listen. I'm saying this for your own good." Silence. "Joe, if you won't speak for yourself, I'll speak for you." Silence. She continued in his voice: "Yes, Echo, I'm sorry. I know you're only . . ." She had barely begun the sentence when he fought his way out of her arms.

"No!" he said through clenched teeth, eyes wild. This was all the participation she required, and she continued in her most reasonable voice.

"Well, then. Not talking at all does no one any good. Listen, Joey. It's a nice idea, but you'd never find a producer or an audience, except perhaps in Nana's nursing home. Believe me, I know." She spoke the words like a lullaby, soothing him back to sleep after a horrible dream. "I'll tell you a story." She patted the floor next to her.

"Once upon a time, long before there were boys, geniuses like Vox Knight filled the theatres with no more than their voices. And they filled the seats too. *A Thousand and One Knights,* Vox's greatest show, ran for three hundred and sixty-five consecutive performances at the Egyptian. Three hundred and sixty-five! Those were the days: one man, a thousand and one voices. Vox was everything: polyphonist, ventriloquist, mimic, comedian, quick-change artist, and he could carry a tune too. A genius. A true artiste." She put her arm around Joe. "And then the dummies came, not boys yet like Narcissus, but life-size dummies, and now there was something more than a voice in the rafters — there was something that trapped the audience's attention, something that you could see from the back of the vast auditorium." She pointed to an imaginary stage and affected the voice of the ordinary punter, who was (as usual) Cockney: "'Lor! That's where those voices are coming from! That mouth!' The old-timers, and Vox wasn't the only one, continued to do their show, the one that had played to the crowned heads of Europe, but the crowds weren't there anymore. Besides: *where was the dummy?* The vogue for Vox, for the lone voice, was over. And that was the end of the great Vox Knight.

"Then the first boy came along: a boy, a real portable boy, not a row of dummies. This was what we had all been waiting for. All you needed was a puppet and a stool. Forget the scenery and all that bother; this was perfect for a ten-minute spot on the end of the pier. And suddenly the boy became the whole focus. Vox knew it the first time we saw Fred Russell and Coster Joe at the Palace. 'Get yourself one of them, my gal!' he said. I can hear him now, good old Pa. And Narcissus came for my twenty-first birthday.

"And since then, nothing has changed. The boy is the act now, you're the straight man, and that's what people want. When *Tonight's the Knight,* his last show for smaller halls, was ailing, Vox and Nana and I, we were living with three other families in one house on the Cut. Now look at us. It's the house that Echo built, and the house that Narcissus built too.

"You have the name, Joe Fisher, you have the talent, and I know you have the technique, but do you have the will, the personality? It's not good for you, sitting in here, writing all the time. When you're ready, Joey, let me put you in front of someone. They'll take my word, of course, but . . ."

"I am ready."

"Show me!" she begged.

"But I have nothing to say with George."

"Yes, it's *trickier* with a boy, isn't it?" If she was mocking him, challenging him, the accompanying laugh was all sweetness. "Be pragmatic, Joey! You want to be the lone voice in unbounded space? If that's your dream, you have to start somewhere: you'll have to seduce people, and perhaps when you've got something worked out with George, then you'll have the opportunity to introduce a little of the other. And now is where we will start. . . . Audition for me."

Joe unwrapped himself from her and walked towards me.

She had done it! She had appealed to him as a mother. He picked me up and sat in the armchair. His fingers entwined with my mechanism, and I was just about to speak when she interrupted.

"Joe. You'll want me to tell you exactly what I think, of course you will, but remember: I am also a mother. Oh, this is so exciting! Begin."

"He's got no material," I complained. "Nothing. He just reads, and writes those books all day, leaves me sitting here . . . like a dummy." I looked at her, then at him, and crossed my eyes in boredom.

"Splendid!" said Echo, clapping her hands.

"Is she going to comment on every single thing that I do?" I asked. He nodded. "Guess we won't have to wait for the review in tomorrow's papers."

"Speak to *each other*," she implored.

"He doesn't want to talk," I said. Joe was looking far away, out of the window, his head turned from me. He sipped from a glass of water.

"Joe, say something. You have to talk."

"He's got nothing to say," I said. "Give him a break. Let him do what *he* wants."

"Joe, you have to talk. George needs someone to spar with; he needs a straight man."

"We don't have any material."

"Do one of my routines. You know them by heart."

"OK, shall we do one?" I asked.

He nodded without enthusiasm, rolling his eyes. He sat me rather too upright and placed himself next to me in a self-consciously formal posture.

"Hello," he said, as though we had never met. "How are you?"

"Very poor."

("Good choice!" said Echo.)

"Are you not feeling well, George?"

"No, I haven't got any money."

"Ah, so you're not poorly, you're poor."

"That's what I said, ainnit? Besides, I can't afford any food."

And so the sketch went on. At length. It was a strange choice of material — corny, childish — and by halfway, even I was bored. We performed proficiently, but we didn't spark as we had in front of the mirror. I looked at her in expectation. Echo hadn't laughed once during the routine and was now at a loss for words. I cleared my throat and had a cigarette. She finally spoke.

"This is difficult, Joe. I have to tell you one thing, and I hope this isn't a surprise: technique for its own sake is empty."

"It's good to move your lips a little, so they know it's you. . . ." My mimicry was ill advised. Now she was irritated.

"Listen. You can't be a great artiste on technique alone. You need more than that. . . ."

"Oh, really," I said. "You need teeth and a tongue and a little patience. Then practise, practise, practise."

"I'm surprised at you. It's very sad that you think that's all it comes down to. And it's naive. What about personality, charisma? What makes a star? What made *me?*"

"Teeth and a tongue," I said. "And a little boy sitting on your knee."

She let this pass, but she was on a slow boil, annoyed by the slight to her fame.

Joe interrupted: "We have one more bit. Could be a good audition."

Echo was still seething and said nothing as Joe put his legs on top of mine, so he was sitting on *my* lap. He moved us closer together, took my right arm and placed it behind his back, wedging it into the belt of his trousers, and grabbed my cap from my head, perching it on his own.

It was the same script we had just performed. I said his lines, in a voice that sounded like nothing I should be made to produce, and he said mine, in a reedy falsetto, his mouth snapping up and down. And then my head was spinning, as he twirled my spine around and around with laughter. Whatever had precisely happened, Echo was beside herself with anger.

She shouted at the top of her voice: "Joseph, I am the greatest living ventriloquiste, certainly the best in England, voted such by my peers three years running. I have respected the traditions and I have forged ahead." She stood up suddenly, borne on her fury. Her maternal feelings had been treading water but were now drowning, pushed under by her wounded pride. "And I will not have my life's work belittled by an amateur, even if he is my son. Here is the truth." She was calmer now, but it was the dignified calm of the slighted, not real calm, and she struggled to moderate her tone. "On a stage, in the halls, you must be nothing but yourself. It is a world free of pretence. And if you can put it over, sell it, then the thing you are selling, and the thing that people love, is you, your *self*. And a great artiste, a great star, will find within himself the personality that wins the laughter, that deserves the applause and the love. It is personality that makes business, and if you don't have it, you will be found out. All the greats have this gift, and they give it freely, share it, pour all that charisma into their song or their turn, their partner or their boy. And through their act, they reach out to the audience, so that the audience can feel their essence, taste it, breathe it in. That is what makes it in the halls. Personality." She was working herself up again. "Why do you think I am telling you this?"

He knew.

"Because you can't become great at anything unless people like you. And that is the problem, Joe, your problem. It hurts me to tell you this, and God knows it must be my fault somehow. This is your problem — and I tell you this because I love you." Her voice was measured and took on the air of a valediction. "With you, there is nothing there, no personality, absolutely nothing. I'm sorry. And I don't think it can come, because it simply isn't within you, because there is none of the world in you. The technique is fine, but technique will get you nowhere if they can see right through you. You are not *believable*. You are not *interesting*. There's nothing there." She added, although it wasn't an afterthought: "It's not a bad gimmick. You should talk only through the boy. Let him take over entirely. He's the interesting one, not you."

And she was right. That was the worst thing. I *was* the interesting one. He had tried to impress her, and she had laughed at him, ridiculing the technical perfection that was the acme of his dreams, the idée fixe of all his writing; he had tried to beat her at her own game, and she had crushed him.

The moment she closed the door behind her, his fingers gripped my spine in fury. He wrenched my head from my body and hurled me towards the door.

I flew across the room like a tomahawk: a blunt, useless, poorly aimed tomahawk.

Fisher the Ventriloquist

"The Fisher men are not to be relied upon, never were. Only the boys, only the boys." He'd heard her say it so often; George loved to be one of her boys. He had beaten her at life, just like she had said.

Half-term was upon them. George passed the last few days in distraction, angry not because he wasn't going home but because he hadn't bothered to read the stupid green book in time to thank her.

Plans crystallized around him, but he paid no attention, quietly resigned to this misfortune in much the same way he submitted to his daily mauling on the games field. A moment's hope that half-term might be spent with the Morrises, visiting some relation in France, was scotched: George didn't have a passport — Fisher holidays were generally tied to Frankie's summer season.

Did he even react when he first heard that he would be staying with the headmaster and his wife, sleeping not in an empty dormitory but in a spare room in their annexed apartment? By the time he heard about it, all was decided. He vaguely remembered saying thank you.

Not going home on Sunday was bad; not going home for half-term was unheard of. With some detachment, he watched the other boys turn giddy with freedom. The final night was odder than any other: the teachers more irritable, their wards wired and unable to sleep, ready to push the enemy further.

After the last assembly, they cheered and ran, spurred by specific instructions to the contrary. Teachers and pupils alike knew that nothing could stop it now, not with all those Jaguars and Range Rovers queuing up in the driveway.

George hid in the library, the one place you were sure not to be found. In the dim natural light, he sat by the big arch windows that overlooked the back lawn. Here, for the first time, too late, he opened the cover of Evie's gift, *Valentine Vox* by Henry Cockton. He considered the unprepossessing cover: florid black ornamentation on a leaf green book, the name *Valentine Vox* etched in gold. He flicked through: 512 pages of close type. A dull half-term unfurled before him. At least there were illustrations: opposite the title page, there was an intriguing plate of ten museumgoers in various states of astonishment, standing around an Egyptian tomb, the centrepiece of which was the head of a sarcophagus. The caption read, "How's your mother?" as though the statue were asking. Perhaps it was a comedy, a book you couldn't judge by its cover. How was his mother? She had known throughout the interval and said nothing.

"And lo!" called Hartley as he burst in. "God said, *fiat* Fisher . . ." He flicked a switch. "And *erat* Fisher." He called back down the corridor, "Eureka!" Hartley sat down, immune to the library's overwhelming disorganization, clapping both hands firmly against his knees in a gesture that said, let us begin. "We're going to have a fairly good half-term, you and I, Young Master Fisher. The situation has been forced upon us, but we will not be found wanting. What are you reading?"

"Something I found on the shelf, sir." George slipped it among other tatty books. He'd get it later.

"There he is," said Hartley's wife as she came in. George saw a kindness in her face that he had not spotted in the previous five weeks. It was pity. "Well, come along, then, let's put him in his room, and we'll see what we can come up with for him this afternoon."

Could she possibly refer to him in the third person all half-term?

Despite their best attempts, the Hartleys knew no more what to do with George than he knew what to do with them: two hundred boys was one thing, one quite another.

Even television had the air of homework, so he escaped to the library whenever he could. He liked to associate himself with this room in the headmaster's mind, for it was part of his master plan to duck games. Emboldened by the superior quality of the food at the Hartleys', George took the first step over dinner on the second night.

"Sir, I was thinking . . ."

"*Were* you, by Jove?" Hartley mopped up some gravy with the crust of his French bread.

"I was thinking, sir, I'd like to work on the library."

"I'm listening."

"Order the books. Put them in a system so they can be found. Put the Dickens together. Under *D*. It's a big mess."

"You'd like to spend your half-term being a librarian?" He didn't look at you, George realized, and when he did, he looked through you. "And that's how you get your . . . *kicks*." He was speaking a vernacular he seemed to think George would really understand. "I can't have you inside all day, you know. I have been entrusted with your entire body, not just your mind. All work and no play makes George a dull boy."

"And then I was thinking, if no one else wanted to, that I could be the librarian, perhaps looking after the library during games, with lending time immediately afterwards."

"Whoa, cowboy!" Hartley weighed the options. "Look here. Donald is marking out the fields for the second half of term." Everyone else called the groundsman Old MacDonald. "If you'll help him outside, then we'll leave you to organize whatever you want inside." His eyes met George's. "But there's no arrangement yet on *being* the librarian. Do we have a deal?"

"We have a deal."

"Let's shake on it."

Since bed was only minutes away, there seemed no harm in one further suggestion. "I was also wondering: do you play cards, sir, or Mrs. Hartley?"

"We play bridge . . . and canasta," said Mrs. Hartley distractedly, assuming he would never have heard of such adult pursuits.

"Eleven take one or thirteen take two?" asked George.

There was a pause. The head let out a polite belch as he polished off his large glass of red wine.

"Clear this lot away, and let's to it," he said.

Next morning, George set about the library. The head checked up on him once or twice, as he had expected, so he made sure to be whistling while he worked.

"We'll get the place cleaned up a bit," said Hartley, inspecting the accumulation of greasy dust on a swiped finger. "You're sure you want to do this? We must be clear that I'm not making you."

"Would you like it in writing, sir?"

"I rather think I would."

There were multiple copies of many titles: seven Last Mohicans, fifteen Men in a Boat, three hundred and three Dalmations, and more Musketeers than you could shake a stick at. Many more books were defaced, lacking covers, bereft of their illustrations, or in desperate need of rebinding to save them from disintegration. These George put in separate piles for his presentation.

By morning's end, he had the library down to its bare essentials: books that could actually be filed and read. There were so few that he reclaimed some of the least damaged from the discard pile to make the holdings look slightly more respectable. The most popular author in the revamped Upside library was Frank Richards, the author of Billy Bunter, edging out Rider Haggard by two.

At lunch, he put on his Wellington boots and trudged out to the playing fields, where he found Old MacDonald leaning on an antique white-marking machine.

"Poor sod!" said Donald when he was within earshot. "Why aren't you home?"

"Great-grandmother died."

Donald pursed his lips and nodded to show he had taken the fact on board. Despite his nickname, he wasn't an old man at all, perhaps in his early thirties, though he did look rather like a farmer, even with the school tie he wore as a belt. He had an intelligent, piercing stare, but the rest of his face was gaunt and weary, from the minute veins that twitched beneath his eyes to his uneven teeth and the patches of stubble on his oddly taut and translucent skin. It was as though he were becoming invisible.

"Poor sod! They all call me Old MacDonald. And you can call me that." He spoke carefully, barely opening his thin lips, as if reluctant to impose too many words or too much noise on the world, as if speaking itself were something of a chore. George was surprised at his gentle manner. He'd expected more of a yokel. There were rumours, evidently false, that the groundsman, who had been spotted tippling from a flask, was a bit simple. "Or Donald, Don, whichever."

"I'm George." George offered his right hand confidently. Donald considered shaking it but only got as far as wiping his hands on his trousers.

"Right." He looked around. "Lines for the rugby and hockey pitches. Can be done by one, easier with two."

Don was a methodical man, not looking for a shortcut. He worked slowly, meticulously explaining as he did: how to do the wheelie that ensured you marked only where you needed lines; how to stretch the string taut across the grass to ensure the line was straight; why the white marker, which smelled moreish like an indelible felt-tip pen, was better for the field than creosote. It felt momentous, as though Don had to pass on knowledge that would otherwise die with him. Regularly, he stopped, cleared his throat, reached into his top pocket, pulled out his tin of rolling tobacco, and rolled a cigarette thoughtfully between his thumbs and fingers. While smoking, he sat in total silence, not inviting conversation, gazing off into the distance, barely seeming to notice the cigarette, let alone the rest of the world. Then he put the butt into a little pewter travelling ashtray, worn smooth with years of use.

"Tea break over," he said. Don took a swig from his flask and then wiped the back of his hand across his lips. "I'm not giving you any of that," he said and smiled.

When they were done, they gazed in satisfaction over the completed hockey field. Apart from anything else, George thought, it was nice for Donald that he was there; otherwise no one would appreciate the effort that had gone into the geometrical lines.

"Best bit," said Don. "Centre spot. Go on." .

George dunked the sponge-on-a-stick into the basin of the marking machine, then daubed it dead centre.

Don produced a striped packet from the recesses of his jacket, which hung on three practice stumps in the pavilion. "Same again tomorrow, George," he said, and handed him a fossilized Everton Mint that had merged with its wrapper.

"OK. Same again tomorrow, then."

George felt grown-up, as he did when he was with Frankie in her world: nothing like he ever felt at school.

Queenie couldn't visit. George twisted the curly telephone cord around his fingers until the base of the phone rose into the air.

"I'm sorry I can't come. It's Evie's funeral. It was the one day we could have the service, and people are coming from all over. It's Frankie's only day off. You don't want to come anyway," said Queenie. He decided to agree. "She's left you some special things, very special things. Frankie has them for you at Christmas. We're going to have a very lovely Christmas. A family Christmas." But no Good Old Des this year, no Evie. "Are you there, George?"

"Yes."

"Did you see the obit in *The Times*? Just small, and a wonderful one in *The Stage*. I'll send you a copy." Above the phone, there was a mantelpiece of bibelots. Among them was a frame surrounded by seashells, in which was a photo of the Hartley family — mother and father and two young children, boy and girl. "George?"

"Yes? Oh, sorry. Will Sylvia come?" He'd had a sudden vision of her long brown hair; the question had asked itself.

"No" came the abrupt, surprised answer, before a pause of recovery. "Well, I shouldn't think so. She and Evie, you know . . ."

It made him sad to remind her of this never-mentioned unhappiness, and he added, to please her, "I'm reading that book Evie gave me. *Valentine Vox*."

"Oh, yes. Your grandpa's favourite. She thought you might like it too."

Forgoing the nightly game of canasta (to the relief of all three of them), he lay in his bedroom and noticed the bookshelves for the first time. The books were neatly divided: a large colour-coded selection of children's Ladybird books, some drab white-spined books on health by authors who paraded their qualifications, and a small corner dedicated to stagecraft and acting, probably for the school play. George had a new appreciation for the careful method of their shelving.

Cleaners mined the lost treasures of the school library: chocolate (hidden and forgotten), coins, an essay on Sir Thomas Wolsey dated seventeen years ago, even a prehistoric packet of cigarettes. The headmaster approved the cataloguing system, a primary rainbow of sticky coloured dots was bought at the local stationer's, and reshelving began.

Afternoons saw George continue his work with Don. He looked forward to their conversations. Don didn't say much about himself, but George had ascertained that he was thirty-six, single, and lived on his own in the compact school-owned bungalow at the end of the driveway. He gave the impression of being perfectly content working at Upside, as handyman, groundsman, dogsbody. Regularly, he would call a tea break, when he sat in blissful silence with his cigarette, a good advertisement for smoking. They talked only when they worked.

"Like books, eh?" Donald called down to George from the top of the pavilion, where some tiles beneath the weather vane had blown loose. George was swinging a hammer around his head, supposedly monitoring the pulley system. "Are they making you tidy up that library?"

"No. I want to be the librarian. It's my plan to get out of games."

"That library's been a black hole for years. So, what are you reading?"

In fact, George wasn't reading anything in particular. The library had given him a good excuse to put *Valentine Vox* aside. Yet he had an urge to say something that Donald hadn't heard of, to impress him.

"It's called *Valentine Vox*."

"What's it about?"

"Well . . ." George realized he didn't know. "I have to read a bit more and then I'll tell you tomorrow."

"OK." Donald was dependable: he wouldn't forget that George had promised a description. "Hey, there's an instamatic in the pocket of my jacket. Take a picture, and then winch it up here: what you did on your holidays. How's this?" Donald stood on the apex of the roof, one foot on the weather vane, and stretched his arms wide.

At first, progress with *Valentine Vox* seemed less than likely, enjoyment out of the question, but he was determined to make headway: for himself, for Evie, and for Donald. The publishers couldn't have tried to make the book any less appealing. The typeface was crammed onto the page in such a way that, he worked out, they could fit an average of about seven hundred words on each page. Seven hundred! Yet somehow, by the end of chapter 3, George was hooked. It certainly wasn't the telling of the story — that was almost counterproductive; it was the events themselves that caught his fancy. He told Donald the next day as they painted and rebuffered the rugby posts.

"It's about a boy, a ventriloquist, who can throw his voice. He makes fun of people, by pretending to be another voice, and they don't realize it's him."

"How?"

"He practises in the fields and does a lot of training. And then in six months' time, he has total command of his voice." The explanation in the book had been wilfully obscure, and George couldn't quite remember it. "I don't know how he does it, but he can do any voice."

"Like an impressionist."

"There's a funny bit where he upsets an election."

"And everyone falls for it?"

"Yes."

"Kids' book, is it?"

"No . . . well, I don't think so. It's old. The print's pretty tiny, but there are pictures."

"I'd like a look at it." Donald stopped for a cigarette.

That evening, alone in the little square room that had obviously once been that of the Hartleys' son, George read on. The writing hadn't picked up, but the things Valentine could do! The control he had over his voice — the way he could ping it around any room, up a chimney, out of a moving carriage, imitate anyone or anything! It was simply astonishing: one of the most impressive things George had ever imagined, let alone read.

However, Valentine did not use his superpower particularly responsibly — he teased a hapless nurse by pretending to be a hidden child: what had the nurse done to deserve this? He continually disrupted a coach trip to London by throwing his voice so people believed a straggler was trying to catch up. He caused an opera to be stopped not once but four times, each time using a different trick: but what was the point? And what would Frankie have had to say about someone who continually disrupted *Peter Pan*? Valentine just liked to watch mayhem descend. It was all rather mean-spirited and self-congratulatory.

And there was one thing that troubled George above all else: Valentine's skill, the very subject of this thick brick of a book — could it actually be done? He fell asleep with the book open on his chest and dreamed indistinctly of voices that called out to him but whose source was unknown.

Next morning, Don flicked through the book, taking particular note of the inscription, and lit a cigarette. When he'd finished, stubbing it out carefully in the pewter ashtray, he asked about the dedication: "Joe?"

"That was my grandpa. Died when my mum was very young."

"Hmm." A swig from his flask left a milky stain around Don's lips. There was a long silence.

"Don? Can you throw your voice?"

"No." Don laughed.

"No, I mean, can anyone throw their voice?"

"It's a trick. People used to talk about it all the time. It was big when I was at school here."

In his surprise, George forgot Valentine: "You were *here?*"

"Still am."

"Did you ever leave?"

"A long time ago. Nineteen fifty. Went to public school — St. Catherine's."

"Was it good?"

"No." Don shook his head. He spoke tersely, used to giving the truth in as unadorned a fashion as possible. "Didn't like it. But that was just me. I wasn't well. You'll have a grand time." He saw George eyeing the flask and offered it to him.

"I can't have that!" said George.

"I know what you think, but it's not booze. It's soothing for my stomach."

"I'll get the book back off you tomorrow," said George.

He walked back past the long-jump pit, trying to imagine getting his body even as far as the sand. Leaves crunched underfoot. It was getting dark early.

Don had given the matter some thought overnight.

"Your physics teacher would be able to explain it better than me," he said, though George doubted whether Poole would have any opinion at all. "Look. Where is my voice coming from, then?"

"From your mouth," said George. They were on some errands, standing on a messy patch of gravel outside a lawn mower shop.

"How can I make my voice come from over there?" Donald pointed into the distance behind George's head. "I can't, and I can't persuade you I can, because you see my mouth moving and you hear sound coming from my mouth. Think about it. You can't train your throat muscles to defy nature and produce a sound far over there without having it *get* there first, can you? Sound waves don't work that way."

"So the book is a load of rubbish."

"The book is fascinating, but in the real world no one can do what he does. But, see over there. . . ." Again he pointed, but this time to the front door of the shop, and George followed with his eyes. As he did, he saw Donald's lips move as he said: "*Over here!* . . . It's called misdirection. The eye moves quicker than the ear and tells the ear where the noise is coming from. The ear follows the eye and believes what it's told. After I tell you where it's from, you look and think that's where it is."

"Wow," said George, unconvinced by Donald's lame attempt at illusion but grateful he had gone to the effort. George watched the mechanics unload the Upside lawn mower from the back of the school van. What Donald was saying made sense, but there was something missing. He couldn't get it out of his head as they did their errands.

"Do you like comics?" Donald asked. George nodded. "The Superman kind or the Beano kind?" Both were illegal at school.

George understood that a voice could not logically be thrown — but a Fisher knew that you could persuade people of almost anything. And Donald had demonstrated the rudiments of the illusion. If you could harness that "power" — make people utterly believe that there was a voice coming from elsewhere — what could you use it for? How far could you go? Certainly the events in *Valentine Vox* were exaggerated, but would someone really have spent so long writing 512 pages, each filled with 700 words, if the whole thing could be dismissed just like that, as a *kids' book?* Were people so very stupid whenever the book was written or was their willingness to believe in Valentine a longing for magic that George could exploit even today?

"I don't know how," he said when he'd been rewarded with two comics for helping load some plants from a nursery, "but I'm going to find out how to do it right."

"Good for you," said Donald, smiling, lighting a cigarette, and leaning up against the back of the van. And then he spoke while smoking for the first time ever. "Think of all the things you could do. But not just stupid stuff like Valentine . . . Do you know what *ventriloquism* means?"

"Making a dummy talk?"

"I looked it up: literally, 'speaking with your stomach.' And the book keeps harping on about abdominal intonation."

"Is that how they do it?"

Don laughed. "That's what they believed a long time ago. You can have a go, but you probably need a full stomach. Do you know where Mrs. Cakebread's is?"

"Over there," said George, as though he could throw his voice.

The rest of the Upsiders returned, full of themselves and life beyond. The corridors lost their ghostly echoes and were once more filled with bickering, with predictable family boasts and the arguments these provoked. George didn't want to talk to anybody. Nobody wanted to talk to him.

That first night, a reading period was allotted after chapel. Everyone sat at his desk in supposed silence, flicking unwillingly through a book whose covers he had never previously opened. With spirits so high, the attempt was doomed. Commander Poole, even more irritable than usual, made his rounds. He marched between desks to inspect chosen reading material, confiscating anything inappropriate: only the Bible, *Great Expectations,* and *Jane's Fighting Ships* seemed to pass muster. By the time he got to George, the Babel of prohibited titles rose high in his hands. "And what's that?"

George said nothing, flipping the pages to reveal the cover.

"I see," said Poole, who had no idea what he was being shown. "Library book, Mr. Librarian?" He made it clear that librarianship was an effeminate pastime that would have seen George drummed out of the navy.

"From home, sir."

"Signature from the headmaster?"

George winced. His eyes stung suddenly, closing against his will.

"I'll have that, thank you very much."

And *Valentine Vox* was gone. Poole's final words: "You can sit there and reflect. These are coming with me."

Nothing else had riled George, not enforced games, not half-term on his own, but this was pettiness. Spite and stupidity had taken the book from him, the book that was a gift from Evie, that was all he had left of her, the book that kept her alive. Staring at a desk scarred and tattooed by years of previous inmates, George was furious for the first time since his arrival. He lifted the lid and felt for a pair of compasses.

Something had changed over half-term. The others — his schoolmates, the staff — had all run off to their homes, but George had stayed. He felt a part of the school, of the building, of the grounds, as never before, but more alienated than ever from its inhabitants. The Hartleys, quiet Don, and George: these belonged. The rest were part-timers, tourists, even Patrick and his father, and he would keep them at arm's length, forget them, boys and staff alike. He had more important things to consider. When Poole was gone, he dug the compasses deep into the underside of his desk.

That night, he found an appropriate substitute for the proscribed book in the most unlikely place of all: the library. He must have been in a daze, bored with cataloguing the endless pile of Bunters, to have missed it before: "Billy Bunter's gifts were few," confided the back cover of *Bunter the Ventriloquist*. "He was no good at games. He was no good in class. He was no good at anything in particular — with a single exception. There was one thing that Billy Bunter could do, and do remarkably well. He could ventriloquize!"

Whatever appeal Bunter, *the fat owl of the remove*, might have had for previous generations was lost on George. Nevertheless, he read until lights-out and beyond, immersing himself in the archaic yet sadly familiar world of Greyfriars, where *beaks* doled out *impot* and *whops*, while Bunter exclaimed, *"Oh, my hat!"* The plot, such as it was, concerned the fattest and laziest member of the community's quest (for reasons of greed) to play on the school team. Ventriloquism was his sole means to this end.

At breakfast, George considered the book's similarities to the confiscated *Vox:* both featured a teenager, older than George (he estimated Valentine to be eighteen and Bunter eternally fifteen), with the wild talent of ventriloquism and mimicry (in Bunter's case unlearned and unexplained, in Vox's achieved only after "a severe course of training"); both were well versed in misdirection. Valentine was essentially a puckish mischief maker who used his art only to baffle the world, to make people look stupid, then stood back and watched anarchy descend. Bunter, on the other hand, was an abused and greedy tub of lard, using his gift to try to get his way, to "avenge all those wrongs and injustices that had roused his indignation." He made fools of his teachers — and didn't Poole deserve the same treatment? — but also used his art to serve his own ends. And if Bunter could use ventriloquism to get into games, why couldn't George use it to get out of them?

The opposing reactions to their talents summed up the difference: whereas Vox's unwitting audiences became *convulsed with mirth,* Bunter's turned on him and *administered kicks* or *six of the best.* At Upside it would undoubtedly be the latter — so, *Best know your lines before you take the stage:* an old Fisher maxim.

George was from a family of magicians — he would cultivate his own weird gift and avenge all those wrongs and injustices that had roused his indignation. His mind was made up on that point. He owed it to Evie and to Valentine.

The next day, his name couldn't be found on any dangling disk. Was he so bad at sports that they had forgotten him altogether?

Not knowing what else to do, he changed into his normal games clothes and walked outside with everyone else. Mr. Morris approached him confidentially: "Donald needs a hand with the swimming-pool cover."

George's heart soared at this mundane piece of information. He didn't know if it was for that day only or forever, and he didn't care. All his scheming to get out of games, or simply his wish at *Peter Pan*, had done the trick. It was as if he had thrown his thoughts.

He found Donald by the pavilion, smoking, staring off into space.

"Can't get rid of me that easily," said George.

They walked slowly to the swimming pool, either side of them whistles, grunts, and the dull thwack of smacked leather. George felt gloriously immune; being Donald's apprentice made him invisible. Donald set about the holes in the turquoise cover without asking for help.

"What shall I do?" asked George.

"Oh, this is pretty easy stuff," said Donald. "Sit and read."

"I don't have anything. Poole confiscated Valentine."

To George's disappointment, Don hardly reacted. "Maybe there's something in the cubicle."

It was a long shot. The cubicle was a row of numbered metal hooks with a bench that ran its length beneath. In front of this was a strip of wood (that covered an average boy from knee to nipple) with saloon doors flapping at either end. Imagining the shivering goose pimples of cold early summer, George peered over the fence. There, a little farther down on the bench, was a tatty green book that he knew without further inspection was *Valentine Vox*. Beneath it, the two comics. George could barely contain himself. "Don! Thanks, Don! How did you get it?"

Donald tapped the side of his nose and winked, turning his attention to the smelly adhesive. "Read to me."

George sat cross-legged on the concrete and opened the book to find Swish's initials on the inside cover. "'In one of the most ancient and populous boroughs in the country of Suffolk, there resided a genius named Jonathan Vox. . . .'"

"All done," Don said finally, as he lit up. George knew he wasn't going to get much out of him, so he idly opened one of the comics. He'd been a fan of these garish American imports ever since Des had brought one home from a business trip, though what he liked was embarrassingly beside the point. Forget the heroes and the superheroes, those mild-mannered Joes who became bats, spiders, or green giants — the real wonders, the real gifts, were on the back pages: the advertisements. These transported him to a different world beyond his wildest dreams: a world of spyglasses, sea monkeys, auto scare bombs, funny chatterboxes, and 250 Magic Tricks. For years he had endured Bazooka Joe bubblegum purely to look at the offer inside, but here, at the back of these comics, was an entire Cash and Carry of fascinating novelties. Normally, he would have dallied over the mysterious Ouija Talking Board, the vibrating matchbox, the see-o-scope and companion exaggeroscope, perhaps the live chameleons, but today he didn't get beyond the very first ad.

"Don!" he shouted. "Don!"

Don turned around, cigarette hanging from his bottom lip. He pulled it off, smarting as he removed a strip of skin. "What?" It was the first time he had seen Don annoyed.

"Look!" George put the page in front of him, unable to resist jabbing his finger and reading aloud: "'IMITATE RADIO FAVORITES! BOYS! Learn Ventriloquism and Apparently Throw Your Voice! Into a trunk, under the bed, under a table, back of the door, into a desk at school, or anywhere. Lots of fun fooling teacher, policeman, peddlers, or friends. THE VENTRILO, a little instrument, fits in the mouth out of sight. It is used in connection with the above, and with the aid of this wonderful DOUBLE THROAT or VENTRILO, you can imitate many kinds of birds, animals, etc. Anyone can use it. Seldom fails. Ventrilo & 32 Page Book. No. 3461. 10c.'" There was an accompanying cartoon — in front of a car, an angry cop; in the backseat, a naughty urchin with a cheeky grin throwing his voice so that the driver appeared to be yelling at the cop, "GET OUTA MY WAY, FAT HEAD BEFORE I PUNCH YOUR NOSE!"

"How much is ten c?" asked George, hyperventilating with excitement.

"About five pence."

"Five pence! *Is that all?* I have five pence."

"It'll take some getting. It's in America."

"Look! You can throw your voice with it!"

"*Seldom fails,*" quoted Don dubiously, but George wasn't

listening. "I'll look into it. If anyone asks, say you mended the pool cover."

The bell rang. It was time for lessons. George was still in his games clothes at the swimming pool.

Two days later, he found a copy of the previous week's *Stage* awaiting his daily visit to the pavilion.

"That's your great-grandmother, then?"

"Yeah."

"Read it to me."

"OK." He cleared his throat and read: "'Some say ventriloquism died many years ago. Perhaps so. But they buried it today. Sadly, I suspect there can be few readers who saw Echo Endor in her heyday. The great, now late, Echo Endor was royalty in a bygone era of music hall and variety entertainment. Though this world, and the colossi that best rode its stages . . .'" (Don corrected him: "bestrode") "'. . . bestrode its stages, is largely forgotten, and though she is now less well known than several of her contemporaries who ventured into film and television, Echo Endor was the most successful of all female ventriloquistes and one of the last great stalwarts of the British variety stage. We shall not see her like again.'"

The lengthy obituary continued with the facts of her career, minutely recounted, before: "'In 1910, her marriage to the great Wallace Fisher, the self-ordained "Tsar of Impresarios," cemented her position at the top of her profession. They had but one child, Joe King Fisher, who also went into the family business, and whose wartime exploits with his dummy, Garrulous George "GC," earned him the famous nickname "Death Wish" Fisher.

"'The long span of her sixty-year career in music halls and variety saw her receive billing with, amongst others, Chaplin, Tommy Trinder, Danny Kaye, and even, at the end of her illustrious career, Cliff and the Shadows!

"'She was voted Ventriloquist of the Year by her peers three years running, the only time a female has received this honour. In 1959, she was awarded the Medal of the Realm of Britain for her charity work, having raised a total of over £250,000, much of which went to Byng House, Essex, the home for retired variety performers. In 1961, she received the OBE for services to British Entertainment. In 1966, she was named one of the British Magic Greats at the British Museum of Magic, where Narcissus is still on display, in a ceremony officiated by Tom Tiddler and Ermintrude.

"'Unfortunately, the microscope of television held no appeal for her, and she died with her mystery intact. Her absence from *The Happiest Night of Your Life* and other shows that continued to support the Good Old Days coincided (not coincidentally) with her running foul of one of the Grades, an unseemly resentment that saw her unwelcome on various of their shows, stages, and screens. Or perhaps her day, anyway, was gone.

"'Echo Endor died peacefully in her sleep on October 10, aged ninety-four, in the bosom of her family. And thus passed a legend. She leaves behind a legacy of laughter and joy, and, in the charming shape of her granddaughter Frankie Fisher, a worthy heir. Narcissus, whose catchphrase "Do you love me? You *know* you do!" was the "Give us a twirl!" or "Shut that door!" of its day, is said to be "voiceless" with sadness.

"'Say her name once more: ECHO ENDOR. Thanks for the memories. Did we love her? You *know* we did.'"

George folded *The Stage* and put it down, his eyes full of tears.

"Well, you're a chip off the old block, aren't you? What was she like?"

"Well, I suppose she got quite difficult towards the end, actually, but she was a grand old lady." It was such a perfect description of her, so preferable to the image he now had of the skin hanging slackly from her arms and elbows. "She was awfully competitive. She beat me at everything, even darts, even from her bed."

There was silence.

"And what about your mother?"

George smiled. "Oh, she's like a character in a fairy story."

"Which one?"

"All of them. Peter Pan, maybe."

"I bet she is. Want to read me some more *Valentine*?"

Two weeks after half-term, the weather was turning cold, and George was more grateful than ever to have an alibi in Don. This was worth the teasing, and George did not respond — there was nothing wrong with being a *farmer*, however the word was sneered, and Don was neither *spaz* nor *alkie*. He kept their conversations a secret even from Patrick. When this one friend, inspired by a spying craze, tried to enlist George in some sound experiments of his own (a string telephone made of two tin cans and a length of twine that wasn't long enough), George politely declined, thinking it very childish, and Patrick went regretfully in search of another participant.

Out of boredom, George even did a little schoolwork from time to time, though he had become so engrossed in *Valentine Vox* and the secrets of ventriloquism generally that he was disinclined to do much of the work set, having discovered that if he applied himself for about ten minutes, in prep or in class, he could keep up quite easily.

His class had been asked to write essays on their families. Alone in the library, inspired by the obituary, he started to write about Evie, who had told him that not all things could be explained, that "some things are just magic"; and Narcissus, her "favourite boy"; and her son, his grandfather whom he never met, the entertainer of the troops. He hadn't even got onto Queenie and Frankie, and already the essay seemed completely inappropriate. He didn't like the way his family read on the page, and he didn't need them paraded before his English class. So he stopped writing, resenting the time it was taking, and in a moment of protest, searched through the few books in the Young Readers section, finding something called *Children Like You*, a very boring looking book with stock black-and-white photographs, from which he copied the following (with appropriate amendments): "My father is called Peter. He works in a bank in the City and goes to work every morning on the 8.12 from

Esher. My mother sees him off at the station after we have all had our breakfast. My day begins with a short walk to school."

As he went on, the changes he made achieved a kind of creativity, as he struggled to let the piece keep its own internal logic while believably describing the day of his fictional family. His father was a great success, doing big things in the City, his mother a devoted homebody. His brother, Ron, was keen on football; and his dog, Rover, chased the neighbour's cat. Everybody else's essay would read like the one from *Children Like You,* with the odd stepparent thrown in for good measure, and this is what he handed in.

Mr. Burgh gave him a solid seven and a half out of ten without comment. There were some corrections of English (and try telling those to the writers of *Children Like You*), so Burgh must have been paying some kind of attention — but not enough to notice, if he even cared, that George had no such family.

A week later came George's birthday. When his name was read during the roll call at lunch, the headmaster allowed himself an ironic chuckle that signified a deluge of mail. There were cards from his whole family (only Sylvia was unaccounted for), from the cast of *Peter Pan,* from Reg. An anonymous ersatz ransom note contained the news, in letters cut from *The Daily Express* (confirming the hand of Queenie), that a chocolate cake, direct from Mrs. Cakebread's, would be delivered for tea.

"It's my birthday," said George, breathing in the familiar brew of turpentine, creosote, paint, and white marker in the pavilion. He found Don in an unusually lively mood.

"I know." Don handed him a wrapped present. "Well, you know how much it was, anyway. Happy birthday."

George ripped off the paper and studied the contents: a thirty-two-page booklet and the tiny Ventrilo, "The Wonder Voice Thrower," precisely as advertised.

It was the key to the kingdom.

Throughout the last two periods of the day, unending double French, George fingered the Ventrilo in his pocket, imagining its potential, feeling its power. Out of class, he found a secret corner in which to experiment. The item in question had turned out to be a rather unprepossessing little object (unpictured in the original advertisement — this should have raised suspicions), comprising a patch of thin white gauze and two small curved pieces of metal around which was stretched a rubber band. The Ventrilo was to be placed on the tongue, then pressed against the roof of the mouth: "Hiss strongly till the sound comes through. Then practice talking and other imitations." So far, George had managed only to spit it out and was yet to experience any profound ventriloquial benefits.

He remembered that he was required to make a list of the people with whom he wanted to share his cake: Patrick should have a slice; he owed Campbell; he certainly wanted to send a piece to Mr. and Mrs. Hartley. But most of all he wanted to find out Don's last name: he couldn't write "Old MacDonald," and just "Don" seemed rude, as if the man were some kind of peasant. It was easily discovered — Don had said he left Upside in 1950.

George skated down the corridors as far as the leavers' boards in the main hall, caressing the Ventrilo lovingly, like a new filling. Having begun to suspect it was useless, he had finally managed to manoeuvre it where the diagram specifically recommended and was hopeful that he might finally get some results.

George traced the interminable list of names (commoners in black type, scholarships in red) and dates back in time, alternately sucking and blowing on the Ventrilo gadget, achieving nothing more than a tuneless whistling. There were about twenty leavers in 1950 — among them, coincidentally, he noticed someone called Hartley. Donald Hartley. In red.

Donald Hartley?

St. Catherine's School.

"Fisher?" boomed a voice offstage.

George had been so lost in the implication of the fact that Donald's last name was Hartley that his shock at the materialization of the very man who had suddenly metamorphosed into Donald's father was too great. He gulped and swallowed nervously; but if he expected anger, Hartley was all bonhomie as usual.

"Looking for inspiration amidst the scholars of yore: a perfectly good activity for a birthday." Something in George's eyes gave him pause. "What is it, boy?" said the headmaster. George's eyes swam with tears as he started to choke. "Something stuck?" George coughed and swallowed again.

"Yes, sir," George answered barely, his eyes streaming.

"Well, you wouldn't want to be unfit for your birthday cake. I'd go and see Matron."

"No, I'll be all right, I think, sir."

"What was it?" What could George say? "Well, I think I can probably imagine. Sweets for the birthday boy, et cetera. So be it."

George massaged his throat as he watched Hartley disappear. No point in going to Matron now.

He lay in bed that night and kneaded his midriff, wondering whether he had a stomachache, and if he did, whether it was from the three slices of cake or the Ventrilo. He had overindulged on the logic that when all was said and done, the Ventrilo was better out than in, and if it was to get out, then eggs, flour, milk, butter, sugar, and chocolate would probably smooth its passage. But the Ventrilo had not yet emerged. And he was by no means certain that he did have a stomachache. In fact, he felt fine. Better than fine.

Somewhere in his belly was the Ventrilo.

Now he was Valentine Vox.

Things would be different in the morning. Again his mind filled with muddled thoughts of voices calling out — but this time it was different: he was the source.

He was the ventriloquist.

4

The Fisher Fol-de-Rols

The debut of the new act was New Year's Eve 1933, at the Trocadero.

Joe had eventually seen sense and relented under constant maternal pressure, though he had done so for reasons of his own.

She had beaten him.

What would be his consolation? I would, he hoped. He put aside his manuals. Through me, he could speak the things he otherwise dared not say; previously, besides, he'd had no one to confide in.

(And so, to make sense of my life, I started this diary. My message in a bottle has washed up on your shore.)

Once he had decided, he thought us ready to perform immediately. Echo scotched that idea — and she was right. It was wonderful when we simply let the words crackle between us, or when I spoke and he said nothing at all, but it didn't add up to anything: it wasn't an act. Though I had plenty of personality, I had no particular character. As I waited in vain for him to develop material, Echo foisted some of her old routines on us, and, as first night beckoned, no better alternative offered itself. Thus it was that we found ourselves doing Echo's routines to her audience at her show.

If Joe had thought to use me as a means of escape, he had not realized how far Echo's shadow stretched. She planned everything: our agent (her agent), our eight-by-tens (her photographer), our bio in the programme (full of outrageous lies and there, there, the great Romando name in bold), our place (far better than we deserved, the penultimate turn before the interval) on the bill (her bill), and our wardrobe (formal). Her motive was obvious — it was she who would be judged and found wanting.

The master of ceremonies, Tubby Jeans, wearing a large chequered suit I should sooner have used as a tablecloth, was under strict instructions from his employer, Echo, to assure the audience that they were in safe hands. She stood behind us as we waited for our introduction. The heat of battle — her element — found her calm and steely eyed, the colonel who, without a flicker of emotion, sacrifices a battalion to win the war.

"Look at him! Ugly tub of lard, but how he works them!" Sweat dripped down the sides of Tubby's face, its glistening progress halted only by bushy muttonchops. "And if things are going badly, I'll be here!"

"Ladies and gentlemen, you knew Vox Knight and his *Thousand and One Knights*," bellowed Tubby, as Joe shifted his weight from one foot to the other. "And you know, you love, Echo Endor. And here is one more from the School of Fishers in *The Ocean Deep*, one *more* from the *First Family of Vocal Gymnastiques*, your new friend, your soon-to-be-favourite, *Joe King Fisher . . . and George!*"

"Go!" said Echo. "Don't let the side down! I love you!"

We were on.

I had never seen so many people in my life. The sidelights and hangings bathed them in an exotic crimson glow, and all those eyes, aisles of eyes, staring at us. There was silence. And a cough. And another. I heard Echo's voice from offstage. She was saying something, which I struggled to hear. She was saying, "Say something."

"Say something!" I hissed to Joe, who stared straight ahead, wearing a stiff smile. "Say something!" I said, much louder, in desperation. The audience exploded into laughter. "Blimey!" I said after a moment's pause. "It don't take much!" Another wave of laughter. Joe didn't move, eyes fixed. When the laughter subsided, I leaned to the side, jiggling up and down, and said to Joe, "I'm gonna need some 'elp, mate. I can't do this all on me own!"

More laughter! This was really happening. We were actually doing it at that moment. We were doing something now.

"Script!" Echo urged from the side of the stage. Joe, as though waking from a trance, turned his head and saw her make a winding motion: *get it going; speed it up!*

And then, in a slightly formal manner, Joe asked me, "And how are you today, George?"

"I'm very well, thank you, Mr. Fisher."

"You're very well, are you?"

"Yes, I'm very well, am I?"

"Yes, you are."

"Well, if you know, why are you asking?"

The ensuing laughter was faint praise compared to their previous raptures, and it was a disappointment to be back on course. We had been about to take them somewhere new, but we retreated and ended up somewhere safe, with something they'd heard before — literally, if they'd seen Echo in the old days. We rattled through the routine and did a funny bowing bit, completely spontaneous, before making our exit to healthy applause. Under special instruction, the entire Drolls cast thronged around us.

"A good recovery," said Echo confidentially, kissing Joe on the cheek and ruffling my hair. "It was touch-and-go for a moment, but I knew you'd pull through. Very respectable."

As the orchestra burst into "I Was Only a Poor Little Daisy," Echo addressed the backstage masses: "Friends, members of the cast, thank you so much for sharing this historic moment. The great Vox Knight is looking down with pride. Frugal man that he was, however, he'd be horrified to hear that Fisher Fol-de-Rols, the Drolls to you and me, is throwing a New Year's after-show to which you are all invited. Now, let's make the rest of the show one to remember."

Enry Edley, who had been billed as the new Albert Chevalier for twenty years, passed on his way to the stage. "Well done, kid," he said in his Cockney wheeze. "Them's big shoes."

I looked down, but I knew what he meant.

The entire second half was designed to make Echo's splendid entrance as dramatic as possible. The ultimate star part, Echo maintained, was not someone in the picture for all ninety minutes, but the person who was talked about for eighty and appeared right at the end, looking her very best. This was the philosophy of all Fisher Fol-de-Rols productions.

Joe and I watched the buildup to the finale from the wings. Echo was, *unmistakably*, a star before whose brilliance the curtain had to be lowered. It had likely been planned that the climax be preceded by acts of negligible talent, with the result that the audience breathed a collective sigh of relief when it heard the familiar first chords of Echo's theme song, "Say Her Name Once More," pouring out its enthusiasm even before the curtain was raised.

I had heard much of her famous grand entrance. Echo appeared separately from her beloved partner, joining him in the middle of the stage after she had dismounted so elegantly from the trapeze that flew her in (at a stately pace and a modest height). But I was quite as excited to see Narcissus.

We were yet to come face-to-face. For a little while, either of us might have been under the mistaken impression that we were being kept apart, but in fact, Narcissus did not live at home. He travelled from venue to venue, under lock and key, to rendezvous with Echo at her next engagement. There he had his own dressing room. (Actually, I won't exaggerate: he had a room in which his clothes were pressed and his hair tidied, and this room he shared with the outstandingly dowdy Diane, dresser to both Echo and Narcissus.) His was the star part: talked about constantly, mentioned in hushed tones by anyone who visited, he would only now finally appear.

In full regalia, Echo looked like the ocean. She was wearing a dazzling deep blue sequined ball gown, which lapped at her body in waves, with a sparkling silver headband to which a stuffed kingfisher, diving into the waters beneath, was secured with a hatpin. A plume of sea green feathers framed her hair. Diane, a short stump of a woman with bandy legs, now brought Narcissus to the stage for a last-minute inspection before he was taken to his mark. Echo took him on her arm, this old boy, her partner.

I couldn't quite believe how antique he was, as if purposefully distressed. He was glassy-eyed, his hair giving him the look of a senile don, and his terrible clacking mouth now bounced uneasily up and down, probably due to worn-out hardware, in a fair impression of Parkinson's. Forget the fake tears, which I (and some of the newer boys) had, Ogilvy should have given him a fake drool. How would he look, straight out of a night in the box, without makeup, his hair not yet coiffed? It didn't bear thinking about.

Echo gave him a cursory once-over, seeing nothing I have just described. She took note only of the accessories, which were perfect: the clothes newly pressed, the shirt crisp and white, the shoes gleaming, the pinstripes immaculate with their razor crease. There were tales of other ventriloquists who had become obsessed with their boys to an unhealthy degree. Echo was not one of these.

"I'll take him. I need him just so," she said, to the surprise of Diane and those around her — Echo only fussed when people least expected it, overestimating the importance of a trivial detail as though she were the only one with the genius to recognize its significance. A stagehand offered to take Narcissus from her, but she slapped away his hand: "Me!" As she walked Narcissus to his spot, she passed us. Narcissus and I hadn't yet been introduced, so I thought it polite to say something, particularly after I had judged his appearance so harshly.

"Have a great show," I said. "Break an egg!"

He stopped in front of me. His lower jaw quivered.

"Nice try. Watch closely, kid. You might learn something."

This was not said in a kind way, and he was gone before it sank in. I turned to Joe, who was looking straight ahead, and then back to the stage. Narcissus was on his spot, and Echo upstage, where she was climbing a ladder for her appointment with the trapeze.

I was numb for the entire performance. I heard the introduction ("Ventriloquism without a safety net!"). I saw her conservative swoop. I heard the audience's unabashed enthusiasm. I saw the bows and felt the rumble that demanded an encore, and then another. I didn't see the standing ovation but heard it announced by the snapping of seats. Yes, all that: but I was numb.

At the party afterwards, we sat in the corner, sulking amidst the popping merriment, unimpressed with the floor show. A lovely figure of a girl with delicate jaw and deep brown eyes, her black hair fashionably bobbed, flitted around the dressing room in a minuscule piece of chiffon over which a purple robe was sashed lazily at the front. She landed, as if by chance, on Joe and gave him the glad eye. After a few moments, Echo snatched her away: "You can't monopolize him all night, Phyllis dear. Come hither and meet someone who can do your career some good. Joe," she added in admonishment, "not your type!" before turning to greet the incoming "Nigel!" Echo had moved on since the matinée idol, though her new companion, a recent find, was almost his double, a coat flapping around him as though a great gale were whipping through the green room.

"Soon as I could, darling, soon as I could!" said Nigel, before his exhalation bathed the room in a smoky Turkish haze.

"You missed it!" said Echo, after he proffered his silver case. I had the horrid impression that she wasn't referring to our début, but Nigel, to his credit, assumed otherwise.

"How was it, Joe? How did it go, old man?" He clapped Joe on the back, holding his cigarette at an arm's stretch away while luxuriating in his own emanations.

"Very well, thank you. How was yours?"

"My female lead, the dread Amelia . . . You're the specialist, but it's I that am acting with a dummy! Let me tell you . . ."

"Tell *me*, Nigel," said Echo as she bore him away.

* * *

There were four more shows that week. We opened the second night with off-the-cuff banter, as we had on the first. Although it went quite as well (in fact, better), Echo again reined us in with frantic mime, this time vacating her post stage left before our turn was done. Before the third show, she told Joe (in front of Tubby, when she could perfectly well have told him at luncheon that afternoon): "I don't know what you're trying at the beginning, but it makes the show look a trifle unprofessional. *If* you don't mind. Thank you, darling."

Without comment, this most enjoyable part of the act was cut. The thought of regurgitating the same mediocre stuff night after night stuck in my craw. Seeing the week out would be agony. The third night was our own fault — we underperformed. Though we did not walk off to the sound of our own footsteps, the journey was inordinately lonely.

"Going from strength to strength, Joey," said Echo in the wings, barely having to raise her voice above the modest applause.

"They *loved* you," sneered Narcissus. I can imagine you get a little jaded in the Indian summer of your career, tired of a younger generation snapping at your heels, but there was no excuse for his behaviour; his spite unsettled me.

Despite this, the first chords of "Say Her Name Once More" drew us magnetically to the stage every night, moths to its footlights. And every night, the same rigmarole: the trapeze, the jokes, the scrupulously well planned ad-libs. And every night, the applause, the ovation, the bouquets and bows.

Oh, she deserved it. She gave herself entirely to her performance. She wrote herself on a huge canvas to be read by all. And he lived too. They drew breath as one.

The end of the run found Joe hugely relieved, and his mood lightened. Back in his room amidst the comfort of his books, he withdrew into his writing, neglecting worldly ends. Although the Fol-de-Rols was over with until the Easter season, there was never a gap in Echo's calendar, and we saw less of her than ever. Joe indicated her colourfully stamped postcard that spoke enthusiastically of spring in Blackpool and a summer season in Brighton, our participation taken for granted.

"Spare us!" he begged no one.

Perhaps another young man could have found salvation in a pal, a confidant, or a girl and a marriage, a family in which he could take refuge. But who would have this awkward, shy man? And how besides could he meet someone? Not at the Fol-de-Rols, that was certain. Green Room Phyllis would have eaten him alive.

I saw it now. It was to be me against Narcissus, and Joe against Echo. We needed all the help we could get. We would never find our true voices if Joe was nothing but a pale imitation of his mother and I of her boy: we wouldn't rise higher on the bill wearing their hand-me-downs. Echo offered him one hand and pushed him down with the other. She had him exactly where she wanted him.

It had to end. At least he had enough rebellion in him to know that. It was time to fend for himself, without his mother, without the passport of the family name, without, even, me.

I was abandoned in my box. For many months.

Resuscitation came for an unlikely reason, from an unlikely source.

There had been a crisis. Due to a shipping mishap, Narcissus would not arrive in time for Echo's opening performance at Daly's Theatre. The telegram had arrived too late for her to call up one of her ventriloquist friends (and they were few enough anyway), and Ogilvy & Son of Brighton were mourning the death of their senior partner and thus unable to offer an immediate replacement. Desperate times call for desperate measures and, as a last resort, Echo had come searching for me, believing that I would *do*.

She brought an accomplice, a large woman, wearing a tent of a dress printed with huge violets, who looked me up and down as though I were standing in front of her in nothing but socks and garters. An attractive woman, the girl next door's ample friend, she had large glasses, a big smile, and a vast, unconquerable range of bosom hidden in the flower show of her marquee. About thirty years old, she spoke with the trace of a West Country accent, and had come to London to stay with her cousin Diane the dresser with the thought of looking for work on or near the stage. She'd become a familiar face at Echo's various London appearances over the past year. Originally, Diane had advised her to avoid the diva, even to avoid looking at her if possible, but Echo had taken a shine to this forthright, motherly woman who seemed more Echo's age than her own. She was called Queenie.

Two hours later, I found myself in Narcissus's dressing room, faced with a travelling steamer trunk that housed a collection of his identical outfits. Various points of view were advanced as to whether I should be dressed like Narcissus, if the audience would silently accept such an extremely poor substitute, or whether, if we let me remain myself, jokes might be inserted to cover for the fact that I obviously wasn't Narcissus. Given the nature of Echo's act (as permanent as the Pyramids, possibly dating from the same era), it was decided that I should be disguised and presented without comment. It was demeaning to have to substitute for that Nasty Narcissus, grotesque to be dressed like him, to pretend to be him. And yet, and yet, *I was out of that box!* How could there not be some novel aspect to the whole situation that would save the day?

Diane had to lavish far more time on me than she had predicted, which put Echo in a tetchy mood, and Queenie did double duty, assisting with any of the star's other demands. The help chatted as they worked, conversations unhindered by the various hairgrips and cigarettes between their lips. When they were finished, the mirror revealed the horrifying transfiguration they had worked on me. I was grey, old, and miserable.

"Poor little devil, covering him in all that stuff!" said Queenie.

"Di!" Echo screeched.

"Bit busy, ma'am!"

"If you think you're busy now . . . Look who's here! Crisis averted!" A delivery boy rushed through the door, wheeling a

large trunk with hotel stickers pasted willy-nilly over every surface and an unmissable red label: *URGENT!*

"Crisis averted, my arm!" moaned Diane, as I was summarily
plucked from the chair. "Twenty minutes to go and his bloody
nibs turns up!"

"I'll take him," said Queenie, groping my innards for a
handhold.

"Set him here," said Diane of Narcissus, very matter-of-fact.
"Right, twenty minutes . . ."

"And counting . . ." In came Echo, sporting little more than
her underwear, a complicated system of wires, weights, and pul-
leys designed to smooth the surface of her dress. The delivery
boy gasped and turned his back.

"Put that on!" shouted a gruff unknown male voice from
Echo's room. She plucked a flying sarong from the air and shim-
mied within. Assured of Narcissus's presence, she glanced at me
and sniffed dismissively.

"Valiant attempt, Di dear, but really . . . I suppose we'd better
put him back as we found him. Queenie, would you mind?"

"No, no, not at all."

My spine was completely out of alignment with her manhan-
dling, my chin resting on my shoulder.

"And do have a care of him, dear," Echo said pointedly. "You
wouldn't want to upset *you know who* . . ."

"No, quite," said Queenie. "Leave it to me." She peeled Narcissus's pinstripes from me. Within seconds Echo was screaming
for help. Di was brushing Narcissus's hair with one hand, her
other in his torso, where she was trying to staple his shirt to the
inside of his back so it stopped rising behind his collar. "I'll go,"
said Queenie. As she got up, my head toppled out of my body,
which flopped back onto the sofa. As my face hit the floor, a tiny
chip of my nose broke off. "Oh, blow!"

"Just go to her," hissed Diane. "We'll see to him later."

And so I stayed in two, face down in the dust, body marooned
on the sofa, until Narcissus was ready.

Was any further humiliation possible?

Only one.

Echo entered in her sea of blue to pick up Narcissus, the vampire with his black coat and overly rouged lips. She balanced him on her arm, administering final touches that did no good whatsoever. As he made his way to the stage, he threw me a look: "Nice try, kid. Better luck next time."

Queenie loved to tell the story: she had been out one night with a group of girlfriends when the blustery night forced an odd left turn away from Leicester Square. They found themselves sheltering beneath the sign of an out-of-the-way place called the Eclectic Room. Without their knocking, a turbaned man addressed them through a small panel in the door, demanding a password.

"We don't know no password," said Renée, the ringleader, giggling.

"Yield to the power of the mind," he intoned. "The name of a town."

"I don't know yer bleedin' password!" said Renée, then, turning to the others, "Come on. They don't want us in there, and I'm drenched."

"Don't be frightened. Yield," said the doorkeeper insistently, with a forceful hypnotic gaze.

"Brighton!" said Queenie, just to prove a point.

The heavy door opened smoothly for them.

"That was never the word," tutted Renée wearily, as they went through.

"Madam," said the doorkeeper, and pointed to a sign to their left: BRIGHTON.

The bill at the Eclectic Room was a series of very respectable cabaret magic acts. Queenie loved a magic show, though her mind froze when she tried to work out how tricks were done. She wanted no more than to enjoy the retreat into illusion. It was the least-popular act of the night that caught her eye.

Although this clean-cut young magician seemed barely old enough to be out, he and his immaculate tails belonged to a more elegant era. Performing in silhouette against the wall, he didn't call attention to himself, preferring not to address the audience, and his tricks, though by no means spectacular, had a particular elegance in harmony with his entire presentation. The audience gave the Chinese rings their marginal approval, but his card tricks were less well received, and she noticed a slight trembling of his hands, a nervousness at odds with the rest of his performance. Renée and crew's attention had drifted elsewhere, and they cast their eyes about to see who might stand them the next drink, but Queenie was still intrigued. For his climax, he faced the audience and spoke forthrightly: "Ladies and gentlemen . . ."

It was then that the mayhem began. A voice called to him from the side of the stage. He pleaded that he was in the middle of his act. Then there was a heckler somewhere in the audience. And another, arguing with him. The house, adding to the general din, turned around to see who had been so rude as to shout.

"Be quiet!" the magician finally yelled into the maelstrom. "All of you!"

There was complete silence. The audience stopped shuffling, unsure where the disturbance had gone. The magician pulled back a curtain stage left: no one. Then, a disembodied voice was heard from stage right; again, there was revealed to be no one.

"Ladies and gentlemen, I am King Fisher. I am an illusionist, a ventriloquist. And I present for your amazement the unique power of vox humana." He bowed, and he was gone.

A smattering of applause mixed with baffled silence. The whole act had been a prelude to this bizarre climax, which had merely left the audience uneasy. The next turn picked up the pieces, but Queenie could think only of King Fisher. She assumed all the voices had been his, that that was the point, and wondered whether he was as lonely as he appeared on the stage. He had brought something out of her: that was how she put it. As the rest of the entertainment ground on, the happy faces in the Eclectic Club left her sad. There was no sign of the young man.

The next day she went to visit her cousin at the Alhambra, dying for a chance to talk about her night out. Diane was only marginally interested until mention of the Fisher name, which caused her to dart into Echo's dressing room and return brandishing an eight-by-ten, signed to his mother by the magician in question. Queenie could hardly believe her luck. He had gone off on his own, Diane said, and even Echo didn't seem to know what he was up to; this raised him further in Queenie's estimation.

They hushed the moment Echo returned, but her beady eye noted the picture's absence. She gathered clues and went on a slow offensive. Queenie, who was beginning to suspect, not to her displeasure, that she was being set up, finally gave in, confessing all on the trip to fetch me from Joe's room that Echo had specifically engineered. She begged Miss Endor's confidence.

"Oh, rot. You're just what this family needs. I thought so the moment I saw you. And please call me Echo. Queenie, listen." It was Echo's final word. "Every magician needs an assistant."

Three Parts for Fisher: Slave of the Ring

The end of term was still three weeks away. Three weeks with Frankie flew by in a quick dissolve of high teas and curtain calls. These would last forever.

Her run of *Peter Pan* was finally coming to an end, climaxing in a sold-out weekend in Plymouth. She then immediately went into rehearsals for her annual pantomime. Year in, year out, it was Once More unto the Breeches: her Christmases full of thigh slapping, fishnets, stubborn props, and "He's behind yer!" — it mattered not which pantomime. Whether there was a beanstalk, a genie, a talking cat, or seven dwarves, there was always a dame (who did a striptease), a villain (who was hissed), a fairy godmother (who was a little boring), a cheeky chappie (who was hilarious, but rather morose backstage), a principal boy (who was Frankie), and some poor twit dressed up as an animal. This year, she was Aladdin at Wimbledon; the best, for all of them, was that she would be at home throughout, ferried back and forth by taxi.

She sent a glossy postcard of the Wimbledon Empire: "Busy in rehearsal, but it's lovely to be home. Reg has moved in as a lodger!

Nice company for Mum. It's going to be a lovely Christmas, and we'll be spending a lot of time together (believe me!)."

She had something up her sleeve.

The return of *Valentine Vox* had not diminished George's resentment. The school felt no less his, and certainly more his than theirs.

The Ventrilo hadn't yet made an appearance. Although George hadn't become an overnight Vox or Bunter, the urge had taken root as certainly as he could picture the Ventrilo inside him. Don's gift had been the Ventrilo itself, but it was the revelation of his true identity that had carried the Ventrilo down, lodged it deep inside. George knew about Echo, and his grandfather. He'd seen Queenie and Mikey, the puppet she used at the kids' parties. He wouldn't fail. It was in his blood: his mission.

Work was an inconvenience, and George sought ways to reduce the burden without affecting his marks. Once he went so far as to experiment with cheating. He wrote a history essay in his free time, scribbled idly elsewhere in his exercise book for thirty minutes, and handed it in to the perenially stale-smelling Mr. Hessenthal. Next day, it was returned with the smile reserved for those who did exactly as they were told. This had saved George revision, time better spent on other business.

After his initial success, cheating became a habit. It was so easy. The first rule: don't look at the teacher. The second: don't tell anyone — people were noticed only when they acted in groups, and George was alone. What else had he been doing in the library all that time, if not working, preparing for the essay or the test at which he had excelled? He plagiarized from books and encyclopaedias, rephrasing appropriately, barely noticing the facts as they were transcribed. Cheating was an art form, and he improvised. He favoured the subtle (tracing the formulas from a sheet below), the imaginative (writing the answers out and hiding them in a semi-opaque file left carelessly on the desk, invisible to all eyes but your own), and the adventurous (complaining about the noise in the class and asking to do your work in the library, where a previously written essay was waiting in the drawer of the desk — this was the fail-safe); he avoided anything risky or obvious (inking key dates on the palm of your hand or copying from somebody else's work — bound to fail).

A by-product was that it made people look stupid: particularly Poole, so pompous in his stand-alone "laboratory" a wet shuffle away from their form room. George was not remotely interested in physics, so he hardly felt that by cheating he was cheating himself — the old maxim. He was cheating Poole. It was revenge. He noted the high grade on the bottom of his essay, considered its inverse proportion to the effort he had made, and wondered if he should make less in future.

Advent calendars appeared. Frankie had sent George the classic model: a glitter-flecked Nativity scene whose daily doors opened to reveal Germanic wooden toys undesirable since the beginning of the century. By Christmas, however, the calendars would be forgotten, jettisoned in school desks, to become sad January reminders of holidays recently past. The big day for Upsiders was the seventeenth, the end of term.

As George popped the doors open one by one, school petered out in a jumble of festive games and carol services. His name appeared on a list of performers for the Christmas entertainment. The bare minimum was more than his audience deserved, but when George spotted Don leaning against the wall bars, the Fisher in him triumphed. He laid into "Li-Fang-Fu," complete with theatrical mime, as if Christmas itself depended on it. For this recitation, the staff rewarded him with an encore, for which he dusted off his old standby "Albert and the Lion." It inspired Hartley to make reference to the Lent term's school play — coincidentally not "Albert" but *Androcles and the Lion.*

"Very good," said Don the next day. "Get that from your mum, do you?"

"Yeah. And my grandma, and Evie. And my Auntie Sylvia. All of my family."

Groundsman and apprentice had given up on *Valentine Vox,* in which situations had begun to repeat themselves monotonously. Instead, Don and George had been reading together from the Ventrilo booklet, which proved most informative, though exceedingly cynical about any mystical aspects of voice throwing. Don allowed himself a rare joke when George admitted the Ventrilo's current location: "Maybe you can keep your mouth closed and talk through your arse — that'd fool people."

Don was Hartley's son; his the young face George had seen in the photos, his the room that George had slept in, surrounded by his old books. But George said nothing. Clearly he was not meant to know or Don would have told him: standard practice in the Fisher family. His silence repaid Don's kindness. Now, however, it felt as if he was keeping a secret from Don. This made for a little self-consciousness; it was as if Don knew.

On the bright, crisp morning before term ended, he entertained the idea that this was his last day at Upside and decided to tell his only confidant.

He found Don cowering in the corner of the unlit pavilion. George had seen Don quiet and less quiet, but never so wretched. The groundsman made no attempt to look up, his cigarette burning deeper orange as he inhaled in the darkness.

"I think this may be my last day here," said George after consideration. There was the soft electric crackle of tobacco. He continued as though Don had asked why. "Well, I just think it's silly me being here. I don't fit in. I don't play games. I'm not much like the others, am I? My family's nothing like theirs. I don't hardly even talk to anyone else. I like being in the library, and with you." Don's face was obscured in the gloom. "I mean, I don't do a lot of work," George continued, electing to omit mention of the cheating. "I don't like the food . . . or the rules . . . or the teachers. I don't have any friends. I miss my family and I'd rather be home. I think everything they do here is stupid."

These were just statements of fact. He wasn't worked up. He hadn't even started on the uniform or the name of the school when he realized that Don was crying, his head in his hands, sobbing to himself. The Fishers cried at the drop of a hat, at the end of almost any movie, at a suggestive piano chord, at the slightest piece of bad (or sometimes good) news. It was the way they were. But as easily as they cried, they knew it was equally hard for others, and George had never seen a man in tears. He didn't know what he should do, but he knew what Queenie would do. He put his arm around Don's shoulder.

"Sorry!" said Don, through some undignified gulps. He reached over his shoulder and clasped George's hand. It came to George in a flash. It was time to break his vow of silence.

"Don, I do know, you know." There was no answer. "I know who you are." Don didn't speak. His eyes were bloodshot, lids trembling. "I worked it out . . . from the leavers' board. You're his son." Don turned away. "OK?" asked George. "It's OK, right? I won't tell anyone, OK?"

Don started crying again but was able to say OK.

Cool winter light flooded the pavilion as Potter barged in. George looked up with the surprise of someone caught cheating.

"I'm afraid Donald is . . . ," he began.

"Donald," said Potter, all concern as he twitched his moustache like a rabbit. "All right, old man?"

"Migraine," mumbled Donald, and shaded his eyes from the light. "Close the door."

"I think you'd better run along, Fisher. Go to Matron and tell her that Donald is poorly."

"Yes, sir," said George. "Bye, Donald."

"Bye," said Donald, though it was little more than a groan.

Matron sniffed unsympathetically, making no secret of her unwillingness to walk an aspirin down three flights of stairs and all the way to the pavilion, and not willing to entrust George with this simplest of tasks.

That night, there was Christmas pudding. One lucky boy waved a ten-pence piece around triumphantly. George paid no attention, playing with rather than eating his dessert, idly flicking currants around the plate until it was removed. He hoped Don knew his secret was safe. Similar worries nagged at him through prep, but by lights-out the thrill of going home took hold, and by morning all else was forgotten.

In rolled the Royces and Rovers after chapel, the front lawn a fortress of trunks and tuck boxes. Among the approaching fleet came a large black taxi, or perhaps a hearse — at any rate, a swollen and luxurious motor — bouncing with dignity over the sleeping policemen. Out stepped Reg, in his chauffeur ensemble, to open the door for Queenie, who declined to emerge, waving imperiously at the headmaster as she ordered Reg to fetch the trunk.

"Yes, milady," said Reg, and came over to George. "You wouldn't believe it," he whispered. "She's drove the whole way here, but she's made me stop at the bottom of the drive so she'd be in the back all regal. And she slipped and she's covered in mud, so she's staying put."

George laughed and shouted, "And be quick about it, my man!" as other parents observed the poor little rich boy's high-handed treatment of the family butler. Reg doffed his cap agreeably, and the Quicke-Johnsons regarded him with curiosity. The headmaster called George over.

"I wondered if, rather than going home, you'd like to stay with us over Christmas. . . . Joke, boy, joke!" George reached out to shake Hartley's leathery paw, imagining it the last time they would ever meet.

"Thank you for half-term, sir. That was very kind. Will you please wish Donald a merry Christmas for me?"

"Run along now," said Hartley, banging his pipe on the sole of his shoe. Scanning the immediate vicinity, he picked a random parent for scrutiny. "Sterling work, Mr. Morgan; bend from the knees!"

George got into the car and kissed Queenie.

"Hello, love," she said. "Mud everywhere. It's like the Somme back here." She settled back in the seat, pulled her spattered fur around her neck, and called to the front in her best House of Windsor: "Wimbledon. Centre Court."

*   *   *

A big surprise, was how Queenie described it, that would make up for half-term. They were going straight to the Empire and would be just in time for the first matinée of *Aladdin*.

"Are we going to stay for the evening too?" asked George, who had not made the mistake of looking behind him as they drove away.

"You wait," said Queenie.

George had rarely known Frankie at home around Christmas (though *always* on Christmas Day itself), and like many children, he couldn't imagine Christmas without a pantomime. But George had grown up with a different perspective. He had been neither paying customer nor player, rather an intermediate with carte blanche when he ventured among the punters. Not for him the family outing, the proscenium arch, and a chair where he slumped with a box of chocolates and a magic wand; his view had always been from the wings or "any free seat" via the pass door. He had known all the in-jokes and precisely how long till the interval. He was able to spot any deviation from the script immediately.

"Georgie!" Frankie exclaimed. They had arrived in plenty of time but seemed to rush backstage. "How you've grown." Tears welled in her eyes. As they hugged, he felt her signalling over his shoulder. He tried to extricate himself to see what was going on, but she held him even tighter: "No, no, no . . . not till we're quite . . ." And then she turned him round, her hand in front of his eyes. She whipped it away with the standard fanfare — "Ta da!" — that accompanied the unwrapping of any gift, the arrival of any main course.

From a cocked finger, Reg dangled a clothes hanger: there hung a grey waistcoat festooned with fake jewels, a white frilly shirt, a pair of shimmering green pantaloons, a silver-sprayed wooden scimitar, and the yellow beehive of a turban.

"Happy Christmas, O Slave of the Ring!" said Frankie. "This Christmas, your stage début."

"What?"

"Scout's honour," said Frankie, waving a programme in front

of him, his name printed clearly among the cast. "No time for rehearsal: here are your lines, get your clobber on."

Frankie had had a *contretemps* — this was the nearest she ever got to admitting to an argument — with the director over the previous Slave of the Ring, who'd done everything except say his lines on cue: the culprit was demoted to the chorus. A sweep of local children's dancing and acting academies yielded no suitable replacement, and Frankie had the bright idea of casting a boy she knew to be more than capable of putting himself over, and what is more, a boy on holiday from school who wanted to be with his mother.

The Slave of the Ring was a small but essential cameo, under no circumstances to be confused with the Slave of the Lamp, played by a pleasant, well-developed older girl, Joanne. The Slave of the Ring saved the day and granted a wish to Aladdin (Frankie); his mum, Widow Twankey (Bernie, a gruff but kindly northern comedian); and his brother, Wishee Washee (Dennis, the host of a children's show George had never seen). He then stuck around to help Aladdin fight off Abanazar. At the successful resolution, he took his bow with Joanne.

Mercifully, the Slave of the Ring did not appear till the last act, and this gave Queenie time to refit George's costume while he learned his lines:

> *O spirits of the wind and sky,*
> *Off to Peking! Make them fly!*
> *Speed through the air like an arrow true —*
> *Aladdin, Widow Twankey, and Wishee Washee too!*

As she rushed by between entrances, Frankie said, "If you forget a line, just make sure the next one rhymes and you're fine. Besides, I'm up there with you. And don't mask anyone." She said she forgot lines all the time, but he knew she didn't. Her every corpse and fluff was scrupulously rehearsed. Spontaneity was reserved only for her interaction with the children, and they loved it.

By George's entrance, the auditorium was littered with sweet wrappers (purchased in the foyer or hurled from the stage by

Widow Twankey) and anxious parents wondered whether to encourage their tired toddlers to volunteer. As he waited backstage for his cue (the end of Abanazar's version of "All Shook Up"), George wondered how close he and Frankie would be on stage: he was used to watching her from a safe distance, and he knew the feelings this summoned within him. The only surprise when he hit his mark, however, was the accompanying pyrotechnical flash and the heat of the follow-spot on his forehead. His mother smiled her brightest smile, and George, standing with his arms folded as he had been told, declaimed, "I am the Slave of the Ring."

"I've read *Lord of the Rings*," said Dennis to the audience. "But I've never heard of this one."

"Oooh," said Bernie. "Nice sword — it's all curvy!"

"Scimitar," corrected Dennis.

"What to?"

"No, that's what it's called. Scimitar!"

"Scimitar to what?"

"I give up."

"And I come to grant you all a wish!" said George, seizing his moment, gesturing expansively with his left arm.

"A wish! A wish! I'll have a million pounds!" said Bernie.

"No, Mum," said Frankie, stamping her foot so flecks of dust swarmed in the footlights. "That's what got us into trouble in the first place. We want to go home."

It was at this point that evil Abanazar emerged and the fight ensued. For this scene, choreographed to a piece of classical music, Frankie had advised George to look interested and stay out of the way. Abanazar, vanquished and hissed from the stage, returned briefly to deliver his valedictory change of heart ("I'll make amends, I'll be astute, I'll join the women's institute"), and the trio sang a victorious chorus of "Take Me Home, Country Roads" before George recited his magical quatrain and off they all went. The curtain call went off without incident, and George's début was adjudged a triumph.

"Phew!" said breathless Frankie, who never took off her makeup between performances, only applying a second mask on top. "And the Oscar goes to . . . !" She handed him a box of After Eights. "You'd better have these, then."

George made tea as Reg hurried Queenie off to her party in Hammersmith. It was hard to believe, amidst all the hurly-burly backstage, that only a few hours ago he had been at Upside, that he was removed by no more than a car ride. He had left school far behind, forgotten it already like a dream, and woken into a grown-up world where he was treated as an equal. No one told him what to do. He didn't have to be anywhere, except on cue in the wings. He could eat whatever he wanted. He could read whatever he wanted. It was truly going to be the best Christmas of all time.

Pantomime was a mysterious upside-down world where old men played ugly women, beautiful women played handsome young men, and George thought it quite normal to be sitting backstage at nine learning poker from a bearded man in a dress. Bernie reminded him of what Hartley might have been if he hadn't gone into headmastering.

There were rules, some as strict, arbitrary, and unfathomable as those at Upside. Whistling was forbidden, certain words unmentionable. At school, you had to wear green; backstage, green was forbidden.

"Why?" George asked Bernie. "There's a green *room*."

"But it isn't green, is it?" said Bernie, as he tried to squeeze his breasts into acceptable curves.

"Why are you called Widow Twankey?"

"'Cos it's the name of the part!"

"Yes, but why is it always Twankey?"

"Jaysus, I don't know, son. Ask your fuckin' teacher."

One rule was never to be forgotten, and it had stayed with George ever since he was a small boy. There was a strict pecking order at the pantomime: the principal boy was at the top (that went without saying, though it was often said), and at the bottom, the very bottom, was the skin part. Whether it was Tommy the cat, tap-dancing his way to London in *Dick Whittington*, Priscilla laying golden eggs in *Mother Goose*, the magic cow in *Jack and the Beanstalk,* or even Nana in *Peter Pan,* the skin part never said a word or sang a note, only mimed. It was quite normal to look down on the skin "actors," these sad masochists happy to swelter in silence, doomed never to reveal their faces. Though these performers could bring a lifeless fur suit gloriously to life, and though the younger half of the audience might even consider them the star of the show, the skin part was the lowest of the low. George was polite to the man who played the giant panda, but no more.

"It won't be just his species that's endangered if he sniffs around my room," said Bernie.

There were other children milling about, the villagers of Old Peking (including the disaffected ex–Slave of the Ring) and some dancing cave rats, who shared a noisy dressing room as far from the stage as possible, but George stayed with Frankie, and that was just as he wanted it.

She started to complain that the orchestra was messing her about; she wouldn't be specific. Bernie, who found this more interesting than the backstage lore, was prepared to be forthright in the privacy of his own dressing room: "They're trying to take a peek up your mum's tunic, sonny. And so would you too, if you were playing that crap night after night. Now pop next door and bring us back a Rich Tea biscuit."

Frankie had banished George while she performed an annual ritual: wrapping Christmas presents, which she laid on the floor as she sat on her knees with rolls of wrapping paper and some Scotch tape. So he went to the green room, where there was always a rather mouldy pile of biscuits and some lukewarm tea.

"They're a bit stale, Bernie."

"I'll dunk 'em."

"Ever done any ventriloquism?" the Slave of the Ring asked of Widow Twankey.

"Bugger me, no. Gottle o' geer? Not on your nelly!" He cursed again as the dunked biscuit belly flopped into his tea and disintegrated as it sank to the bottom. "Hand us a strainer, son," said Bernie, who then strained the contents into another cup, flicking the soggy remains of the biscuit into the bin. He sipped his tea.

"Lovely," he said, and his mood improved. "So, d'ye do any acting at school, son?"

"Not yet. I'll be in the play next term, though, unless I decide not to go back."

Bernie laughed. "Mum know about that, does she?"

"Yes," said George confidently. She didn't, but he assumed that everything he, Frankie, and Queenie wanted was in perfect sync.

"Georgie," shouted the principal boy. "Will you come and do me up?"

"I'll come and do you right up, love," said Bernie.

She was standing at the door with her tunic clasped at the neck. "You, Bernie Mills, are a dirty old man. Georgie, he's a bad influence. Come out of there."

"You'd understand if you were in the orchestra, my lad!"

"Bernie!" she growled. "Stop."

Frankie breathed a sigh of relief as she shut the dressing-room door behind them. Then she clapped her hands together and squealed: a pile of Christmas presents lay beneath the radiator. "Look! But don't touch!"

A muffled moan of frustration came from the adjacent dressing room.

There was only one performance on Christmas Eve, and the show was down by seven p.m. Frankie and George hadn't been home much until then — every day began with a hearty breakfast before the daily dash to Wimbledon, and they rarely returned before midnight — and that night was the first they spent together as a family.

Already Reg was one of them, as though there had been a space reserved for him. He had taken the spare room, although there were still no curtains, and George wondered how he slept in the morning. As Frankie had suggested, Reg was more than a lodger; he was a friend for Queenie, a chauffeur for her jobs, but also someone she could look after. He took a special pleasure in settling into the old leather armchair by the fire — in other houses, it would have certainly been called the man's chair — where he philosophically worked a toothpick round his gums.

Frankie made a great show of domesticity at family gatherings. She solicitously offered tangerines, nuts, tea, sandwiches. "Here's my favourite bit coming up," she said, glancing at the television as she left the room to fetch another round of mince pies. When she'd finally settled down, the movie done, Reg announced an early Christmas present for Queenie, who raised her eyebrows: "On Christmas Eve? Aren't I special." Reg handed her a small package, which she unwrapped. She smiled at him, and her eyes filled with tears.

"Do you really want an old girl like me?" she asked, as Reg made to kneel in front of her. "Stop, you'll never get back up!"

"You'd make me the happiest man in the world. I've waited too long, girl. We've been apart too long. It's now or never."

"Of course I will. Come over here."

"Oh, Mum!" said Frankie, dabbing the corners of her eyes with a serviette. "Did you know? She knew!"

"Well, I may have had an inkling . . . ," said Queenie, who wouldn't let go of Reg's hand, which she had firmly in her lap.

"You'll have to call him Uncle Reg now," said Frankie to George, sobbing happiness.

"No Uncles here, not for a grown lad," said Reg, who poured everyone, including the grown lad, a celebratory drop of scotch. "George, you'd make an ideal best man."

"You'll have to give a speech, mind," said Queenie.

"Unaccustomed as I am . . . ," intoned Reg. Everyone laughed — the generosity of the house was such that anything offered as humour, however unoriginal, was suitably rewarded, particularly at Christmas. "I've been waiting a long time for this," said Reg, toasting his good fortune. "Too long."

Caught up in the moment, George remembered what was missing. "I wish Evie could have been here to see this."

There was dead silence, silence as had never been heard among Fishers unless mandated by a script. Queenie, glancing at Reg, seemed on the point of an announcement, but Frankie interrupted: "Yes, if only Evie were here, eh?"

"God rest her soul," said Reg, as a toast. "This is for you, Echo Endor, wherever you are." He said it with a smile, but as he tipped his glass forward in salute, it seemed to angle away from heaven.

George always had trouble sleeping on Christmas Eve, but this year was different. *Aladdin* had him exhausted, and he woke later than he ever had.

"Look at Sleepyhead," said Reg, from a breakfast table laden with smoked salmon, bubbling with champagne.

A fire roared throughout the day, and everything possible was done to keep the world at bay, to keep Christmas in its Victorian time capsule. When the phone rang in the early afternoon, only Reg, in his yellow crown, was fool enough to answer. "I'm cooking," Queenie yelled. "They can call back." The day turned slowly through stockings, pillowcases, the women cooking while the men relaxed, and then a late lunch, punctuated by crackers and a flaming pudding from which each family member received the traditional silver threepenny bit. (The coins weren't baked into the pudding like at Upside. Queenie palmed them into each serving to make sure nobody was disappointed.) By the last bite, everyone had lost the will for anything but sleep.

Queenie had evidently saved a little treat for herself and Reg. "Shall I?" she asked.

"Yes," he said. "You should." Queenie excused herself and went to the phone, while Frankie and George amused themselves with a little plastic puzzle, of an impossible factor of difficulty due to the cheapness of its manufacture, recently fallen from a cracker. Reg looked at his fiancée with pride as she dialled, but when she didn't turn round with a smile of her own, he grew more serious.

On her return, she simply shook her head. "No, I'm afraid not. She won't."

"Not *yet*," said Reg.

"She won't talk *yet*," said Queenie. That was her only glimmer of hope.

"Who?" asked George. Frankie frowned and shook her head confidentially.

"Not even now," said Reg, shaking his head.

"*Who?*"

"Come on, Mum," said Frankie, her attention elsewhere. "It's all right. She'll come round."

"*Who?*" asked George. This would never have happened with Evie alive. They all looked at him.

Frankie sighed and stopped trying to get the tiny metal balls to drop into the correct holes. "Sylvia," she said.

"My daughter," said Reg. "The daughter I don't know." Reg felt Frankie's and Queenie's eyes on him and asked innocently: "What? The boy's old enough. George, I've been in love with your beautiful grandma since the war, and Sylvia is our daughter."

It was like a light at the end of a tunnel George hadn't known he was in: Sylvia and his mother, so different; Reg, so strangely familiar. "Why haven't you seen her?" he asked involuntarily.

Frankie was nodding, her eyes half closed in scrutiny of the situation. "Tell him if you have to," she said. "But not a bad word about Evie. I won't hear it."

"Just the truth," said Queenie, as though on oath. "George, Frankie's father was away in the war, and the long and the short of it is that Reg and I, *we*, fell in love. And we were blessed with Sylvia. And then Joe died. . . ." She reached for Reg's hand. "And that made for a horrible guilt every day. Not only that, but . . ." She looked at Frankie. "Evie made me feel it. I'm sorry, but she did. We depended on her, me and Frankie and Sylvia, for everything. And after we got the bad news, Evie forbade me to see Reg at all, wouldn't hear his name."

"She did more than that," said Reg firmly, as he massaged Queenie's engagement ring around her finger.

"You don't know," said Frankie, looking away.

"George," said Reg. "I did quite a stretch in jail."

George gave a cry of disbelief. "What for?"

Reg nodded, acknowledging that it was a reasonable question. "Looting."

"All you did was rescue stuff," said Queenie.

"You called it rescuing; they called it looting. Trouble *is*, they were right. I thought it was fair game, kind of a public service, if you like. The question is: how did they find out?"

"Mum! Reg!" said Frankie through gritted teeth. "It's not needed anymore. It doesn't help." It was as though Evie had bequeathed Frankie all her influence.

"No, you're right, darling. Anyway, Evie put her foot down," said Queenie. "She said she'd take Frankie. And I *had* to stay, I had to, for the girls. There was no choice." Then she added with a smile, "I was getting no help from the Prisoner of Zenda here."

"Yes," admitted Reg, counting passing years on his fingers, "'cos then I was away for a little longer, like. Completely unrelated," he assured them, adding in mitigation: "Well, it was a difficult time. I didn't have a lot to live for."

"My marriage had been quite difficult for both me and Joe," said Queenie. "We were rather thrown together. But with Reg . . ." She looked at him circumspectly and smiled. "Well, hard to believe now, I know, but . . ." It was easy to tell the story; she had been practising for so long. "Evie wanted me to stay lonely, in memory of her son. And that was hard when I'd found someone, but it was the only way she'd put up with Sylvia, and *put up* was all she ever did. And when we could, when he was back out, Reg and I did see each other, though she could never know about it — and New Year that year, we went away together when you were up in Edinburgh, and she found out. Through nobody's fault, I'm sure." Frankie was staring at the game from the cracker as though she could make the balls slot home with her mental energy alone. "And she told Sylvia there and then, told her what she'd told me never to tell her."

"And the girl upped and went," said Reg. "Don't want nothing to do with us."

"*Yet,*" said Queenie.

"Where there's a will, there's a way," said Reg.

There was silence. Frankie was chewing the inside of her cheek. "Merry Christmas," she said with a smile around the table, as she sought permission to end the conversation. "And God bless us, each and every one."

But Queenie wasn't quite done. "And, Georgie, that's why when you said it was a shame that Evie wasn't here to see it, well, I had to explain that it could never have been. Sad to say: it's only because she's not that we can. And he waited for me all those years."

"We should have run away years ago and eloped," said Reg.

"Anteloped?"

"Anteloped. Back then. Mind you, it got a bit easier when she couldn't get out of bed no more."

"Reg!" said Frankie in mock horror. She had regained her equilibrium almost immediately. "Can we get back to the business of Christmas?"

"It's better out in the open," said Queenie. "We wouldn't want to keep anything from you, would we, Georgie?"

"That's right," said Reg.

"There's a Christmas to be had!" exclaimed Frankie. The three of them started moving dishes to the kitchen.

George sat back, weighed down by turkey, brandy butter, news. Strangest of all, none of it was unexpected. He was happy for Queenie and Reg, sad for Sylvia, relieved that everything was known. It was Evie he was muddled about — no wonder there had always been friction with Queenie, living in the same house all that time, juggling the two sisters; and Frankie — she'd known all along and pretended otherwise, just like during the interval at *Peter Pan.* Presumably, she had her reasons; perhaps she was just being kind, thinking George too young.

Exhausted, they sat back and recounted the day to one another, sorting through the mountain of wrapping paper, Queenie separating the reusable from the useless, folding the former as neatly as possible, and Reg torching the rest.

The subject turned to Upside, Reg pretending to choke on his cold turkey when George said that he helped the groundsman. "What is it, a slave camp?" George changed the subject when they asked about schoolwork, and started to tell them about *Valentine Vox,* how the book got him interested in ventriloquism; he was just about to tell them about the Ventrilo, when Frankie clapped her hands and interrupted.

"We'll have to follow family tradition and buy you a dummy. That's what Evie would have wanted. But you can't really have schoolboys anymore. They look a bit old-fashioned, creepy."

"You want something like what Queenie's got," said Reg, referring to Mikey, the bright green monkey who was a cross between a fur rug and an alien.

"Thank you," said George. "But I was thinking of the other kind of ventriloquism, not with the figure — not that there's anything wrong with that, of course. . . ."

"Perish the thought!" said Queenie, in an impression of Evie, which honoured her memory as it lightly mocked her. It was Queenie's recognition that despite everything, regular attitudes had reestablished themselves, that the family compass hadn't lost magnetic north.

"I want to make voices appear out of nowhere, so people can't believe their own ears. I want to make a voice come from behind there" — he pointed to the grandfather clock — "and over there, and over there."

"Blimey," said Reg, with a splutter of scotch. "You're not just a chip, you're the 'ole bleedin' block!"

"Darling, that's wonderful," said Frankie, as she crawled over to hug him.

George hadn't been expecting such an ovation. He'd thought they would react as they had when he had told them he was building a large model train set in his bedroom. Queenie, who hadn't said a word, left, returning with a stack of books that she placed on the floor. It was Frankie who spoke.

"You remember Evie had some special things for you? Here they are. You never knew my dad. Death Wish Fisher! All his life, he had one dream — just what you've been talking about. And when Evie was looking through her things, she found his notebooks, on how to do magic and all sorts, in his tiny writing. His life's work, I reckon."

Frankie pulled out the first book. What had once been black with a burgundy cloth binding was now washed-out grey and pink. It was tied together with string, and the covers, acting more as a portfolio around the interleaved extra pages, were badly bowed. Queenie produced her always handy nail scissors, and Frankie cut the string, declaring the book *open,* and turned to a page of faded blue ink.

"See, look. And . . ." On the first page, there was the date 1940 and the inscription:

> *Imaginations, fantasies, illusions,*
> *In which the things that cannot be take shape,*
> *And seem to be, and for the moment are.*

"Longfellow, I think," said Queenie. "He loved his little bits of poetry: Shakespeare and that. Always quoting Dickens too, he was." Beneath that was written in the same faded ink: *For my Grandson.* "And that," she added, "is you. And if anyone knew how to throw his voice, Joe Fisher did."

"Shall I tell you what I always remember about him?" His handwriting had tripped a memory in Frankie. "His voice, reading to me, when I was just a baby."

"What was he reading?" asked Reg. "You remember?"

"I do, yes. Beatrix Potter. We had a lovely set of those, a little miniature library. I wonder what's happened to them."

Queenie shrugged. George, however, was barely listening. The books were calling out to him, and he was already putting them in chronological order. Gifts had appeared from unexpected places this Christmas, but his family had saved the best present for last.

Boxing Day was back to work.

The pantomime lingered on almost until the beginning of term, adapting its references from Christmas to New Year to Back to School. Audiences dwindled as Christmas became an expensive memory.

Also lingering was Ricky Mitchell, Des's nephew and successor. A slightly overweight man of thirty-three, with a neatly cropped beard too grown-up for his boyish pudgy face, he had been little more than the office boy at the Mitchell agency, but the further Des had sunk into cosy retirement in the bosom of the Fishers, the more Ricky had insinuated himself, until his uncle relented and left him the company. Ricky had also inherited those clients (one of whom was Frankie) who stayed out of loyalty or laziness after his uncle's death. Des's stylish sleight of hand had been to make the nuts and bolts of business vanish — Frankie should worry about nothing but her art — but Ricky had no such trick up his sleeve. He thought only of the lowest common denominator, the bottom line: meat and potatoes, he once said, were his bread and butter. He was always on the lookout for, and ready to discuss at length, an angle, a package, a strategy, an extra percentage point (as, in his civilian life, he was obsessed with a better rate and a quicker route). Inviting himself into the dressing room, he would expect from Frankie a level of interest in, and an understanding of, percentages, net and gross, deposits and back end, box office trends, and taxes that his golden goose was quite unable to give, and that was perhaps beyond her. George found him a bore, laughing at the way he shaved his beard high so it gave the impression of a jawline, but Frankie was flattered, and somewhat relieved, by the plans Ricky had for her and, by encouraging him to involve her, flattered him in return.

Though the excitement of the stage never wore off, George had a new focus. He lived in Frankie's dressing room, no longer interested in pestering the dame for information he didn't have. Frankie chatted away, in between Ricky's frequent interruptions, but George's attention was elsewhere. He was reading his grandfather's book in bed, backstage, in the sitting room, over breakfast. He wanted to learn everything his grandfather had to teach.

Until now, Joe King Fisher had been a legend. George had stared at the medals and the famous photo above the fireplace: Joe in his uniform, little Frankie perched between his outspread legs, saluting. The two George Crosses were displayed close by, the most frequently dusted items in the house. *For Gallantry*, said the medal, as St. George hacked at the dragon. But who was this gallant hero?

Now here he was, the man himself in inky relief. He was never spoken of without reverence in the Fisher family: they idolized him, though the worship came exclusively from Frankie and Evie, who had regularly referred to him as "our war hero." George remembered sitting on Evie's bed while she flicked through her crisp yellowed press cuttings, black-and-white memories protected by see-through leaves. The whole story of their family was told in those gold-covered albums, Evie's lifeblood. Predating Joe was the Echo Endor Story, and even some dusty mementos of her father, Vox. She had looked back at the pictures of herself when she was the great Echo and told George the stories that accompanied every one.

"Why can't I call you Echo?" he once asked.

"Because now I am just an Echo, a memory, and I certainly don't want to be reminded of the fact."

After the war, there was more Echo, mute colours on stylish show bills, elegantly designed, and even a few polite mentions of Queenie (mainly from local papers); then came the rise of Frankie Fisher and a different kind of memento, on garish glossier pages.

Evie told often how Joe had answered his country's call as an entertainer for the troops. He hadn't thought twice: he had gone to serve as soon as he could, and this had taken him to the most dangerous forward positions. There was Joe with his famous dummy — Evie always called them "boys," though Frankie thought this a little ghoulish — pictures of the two of them with bravely smiling locals outside a bombed-out church, performing on a jerry-rigged stage to a company of soldiers, receiving the thanks of a mayor with a comically waxed moustache. Joe didn't age. His years of fame had been cut short. And he had done the art a great service too, explained Evie, making it brave and heroic in a time of crisis. Alas, he had been too brave.

The rest of the story had changed a little in the telling, adapted regularly to best suit the listener. The bare facts: in 1944, Joe "Death Wish" Fisher was performing to Canadian soldiers in Italy, when they were bombed. Many died. In the salvage operation, the few survivors, searching without hope, were amazed to see small black shoes sticking out from some rubble and, fearing it to be a local urchin, cleared the debris. It was Joe's ventriloquist dummy, his body thrown through the air by the explosion.

Joe Fisher was posthumously awarded the George Cross. "The least likely person ever to be awarded anything," said Evie, though she was unspeakably proud. Garrulous George, on the other hand, was sent to a field hospital. His stay there provided some of the most poignant clippings in the scrapbook, for in these it was as if he had become Joe, as if the hopes of England were on a brave human of real flesh and blood pulling through. He was a symbol of triumph against all odds, of Allied survival against the evil onslaught of Nazism.

Off camera, they shipped in a new tailor-made Tommy's uniform, had a makeup artist restore George's face, and, in the interests of morale, announced his perfect recovery. For the subsequent photo call, a replica George Cross, in recognition of George and Joe's bravery, was pinned to his lapel, an honorary award that provoked humourless debate in the letters pages of leading newspapers. "Whatever next, a Victoria Cross for milady's maid?" demanded a brigadier, who suggested that the newly founded Dickin Medal for brave animals — intrepid sniffer dogs, valiant carrier pigeons — might be more the ticket. The dummy, however, was no more animal than he was human, and, if only because of his name, an honorary George Cross was the popular choice.

"What does it take to get a George Cross?" asked *The Herald* of the plucky invalid.

"A Nazi with a bayonet," Garrulous George replied from his sickbed. "But I'm not cross; I'm cock-a-hoop!"

Britain's secret weapon was flown back to England and displayed in the Imperial War Museum: a national treasure. After his exhibition, he was returned to a sad but grateful Fisher family in an official ceremony, where, at Echo's fingertips, he delivered a eulogy to the bravery of Joe Fisher and expressed his gratitude to the country for his decoration. His exploits were over, his mark on the world made, and he was returned to the safety of his box. That was where he stayed, in his Tommy clothes, until the Fishers started to feel the pinch and agreed to sell him after all. They could still see him, behind glass, in the rather eccentric Armed Forces Museum, but since Evie had taken to her bed, it was a grave they tended less and less often. No such expedition had ever been suggested to George.

Though the dummy was no longer in the house, he was still part of the family, the bravest boy in the world, the boy that all Fisher children had to live up to.

"A learner should only move on when he has totally mastered a given effect," advised his grandfather's first notebook, and George vowed to obey this rule. Though he was desperate to get to the instructions on voice throwing, he mastered the urge to flip ahead. He began always to carry a pack of cards, another early instruction.

After a few days, he predicted to Frankie that by his fifteenth birthday he would know all his grandfather had known.

"You'll be like my son *and* my father," she exclaimed in delight.

As the holiday ended, otherwise unremarkable pieces of domestic trivia became sources of unexpected sadness. George kept reminding himself to savour every moment.

5

Behind Enemy Lines

I had two functions in the dressing room. For Queenie, I was a surrogate; for Echo, bait.

Echo encouraged Queenie to have a go with me. Apparently, we made *an adorable pair.*

"I couldn't, Echo! I can't do the lips."

Echo dismissed this: "Just turn your head a little, move *his* lips, and that's where everyone looks. It's called *misdirection.* Oldest trick in the book."

And so she toyed with me. It was not fun. You know what it's like when a child practises the violin, that terrible hesitant cater-wauling? Well, now imagine *being* the violin. Imagine being scraped, dropped, fiddled with, mauled. Echo had gone so far as to bring in some of her old practice scripts, routines even more in-fantile than the chestnuts Joe and I had performed in the Drolls.

Queenie was practising ventriloquism, yes, but she was also practising for Joe. His future was in her every touch. I had been drafted in as an understudy for rehearsal while the main actor fin-ished a previous engagement elsewhere. Though she made each manipulation with affection (and even love — for it was love that made her so determined), I watched a web woven around him.

Queenie was what they call in the trade *a natural*. Though she would never be adept technically, she had a quality that transcended all — children loved her. She had been fiddling with me three days, *three days* mind you, when that magnificent old ham Lex Lyon unexpectedly deposited his son with us while he went to *manjari*. Fifteen minutes of friendly banter passed with the cheeky little chap. I may have been involved in some of it, asking if he liked school and so on, but my major contribution was turning my head from side to side and smoking a cigarette, while Queenie involved the little shaver in half-witted conversation.

"You, my dear, have a gift," said Echo, observing unseen over our shoulders.

"Oh, I was only playing around."

"Precisely," said Echo, swooping the room as she searched eagle-eyed for her replacement kingfisher. "You'll make money with it."

"Oh, don't be silly. I don't even know what I'm doing."

"Nor do children. But they like you. Leave it to Echo."

I gulped. For Echo, I was bait, and with that woman playing Cupid, Joe stood little chance. He'd need all his wits about him, not to mention a considerable slice of good fortune, for this to end in anything but marriage.

And then, true to form, there he was, between the two shows on Saturday: a lamb to the slaughter.

"Look what the cat dragged in!" said Diane. Rain drummed on the skylight, and Joe's newspaper had been doubling unsuccessfully as an umbrella.

I was on Queenie's lap. She was flustered, as though we'd been caught in flagrante, and this she communicated through her fingertips.

"Visitor," announced Diane. Echo ignored her, but when Diane added, "Family!" the diva immediately materialized.

"Joe, have a seat. You're soaked through. Sit down. A cup of tea . . ." Echo threw a towel over his head and stood behind him, talking to him, about him, as she dried his hair, making a fuss as never before. The end of her monologue coincided with her growing bored, and she whipped the towel away like a tablecloth from beneath a set of china. ". . . and I don't think you've met Diane's young cousin Queenie." His hair was sticking up at various angles, still held by the remains of the Brylcreem that hadn't been dried away. "She's been . . ." Echo pointed high-handedly, indicating the contents of Queenie's lap: me.

"I hope you don't mind. I've been playing with your . . . George."

"Not at all." He sat down next to her. "I came to take him home. I was *told* he was getting in the way."

"*In the way?*" asked Echo in feigned innocence. Her work was done. Whether a horse drinks or not is no fault of the person who has generously bothered to lead him to water. If more persuasion was required, it could be done behind the scenes. "Lovely! She's got to grips with George, Joey. Children adore her!" And then she was gone. "Di!" came her immediate cry. Out trooped Di. Queenie found herself alone with him at last, separated only by me. And that was the way it was going to stay.

"Oh, look, his nose is a bit . . . ," Joe observed.

"My fault!" admitted clumsy Queenie. My head lolled to one side. "Can I tell you something? I've seen your act."

"The Drolls?"

"No, you on your own. At the Eclectic Room."

"The Eclectic Room. Oh, well, I'm afraid they had to give me the old tin-tack. Two nights running I started a fight and the police got called in."

"With the voices at the end?" Queenie kicked herself for bringing it up. "I liked that bit. I liked the whole thing."

He had to change the subject. "Let me have a look at him, then." He gazed at me fondly, as he never had before; it was as uncharacteristic as Echo's recent hairstyling routine. "Hello, old fellow," he said as he picked me up.

"Hello, Queenie! Hello, Joe!" I said. Her necklace fell between her breasts on a trampoline of black brocade so taut that if flicked, the locket would have bounced two or three times.

"Hello, George," said Queenie. "How do you do that? How do you do that so well?"

"How does he do what?" I said. She laughed. "It's me doing all the work," I added in exasperation. "And if you don't know that, then you don't know nuffink!" I turned round to Joe. "She don't know nuffink! They always give *you* all the credit. What about me? It's unfair!" She wasn't looking at me at all but scrutinizing his lips, watching his Adam's apple.

"All right, old boy," he said. "Calm down, calm down. And she's been having a go with you, George, has she?"

"Has she ever!" I said.

Queenie laughed, pretending to be shocked by the innuendo.

"And how do you like it?" he asked. I said nothing — but the question had not been intended for me.

"Oh, I'm no good. But Echo thinks I'm all right. She says I should take him to Christmas parties and such, for children. But I've no idea how you do those lips. Echo said you might give me a lesson or two."

"She did, did she?" Joe asked sheepishly before requesting rather formally that she show him how she was getting on. She reluctantly agreed. Though he kept a straight face, I'm sure he must have winced throughout what followed, and I the unwitting agent of this catastrophe masquerading as entertainment. However, there was a bright side to the shambles. I knew his standards. He would see everything for what it was. By the end, however, Joe was smiling.

"Echo's right. You're a natural. It's all there."

"Oh, you're just being nice."

"Well, I have some notes you might find interesting. It's all quite straightforward. You just have to learn a few simple substitutions. Tricks of the trade."

Queenie and Joe's first negotiation was almost complete. Echo and Diane passed through on their way to the stage.

"Bake an egg," I said, as Echo passed by with Narcissus on her arm.

"Thank you," said Narcissus, bowing graciously.

Everything was going exactly as they had planned. Perhaps his mother was right, despite her Machiavelli impression. Perhaps Queenie was just what Joe needed. Echo had been right about the ventriloquism; perhaps she was right about everything. How depressing.

"I must dash. I'm at the Razzle-Dazzle for two weeks: just a warm-up, but I do get my own spot every night."

"Can I come and see you?" She put me down on the sofa.

"I'd rather . . . It's not very . . . I'm not . . . You see, I'll only play places that I'm sure aren't booking me because . . ." He gesticulated at the empty dressing room that was Echo's. "Go on, then," said Joe with a shrug of decision. "Why not?"

"Do you want to take George?" she asked.

"No, I really don't need him. You hang on to him until we meet again for a lesson or two." He got up to leave, but she stopped him.

"Your hair, Joe. It's a little . . ." The mirror confirmed this. "It's stopped raining now too. Hang on a mo." She ran next door into Lex Lyon's dressing room and returned with pilfered Brylcreem, then borrowed one of Narcissus's combs. "You sit down here. I've done a bit of hairdressing in my time."

He sat in Narcissus's chair, in front of Narcissus's mirror, surrounded by Narcissus's things. What Echo had started with the towel, Queenie now finished. That was how it was going to be: he was being passed on, handed down. He had no idea what he was getting into.

After the good-byes, Queenie made straight for me, picked me up, and crushed me to her.

"And? And?" said Echo five minutes later. She swam in from stage like the tide, leaving starfish and sequins in her wake. Diane put Narcissus back in his chair, tutting with distaste to see his comb besmirched with Brylcreem. "And? And? And?" insisted Echo. "Be not coy!"

"*And* he said he'd help me with a few lessons," said Queenie, as though her heart had not soared at the offer. She and Echo were in league, but Queenie was determined to enjoy her innermost feelings in private. "He invited me to see him at the Razzle-Dazzle."

"That fleapit. Ha!" said Echo; she snorted and left.

Queenie took me by bus back to the unspectacular beige surroundings of her boardinghouse. She'd done her best to pretty the room up, but it had resisted her attempts.

Finally, after twelve nights, he came and lessons got under way. I call them lessons (and teaching did occur — he showed her how the alphabet broke up into easy and hard, how simple were the substitutions for the hard letters, how a relaxed smile was better than a fixed grimace), but, though the avowed purpose was to get Queenie's act shipshape for the glittering career as a children's party entertainer for which Echo had her marked down, it was all a polite excuse for them to be together. Progress, on all fronts, was slow.

Queenie told Joe she was wondering whether she could use *me* for her act, for which she even suggested changing my name, "for the children." Pip Squeak, she said, had been Echo's suggestion. The nerve of it! Couldn't he see the irony? Couldn't he see she was in league with the enemy?

"I don't want to be Pip Squeak," I said, trembling on Joe's knee. I wanted to be a children's entertainer even less than he did.

"No, you're George, and I christened you that," he said with a smile. "Perhaps you need your own boy, Queenie."

"I'll have to look into it," said Queenie, keen not to offend. "Are they dear?"

"I'll tell you what. Why don't you practise with George, and if you get an engagement, use him until you get your own."

Thus continued their ponderous courtship. Neither of them had a great deal of experience with the opposite sex. Queenie had dreams of imposing herself physically upon someone — I had experienced them momentarily — but was too demure to bring this about. Further, she did not respond well to romance, nor had she ever sought to spark it in others. Flowers, yes, if trimmed and put in water immediately, but no poetry. Her straightforward manner punctured any party balloon lobbed in her direction; people took the hint and stood off.

All was quite proper, and there was little prospect of progress. Both were waiting to be asked, and neither knew the question.

One night, Queenie went with a friend to see Joe at the Beauchamp, where he had finally secured proper billing. The two girls, dressed to the nines, set off like gamblers on their way to a casino, but Queenie came home earlier than I had expected, an amateur who had bet her entire allowance on the first spin of the roulette wheel and lost.

"Anything?" asked Diane one day, her forthrightness a relief amidst all the dithering. "Young Lochinvar. Any progress?" She stabbed her cigarette into a shell ashtray. "It's been months now." Had it? "Nothing?"

"Why the interest?"

"Her Highness asked. She's requested an audience with you. We're out of town, Brighton, from tomorrow. Perhaps you should pop down."

"What is it? Birds and the bees?"

Diane lit another cigarette, shrugged, and looked at the rain-flecked window. "Might be nice this time of year."

The next lesson took place a week later in the early evening. Queenie helped them both to an ominous sherry, and we all sat down on the sofa. He could smell unusual perfume about her, spotting the source on her dressing table: a decanter labelled *Denholm's of Brighton*, his mother's favourite perfumer. Both bars of the fire kept the room rather too warm; flowers were arranged with precision in the only vase. Queenie did not mention that she had seen Echo, but she did mention his engagement at the Beauchamp.

"Oh, I thought that was an awful shame," she said. "It went well apart from the technical difficulty. But the people will interrupt, won't they?"

"Well, you'll have to get used to that at your parties." They laughed at the thought of children, then stopped laughing at the same thought. "On to business," said Joe abruptly, and the lesson began. There was no doubt about it: Queenie was coming along — she had the basics, her handling had improved, and she was easily qualified to take children's minds off cake for fifteen minutes — but today her performance was particularly cackhanded. By this stage, Joe had even given up using me for demonstration; he merely held up his hand like a little ostrich head and talked to it. Lessons would soon be over.

She put me aside, got up, and poured two more sherries. When she sat down again, there was silence.

"Well, perhaps I'd better . . . ," said Joe, the full glass of sherry in his hand.

"If you like," said Queenie, but hurriedly thinking better of it: "Let's just finish our drinks."

After a moment of decision, Queenie took Joe's hand in hers.

"Queenie," said Joe in polite resistance.

"Shh!" she said. They sat without moving. She put her hand on his leg.

"Queenie!" I said, without moving my lips. It went unheeded, unlaughed at. I had meant to defuse the situation, put the brakes on before it was too late. As it was, I watched the crash from a horrifying vantage point. She leaned over, took his right hand, and moved it to her bosom, placing his fingertips just inside the neck of her dress.

"Go on, then . . . ," she said. His progress was not quite as she had planned, so she leaned over, moving her hand across his lap until it settled, and put her lips to his. They kissed without seeming to move. She moaned rather self-consciously, took his other hand, and placed it on her leg. If he moved his hand three inches farther up beneath her skirt, he would reach the top of her stockings, feel the clasps of her suspender belt, the handful of flesh above, which spilled over like a bag half full of water.

"Queenie," said Joe, his resistance less persuasive.

"I know," she said. "I know." She stroked his hair and pulled his head to her bosom, where he rested happily, looking straight at me. They made a bizarre tableau in front of my very eyes, a surrealist Madonna and Child. "Oh, hold on!" she said merrily. She quickly got up and turned off the light, plunging the room into darkness. "Come here."

The sofa shifted as he got up, led by her hand, and the bed creaked as one of them, both of them, landed upon it. She murmured his name. It was then that the noise began, slowly at first: grunts, creaks, and sighs. I thought of stockings, flesh, tan underwear, ballooning cami-knickers, and a brassiere the strap alone of which was two inches wide.

The only light, the glow from the bars of the heater, bathed me in a hellish glow.

"Those eyes," she said, suddenly looking over at me with a laugh. "I'm not having those eyes on me!" She got up and turned me round so my head was facing the cushion.

I remember nothing more.

Next thing I knew, it was daylight and my box was open beside me.

"*All night?*" asked Diane.

"No, of course not. He had to go to the Beauchamp." Queenie brushed out the bottom of the box with her hand and smoothed the lining.

"And?"

"Nosy!" But Queenie's tone answered the question perfectly well enough. And where were we going? Not out of the frying pan into the fire? After all I'd gone through last night, it surely couldn't be that I was being taken to a children's party today.

"My very own cousin Queenie!" Diane feigned surprise.

"Well, I just did what Echo told me," said Queenie, picking me up by the hole in my back.

"I wasn't privy to those pearls of wisdom," said Diane, thinking it less than she deserved.

"Oh, you know . . ." The sentence and I dangled in midair while Queenie decided how specific to be. "She told me to, to, *to take him in hand.*" She gave the last few words a confidential emphasis as she hoisted my feet over my head.

"And did you?"

"Yes, I did." She put me into my box, bottom first.

"And more than that?"

"And more." She patted me on the head.

Was it really, on top of everything, to be a children's party?

"Queenie!" said Diane. It was the last thing I heard as the lid slammed and the key turned in the lock.

I was trapped.

Three Parts for Fisher: Androcles

At Charing Cross Station, nothing had changed. Potter was propping up the same bar, drinking the same beer with the same purpose, while the same boys waited to get the same train to the same school. George's escort, however, was different. Reg, too proud to ask for a porter, scraped the edge of the trunk along the platform, while George carried his tuck box.

"We'll come and visit Sunday after next," said Reg. "And I want to see some of your tricks then. Oh, and here's a little going-away present from Henridge's. They're a bit special: stripper deck. Have a shufti." George was unbearably moved, so much so that his thanks seemed rather nonchalant. Neither knew whether to shake hands or embrace, an indecision further muddled by the self-consciousness they felt in front of the watching schoolboys. It was up to George to set the tone, so he wrapped both arms around Reg's midriff and clung on as long as possible. He'd never had a grandfather.

Potter herded the boys towards the train, and George lost Reg, who was under strict instructions not to stand and wave, in a forest of bodies.

"Hello, Fish," said Campbell, without enthusiasm. "What's that about tricks?"

"Nothing," said George.

Secrets were of paramount importance at Upside.

Chapel was more sombre than usual, prayers a little more earnest. Inevitably, many found themselves regretting opportunities wasted at home, moments in which they had allowed themselves to take freedom for granted. George had a deck of cards in his pocket, and as they sang and prayed, he fingered its edge.

He was never without cards now, and whenever he had a spare hand, he practised the various sleights. His hand was barely large enough to palm a card, but, according to the book, the principle was the same: learn it now, and you'd be a master when you grew into it. His arm dangled, as if idly, between two chairs. When he fumbled the card, he waited until the next prayer to pick it up. He had made no progress by the blessing, but that was the proof: all he needed was one card and the Lent term would fly by.

Commander Poole made his usual tour of duty during prep. George flipped over his cover: "Library book, sir," but he was concentrating on the ace of spades in his right hand. At one point, it fell to the floor. George gasped and Poole noticed.

"Bookmark, sir," said George, and picked it up.

After lunch the next day, he happily changed into his games clothes in the dressing room without checking the board, barely registering the chatter around him, about how the first eleven would shape up, how the goals didn't have nets yet.

Steering the farthest course from the football pitches, George watched his cold breath in the air and turned the corner towards the pavilion. He had barely thought of Don over the holidays and now found himself wondering whether Don had spent Christmas with his parents or alone in his cottage at the end of the driveway. He looked forward to exchanging a few of his tricks for some newly discovered distant-voice lore.

The glass on the door rattled as George pushed it open. Don wasn't there, nor his coat, nor any evidence of him. The kettle didn't look as if it had been used in weeks, and there were a couple of mugs ringed at the bottom with the brown tar of instant coffee. No sign of life at all. Even the tiny fan heater hadn't been used, its flex wrapped around itself as though it had left and returned. George poked around but found only Don's portable ashtray sitting on one of the chairs. He opened the lid. There were three stale butts. Where was he tapping his ashes?

George took the deck from his pocket to entertain himself, but after a while it seemed selfish sitting in the pavilion when Don might be hard at work somewhere, so he went to look for him, pocketing the ashtray in case Don had forgotten it. It was hard to avoid the games fields, since this was exactly where he thought Don might be, either on the lawn mower or raking leaves by the all-weather pitch, and George's search took him by a blue versus green football game, where Mr. Wilding was repeatedly blowing an abrasive whistle.

Poor sods, thought George, thanking God that he'd had the wherewithal to avoid this fiasco. The word in the dressing room had been right: there were no nets on the goals, no corner flags, and, in fact, no lines. There were just white wooden goals, nothing else. Where was Don? And why weren't the pitches ready?

He had just turned back to school when Wilding shouted, "Fisher! Why aren't you on this pitch?" George wondered what he was talking about. He wasn't there because he didn't play games, because he worked with Don. He didn't answer. "Fisher, get over here." Wilding was sufficiently riled by the indignity of playing on an unmarked field, so George scratched his head, trying to look unconcerned, and approached. "Run!" shouted Wilding, and George broke into a saunter. Twenty-one players stared at him.

"Why are you late?"

"I didn't know I was meant to be here."

"Didn't you even bother to look at the games board? Where are your boots?" George shrugged. "Well, then you'll have to go in goal. Get in there." Goalkeeper was the most dreadful position of all, where any attempt to avoid the ball resulted in disaster. His team sneered as he mooched towards the goalposts.

"You'd better not let any in," said Fisher Major at left back. Punishment, however, came from Wilding, detention the consequence of his abject display.

Despite the humiliation, George felt a sense of achievement as he walked back into school, shunned by every other games participant, his hands frozen purple. Surely that would never happen again: Don would return and he would once more be spared. George checked whether his name was indeed dangling on the games board. Bizarrely, it was. While he was pondering this anomaly, Hartley bellowed his name down the corridor. George remembered the trepidation he had once felt on being summoned to the headmaster's study, feeling no such thing now. He left it a polite minute and then knocked.

"Come!" mumbled through clenched teeth and pipe. George reeled on entry, nauseated by the overstewed tobacco. Hartley considered him and clicked his pipe against his stained lower teeth. "Once upon a time there was a schoolboy called George Fisher. Did you have an enjoyable Christmas?"

"Yes, thank you, sir. You?"

"Yes, I did, thankyousoverymuchforasking. Now . . ." The "now" took George by surprise, as did the subsequent pause. "Sad news, I'm afraid. Donald has left us here at Upside, gone elsewhere . . . rather unexpectedly, in fact . . . and his place will be taken by Mr. Blackstock. Mr. Blackstock is not sympathetic to your assistance, so I'm afraid it's . . ." He looked up. ". . . back to games for *you*." He gave the last word particular force, and suddenly it was all about *you* and *I*, as he prodded in George's direction with the stubby end of his meerschaum. "*You* don't like it. *I* know it. But *I* say it's up to *you* to make the best of it."

"Where did he go?" George had barely begun to consider the implications of compulsory daily games.

"Where did he *go?*"

"Yes, I was wondering where he went, if he was all right."

"Well, I . . ." George had never before seen Hartley lost for words. This grizzly bear of a man looked out of the window not knowing how to evade the question. Schoolmasters had a tendency of reverting to type at such moments — punishing someone, tell-ing him off — but Hartley wasn't like that, and Don wasn't just the groundsman. "Your solicitude does you credit." He drummed both hands on his desk and delivered an official diagnosis, rather as a doctor than a concerned father. "Donald is of an *unpredict-able* disposition, and I'm afraid that he was unable to continue his work for us. I can say no more." He smiled, though it wasn't a real smile: he stretched his mouth as wide open as possible in contemplation and combed his beard with his fingers.

"Can I see him? Is he here?"

"Is he here? Why would he be here?" George didn't say any-thing. He didn't want to annoy Hartley, but he couldn't unknow what he had discovered. "*I* know you don't want to play games. *You* know you don't want to. But *you* can't sit in the library all afternoon. I'm afraid that is the way it's going to be."

George bit the side of his lip. This wasn't about games! Where was Donald? He left the study as though he had just been caned, but it was his soul that was beaten. One thing had made all the rest worth it; that was gone.

He couldn't rid himself of his last image of Donald, weep-ing in the gloom of the pavilion. He had no reason to doubt that Hartley was telling him the truth, but had Donald recovered? Was he well? Was he alive? Was it because George had forgotten him over Christmas?

The boys and teachers ignored George as though he were in-visible. He felt like the tramp who lived at the back of the tube station by their house or the mad old trout who talked to herself as she pushed a doll in a pram down the High Street. George had interrupted her monologue once to say hello, and she had bared her fangs like a wild dog.

There were two lessons left before dinner, a double English class for which he was meant to have written an essay on what he did in his holidays. He hadn't done it and he couldn't have cared less — he'd say he forgot. That could work once a term. He went to the tuck box room and opened his box. He pulled down the secret compartment, in which he had hidden the first two of the notebooks, his project for the Lent term, and got out the first volume.

In his right hand, he took a pack of playing cards.

Word of the library's new status as a functioning literary concern had spread among the board of governors, causing an influx of books over Christmas. Rather than donations, these were grandly called *bequests*, which was, as a cursory glance revealed, a euphemism for books that would have been left unsold at a jumble sale. As he flipped through them under the supervision of Mr. Burgh, the English teacher, George sighed. Everything he had weeded out was being thrown back over the fence — this time with a pompous bookplate: *Donated to the Upside Library by Brigadier Sir James Holyoke, KG (1932–1936).* The book in this instance: *The Boy's Own Book of Knots* (with a large piece of masking tape where the spine had once been).

"We're going to have to throw a lot of these out," said George.

"Nonsense," said Mr. Burgh, who saw the library as his own private source of free secondhand books. "They'll all have to be catalogued," he said, sniffing through for attractive titles, presumably referring to any of the books that didn't leave with him.

I did my best, thought George. *That's my work with the library done.*

"And look," said Burgh, "here's something handy. *Androcles and the Lion.* We'll need all the copies we can get." Burgh had one of those faces that would never look old. A dense growth of sideburn did nothing to make him look more mature, since the rest of his chin and cheek was incapable of facial growth. To nickname him Babyface would have been too easy: this recent arrival, in reference to the way he twittered, was called, simply, Bird. The similarity to his name afforded the extra frisson of calling him Bird to his face and him not noticing. "Auditions draw nigh, Fisher. You'll be auditioning, of course."

The school play: *Androcles and the Lion.* Only last term,

George's reaction would have been: *Maybe it won't be so bad,* but now it was: *How much worse is this going to be than I can even imagine?* "Well, I say audition, but of course you're a shoo-in." Rehearsals, time, work, human interaction. Bird saw George's reluctance. "As well as acting, I thought you might like to be my assistant director. Perhaps we could even get your esteemed mother down here to show us yokels how it's done." He drummed his fingers. "And, frankly, I don't know how someone could put their all into being an assistant director and so on, with the scenery, the costumes to pick up, and the lines to learn, while being out on a games field every afternoon." It was a bribe. "And how you've managed to get detention this early in term, I have no idea," said Mr. Burgh. "Quite a feat."

"Yes, I'm . . . rather proud of it," said George, in the manner of James Mason.

"It's nothing to be proud of. And no one likes a smart aleck." There was a moment's silence. "The offer stands."

Due to the library's recent accessions, detention had been moved to an undecorated room that had not yet been allotted to a form.

"What are you here for?" Poole asked irritably.

"I was late for football practice. I didn't have any boots." *Why? What are you here for?* he wanted to ask.

"Ah, yes. Your alibi has gone walkabout, and now there's nothing left for you but to play games with the hoi polloi. Terrible for you. Copy out of this."

George sat down behind a stack of foolscap at the middle desk and prepared himself for fifty minutes of tedium, copying out a physics book called *How Sound Works.* Zigzags emanated from a white radio antenna on the bright purple cover, and below the title there was a drawing of a human ear about to be speared by a quiver of arrows. He opened the thumbed textbook just where the laminate was peeling. It had reached the point, only two days into the new term, when he didn't care anymore. He was beginning to sympathize with Bunter.

"Diagrams as well," said Poole, who was marking books without interest, his technique to scan each page, pick a random mistake, and obliterate it with a long red line that was understood to apply to all possible surrounding errors.

Copying had become such a habit for George that when he started his transcription of "The Behaviour of Sound Waves," he was able to put the work over to one side of his brain, so he could think with the other. After a few minutes, he read back what he had written. In his handwriting, it became slightly interesting.

Sound waves, which he had never considered in specific terms, travelled in three distinct, easily explained ways: reflection, refraction, and diffraction. And that apparently was it, as dictated by Science — they didn't hop round a corner inaudibly and manifest themselves in a cupboard.

Poole was standing over George's shoulder. "And the equations?" he asked, and sat down again.

It was just as Donald had said, and George had known, though he had been so seduced by the possibility that he had deferred believing the obvious truth: no one under any circumstances could make his voice come from anywhere other than his mouth. That was *how sound worked* — here it was in black and white.

George started to reproduce a list of equations: Speed, Frequency, and Wavelength. *Speed equals distance (meters travelled) divided by time. Frequency equals cycles divided by time. Wavelength equals velocity divided by frequency.*

Clearly Vox and Bunter were fictions, fantasies. Their authors (grown men and, presumably, not idiots) had no special insight into, or belief in, voice throwing; they just thought it a good literary device to cause the required mayhem. *Radio waves travel at 300,000 kms.* Yet George thought it likely that the effect of their tricks, if it were possible they be performed, was accurately described. In their fictional worlds, Vox and Bunter could throw their voices and were brilliant mimics. *300,000 kms equals the speed of light.* In the real world, the grim Don-less world of Upside, George couldn't, and certainly wasn't.

He had been reproducing his text on autopilot when he looked down at his work, suddenly conscious: *radio!* What if Bunter or Valentine had had use of the radio? Weren't voices thrown every day at 300,000 kms? George couldn't mimic (or even throw his voice), but he had one thing in his favour: *radio waves travel at the speed of light.* Vox and Bunter hadn't needed it, but think what they could have achieved if they'd . . . He would find a way to harness that power.

"Fisher," said Poole. "You can stop now. Thank you. Bring your pages here." George did as he was told, but, to Poole's annoyance, loitered. "Well? Off with you."

"Can I hang on to the book, sir?"

"Why?"

"I was . . ." He didn't want to say he was enjoying it, in case it appeared confrontational, but couldn't think of what else to say. He took one lingering look at the purple cover. Perhaps *How Sound Works* had done its job: it had taught him that throwing your voice wasn't out of the question at all — it just required new technology.

"Nothing," he said, and left.

Term continued as miserably as it had started. He cheated as often as possible and practised his sleight of hand with the bought time. *Androcles* at least spared him daily hell on the football field.

He'd read the play and hadn't enjoyed it. There was some fairly funny business at the beginning, when Androcles and his nagging wife were confronted with the stricken lion, but after this promising prologue, things took a sharp nosedive as the Romans herded the captive Christians to the gates of Rome (act 1) and escorted them to meet their fate at the Colosseum (act 2). The introduction of the characters was painfully schematic: the proud beauty (ready to die for her principles), the belligerent strongman (unable to turn the other cheek), and the useless coward (only thinking about himself). Everything worked out nicely in the end, with the buffoonish emperor's ludicrous reversal on Christianity, and no one (except the coward, offstage) dying; Androcles and his old friend the lion waltzed around the Colosseum to the applause of all, and curtain.

In the middle of the play, the writer, despite his best attempts with the animal-loving Androcles, whom he had provided with a modicum of funny lines, committed the greatest sin of all: he resorted to *speechifying,* as Frankie called it scornfully, to make his point. When *speechifying* started, drama and comedy went out of the window. Between the prologue and the final reappearance of the lion — now called Tommy, like the cat in *Dick Whittington:* it was just another skin part — the play sagged like a giant blancmange. Judicious cuts were required.

To Bird, however, the play was a masterpiece, the perfect marriage of form and content.

"When *we* put it on at school," he said, confirming everyone's suspicion that Bird was reliving his youth, would rather be in the play than directing it, and, QED, was going to be a terrible director, "we had a marvellous lead. Of course, I was only one of the slaves, but I'll be looking to inspire you with a little of the spirit of that production."

George had inferred that the title role was his for the taking. Seeing the audition call on the notice board, he realized to his momentary horror that there were two title roles, but Bird had only one in mind: George would be Androcles without audition. The line of hopefuls outside the gymnasium stretched almost to the dining room.

"You going in, Minor? Gonna be one of the girls?" sniggered Fisher Major. If only Bird would cast *him* as one of the girls, but that great brute could never pull it off. Besides, the female parts would be given to the nine-year-olds, who would be less self-conscious in a dress.

"Who's for the skin part?" George asked Bird on an inspiration. He had finally located the director nesting in the masters' common room, a grey hiding hole where the armchairs smelled of linseed oil and liniment.

"The what?"

"The lion."

"The *skin* part? You're going to have to talk English; we don't understand your backstage slang here in the real world. Anyway, for the lion, let's see, we have Jonty Smith, Patrick Morris, Campbell, and . . ."

"Fisher Major. He auditioned. He'd be good."

"I thought Ferrovius the strongman for him."

"Shouldn't Ferrovius be someone bigger?" suggested George. "Someone from the first fifteen. They don't have to be awfully good. That makes it funny."

"He's right, he's right," Burgh said to himself. "Who do you think?"

The play was cast in half an hour and a list displayed on the school notice board, around which a scrum quickly formed. Those who had already read their fates passed George on their way back. "Fisher, you're the main part," one of them said.

The read-through was deadly boring, a boredom exacerbated (and protracted) by Bird's repetitions of many lines in an improved form and his enthusiastic laughter at jokes no one else was enjoying. Rehearsals were no better. The cast quickly divided into two groups — those who liked the idea of acting (slightly over 50 percent) and those who were there for the fringe benefits, cared little for the play's success, and, ring-led by Fisher Major, preferred to rile the director.

As assistant director, George attended all rehearsals, but his title meant little. According to Bird, an actor should deliver his lines while standing completely still with one arm raised; everybody listening should stand with his arms at his sides. This was Bird's one directorial note. Apparently, he thought the play a series of tableaux vivants. Cuts had been made, but these had not solved the obvious problems.

First night was only six weeks away. George liked to sit on top of the wall bars in the gymnasium, turning a card round in his hands. From this vantage point, he was afforded a bird's-eye view of the director's bald patch and Fisher Major crawling around in his shorts. He felt safe up here — if someone came for him, he could easily repel him with his feet. He looked out across the fields.

One day he saw Donald's old van disappearing around a corner. To Bird's annoyance, George excused himself and rushed out, only to see Blackstock, Don's surly replacement, emerge from the van, picking his nose unselfconsciously. From the Pope window, George had spied smoke rising from the chimney of the house at the end of the driveway: *someone* was living there. He imagined this was Blackstock, assuming Don's possessions one by one.

On an afternoon in early February, a parcel arrived for George. He didn't recognize the red felt-tip pen or the style of packaging (slack kitchen string tied in knots). Perhaps something from Sylvia, he hoped — she had been on his mind since Christmas, and he kept turning over the phrasing of a postcard he wanted to send her — but the very placement of the stamps, an array of seemingly random amounts, didn't seem right.

Normally there was quite a procedure involved in getting a package, so it was odd too that this one was lying idly outside the headmaster's study. Perhaps the post had just arrived. He took it to the tuck box room and opened it to find a box, on which there was a note: "The closest we're going to get! Happy Late Christmas, Don."

Inside, wrapped in inappropriate pink tissue paper, were two black walkie-talkies, secondhand. They were too heavy to be toys; rather, they were intriguingly official, military transistor two-way radios, with sturdy leather straps on the backs of their leather cases, bought from one of those stores whose windows were dressed in camouflage, khaki combats, and netting. There was a thumb-operated Push to Talk button — its function self-evident — but also something called a DX switch, a fine channel tuner, a phone plug-in, an AG/FG mode: and no accompanying manual. Their antennae extended nearly three feet and wobbled like the teeterboard at the circus. Any other young Upsider would have immediately found a friend to see if they worked, to test their range, but George stuffed them into his tuck box.

"The closest we're going to get!" Don had written, presumably referring to the fact that having one walkie-talkie in one room and one in another was the only way you could really throw your voice.

Wherever Don was, he was able to read George's mind. George had worked out the need for new technology, and Don had come to the same conclusion. George was still within Donald's range.

But when George read the note again, it made him sad: "The closest we're going to get!" What if it referred not to distant voice but to George and Don, to the fact that sending a package to George at school was the closest they would get to each other? Or what if Don meant that the closest they would ever get to communication would be talking through walkie-talkies? In that case, was it at least an invitation to communicate?

And where was Don, anyway? George didn't know what to think, but like the great detective himself, he surveyed the package for clues. He had only ever seen Donald write little notes to himself with a stubby pencil he kept in his jacket, but this was definitely the same hand, disguised by the childishness of the red felt-tip. The school address was clear enough, and there was no return address — of course not; that would be too easy. Besides, Holmes's analytical prowess didn't require that kind of assistance. The postmark should be his first step, but it was too smudged to reveal anything.

He turned the brown paper around, his mind unfurling narratives involving a local newspaper, used as extra padding that would give away the geographical origin of the package, perhaps even the date. Holmes always analyzed the watermark on a piece of paper, but there would be none on this coarse brown wrapping, and George decided to turn his attention back to the stamps.

It was bad luck that he couldn't make anything out of the postmark. Then he looked again. Suddenly, he was explaining himself to Watson in "The Case of the Unexpected Package."

"Eliminate the impossible, my dear fellow, and you must be left with the truth.

"The package was not announced at lunch, neither vetted by the headmaster nor by the matron — an ugly-looking woman I should not want to meet in a dark alley — for the simple reason that the package *did not arrive by the mail.* The British postal system knew nothing of this delivery. Look at these stamps, their motley configuration. Observe how the ink of the postmark has not sullied the brown paper — these stamps have been steamed from another envelope and affixed to the parcel with some paper glue, used, to judge by the amount, by a man of a melancholic disposition in his mid-to-late thirties.

"Oh, Holmes, how can you possibly . . .

"The package, Watson, was delivered *by hand.* It was carried — like *so* — by this string so impulsively tied around the parcel. This I deduce from the slackness of the twine. Further, from this slackness I surmise that the parcel was not wrapped anywhere in the school, and, safely assuming it came from outside, that it was not transported in an automobile and brought the short distance from the automobile to the desk outside the headmaster's office, but rather carried a fair way: say, the length of the school driveway.

"The man who delivered this package by hand, Watson, must have been dropped off at the end of the driveway and walked the remaining distance, for I see no traces of mud, none of the scuffing one might normally associate with a walk through the woods, the only other mode of ingress. And the plot thickens: didn't the erstwhile groundsman have a house at the end of the driveway? And would a total stranger have licence to walk the entire length of the driveway in *broad daylight?* My case is made!"

"Fisher, what on earth . . . ?" It was, unfortunately, Mr. Morris, whose attitude had changed noticeably since George's friendship with his son had fizzled. And *what* on earth? George was caught red-handed in dream world, walking up and down the tuck box room, gesticulating in grand Rathbonian manner.

"School play, sir. Learning my lines."

"Well, tidy up that brown paper and get to class."

George had the solution. Despite Hartley's implication, Don had never moved. George would have to see for himself.

"The closest we're going to get!" George wandered to his next class, for which he had already copied out the answers to a spelling test, and considered this sentence. If Don still lived at the end of the driveway, he couldn't be much closer; legally, however, he couldn't be farther away. Beyond the school boundary (the conker trees), an inch was as good as a mile. Attempting it by daylight would be a suicide mission. It would have to be done in the dark.

That evening, he ambled nonchalantly out of prep, informing Mr. Wilding that he had to do some work on *Androcles,* implying as vaguely as possible that Mr. Burgh had ordained this absence. Plays gave a boy licence. Wilding, who had given George up as a sporting lost cause, didn't care either way.

George went down to the tuck boxes, got his walkie-talkies, put on his blazer in the changing room, and left by the gravel path behind the school, tiptoeing by the headmaster's office. The side gate was locked, but he clambered over without too much difficulty. The air beyond felt crisp. He set off down the driveway, feeling liberated, as good as he had since he had arrived back at Upside.

Although he'd never walked it in the dark, the drive, with its speed bumps and SLOW CHILDREN signs painted thick on the asphalt, was familiar from the daily morning constitutional. Beyond the conker trees, however, all was foreign. It was one thing to travel its length the other way in a car when driving back from a holiday; it was short enough when the grey hulk of the school was the last thing you wanted to see. But this way, and by foot, every slight bend revealed another unfamiliar piece of driveway, another snaking stretch of tarmac: it was farther, and colder, than he had imagined. Deeper into the woods he went, like one of the babes, until the trees arched over the driveway and obscured the stars. To his right, a rustling: a bird, perhaps, or a squirrel, but perhaps something larger, more dangerous. With everything so unfamiliar in the gloom, he began to wonder whether he had somehow taken a wrong turn, but there were only two ways — to the road and to the school, and the school was behind him. It would seem shorter on the way home, he told himself. Didn't it always?

If Don was still in the cottage, George knew that there would be no problem, but if it wasn't Don, or if somebody else saw him, one thing was certain: George was doing the most illegal thing you could do at Upside. He was out of bounds. Not only that, but he was almost *to the road*. He had lied to get out of prep and jumped over a gate that was locked for a perfectly good reason: to keep him inside. Expulsion was the only punishment for such a crime. The enormity of this hit him in an instant, immediately followed by the defiant thought: *Expel me.*

He heard the distant hum of a car engine, which he assumed to be coming from the road at the end of the driveway. At first it was just a yellow glow in the distance, but as the car approached, the headlights became more distinct, like searchlights, and George ran behind one of the larger oaks, holding his breath. The tree split the main beam and threw the lights onto the sludge and leaves around his feet. He saw a tiny pair of eyes reflect deeper in the wood as he waited until the car's rear lights disappeared towards the school. What was he going to have to do next? Pull a thorn from a lion's paw? He went back to the drive, looking up every now and then to check for any other car. None came.

Nobody, to George's knowledge, had ever been expelled from Upside. Bullying, violence, cheating: all merited the ultimate humiliation, yet these were common occurrences and went unnoticed. The Blackout Society discussed it in hushed tones after lights-out; they subconsciously feared that the punishment would unmask them in front of their parents, but George couldn't sympathize, for Queenie and Frankie were on his side. He'd tell them what was what. So *Expel me*, he thought. Where was the threat? He didn't want to be at Upside. He knew he didn't belong there. He couldn't even quite put his finger on why he was there at all. He had so little to offer the school, except the possibility of some red ink for its scholarship board, and yet there he was, encouraged to do prep, be in the play, brush his teeth, and go to bed at the same time as everyone else. To deprive him of Upside, or vice versa, would make no difference at all.

George had meant to hatch a plan as he walked. But the night had affected his mind — the sounds, the dark, the car, thoughts

of expulsion — and he had nothing. What if Don wasn't there?
What if Don *was* there? What if?

And if George was caught and got cold feet about expulsion,
he could always say he was running away. Going out of bounds
was very punishable, but going out of bounds *to run away* was a
guarantee that all would be forgiven. This last resort spoke badly
not of the troubled child himself, but of what he was running away
from. In such a situation, there would be a discreet word with the
parents, a week's sabbatical for their son, perhaps, but no punishment as such. And wasn't suspension or expulsion a kind of reward for a runaway? George felt like a man with nothing to lose.

Finally — the walk must have only been about half a mile in
all, but it couldn't have ended soon enough — the trees parted,
opening on a storybook view of the cottage. A plume of smoke
curled from the chimney. There were lights on downstairs. The
van wasn't in the driveway, but this was to be expected: Mr.
Blackstock had inherited that.

A nondescript pair of Wellington boots sat outside the back
door. George approached cautiously, aware of every crunch of
gravel, past a washing carousel from which hung dungarees and
a couple of tea towels. A shadow moved in the kitchen; George
could hear voices, perhaps a radio. He walked around the back
of the house. The curtains were drawn.

He continued to the far side, which faced the road. He could
hear a TV, see its ghostly glow in the sitting room, and he put one
eye to the crack in the curtains. The news broadcast to an empty
chair and a table, on which sat a dinner tray. There were books,
plenty of books, and little that suggested the attention of a woman:
everything pointed to a comfortless life of contemplation — Don's.
The embers of a fire burned behind a guard, and a pile of moving
boxes was stacked to the right. George had come just in time: he
was moving out. On the mantelpiece, a large carriage clock had
stopped at ten minutes past midnight. That wasn't the real time,
but it reminded him that he had to be back in school before his
absence was noticed, and that he still had to tackle the driveway
again.

A toilet flushed. A shadow came back into the room, and George darted out of view, kicking himself for not waiting a moment longer to confirm his suspicions. It was now or never. He peeked his head round again and saw a man's back. It was certainly not Don, but at that moment Don walked into the room and turned the television off.

George scurried around to the other side of the house as they talked. On an inspiration, with the two men safely in the other room, George went to the scullery door. Opening it as quietly as he could, he walked into a small spartan kitchen with a sink full of suds, peeling lino, a fridge door covered in photos and newspaper cuttings, and an electric kettle about to boil. Hearing muffled conversation from the sitting room, he took one of the walkie-talkies out of his pocket and placed it on the table. As his eyes surveyed the room, he took a closer look at the fridge.

The main photo, the epicentre of the collage around which all the other pictures and yellowed cuttings were arranged, was a picture of him, taken during the entertainment at the end of the previous term. He was holding forth, one arm raised, in the gymnasium.

The sheer weirdness of its presence startled George. He stood transfixed, unable to see anything else on the fridge clearly, and at that moment, when he was incapable of any movement, the door opened. He turned around, and there was Donald, who was looking over his shoulder, listening to something being said from the other room. Donald looked pale, cold. They faced each other. They froze. The other man spoke from the sitting room, but neither heard what he said.

Donald looked at George without any change of expression, as though he were seeing a familiar ghost. Behind him, the voice pressed its case through the open door. Donald still didn't move. George glanced at the walkie-talkie on the table, looked into Donald's empty eyes one last time, and bolted out of the house.

"Everything OK?" called the voice, which George didn't recognize. George ran round the corner, where he hid behind a tree, heart pounding.

"Yes," said Donald, snapping out of his trance. "Door came open." He popped his head outside and scanned the back garden. George heard the door close and sprinted, hoping against hope that oncoming headlights would not send him scurrying back into the undergrowth.

Breathless, he got to the side gate, managing to get one foot onto the latch. He hoisted himself up, the faint smell of a bonfire in the air. Swinging one leg over and then the other, he groped for the latch on the other side with his right foot so he could balance before he dropped to the ground. Miraculously, his foot steadied on something. He then realized that his right foot was not so much balancing on as being held by something, something that wobbled slightly — a hand. There was nothing for it now, so he swung his other leg over and leaned backwards, to find himself sitting on someone's shoulder.

"Mr. Fisher, I presume!" said Hartley, who had been enjoying his evening pipe in the fresh air. "Nice of you to drop by. The very last thing I expect to see when I am taking my nightly walk is a boy's leg fishing for a hold on the gate." He let George to the ground. "It's all a bit Brideshead, isn't it?"

George said nothing. Faced with silence, Hartley could moderate his temper only with his measured tone. "What did you think you were doing?"

"I was running away," said George without hesitation.

"Then you have a poor sense of direction."

"I thought better of it."

"You thought better of it," repeated Hartley, nodding. "You were running away, and you thought better of it." George fixed his stare on the gravel. He wondered if he'd feel less miserable if he told the truth.

"How far did you get?"

"Not very. The conker trees."

"And why were you running away?"

"I'm not happy." He expected a caning. That was the least of it.

"You're *not happy.* No, I understand that." There was silence as they walked back towards the school. "A lot of boys and parents *are* happy with Upside: the abundant facilities, the competitive fees, the low death rate. How can we, the powers-that-be here at Upside, make you, George Fisher, happy?"

"I don't know."

They walked into the school through one of the doors that the boys were not allowed to use. It was the shortcut to the headmaster's study, where George's punishment awaited. He hadn't done enough to deserve expulsion or suspension, and because he hadn't actually run away, there would be little sympathy for him. He was merely going to be punished, whipped like a dog. When he moved to the headmaster's study, however, Hartley peeled away towards his own living quarters.

"You don't know how we can make you happy?" asked the headmaster. George shook his head. "Well," said Hartley through his teeth, before walking away, "if you find out, get back to me."

6

The King and Queenie Show

Very rarely, when things seem not to be able to get any worse, they don't.

It was Joe who took me from the box. We were back at Cadogan Grove, in the dining room, where we had first met. I was home! Home amidst the silver frames, the earthy colours, and the drapery; home, where I could do my best for the man I was made for.

"Pop you up here, George! Wouldn't want you to miss all the fun! You didn't want to go to those children's parties, anyway, did you, old boy?" he asked rhetorically, as I took my place on the sideboard among the decanters and bottles. "You don't want sticky fingers in your hair. Queenie, it's time for George to come home. But we didn't want to leave you empty-handed, so . . ."

From beneath the table he produced a box, a Romando box, identical to mine: the same two brass catches, the same keyhole, and doubtless the lining I knew so well.

"You never!" Queenie gasped. On top of the box was an engraved brass plate on which was written in that familiar swirling script: *For Queenie Brown. Romando Theatrical Properties of Henley. "Pip Squeak."* "Joe! Oh, thank you!"

Out of the box, she took a boy. My doppelgänger! My saviour! The same crest on the same forest green blazer, the same mop of hair beneath the same red school cap, the same black leather shoes over socks that didn't match. Queenie compared us. "They're perfect little twins! He's adorable."

Then I saw his face. He had the same (independently winking) bright staring eyes and the same permanently flared nostrils, but he didn't look quite the same as I: a little blanker, not quite as live a wire. He might have been like me, very like me indeed, but somewhere among all those hieroglyphs there was a crucial difference: only one of us was V/IX/30. On the final day of judgement, we would not be mistaken.

"Pip," said Queenie. "Pip Squeak!" Joe laughed. Here he finally was. Pip Squeak. My younger brother.

"Can I offer to . . . ?" she asked with caution.

"Absolutely not," said Joe. "Compliments of the Fisher family. We should introduce them."

Joe caressed my levers. I shuddered as my mechanism stuttered into gear, a car on a cold morning.

"Now, George," said Queenie. "I'd like you to meet someone."

"Hello, Pip Squeak!" I said, and winked. Close up, he was a handsome kid, and he wouldn't have the easiest start in life, groped by Queenie, smeared by the birthday boy. He'd look up to me as an elder brother, of course he would, the prefect who knew the ropes, as I had looked up to Narcissus before he had put me so firmly in my place. "I'm George."

"Ho, Geo." Poor devil. He was only a baby. He could barely talk.

"Turn and face him a little more, then you can be a bit freer," Joe advised Queenie.

"You're rather handsome, aren't you?" I said, turning my attention to the lad.

"I look like you."

"My point exactly!" I made a show of yawning. "Are you tired? I am. I didn't get a wink of sleep."

"Hey!" said Queenie. "Not fair." She was laughing at me, at him, at her boys. "I thought you were going to be my perfect little gentleman, George."

Echo exploded into the house with the report of slamming doors, homing in on us like a guided missile.

"Success? Success? Joe? Does Pip Squeak fit the bill?" I nodded. "Success, Queenie, success?" Queenie smiled and nodded too in recognition of a quite different achievement. "Really, dear? Oh, I am relieved." It was Echo who put the pause that followed out of its misery. "And I had an idea: should the two of you ever have the whim to do an act together . . ." Picturing the names in lights, she traced the perimeter of an imaginary billboard in midair: "King and Queenie." She repeated it in exactly the same voice with exactly the same mime. She was ready to do this endlessly until everyone acquiesced.

Echo finally had her Pip Squeak. I had only narrowly escaped the name, but now there he was, Pip Squeak, sitting in front of me. And doubtless it was only a matter of time before she had her "King and Queenie" too.

Queenie was unexpectedly cast in *The Count of Luxembourg*, and Joe found himself somewhat relieved by her imminent departure for Edinburgh. It gave him time to think.

In the ten days before she left, there was no repeat of that final lesson, and certainly none in Joe's room, a haven to which only the two of us were admitted and which I never left.

I was set back in my original chair. The room, the books, the desk, the dust: all was as it had been. What had changed was his attitude. For whatever reason, he was glad to have me back, and more than ever I found myself his confidant.

At first, we danced around the key issue. I didn't want to rush him, yet I couldn't let him be the unwitting victim of Echo's manoeuvres. She had handed him off to Queenie. She had arranged every minute of the relationship, just as she had managed the beginning of our career together at the Drolls. The wise bet was that she had bought Queenie the perfume and told her which brand of sherry to buy. One hoped she had shied away from advising Queenie on precise *techniques,* but it was only a hope. If Echo and Queenie were in league now, they would always be in league. He had let himself be trapped again.

There was still time to escape, to make for the high seas. Only I could help. But I was happy to bide my time. Softly softly catchee monkey.

But, of course, I didn't even have to say a word. He knew it already: he simply had to work it out for, admit it to, himself. At first he blamed me, then he blamed himself; only finally did he blame Queenie. Although he was in touch with her, this had all gone unmentioned. It wasn't the kind of thing you scribbled on a postcard.

"There's only one way," he announced. "I'm going to Scotland." He threw some clothes in a small brown suitcase and was gone.

On his return three days later, he made straight for his desk and wrote, always wrote. The postcards from Scotland, all thistles, kilts, and jokes about Gretna Green, dried up long before Queenie's run was over. She returned to London but didn't visit.

One day Echo was at the door.

"I've heard," she said pointedly in mock-chiding tone. Her expression changed suddenly with the ludicrous theatricality she expended even on the smallest of moments. "Diane told me. Congratulations are in order."

Joe looked up but said nothing.

"Surprisingly rakish of you, if you'll forgive me." She stood over him at the desk. "There's no shame in it at all. We live in a world, a *demimonde* so-called, where these things are awfully run-of-the-mill."

There was a pause.

"Echo?" he asked. "You pushed her towards me, didn't you? You planned it all —"

Echo pished this with a dismissive hand. "The girl was besotted with you, *smitten,*" she said blithely, and twirled around on the spot, a debutante dancing her first waltz with a dashing nobleman. "Oh, it was so *romantic*. She must have seen you onstage in your evening dress and just fallen head-over-heels in love with you there and then." The waltz suddenly crashed to a halt. "But waiting for you would have been . . . A mother knows what's best, sometimes. Besides," she added matter-of-factly, "I wasn't expecting her to be quite *that* successful." Joe did nothing to fill the silence. "Hadn't you better see her? A little bird tells me she's waiting to hear from you. Darling, there is so much more to say, but congratulations. It's just what you need. She'll be excellent for you. Joe, you have my approval!" Out she went. She came back in. "And one more thing. *Demimonde* though it may be, bohemians and children of paradise though we undoubtedly are, speed and timing are of the essence, for obvious reasons. Chop chop!"

She was gone. Joe threw his head back, closed his eyes, opened his mouth, and exhaled for ten full seconds. Lost in thought, he stared ahead through the tears.

The wedding of Joe Fisher and Queenie Brown took place at St. Mary in the Meadows, Islington, on the fifth day of December 1935. It was a hastily arranged family affair, but the reviews were good, even for Reverend Wooley's sermon, with its obligatory chuckling reference to Evangeline's heathen pseudonym.

Queenie's digs were no longer considered appropriate, and since the newlyweds could not afford a house of their own, she moved into the Fisher residence. The invasion was almost complete. Joe relocated his bed within two feet of hers in a quainter room on the second floor but kept his bedroom as our den, sensibly defending this last bastion of privacy.

With the marriage came new financial concerns. They'd be a double act, all right, as Echo had suggested, and so should I: at children's parties, King and Queenie, George and Pip Squeak. I was pleased to see him engrossed in a project, whatever its nature, particularly one that included me. I even opened my heart to the rehearsals. We had had dreams, of course, but now we had to adapt and be as good as we could at what was required. We could no longer headline the Theatre Royal, but we might perhaps live on in the hearts of some children. These were different responsibilities, and I respected his wishes. Reflection would be fatal, and Joe was determined to move forwards into this new life without it. For all I know, he would have described himself as *happy*.

And then, just when I had forgotten all about it, Queenie went to the hospital. She had assumed a kind of queenly grandeur as her stomach grew and her bosoms inflated to the size of hot-air balloons, but I had ignored it, preferring to concentrate on our pitiful little entertainment. That there was a reason for her great size (I just took her to be an ever-increasing parody of her original shape) had almost slipped my mind.

She returned looking radiant, vastly slimmer. It was the most beautiful I ever saw her, as she was pushed into the house in a bath chair. That night Joe, Queenie, Pip, and I sat on the carpet in the parlour in front of a roaring fire, and she said, "Look what I have for you, George."

And out of a bundle of white blankets poked a little bald head. Given my negative feelings about children, their parties and their fingerprints, I didn't quite know how to react when confronted with this pink lump, this baby girl. Yet my heart melted. She was so beautifully unspoilt: I wished only that she could remain so, free of the crippling shyness, the loneliness that had blighted her father's life.

Perhaps she could be his saviour; I didn't believe that for a minute. In this ludicrous, necessary union, he had to hide himself away more than ever, as if his true nature were monstrous.

"How about Francesca?" said Queenie, who couldn't stop smiling a worn-out smile.

"Yes, I like that," said Joe, who was smoking incessantly now. He was such a banal monster — a man who preferred his own company, his best attempts doomed to failure. "Frankie Fisher."

Frankie Fisher — my little assistant.

* * *

Marriage wasn't, nor can it ever be, a cure. Theirs was a practical arrangement of friendliness but no great passion. They slept in the same room but not in the same bed — and one never kept the other awake. It was even money Frankie would be an only child.

Joe was still happiest in his private room, and in this Queenie humoured him, without remark, for she was happiest with the baby; the baby, it was assumed, was happiest with her. Joe did his best, but Queenie was better with children: she was the natural. She wasn't scared that Frankie would snap in her hands, suffocate in her arms, tumble and shatter on the floor. Queenie handled her with calm, loving authority, never in doubt as to the right course of action. She left Joe to look on and occasionally test the water with his elbow. Eventually, he was allowed to shoulder a modicum of responsibility, but not before it had become clear that Frankie was essentially someone else's. He had pictured himself walking the corridor late at night, when he returned from his smokers, book in one hand, baby in the other, but somehow this never happened. On his return, Queenie would shoo him off to bed: "Let me, Joe. That's woman's work. . . . You go and sleep. You've had a busy night."

When Queenie allowed, I sat on one of Joe's knees, Frankie on the other, and we bounced and played. (We were at least considered up to this.) Most of our early attempts at entertainment went over her head, but gradually things improved. She made the slow transition from nearly bald in the cradle, to blond in the cot, before the curls graduated to brown by the time she slept in her own little bed.

One day Joe brought home a miniature library of Beatrix Potter in a smart presentation box. Over the next year, we read every book to her. I played the frogs and the rabbits, the squirrels, the town mice, the flopsy bunnies, and the kittens, while Joe was narrator, pig, and farmer.

Echo flitted through infrequently with a knitted offering "to placate the baby gods." She cooed circumspectly without quite taking Frankie to her bosom, giving the impression that she would be willing to show the child more affection when it was old enough to have something to offer in exchange. She suggested that she pay for a nanny on the basis that no performer should be hampered by his offspring: it was unprofessional to be accompanied by baby, even if she travelled in a smart carry-cot bought for her at great expense by her grandmother. Queenie, however, was not prepared to sacrifice Frankie to the success of *The King and Queenie Show,* and a trial run revealed that Frankie slept quite soundly provided she could hear her mother's voice. She snoozed next to me through many a show in the back of the silk cabinet, which seemed designed to hide boy and baby. She practically grew up there. Her first word, "wholemeal," turned out, on further investigation, to be "old mill," the picture that was the result of one of Queenie's "tricks."

The parties were our bread and butter. At first, I rather enjoyed the hustle and bustle, provided I remained at arm's length from the audience. Ventriloquism was the centrepiece, but the act was infinitely adaptable. The night before an engagement, Queenie hummed to herself at the kitchen table as she picked adroitly from *the menu,* shuffling the programme until she was happy, always managing to magic up some appropriate doggerel for the final flourish.

And what were they paying for, these party-throwing parents? It was Queenie who delivered the rhyming prologue ("Let's take a trip together / To the Land of Make Believe"), she who took charge of the children, and Joe, silent figure of mystery dressed in black tie, who showed them the effects. A typical programme included (in order of appearance) magic painting, Joe's card tricks, monkey spelling and sewing, paper tearing, and then — the moment we've all been waiting for — ventriloquism, as performed by Joe and me, which brought the first half to a close (before I was put safely out of harm's way). The interval (cake and the blowing out of candles) was followed by the silk cabinet, and then audience participation courtesy of Queenie and Pip Squeak, thrust into the fizzy lemon and limelight. It was bound to be a disaster following so closely the cutting of cake, and I was well out of it. The grand finale involved all four of us in a ventriloquial duel, on which the audience voted. Joe pulled out all the tricks (we both smoked, he drank, and I talked), but Queenie always won. It was exactly as Echo had predicted: the kids liked her more. Kids didn't care about mistakes; they just wanted to be in on the joke. After a second helping of cake, an invoice and two guineas exchanged hands (Queenie was the business manager), and we were back in our boxes and carry-cots, and on our way.

Simple stuff, perhaps, and somewhat beneath me. But I didn't complain. *The King and Queenie Show* was a group effort, and whatever the material, I was out in the world. At first, things seemed to be looking up. I was extra super during the first few parties, an added twinkle in my eye.

It couldn't last. Though we enjoyed the occasional Rotarian or rest home engagement, our greatest success was among children. But the triumph was not Joe's and mine. The kids wanted more tearing, more mess, more of their Auntie Queenie. Card tricks left them cold.

Joe was too good, his skill an irrelevance. Soon it was evident that Joe was an irrelevance too, and he knew it. One afternoon, an argument broke out in the middle of our routine. Queenie strode into the thick of it, but Joe and I simply continued with the act. Tempers frayed, cake flew, icing splattered; on we went regardless.

"This is stupid," Joe said unexpectedly, though the row was such that I could barely hear him. "Shall we stop?"

"Would anyone notice?"

"We might as well not be here," said Joe, as we returned to the script.

It was true.

Three Parts for Fisher: The Skin Part

The lone criminal could get away with anything.

That night, George felt the lump of the walkie-talkie beneath his pillow, waiting for Don to communicate.

The persistent wind announced a bracing morning walk. At break, he went far away from the all-weather pitch and turned the walkie-talkie up as loud as possible. There was nothing but static and a stray foreign radio station that wormed its way into his reception. What good is one walkie-talkie if the person with the other one isn't talking to you?

After rehearsal, George went to the first-form garden and placed the walkie-talkie on the bench in front of him. The gadget sat lifeless on its stone seat. Perhaps he should ask a question?

Clasping the walkie-talkie in his right hand, his thumb poised, he closed his eyes and pushed the Talk button.

"Ventrilo to Don. Ventrilo to Don." He overenunciated in the way that he felt was required of the walkie-talker. "Do-ah you-ah receive-ah me-ah?" He let the button go. Silence. "Ventrilo to Don? Ventrilo to Don?" Nothing. "Over and out."

He left it where it was and paced the perimeter of the frostbitten garden, where, in better weather, the smaller boys grew watercress and runner beans. He was making his way slowly, measuring the boundary by foot, when the walkie-talkie burst into life. For one second, perhaps two, white noise blared into the garden. By the time George reached it, the walkie-talkie was as dead as before. He started another lap. When the miniature obelisk again started to belch, he ran towards it, but again the white noise stopped. George pushed the button. "Come in, Don. Don? Don? Is that you?" But there was nothing. Were they out of range? He ran to the woods at the side of the driveway. If that noise was interference, perhaps they were out of range by inches only. "Don? Don?"

Nothing: no message, no sign, no word at all.

The next day he strayed as near Don's house as possible, within the legal means, but he felt monitored, assuming Hartley had warned the common room that the runaway might try a repeat performance. George ended up behind the squash courts, ankle deep in a rainbow of illegal sweet wrappers and crushed cans of Shandy Bass.

His monologue began as formally as before, as he kept to what he imagined was the walkie-talkie script, but soon he was pressing Talk at will, releasing it when he deserved a reply. In staccato sentences, he gave his report on the last few days: the deduction, the conclusion, the escape, and the capture. The gaps grew as he waited for a response with increasing pessimism. As he trudged to the afternoon's rehearsal, he resorted to inflicting white noise on Don in short sharp bursts in the hope of provoking him into retaliation.

The next day, it was all or nothing. His half-holiday slowly vanished as the full cast run-through dragged tediously on. It was almost dark: another day gone without contact. Finally, with Bird's desperate plea to learn their lines, they were dismissed. George found it easier to go unobserved in the half-light, and he allowed himself to talk into the transmitter long before he got to the squash courts, chatting about the play, his bargain with Bird, his lines. He walked past the new development, a medieval ruin in the late-afternoon gloom. "And what about the assembly hall? The foundations took my whole first term . . . then the two stories went up, and they closed them in just before Christmas and now they've just stopped! Did they run out of money?"

Giving Donald the chance to respond, George pictured himself walking down the path, acting exactly as he was acting now, speaking the same words into the air but without the excuse of a walkie-talkie. *I keep talking, but I don't even know if anyone is listening. I might as well be talking to myself.* There was a boy called Fletcher who conducted a nonexistent orchestra, and a first-former who whispered conversations to his imaginary friend and asked for two plates at meals. And now there was George.

It was cold behind the squash courts, dark, though not quite time for dinner. George kicked at the rubbish and heard the echoing squeaks and grunts as two men smashed a ball around the walls. He picked his way through the debris using his key-ring flashlight. Something caught his eye: a shiny magazine, folded, called *Wing.* The cover revealed a partially naked woman, of Matron's age and demeanour, shoehorned into a tight black rubber dress with a slit up the middle so she could possibly move her legs. He picked it up; the word *wing* became *Swinger.*

"It's a right mess back here. There's some real treasure. . . . Naked ladies . . . sweet wrappers . . . a rugby shirt . . . Anyway . . . here I am, broadcasting from my office again. . . . Ventrilo calling, Ventrilo calling Secret Friend. . . . I'm going to ask you something. . . . You don't have to answer. . . . In fact, you won't answer, will you? . . . Why are you still living at the end of the driveway but not doing your job? And why does Hartley say you've gone? That's all I want to know . . . except that you're OK. . . . I really don't know why I'm standing behind this squash court. . . . It's freezing and it's totally dark now. . . . Nobody could see me if I was walking through the middle of the path. . . . So I'll go. . . ." He took another idle glance at *Swinger* and pushed it between a couple of stray slats of corrugated iron, his should he ever want it. "No one would believe that I'm really talking to anybody anyway. . . . And I'm not, really, am I? Is there anybody there? I'm walking out in the open. . . . Anybody could see me if it wasn't dark. . . . Is there anybody there?" George shouted up into the night sky without bothering to Push to Talk: "Why aren't you listening?"

He hadn't heard the bell, but he decided it was time for supper. He kept pushing the button, to rile anyone on the other end, but as he got nearer the school, he said: "I'll recite some lines and that will be my last transmission, then the national anthem, then shutdown. . . . You can test me on my lines. . . ."

He walked up and down the path, reciting all the lines he could remember, imagining the other parts. He was finishing with a longer speech when the bell rang. There was no one around as he went through the griffin door into school, and he decided to put the walkie-talkie away in the secret compartment, this time forever.

Inside the tuck box room, there was a small crowd of the type that gathers in the hope that a scuffle will turn into a fight. However, far from baiting or teasing, this crowd was completely still. A forest of green and grey crouched around his tuck box.

"Shh!" said Beattie. "Listen. It'll do it again. Shh!" George made a mental inventory of the box's contents. There was nothing that could make noise.

"It must be a radio," said a fat boy who, unable to get ringside, was anxious not to be impressed.

"Or an animal?" suggested another.

"Radios don't turn themselves on and off," said another. "Animals don't talk: fact! I heard a voice."

"Shh!" said Beattie, the High Priest of the Tuck Box, as he listened for further signs.

"It went on for ages just now," said another. They had forgotten about the bell.

"What did it say?"

"Oh, I don't know. Something about . . ."

"Just open it and find out!" Breaking into someone else's box was a cardinal sin in a world where boxes were not to be locked, but they had to know.

"No," said Beattie. "It's not ours."

No one had noticed the owner standing close by. George hit the Push to Talk button. Sure enough, audible static emanated from the tuck box. Beattie and the other initiates jumped as if electrically shocked.

"Jesus!" said Beattie. "You see?"

"That wasn't a voice," complained the obnoxious Fat Boy. "That was just a noise."

"It was voices before."

"Rubbish," said Fat Boy. "Where's Fisher? Let's ask him."

"Open it!" they all shouted, on the basis that whatever was in there certainly wasn't legal and that it would be in the school's best interests if it were reported, and surrendered, as soon as possible.

It had been worse than talking to himself, George thought. They had heard him reciting his lines and heaven knows how much else. Disguised by the crackle of reception, however, his voice had apparently not given him away. Above all, the walkie-talkie must remain a secret.

Just as Beattie was about to open the lid, George, who had weighed up the alternatives, retreated into the corridor and shouted into his walkie-talkie, "Thief! Thief!" There was a scream. Attention had now turned away from the tuck box to the medium, who appeared a little shaken. Everybody had heard.

"I didn't even touch it!" said Beattie, who saw George reenter, having hidden his walkie-talkie. "Here's the answer. What's in there?"

"Open it! Open it!"

As the chant grew in ferocity, George clambered up onto the box and sat down, wondering who would be the first to dare lay a finger on him. Just as this looked a real threat, a voice bellowed, "Silence!" from the door, and the chant stopped. There stood Mr. Morris, arms folded. "What on earth is going on?" Everyone answered at once, those who had been there from the beginning and those who had been lured more recently by the communal chanting. "Silence. Didn't you hear the bell? Beattie, you for one should

know better." Again, everybody spoke; only George remained silent. Once Morris had regained control, he said: "I am starting to
lose my temper. Fisher, what is wrong here?"

"I came into the room and they were breaking into my box.
They tried to get me to open it, but I didn't want to."

In his overexcitement, Beattie garbled a barely comprehens-
ible explanation. "Sir, there were voices coming out of this room,
but there was nobody here, so . . ."

"Fisher, get down now. Beattie, stay. Fisher, stay. Everybody
else, go and wash your hands." Disappointed to miss the denoue-
ment, the spectators traipsed to join the dinner parade. Morris
moved towards the tuck box. "Is there a radio in here, Fisher?"

"No." Partly a lie.

"Are there voices coming from this box?"

"I shouldn't think so."

"Open it, sir, you'll see!" said Beattie.

"I don't need any help from *you.* Can I look inside your box,
Fisher?"

George thought it best to play it cool, though he realized the
game was up. "Sure."

With a degree of formality, and a look of concentration that
suggested he was cracking a safe, Morris opened the lid. George
peered inside with trepidation, knowing what he would see.

It wasn't there.

Morris, a customs official by no means convinced that the victim of his random search is breaking the law, took a cursory look.
"Empty it out." George reached inside and removed the contents:
two books (both vetted by the headmaster), two of his grandfather's notebooks, a pack of stripper cards, a pack of normal cards,
two marbles, three handkerchiefs, four pieces of rope (knotted).

"Do you have a top hat and a dove in there as well?"

"No, sir. That's all." George couldn't believe his luck. But it
wasn't luck at all: it was Don's good sense that had hidden the
walkie-talkie in the secret compartment. And now *Beattie* was
hearing voices. It reminded him of *Gaslight,* Evie's favourite film
of all time. It reminded him of *Valentine Vox.* He had thrown

his voice without even knowing. The walkie-talkies had given a glimpse of their true potential.

"Satisfied, Beattie?" asked Morris.

Unconvinced, Beattie poked his nose in. "We all heard them, sir," said Beattie weakly, looking around for any other possible source.

Morris replied with the resigned tone with which he conjugated the verb *être:* "They couldn't have come from the box; there's nothing in the box. Beattie, see me tomorrow. Fisher, put all this away. To dinner, both of you."

Beattie glared as he departed. Alone again, George opened the secret compartment. There was the other walkie-talkie. Secured to it with a rubber band was a note. In Don's trademark pencil, simply: "SORRY."

That single word said *Over and out.* The chance of communication with Don disappeared with it; Don had moved on, abandoned him. George was no longer within the possible sphere of his influence. He pictured the empty house at the bottom of the driveway, the carousel spinning helplessly in the heavy winds, unencumbered by damp clothes.

Bird suggested that George, in his role as assistant director, accompany him to choose the costumes. George agreed enthusiastically, not because he cared but because he wanted a look at the house by daylight, to confirm his suspicions.

Bird was twittering away about the costume shop as they drove off. At the end of the driveway, three removals men were enjoying a cigarette beside a large van. No sign of Don.

"Ah, moving day," said Bird, interrupting his monologue to call out, "Dennis, erm, Mr. Blackstock." So that's how it was. Bird rolled down his window. Blackstock emerged from the house, mopping a sweating brow with a tea towel. "Everything OK?" chirped Bird. "Welcoming committee, et cetera. Can't stop to give a hand now, on our way to Henley, but perhaps when we get back, if you need anything . . ."

"We'll still be hard at it. Oi! You lot!" Blackstock shouted. "I'm not paying you to smoke!"

"Righto, then," said Bird, rolling up the window. "Always nice to offer. So, were you listening to a word I was saying? About Romando's."

"Romando's?" George knew he'd heard the name, perhaps on TV.

"I thought so. You were off in la-la land. Henley's a bit of a haul, but the school has been getting costumes there for many years. The last performance of *Androcles* was before you were even born, so we're going to look at those costumes and see if we can use them again." George itched at the thought.

Romando's Costumes sat in the grim grey corner of an industrial estate on the outskirts of town, looking as far removed from George's idea of a theatrical costumier as possible. Those he'd frequented with Frankie were colourful places overflowing with linens and crinoline, smelling of carbolic and mothballs, presided over by meek bespectacled men with firm ideas on inside leg measurement and what read well from the gods. Bird led the way through a plain white door with the small sign: ROMANDO'S COSTUME COMPANY, SINCE 1878. A woman sat behind the counter, chewing gum.

"You'll be Phil's two p.m., will you? Upside?"

"Yes, we will. Sit down, George." George hated when they pretended they called you by your Christian name.

"That your son, is it? That your dad?" she asked, idly flicking through the *TV Times*.

"No," they both said at the same time, equally displeased at being familied.

"But this young man is the main part in our upcoming production," said Bird in a stiff attempt at conversational bonhomie. He was unable to look straight at the receptionist. Bird fitted in perfectly at Upside, where everything was relic and ritual, but in the real world, the world of a theatrical costumier's, he was as lifelike as a waxwork.

"I'll just call through to Phil," said the woman, who bellowed "Phil" at the top of her voice.

In came Phil, a hulk of a man in white overalls. "Another year, another production," he said without enthusiasm. "No Mr. Allen?"

"No, he left us for pastures new. I'm doing the play this term."

"Well, no harm, I suppose. And who's this fella?" asked Phil, referring to George. "The new headmaster? Well, come through here and look. I've got them all laid out."

The back room did at least appear more recognizably theatrical, with pictures of previous Romando-costumed productions on the walls and racks of costumes with scraps of paper pinned to them noting sizes and the plays for which they were intended. Bird had brought measurements with him and matched these to the various costumes, although Phil didn't seem much bothered by the schoolteacher's opinions: these were the costumes Upside would be getting whether it liked them or not.

Bird, in the awkwardness of negotiation, had forgotten George, who was following the haphazard timeline of photos around the wall. He always felt at home with old theatrical pictures and, sure enough, as he travelled back and forth among the overly made up and painfully smiling, through the seven ages of twentieth-century live entertainment, he saw a framed advertisement for Romando's Theatrical Properties from the early 1940s, clipped from the pages of a magazine. It was a picture he knew well from the family scrapbooks. At the top it said, *Romando's: Fighting from the Front,* and beneath this there was a picture of Joe King Fisher and his dummy, George's namesake. Of course. Romando.

Bird and Phil were bickering over price and date.

"Never been any trouble before," said Phil shirtily. "Mr. Allen always used to . . ."

"Excuse me," said George. "This is the old Romando's that makes ventriloquist figures."

"Was." Phil tutted at the interruption. "*Was.*"

"Ah," said Bird, who thought he was being rather clever. "Yes. Look at that. That's a picture of George's grandfather."

"Really? Oh, yes, he looks like him," said Phil.

"Joe King Fisher," said Bird. "A legend."

"Oh, him," said Phil, wiping his nose on his sleeve. "No, I meant he looks like the dummy. Just a joke, son, just a joke."

"This where they made him, then?" asked George. "The one I look like."

Phil sighed. "Yes and no. That was in the old place, before everything moved out here. Old Romando used to build all the ventriloquist stuff before the war — family business it was, all hand done, very nice, top-notch. Well, he died, his widow couldn't keep it going, the son lost interest, and Romando's was just going under when CoCo, the Costume Company, bought them out lock, stock, and barrel, everything, merged the two businesses, and moved them out here. Kept the old name, though. Your granddad, was he?"

"Yes, but I never knew him."

"Well, that George was one of Romando's." Phil peered at the picture. "Yes, looks just like all the other ones we have. Got a room full of the things. No one wants them anymore. And they're falling apart. Weren't built to last."

"He's going strong. But he's in a case in a museum."

"The boy in the bubble, eh?" said Phil. "Bet he doesn't say much in there." George laughed. "So if that's your grandfather, then your mum must be . . ."

"Frankie Fisher." George beamed.

"Frankie! What a gal. Oh, I'm a great fan, a great fan. Frankie and I have worked together, oh yes. Now, let me see . . . Look!" Just behind one of the doors was a picture of George's beautiful mother, in gala evening dress, signed: "Phil — I Should Coco! Your friend, Frankie."

"Now, about the lion costume . . . ," Bird put in twice before he was finally heard. He was mystified by the easygoing nature of George and Phil's banter despite the great discrepancy in age and social status, and irked that the two of them could communicate so casually to his exclusion.

"There's nothing wrong with this one!" said Phil. "It was quite all right last time."

"I think we should have an allover costume," said George, his only thought Fisher Major's discomfort. "With the head totally covered. A really big frightening lion."

"It'll be hot in there," said Bird.

"It'll look fantastic," said George, devil's advocate.

"And you won't be able to see his face," said Bird.

"Saves acting."

"I have the very thing," said Phil. "From a musical of *The Just So Stories*, recently come down. You look at this."

Where Bird had been unsuccessful, George, with constant reference to Frankie, was able to sweet-talk Phil into altering the costumes in time, mixing and matching in a way that had been expressly forbidden, and delivering them to the school. Bird should have been delighted, but he was in a foul mood on their return.

"Well, at least it's going to *look* all right," said George as he gazed out of the window. Bird didn't answer.

At the end of the driveway, the moving van was gone. Lights shone in the kitchen, and a pile of neatly broken-down boxes sat to the side of the front door.

The nearer they got to the first performance, the worse it was. The great director was now convinced he could play each part better than its current actor — if you did exactly as he showed you, no more and no less, then you were acting well. Certain things weren't bad — not good, but not bad — yet Bird couldn't leave well enough alone. He snidely referred to George as Gielgud and peppered his notes with unnecessary asides: "Your mother would be ashamed of you." There were many ways George could improve. He wasn't putting much into it, nor was he even particularly well cast for the part, but at least he had the basics covered — he knew his lines, he lifted one arm (as required) and faced forwards (his own idea) when he spoke, he projected. There were others in greater need of Bird's master class.

George wrote to Frankie that he wanted to get out of *Andro-cles*. It was boring. She replied that his behaviour was unprofessional. He was a Fisher. It wasn't only he who would be on that stage, but all Fishers before him: Frankie, Echo, Joe, Queenie, and even Vox. The show must go on. Besides, she couldn't wait for his first starring role, and he couldn't let her down. He loved it when she resorted to blackmail.

But George simply couldn't picture himself walking onto the stage accompanied by nine-year-old James Pardew (in the role of Megaera, his wife). He didn't know why, but he knew first night would never come.

Rehearsals became unbearable. His one solace was watching Fisher Major sweat and toil in his *Just So* costume, a fantastically heavy bodysuit of fur, done in bright African orange, with a generous autumn brown mane, its wearer further burdened by the mass of a fur mantlet and a tail that seemed weighted with lead. At its arrival, Fisher Major, ignorant of the indignities of the skin part, had thought himself rather superior for having such an elaborate costume. Bird sensibly considered it silly to dirty the suit during rehearsals, but George had managed to persuade him that there was an art to wearing the costume properly, that the other actors had to know what to expect, and that it would surely be worth an extra cleaning to have the boy playing Lion be as good a Lion as he could possibly be. So Fisher huffed and puffed through every rehearsal — he had grown tired of his skin long before the other boys had even visited the under-matron to check that their fittings were acceptable — and his temper grew shorter as first night beckoned.

There was one other great advantage to the costume: Major's face was totally covered. The first time George threw his voice into the lion suit was a success. While demonstrating how to salute and bow in the correct Roman manner, Bird had inadvertently knocked over his prop, a lectern. With everyone's attention on this pratfall, George put his hand over his mouth, cackled, said, "Nice one!" and turned in shock to look at the lion suit. The room hushed, out of either respect for Fisher Major or fear of Bird's reprisal.

"Thank you, Fisher Major," the director said as calmly as he could. "That will be detention for you next week."

"But . . . but . . . ," came a muffled voice from the depths of the lion's furry orange face, as the occupant tried unsuccessfully to remove his prosthetic head.

"Shut it!" said Burgh.

"But . . ." The lion scratched furiously, as though the costume were infested with nits.

"On all fours. And don't you dare take that head off. You, *Olivier.* Wipe that smile off your face, and let's move on to the final act."

First night loomed. Even the weather boded ill. Winds whipped through Pope even though the windows, which rattled in their frames, were shut tight. As branches knocked to get in from the cold, George lay in bed, devising a way to combine all his talents for a truly remarkable coup de théâtre.

The following Thursday, his form was required to write their weekly history essay, without reference to textbooks.

"Library for you, then, Fisher?" said Hessenthal unexpectedly. George had started a trend where certain of the pupils disappeared to do their work in various corners of the school, converging back on the classroom with their finished essays when the bell went.

"All right," said George, pleased to be saved the bother of asking. He went to the library, turned on the light, got out his playing cards, sat down at his usual desk, and, as per his usual routine, opened the lid. There, where only one hour before he had left his essay, was a note from the headmaster: "Do Not Pass GO! Do Not Collect 200 POUNDS! Straight to my study."

George put his head in his hands and breathed as deeply as he could. What was the worst thing that could happen? What possible excuse did he have?

In his office, Hartley stood wreathed in his own emissions, his face reflected in the window behind the desk. He had his hands behind his back and was perfectly still. The atmosphere was oppressive, the study heavy with a fog that hovered in the dim light.

"What have you got to say for yourself?" asked the headmaster.

One excuse was all George needed. One really good excuse. His grandmother's death? Overwork because of the play? Bullying at the hands of Fisher Major? Homesickness? Don? Don! How low would he stoop? "Think carefully before you speak," said Hartley. "Once more: what have you got to say for yourself?"

"Sorry."

"A cheat never prospers." Hartley turned around, his frame almost entirely obscured in the haze, so his face appeared disembodied. "When someone cheats, I am upset. First I am upset by my own bad judgement — perhaps he can't cope with the demands, perhaps he never could, perhaps he's simply not *up to it*." George nodded, a lump in his throat. Hartley didn't look him in the eyes. "But when someone cheats who I know *can* cope with the demands, who *is* up to it, then I look for another reason, and when I can't find an obvious one, and if he can't offer me one, I assume the worst — that he is doing it only because he can, that he is lazy, that he is destructive, that he is *bad*." George was close to tears. There was steel in the certainty of Hartley's conclusions. He pierced George with a gimlet eye. "If I *ever* catch you doing this, or hear of anything like it again . . . Do you understand?" George nodded. "Do you understand?"

"Yes, sir." He could barely get it out.

"OK." Hartley exhaled and then sucked on his pipe thoughtfully. "Your history teacher wants you off the play . . ." Hartley left a gap here, but George knew too well to protest. ". . . but Mr. Burgh will say there's no reason he and the school should be punished on your behalf, and he'll be right. So, there is going to be a tug-of-war between Mr. Hessenthal and Mr. Burgh, with you in the middle. And I don't know what the result will be. In the meanwhile, I have written a letter to your mother and grandmother. Here it sits on my desk, with a stamp, waiting to be sent. Do you see it?" George nodded. "Mark it and go."

For the first time, first night seemed an unavoidable certainty. George expected Bird's full support. If Hessenthal had his way, the play would have to be cancelled. No one else could play

Androcles, let alone at such short notice, and the costumes were rented, the programmes copied. The show would now, he was sure, go on. And centre stage, George could win everyone over, even the headmaster.

But that afternoon, he arrived at the gym for the first costume rehearsal to find that Hessenthal had triumphed. Bird hadn't stood up for George, as Hartley and George had assumed he would, for there was one person, and only one, who could step into the role at such short notice — Bird himself. It was the perfect excuse for Bird to put all that great rehearsal acting into use: fate had cast him in the part he had craved since his schooldays.

"Mr. Wilding will take the rehearsal tomorrow. I have to get myself fitted for a toga!" said Bird, his beady eyes dancing with happiness. No reason was given for the replacement of the leading man, and all eyes were on George, who burned with shame. If they were going to treat him like an outcast, he would behave like one. He had no reason to be at the rehearsal any longer, so he turned and left, the only thought in his mind to go and hide under the Ping-Pong table with a pack of cards.

"Hold on, Fisher," said Bird, who, despite being atwitter with excitement, was trying to behave as if there was nothing out of the ordinary in a thirty-five-year-old man hijacking the main part of the school play. "There's still something for you." George turned around and took his hands out of his pockets. "I'm afraid that your namesake, the bigger Fisher, has developed a rather nasty skin complaint from the lion suit and is confined to the sanatorium, so we're going to need someone to step into his paws, as it were. They've just disinfected the offending costume, so perhaps you could pop up to Matron and suit up, and we'll go from my first entry." George stared ahead. "Hurry up, boy, and don't look so ungrateful. Mr. Hessenthal didn't like the idea, but I persuaded him, so perhaps a little thanks are in order! Now, we'll go back to the top, and I'm coming in over here. . . ."

George left the gym and walked up the back stairs to Matron.

The show could rot in hell. There was absolutely no point in staying. He saw that now.

In Pope that night, everyone wanted to know what had happened. They knew nothing beyond the fact that after George had gone off to the library, Hessenthal had said, "And let that be a lesson to the rest of you." George wouldn't talk. They had only ever liked him when he was in trouble or when he had something they wanted.

The wind rattled the glass again, howling at the windows. In the middle of the night, they were woken up by a thunderous crash.

"What was that?" asked a sleepy voice.

"Wow!"

"Lightning?"

"Go to sleep."

In the morning light, a throng of tartan dressing gowns crowded Pope's windows. A tree had uprooted and fallen, smashing into the new assembly hall, demolishing the top of the one standing wall and taking with it much of the scaffolding, some of which had rolled as far as the driveway. What was left jutted out of the building like the teeth of a broken comb, and it was only a matter of time before the rest of the teetering wall fell, taking with it the whole facing side.

Serves them right, thought George. He had so far managed not to wear the lion suit: the material was so thick that it had taken an unearthly time to dry after its disinfection. He had to find a way to get out of the skin part for good. What would Valentine Vox have done?

The wind was too dangerous for their morning walk. The headmaster was not at breakfast, nor were many of the teachers. Afterwards, George, under the pretence of wiping off the tables, waited till the dining room was empty and, seeing Hartley and the crowd of teachers outside scrutinizing the ruin, walked into the headmaster's office, picked up the telephone, and dialled. Queenie answered.

"Listen, it's George," he said in a rapid stage whisper.

"Georgie, darling, how are you? I was only saying . . ."

"No time. You know how you and Reg said you'd come and pick me up if I wanted? Tonight. Six p.m. End of the driveway."

"George, are you all right?"

"Yes, I'm fine. Six p.m. Tonight. End of the driveway."

"Are you in trouble?"

"Not as much as I'll be in if you're not there. OK?"

He put the phone down, picked up the headmaster's letter, and left unnoticed.

Everyone was talking about the wall, the time, the upset, the cost. Teachers spoke of insurance and shoddy work; pupils of the noise, the excitement, the crash and the one that was bound to follow. First the builders were coming, then it was the fire department, then the army. At a hastily convened assembly, Hartley announced that no one was allowed within fifty feet of the new development. George didn't hear this. He wasn't there.

He'd left by the front door and sprinted towards the disaster area. It was one of those days when an umbrella could carry you off into the distance; the wall that remained rocked uncertainly. The oak tree, the wriggling roots of which were raw and new where they had been wrenched from the ground, had fallen directly onto the top storey. If the tree fell farther — and there could be no doubt that it would — the whole structure would collapse and the only option would be to demolish it and start construction again. George hurled one of the walkie-talkies as far into the centre of the crumbling ruin as he could and ran back into the school, just in time to merge unnoticed into a line of boys passing the changing room.

Even the teachers were distracted by the impending collapse, and it was hard to either get or pay attention. Break was spent at windows, looking out at the wall as it swayed precariously. Fire chiefs held on to their yellow hats and shrugged. A section of scaffolding flew off with a jangling crash, and a murmur of admiration went around the school. Still the wall clung on.

After lunch the wind had died down somewhat, and the boys,

strictly monitored, were allowed outside at the safe distance of the all-weather pitch. George slipped away, walking behind the squash court. Here he sheltered from the wind, and here he intended to wait, till the collapse or till his dash for the end of the driveway, whichever came first.

He had some playing cards in his pocket, but out of boredom, he felt around for the hidden copy of *Swinger*. Despite its glossy cover, the print quality was only a few steps above a photocopy, but the activities on its pages were clear enough. George struggled to make sense of what was on offer: DP, TS, SM, Fr. The only one he understood was XXX. A woman with lustrous dark brown hair offered a sensuous massage in luxurious surroundings adjacent to Kings Cross. *Just ask for Sylvia.* George thought of his aunt, her warm voice, her dark hair, but the woman in the picture was hard and brittle, nothing like her. George had never sent the postcard he had been writing in his head. Beneath Sylvia, a woman in old-fashioned underwear looked at the lens, coaxing her camera-shy breasts towards the viewer.

He was just about to reposition himself in his Y-fronts when the rest of the wall fell with a groaning crash, blowing dust towards him. He didn't dare move in case someone saw him, and he half feared that the impact would bring the squash court down around his ears. He ran for the copse without looking back. All eyes would be fixed out of the windows, he knew, so he made sure to keep the squash courts between him and the school.

Once in the copse, he shinned up the nearest tree, from where he had a perfect view of the new assembly hall, which now lay in ruins beneath a cloud of dust. Gravity had done its worst. There was nothing left to fall.

The sun had the nerve to come out for the first time in days. The headmaster and Mr. Blackstock emerged from the school, shaking their heads, gazing on the wreckage, as a steady trickle of teachers joined them. After a brief conversation, Blackstock started to erect a makeshift cordon around the area. George remembered his mission. The opportunity had presented itself; the spirit of Vox rose from deep within him.

"Help!" he moaned into his walkie-talkie. "Help!"

Nothing happened. He would need more volume, much more.

"Help!" he shouted. "Help! Anybody!"

Blackstock stopped, still as a statue.

"Help!" George said again, more feebly this time. He knew there would be some crackle on the voice, but he hoped that the walkie-talkie was buried so far down that this would not be noticed, that it would just sound muffled. Blackstock ventured as near as he dared to the rubble and started shouting. Everybody else ran towards him. George could hear only the shouts. He dubbed their conversation:

"What is it, Blackstock?"

"You're not going to like it, Headmaster. A child."

"Surely not!"

"No doubt about it. I heard his feeble voice."

"How long can he go without water?"

In reality, everyone was shouting at one another. It *was* mayhem. There was Bird, running around in an overcoat, which he had hastily thrown over his brand-new Roman toga, and next to him Hessenthal: what would *he* be feeling when they found out who was missing? The headmaster yelled, and Bird flitted to him before being dispatched on Hartley's bidding. George delighted to see these little men under his control. This was how Valentine had felt.

"Help!" George said again. And again everybody stopped whatever he was doing. "Help!" They had all heard it now. A school assembly would undoubtedly be called. Realizing who was absent, would they put two and two together, or would they just think he had been so foolish as to go precisely where he shouldn't have?

Sirens screamed down the main drive, and George realized that this meant real trouble: when the outside world got involved, it was all over. In the world outside books, the victims didn't smile and say, "Oh, Vox, you devil!" They took revenge. George had to stay outside till 5:30, when, under the cover of darkness, he would escape to his rendezvous.

He'd let them stew for a bit. He got himself comfortable among the branches of the tree and took *Swinger* out of his back pocket. The firemen, standing out in their bright oranges and yellows against the grey of the rubble and the browns of the Upside staff, started carefully to remove the bricks and concrete, all the while calling out, trying to see where the voice might have come from.

George allowed himself one further "Help!" but this did not have the intended effect; perhaps they hadn't heard. When the bell went for afternoon lessons, the crowd of teachers slowly dissipated, but the firemen kept working. As it grew dark, they trained their high beams on the area. He didn't bother to tease them anymore, as they worked diligently, like ants around their hill. One of the firemen got the attention of the others, and they gathered around. Another went into the school. The rest were giving up for the day. They hadn't found the missing boy; perhaps they feared the worst.

George huddled into the crook of the tree. He noted with satisfaction that his watch read nearly five p.m. All was silent in the copse. Lights glowed all over the school.

His walkie-talkie spluttered to life. Startled, he grabbed on to a branch.

"George Fisher . . . can you hear me?" The static made the tone of Hartley's voice harsher than George had ever heard it. "Answer me and quickly. NOW!"

"Yes, come in, Headmaster. I am reading you. *Over.*" George didn't care anymore. He would be gone in less than an hour. They could do nothing.

"Where are you, Fisher?"

George started to climb down. He swung off the last two branches and fell to the ground.

"Where are you, Fisher? *Over,*" the headmaster repeated. "Are you in the school?"

"No."

"I will meet you and your grandmother at the bottom of the driveway at six o'clock. We'll have an end to this once and for all. Over and *out.*"

Hartley knew, but Queenie would be George's salvation. Nothing would happen as long as she and Reg were on time.

George took the longest way he could find through the woods. He thought about his time at Upside, about how he'd come to be there, how it was all ending, and what he would miss. Now Don wasn't there, there was nothing. But he had let Hartley down. He sang to himself.

Miraculously, at 5:50 p.m., Reg's car was waiting. George sprinted blindly towards it to avoid any ambush on the way. Queenie was driving, and she waved to George out of the window. The back door opened.

Inside was Hartley, sitting calmly on the backseat. Reg and Queenie both wore their poker faces.

"Ah!" said Hartley, whose tone had none of its previous harshness. "Here he is! The Guglielmo Marconi of Upside. Climb aboard." George got in, realizing that the car was going nowhere.

"Hello, Reg, Queenie," he said.

"Hello, George," they both answered contritely.

"Firstly, here is this," said the headmaster. He handed George the walkie-talkie, covered in brick dust. "Sturdy little things. Military issue, I should think."

"Donald gave them to me."

"Did he? Did he?" Hartley nodded. His tone was wistful. "So this is a getaway car, is it?" No one said anything. "You never did get back to me, George, with the answer to that question."

"What was that?"

"About what we could do to make your life happier."

George thought about it. "Well, I'm happier now."

There was silence.

"Have it your own way. We did our best. All it remains for me to say is good-bye, George, good-bye, Mr. and Mrs. . . . ."

"Queenie and Reg," said Queenie.

"Queenie and Reg," said the headmaster with resignation.

"One thing," said George. He took the envelope out of his back pocket. Hartley refused it with a shake of his head, opened the door, and walked back up the driveway.

*   *   *

They sat quietly in the car for a few moments.

"Seemed like a nice chap, really," said Reg.

"Yes. Quite nice," said Queenie. "You drive, Reg. I'll sit in the back with Georgie."

George was shattered: it was all he could do to comprehend that he was going home. "You rang the headmaster, didn't you?" he asked her.

"Of course we did, darling. We were so worried."

"What did he say?"

"He told us to come just like you said."

"And you don't have to go back there again," said Reg. "Bugger that for a game of soldiers! Learn a trade!"

"Shh!" said Queenie. "We don't know what will happen. We don't even know what happened." Queenie asked George to tell her everything, and he did. "Well," she said in summation. "It was an experiment: an experiment that failed. Everyone tried their best. There's nothing more to say."

He fell asleep just as they entered the suburbs of London. The last thing he remembered Queenie saying before he finally succumbed was, "I can't imagine what Frankie will say. A Fisher in the skin part! Honestly!"

He woke up as the car arrived at 34, Cadogan Grove, only one thought in his mind: *It's time to grow up.*

7

The Moment When I Come Alive

Joe supplemented the family income with the odd spot of close-up magic. There was no call for me to accompany him.

One evening, however, I was delighted to find myself in the insalubrious backstage of an unfamiliar establishment in the West End. A large sign above the dressing room read, THE DRURY MANAGEMENT REQUESTS: NO GUESTS BACKSTAGE!

"Needs must," said Joe, as he spruced me up.

In bowled the impresario, announcing himself with a fanfare of sneezes. "You're the dep?" A large man whose cold made him huddle inside his pumice skin, he squinted at a piece of paper, eyes welling with tears, mouth open in anticipation of another blast. "Joking Fisher? Funny man?"

"Joe Fisher. King is my middle name."

"Joe King. Joking. Very good. A gag, is it?" Joe shook his head, and the man mulled the name for a further second, put his handkerchief to his peeled-wallpaper nose, and trumpeted. "Why don't you ditch the Joe? King Fisher."

". . . and George," I added.

"Just *George?*" he asked, disappointed.

I looked at Joe, wondering what else I should be. "George Fisher?" I suggested, but he was looking for something more.

"Have it your own way. I'm Maurice Large. Max. Decimated by the flu, we've been: hence your good self." He sneezed again and moaned in self-pity. "And you're on . . . soon. . . ." The orchestra broke into a waltz. "Make that now!" And it was less than a minute later that the chairman proclaimed: "You want them! You deserve them! Joking Fisher and Gorgeous, Garrulous Geeeeeeeeee-orge!"

Gorgeous, Garrulous George — that was what Large had wanted: adjectives, alliterative adjectives. And I liked it! On we swiftly went, without time to get nervous. Joe put his leg on the chair, and I landed with a bump on his waiting thigh. We peered out into the orchestra, trying to get a feeling for the size of the place, but could make out nothing beyond the pit, where the bandleader, his baton poised, his face a question mark, attended us nervously, letting us know that he could strike up some exit music at any moment.

I scratched the side of my face and wore my bored expression. There were a couple of titters, which were shortly replaced by the throat clearing and coughing of growing unease. Joe leaned down, and I whispered, "Rhubarb, rhubarb, rhubarb." He shook his head, shrugging. Still we did nothing. I could picture Max Large pacing the wings, wiping his sweaty forehead with his snot-drenched handkerchief, thinking he'd made a big mistake. We shouldn't let it go so far as "Geddorf!" but I liked the worried coughs. We could end it all at any moment. We would.

"Ooh, sorry!" I finally said, pointing at Joe and mugging. "I haven't had him long!" There was laughter, mostly of relief.

"Ladies and gentlemen," announced Joe, seeking some decorum. "Please, ladies and gentlemen . . ."

"Oi!" I stage-whispered through a clenched smile. "We haven't rehearsed!" The audience laughed again.

"We don't need to rehearse," quoth he.

"Don't need to rehearse? That's easy for you to say! I need all the help I can get. Sorry, ladies and gentlemen, he hasn't been out recently." Another big laugh. "What about the script? My lines?" This was an aside, hissed loudly enough that they could hear me under the balcony.

"Leave it to me. Don't worry yourself," he said, and cocked an amusing eyebrow towards the stalls.

"Leave it to you?" I exclaimed in exasperation. "Leave it to you? The last time I left it to you . . ." I kept moving my mouth, but no sound came. It was a good gag: the audience loved it. Finally, after much silent up and down, I spoke again, chastened: "OK, Joe. I'll leave it to you." I cleared my throat, newly serious. I cleared my throat again. "Ladies and gentlemen!" I shouted this rather, coughed, and then apologized: "Good lord, I think I may be coming down with something. . . . Ladies and gentlemen, may I present to you my partner, Joe." Joe bowed.

". . . In case there's any doubt who's in charge," said Joe to a round of applause, and we were up and running.

We eased our way through a selection of adult jokes: high society was the upper crust, made from crumbs and held together by dough; the definition of a bachelor — footloose and fiancée free. When an audience begins to laugh, the fun begins. A good performer can ride the wave, and Joe knew how to draw out the laughter, to dampen it, to let it ascend slowly and then crash; they were in the palm of his hand as surely as I was at his fingertips. And the wonder of it was, we were making it up, going where the laughter took us. There was material, of course, but we weren't reciting lines. We were actually living, as we had during those few precious moments at the Drolls. I had never thought we could pull this off, but it was simply a matter of confidence, of letting ourselves go. It was the performance of our lives, resulting in a call for an encore that Joe ignored. Echo was wrong: the audience hadn't simply seen through him. He had touched them. They had believed in him. They had breathed him in. I was delighted, as was Max Large, whose cold seemed much improved.

"You've done this before, my lad. Where have you been hiding?"

"Just starting out. I have an entertainment for children's parties," said Joe.

"Dearie me. Here's five crown. Same time tomorrow."

Since there was nothing booked in the next afternoon, we were able to escape to the Drury a little earlier. The rest of the bill was run-of-the-mill, with emphasis on the brash: several deep-voiced women sang throatily and made saucy comments; a juggler made a lot of jokes about his balls. Backstage, Joe was a little out of his depth, but once on, he was in charge. Again we left to an ovation.

"Someone for you to meet, Fisher," said Max Large, as he rushed by, handing Joe a card. "They've had a lot of luck with vents. Look smart and be nice to the secretary."

"'Duke Duval,'" read Joe. "'Duke Edwardes and Franchot Duval. Representation to the Stars. Wardour Street.' Thanks. We'll go tomorrow afternoon."

Ten chairs lined Duke Duval's waiting room and all were taken. This wasn't the "special look" we had expected: it was a *cattle call*. Joe had turned himself out nicely, as instructed, but he needn't have bothered; no one would notice.

Beneath a sign that said NO ANIMALS — NO EXCEPTIONS, an unimpressed secretary sat behind a desk, doling out numbers. She dangled a spare hand over a pile of forms while she continued her more pressing work, and recited, "Name there . . . Name of act . . . Address . . . Previous representation . . ." As she called the next number, I found myself sitting on Joe's lap, eyeing the competition. Another hopeful joined us — unfortunately another ventriloquist, his act in his case.

"Just under the wire, Bobbie," said the secretary to this most recent arrival, a handsome young man with a straight nose and wide sparkling eyes: paint him gold and he'd have the face of an Egyptian sarcophagus. "I can just squeeze you in."

"I'm sure I can fit. I'm only small." He crowned his remark with the sauciest of smiles before adding confidentially, "Worry not, petal. We're here on other business!" Then, mocking the tense atmosphere of the audition, he mouthed, *We'll just take a seat,* pointing ornately at a newly vacated chair and making a solemn bow of apology to the room. He sat down directly opposite us, opened a rather scruffy suitcase, and, in playful imitation, put his boy on his knee.

But hold on a second: *it wasn't a boy at all!*

There weren't many men with female dolls. In fact, there weren't many female dolls, full stop. Beyond the curiosity value, however, there was something magnetic about her. I didn't dare, but how I longed to stare. If only I could get a proper look.

"Aye, aye, Bobbie," said an emerging auditionee.

"How did it *come off,* Bill?" Bobbie placed inverted commas around any words that took his fancy. I had never seen such archness off a stage, even in Echo. You couldn't take your eyes off him. Or her.

"Number twenty-three. Rollo Rothschild," came the announcement. Up stood a tiny man, nervously wringing the life out of some sheet music. How I wished Joe had brought a book — what better camouflage when you're trying to sneak a peek at a young lady? Luckily, he found a small stack of *The Stage* and, clipping one page to my right hand, holding the other side with his left, started reading a drab editorial about the possible consequences of a war to the West End. This did not quite obscure my view of the new arrival, and if I kept my head down yet looked up as far as I could, my view was perfect. Quite perfect.

Perhaps she's a Romando, I thought. *Perhaps I see a little of myself in her.* But no, she was nothing like. Her beautiful blond hair fell from her black hat in a frame of ringlets about her face, and she had the loveliest complexion I had ever seen, as smooth as a snooker ball. I wanted to reach out and touch it. Her colouring was beautiful too; her lips the gentlest, one might almost say *most human,* red, her eyes a twinkling green. *Come on, George, behave,* I said to myself, but I couldn't tear my gaze from her, and I lingered over her ruffled green shirt and her charmingly baggy jodhpurs. (Oh, I forgot to mention she was dressed for the hunt! Trousers cover a multitude of sins.) She was truly a superior sort of being, and with her in sight, the purgatory of the waiting room, despite the slow turnover, seemed rather nearer heaven than hell.

Inevitably, she caught me peeping. I ducked down behind *The Stage*, scared that her indignation would burn a hole through the newspaper, and vowed to stop embarrassing us both, though I couldn't resist catching the odd glimpse as the minutes ticked by.

"Number twenty-seven. Zona Hallett, please," announced the secretary, making a show of prepping her handbag for her evening departure. *Funny name for a fella*, I thought, as a rather serious-looking young man presented himself.

Finally there was only the four of us. It was the ideal moment to start a conversation, and I was just wondering how to manage it, when Bobbie himself addressed me. "Hello, you," he said with a mischievous grin.

I started. It's difficult for me to be urbane under the best of circumstances, but I was able to collect myself and affect a rather upper-class "Hell-o."

"I think he likes my little friend," Bobbie said to Joe. "He's been trying to catch her eye."

I unsuccessfully denied the charges with a frantic shake of my head.

"I can't help you there, old boy," Joe said to me. "You're guilty as charged." They introduced each other: Bobbie Sheridan, Joe Fisher.

"And?" I looked up at Joe. "And? What am I? A dummy?"

"And this is George," he said, giving me my cue to say hello.

"Delighted to have the opportunity to make your acquaintance, Miss . . . er . . ."

"This is Belle," Bobbie said. I bowed, and my cap fell to the ground. Joe bent down and picked it up. "Aren't you boys good?" said Bobbie. "Leave me and Belle in the shade, you two."

"Practise, practise, practise," I said.

"That's what they tell me," said Bobbie with a sigh. "But I'm afraid Belle is the *laziest* girl in town."

I couldn't take my eyes from her.

From the office beyond came the last of the other auditionees. A large man with a walrus moustache clapped him on the back in consolation as his associate, a smaller man with the trace of a foreign accent, commiserated, "Not what we require today, Zona."

"Tomorrow, though. Always tomorrow," said the larger man cheerfully, shepherding the reject to the exit. He surveyed the room. "Bobbie, my dear boy, and . . ." He turned his attention to us. "Here for the concert party?"

"I'm number twenty-eight, Joe Fisher, sent by Max Large at the Drury."

"Maurice's boy! But surely you didn't have to sit through this whole sorry cavalcade! For the love of Mike, whatever must you think of us? I'm Duke Edwardes and this is Duval." He pointed to the petit man in the beret whose attention was elsewhere. "Duval!"

"Two ventriloquists in a room is one too many," sniffed his partner without looking up.

"He's not just a ventriloquist," said Bobbie. "It's more like a double act those two have. They're a right pair. Siamese twins."

"Is he any good?" asked Duval, unimpressed.

"Actually," said Bobbie. "He's bloody marvellous. The best I've ever seen."

I could have blushed.

"There you have it," said Duke, clapping his hands in celebration. "The best that Bobbie Sheridan, the jewel in Duke Duval's crown, has ever seen."

"Can I invite you to the Drury tonight?" asked Joe. "We're only subbing, and I don't know for how much longer."

"The Drury," groaned Duval, at the same moment that Bobbie cooed, "The Drury!" as though we were off to Ascot and he was picking the champagne. "Just like old times. We'll come!"

Being seen is a concept hallowed among performers. Large made sure that word was out, and an aura attached itself to us among those at the Drury whose health still allowed them to perform. Our act surpassed all expectations, even mine.

Despite the posted warnings backstage, a certain calibre of guest was most welcome. The Duke Duval party was it. I lay on the sideboard beneath a parade of yellow lights.

"I told you," said Bobbie, waving a chic cigarette holder like a magic wand. "He's simply splendid. All he has to do is be himself."

What praise! The only disappointment was the lack of Belle.

"Duval! Do please pay attention!" said Duke in frustration to his partner, who was inspecting the various surfaces on which he might risk sitting. "We are paying this boy court, in the hope of wooing him into our stable that he may better thrive under our caring wings."

"He's a horse? We're birds?" groused the tetchy Duval as he whipped crumbs from a chair with his handkerchief. "Do calm down. You'll do yourself a mischief."

"Will you at least give the *illusion* that you are interested?"

"Sorry, sorry. Most enjoyable. Particularly the bit with the dummy . . ."

"Duval, you're a misery, and I don't know why we put up with you," said Bobbie, looking only at Joe. "Joe, take no notice. It was top drawer, bloody marvellous. You are a dark horse, aren't you? Where have you squirreled yourself away?"

"Family in the business?" enquired Duke.

"Any professional engagements?" asked Duval.

"Nothing much. Children's parties," answered Joe.

"Ch —" Bobbie squealed in horror. This admission was the final straw that forced the firm's hand.

"Duke Duval at your service, sir," said the former with a bow. "We would like to offer you the usual terms in return for the great honour of offering you representation. You do the show. We do the business. Our whole team is at your disposal." Duke conjured visions of an office teeming with dedicated employees, but the whole staff clearly consisted of the nice man, the grumpy man, and their indifferent secretary.

Large, who had stood politely aside, offered a simple caveat: "He is under contract to the Drury until the end of the month."

"In writing?" asked Duval. Large coughed. "Null and void," said Duval, offering his legal verdict. "Null and void. We will, however, lend him back at preferential rates . . ."

". . . Other commitments permitting," added Duke. "No hard feelings, Maurice. Business is business."

"I'll drink to that," said Large, and left to find a bottle.

"You know what you're doing up there," said Duke, leaning forward and tapping his nose. "But do you know what you're doing back here? You'll need a hand. Someone to show you the ropes. You'll be happy to help him, won't you, Bobbie?"

"Delighted," said Bobbie, who was sitting back in his chair, knees tightly together, looking at us intently, trying to find the answer to a riddle. "I'll follow him round a bit . . . *make suggestions.*"

"Yes, I'm sure you will," said Duval, who had had enough.

"Perhaps we could come to see you, Bobbie," said Joe.

"Moi?" said Bobbie, ten fingers to his bosom.

"The Bijou? Heard of it?" asked Duke.

"Of course he's never heard of the Bijou," said Bobbie. "Well, here's a card, and you'll find us there. I'll leave your name backstage tonight. Show begins at midnight. I must be off to pick up the tools of my trade. And Joe, you were just wonderful."

And with some flamboyant scarf-furling, followed by furious bickering in the corridor, the circus left town.

Large returned with a bottle of hock. "Departed?" he asked without disappointment, as he poured two generous glasses. "Went well, my boy, very well. Why didn't you tell them about your mother?" Joe didn't answer. "Maurice Large knows what's what. Talent like that don't come from nowhere. But perhaps you're making your own way. Admirable, of course, but promoters like a crowd. Ah well, let's drink to you: another graduate from Large's Drury Academy. You're on the way up, my boy."

Straight to the top.

Joe separated the two parts of his life like black and white chess pieces. Queenie and Echo knew nothing about his nocturnal career, except that he was making money, and Duke Duval and Bobbie knew nothing of life at Cadogan Grove. But Joe could not divide his attention equally; as the parties went downhill for us, our twilight career took off, and this was where he threw all our energies. It was irresistible: a secret world where he was welcome, where he felt alive. And he always took the money home. He was working for the family; that was how he thought of it.

We arrived at the Gaiety Gala one night to find my name prominently displayed on a flyer that had been sent to our backstage room. Our first billing. Rather than Joe King Fisher, it said "Garrulous George *& His Assistant.*" It had always been Joe's worst nightmare that I took over the act, but now he saw the benefit of allowing my name above his — he could hide behind me. That, remarked Bobbie, was *top billing.*

Bobbie was a constant backstage presence, bringing various friends, *contacts*, with him, feting us before them. How unusual he was, his conversation like patter, sparking this way and that, threaded with cheeky puns. He made us feel magnetic, worth the attention, deserving of the praise and applause; and how fond he was of me, always stealing my cap and ruffling my hair, popping one of his cigarettes into my top pocket. *My Georgie*, he used to introduce me to his friends after the show, *my Georgie*. But he never brought Belle backstage, and I was yet to see them perform. How else could I meet her, spend time with her? I could but wait and hope.

In the meantime, I had the ecstatic reward of our show, when we truly lived and breathed.

Cadogan Grove offered only slow suffocation. The middle of the night found me planning and scheming as the noises of the house whirred around me. I'd have rather stayed in the dressing room overnight, but of course we had to go home, ready for the next day's misery. No vampire was ever happier at dusk, and I didn't even have until dawn. My night ended when the last curtain fell.

One night, I dreamed that I felt movement beneath my clothes. What was at first a pleasant tickle soon developed into the tingle that might at any moment become a searing cramp. I looked down to see flesh creeping over me, covering the papier-mâché of my hands, biting into me. The sensation was as agonizing as the reverse, a flaying of the entire human body with the victim fully conscious. Nerves shot through my body, tendons hooked themselves to me, and nails pierced the skin at the ends of my fingers and toes, tearing their way towards the air as if gasping for breath. I tried to scream but I couldn't, and with no rescue at hand, I lay helplessly writhing in my agonies until the metamorphosis was complete.

I got up slowly, moving cautiously, as though I were learning to walk, frightened that my legs might flip around the wrong way or buckle beneath me. I walked past Frankie's room — there she was, sound asleep, so fragile, so vulnerable that I barely trusted myself around her — then to Queenie's room. I opened the door a crack to see her lying in bed, breathing heavily, the lamplight from the street falling on her face. And across the room, Joe. I dared not look closer, for fear of what I might find.

I put the few things I knew I needed into my box, now my briefcase, and left through the front door. *Good-bye, Cadogan Grove; no one needs me here; not now, no longer. Best leave while the going's good.*

On the empty street, a horrible thought — I had been special, a Romando Boy; now I was nothing, a nobody, another tiny speck of flesh on the back of the world. I hailed a cab. Out of nowhere, one appeared. The driver pulled down his window. "Yes, guv," he said. "Hop in the back." But his mouth clacked up and down as he beckoned me, and I ran.

"Help me!" I shouted to a policeman. "I want to be a boy again!"

"We've just had a call from the British Museum," he said. "Your mummy is waiting for you there." He blew on his whistle, but as he turned around, he fell over, his head rolling towards the gutter, saved from the wheels of an oncoming car only by the strings of his mechanism.

I came back to consciousness to the sound of screaming, but it was only in my head.

I even dragged Belle into my nightmares. She was real, human, a magnificent equestrienne in full point-to-point regalia, thirsting for the hunt. She sat in front of me, staring imperiously, drumming her crop on her leg.

"The thrill of the unknown," she said to me, her voice throaty and calm. "And what happens when a boy puts himself in flesh?"

I was determined to remain chipper, utterly terrified of her power over me. "He gets some sweets?"

"Think again, dummy."

"I give up."

She opened her legs and tapped her crop where the material stretched tightest. "When wood joins with flesh," she said, "wood becomes flesh."

I gulped. "So it's like scissors, paper, stone — but you're throwing wood and flesh in there, which opens up the game entirely. I get it now. Wood burns paper? Stone bruises flesh? Flesh crumples paper?"

"Wood *becomes* flesh. Do you understand?"

"Yes," I said weakly.

"Do you want me?"

"Yes."

"You know what will happen."

"Yes."

"Just like being born."

Her hair fell down around her face as she took off her immaculate riding hat. My previous nightmare vividly recalled itself as she unbuttoned her green shirt.

Then I woke up.

One morning, Queenie laid me on the kitchen table. I couldn't stand another party, but the bookings kept coming in.

"Joe," she called upstairs. "Joe. Are you ready?" He had taken to sleeping on the put-you-up in his own room when we came back so very late. We must have been running behind, for there was already a pile of props — Pip's box, the silk cabinet — by the door. Even Frankie was ready. Queenie opened my box to pack me up but, thinking better of it, decided on a little practice to pass the time. Both of my nightmares collided in one gruesome moment as her hands slipped inside. What is more, she was making me chat to her as though nothing was happening, making idiotic small talk, asking me, "What's your name?" (Doubly muddling because my name, in the dialogue, was Watts.)

"Hello," said Joe rather sheepishly, unshaven in his dressing gown, standing at the door, where he had been observing us.

"Joe," said Queenie, frowning. "The car will be here any . . . Oh, my poor boy! Sit down. You look awful."

"I think you'll have to go on your own. . . . I can't make it."

"Oh, lord. What if they complain?"

"They won't. You can do without me, anyway."

"Mr. Wilkins particularly said . . ."

"Well, sod Mr. Wilkins!" he shouted. "I can't go." He sat at the table, his head in his hands. "I'm sorry. My head is pounding. I feel terrible."

The doorbell rang. "Oh, dear," she said. "That'll be the Fleet car now. I'll have him give me a hand into the motor. You go to your room. You shouldn't be up."

He shuffled out. Queenie returned with the regular driver.

"No Mr. Fisher today, then?" the man with the greased black hair asked casually.

"I'm afraid he's indisposed."

"Touch of that tummy that's going around," he said, as he helped with the cases. "So you're flying solo today."

"Yes, I suppose so."

"Bringing the little toddler with you?"

"No, she'll have to stay with her grandmother today. . . . No, not that one, thank you," she said, indicating my box. "No point taking that today."

"Just *The Queenie Show* today, then, Mrs. Fisher."

"Yes, I suppose so, Mr. . . . er . . . And please call me Queenie."

"Thank you, Queenie," he said, as he held the front door open with his foot. "You can call me Reg."

*   *   *

Joe emerged sooner than expected, looking a great deal fresher.

"Come on, old boy," he said, as we left. "Something special tonight."

"So what's the secret?" Joe was asking, as my lid opened on arrival.

"Well, look," said Bobbie. "She's American and she's wood. Her face is carved. That's why it's so smooth. I had her made by a clever chap in Chicago. Lovely sympathetic expression. Ah, Belle!"

And there she was before me. Of course I had always *known* we were different — she was from the New World, the brave New World; an American Belle if ever there was one.

"Not that there's anything wrong with my Georgie. He's perfect the way he is, but a girl like Belle . . ." Bobbie drew an imaginary veil over his nose and mouth. ". . . Sugar and spice and all things nice, you know; a girl needs a little extra assistance."

"Enough with the small talk," I said. "Let me woo!"

"Impetuous!" said Bobbie, slapping my knee with an imaginary fan. "Dost thou dare impugn a lady's virtue?" He put his hand to his forehead in a mock swoon.

"I dost."

"You'll get your chance, George," said Joe. "Tonight. We're all going onstage together."

"A baking powder?"

"We're going onstage together — you can say what you want to Belle when we're up there. We don't want to waste any of the magic in the green room."

"No," said Bobbie. "I've wasted quite enough of my magic back here! *We*," he said, pointing to Belle, "are going to make ourselves presentable. See you boys on stage."

Once we were alone, Joe inspected himself in the mirror and caught my eye.

"A boy can be nervous, can't he?" I gulped. "It's my first time."

The spacious backstage afforded us ample opportunity for privacy. Joe and Bobbie were to enter from different sides, so we took our place in the wings stage left. Joe cleared his throat rather more forcefully than usual as the chairman announced: "My lords, ladies and gentlemen. Order! Order! Welcome to this evening's benefit, a unique entertainment in the annals of the Gaiety Gala. Tonight, two great favourites. You have enjoyed them separately . . ."

"Oooh!" went the crowd.

"And now you can enjoy them together! Hush! Hush!" begged the chairman when the house cheered. "There are ladies present." A roomful of men cheered. "May I present to you — in their début on the same stage — firstly, Gorgeous, Garrulous George and his assistant, King Fisher . . ." The curtain swept up, and we walked on to terrific applause, assuming our usual position. ". . . who will be joined by that Veritable Venus of Ventriloquial Virtuosity: none other than the very beautiful, the very bawdy, the very *British* Bobbie Sheridan and everybody's favourite wooden Dame Sans Merci, Belle!"

On they swept to an even greater roar. I had eyes for no one but Belle — her poise, her grace, her jodhpurs — and it was only after I managed to wrench my gaze away that I noticed she was carried by a tall, elegant woman wearing a flowing white gown and a sparkling tiara. Who was this mysterious interloper? Where on earth was Bobbie? Sitting down demurely, with Belle on her lap, the ventriloquiste threw me a refined smile. She really was most attractive. And familiar . . .

Hold on a mo, I thought.

Laughter rippled through the crowd.

Our first words were bound to bring the house down. There are certain moments when you can't go wrong. *I don't like yours!* for example. Bingo!

I kept looking at her to make sure, then back at Joe. Joe attempted to get the ball rolling, but, certain I wasn't mistaken, I wanted to make sure I wasn't putting my foot in it. "Joe!" I said, and gesticulated over my shoulder. "What happened to Bobbie?"

"What do you mean, what happened to Bobbie?"

"Well, he's . . ." I wasn't sure I could brazen it out as Joe was prepared to. I lowered my voice so everyone in the house could hear me perfectly clearly: *"He's wearing a dress!"* There was a huge cheer. Bobbie was pretending not to notice a word, admiring his makeup in a little compact. I could barely make myself heard over the audience's rowdy approval.

"Doesn't she look lovely, George?"

"Oh yes, she *looks* lovely!" Then I added sotto voce, "Why didn't you tell me?"

"And Belle . . . Now, *she* really does look lovely, doesn't she?"

"Oh, yes," I enthused. Joe whistled to himself, not innocently. I did my special reserve triple take. "Hold on hold on hold on hold on. Do you mean to tell me . . ." Big laughs.

And then she spoke, the first time ever I heard her voice. "Makes you wonder though, doesn't it, George?" she said. Her voice was soft, almost tragic in its innocence, with the slightest hint of an American accent, and my heart melted. Belle batted her lovely eyelashes at me, and the crowd started to whistle. Bobbie was doing a good job — gimmick acts can sometimes rely a little too much on the device at the expense of the basics, but not this one. The house was spellbound. So was I. "It's what's inside that counts," said Belle. "We're all the same. That's the beauty of it."

I gulped and stuttered, "Hello, B . . . B . . . B . . . B . . ."

"Belle," she said.

"Ding dong!" I kicked my legs out underneath me.

"You're blushing, George."

I loved the way she said my name. If only she would call me *my Georgie,* like Bobbie. Joe loosened my collar.

"These two boys don't know quite *what* to think," said Bobbie, to whoops of encouragement. "Perhaps Belle and I can do a little song for the lads at the back. So, boys, you just stand there and look handsome . . . and, maestro, how about a little 'I Would If I Could But I Know That I Can't'?"

The band started up, and Belle's dainty feet pointed right and left in a gesture at dance. As the first verse began ("My mother knew it from the minute I was born"), I wondered at Bobbie's poise and beauty, the source of Belle's. The crowd sang along in the chorus, and Belle swished her crop, taking a few lines here and there. They really were the perfect partnership. It was only a pity the song had to end, but by the last chord, I was raring to go.

We were on stage for twenty glorious minutes, the longest Joe and I had ever performed, and applauded back three times. Backstage, there was bubbly and more congratulations. Joe placed me next to Belle beneath the dressing-room mirror.

"We'll leave those two lovebirds to themselves, I reckon," said Bobbie.

Belle and I sat together, basking in the afterglow, watched over by our partners and their friends.

And so it was the next night, the next night, and the night after that. It became a beautiful habit, a ritual of courtship: we were Romeo and Juliet, Tristan and Isolde, Heloise and Abelard, Laurel and Hardy. To my great joy, Joe stopped taking me home — presumably Queenie and Pip were able to cope with the parties on their own — and my nocturnal torment came to an end. Long might it last.

After the Saturday night, a three-show triumph, we were taken to a grand restaurant, shimmering with crystal and candles. As a symbol of the evening's success — box office records — Belle and I were seated at the head of our party, hand in hand, on matching wooden high chairs, she wearing Bobbie's tiara and I covered in streamers from a high-spirited backstage ambush. Our presence drew queer looks from well-dressed Charlies at adjacent tables, but these were dismissed by Ralph Ward, the sturdy, elated owner of the Gaiety Gala, and 50 percent of the team of Duke Duval, the other half even gloomier than usual. The bandleader, Fred Sharp, with his companion, and the chairman, a Cockney called Len, rounded out our party. Bobbie was wearing a light purple blazer with a white shirt and an aquamarine tie, a hint of slap still sparkling about his cheeks. Drinks were arriving freely, and his movements were even more languid than usual.

"To the greatest team the Gaiety has ever known," said Ward, and raised his flute high, merrily slopping champers all over the table.

"Yes," said Duke. "To the two of you, the four of you. A triumph, my dears, a triumph."

"Here's how!" toasted Len, his nose as brutalized as Bobbie's was perfect.

"Aye," said Duval, tossing a cigarette butt into a nearby wineglass to fizz in the dregs. "A shame it all has to end."

"Now," said Bobbie, pointing a long forefinger in accusation, "*you* are going to be quiet. I am not having tonight spoiled by that bloody war. It's going to ruin us all sooner or later, but tonight we will live as we may. What's life without a good bayonet, anyway?" And he squealed as if jabbed from below.

"Hear, hear!" said Duke, and raised his glass to the rest of the table. "Hear, hear!"

"A last hurrah, is it?" said Duval. "Before the bombs fall?"

Bobbie almost cracked a plate with his knife. The restaurant, in our immediate vicinity, fell quiet. "You stop," he said sharply. "Or I go."

"Franchot, dear," said Duke, whispering into his ear, as the other diners strained to hear. "Do please, please, let us be. Go home if you can't get into the swing."

"I wish this one would hurry up and start," said Duval. "It'll be a relief. Wasn't like this last time." He lit another cigarette.

"We wouldn't know. We can't remember that far back," said Ward, and raised his glass towards us at the end of the table. "To George! To Belle! To business!"

Duval subdued, conversation resumed. Joe was getting drunk. Bobbie always had a slight air of inebriation about him in his parodies of grandiloquence and lavishness of gesture. Sobriety reined him in unfairly, and drink gave him an acceptable excuse to be as he truly was. Joe, on the other hand, being fundamentally shy, and without me at hand to help him along with the quips, fielded questions politely and kept drinking. It was the kind of establishment where, when one of the clientele took so much as a sip, his glass was immediately, almost supernaturally, replenished. The champagne disappeared, but this only meant a change to red wine.

"No more bubbles?" asked Joe. Echo and Queenie would never have heard him say anything like it.

"No more bubbles," said Bobbie with an overabundance of sympathy.

"Bubbles!" said Joe. "Bubbles!"

"Oh, let him have bubbles," said Ward, and motioned to a waiter.

"But I do like this one," said Joe. "Fruity."

"Very fruity," said Ward, and dismissed the waiter.

Despite the merriment, Duval was still not quite done. Out of the blue, while a lengthy debate raged as to whether someone I had never heard of was the greatest living Englishman, Duval lobbed a question at Joe: "And when were you going to tell us about Echo Endor?"

"Oh, I can tell you about Echo Endor!" said Bobbie with a shriek of amusement. "An absolutely marvellous old star. Worked with her once, and I've rather modelled myself on her. Old-fashioned, I hear you say? What? What?"

"I asked Joe," said Duval, cutting Bobbie short.

"Oh," said Joe, raising his empty wineglass. "She's my mother."

"I knew there was a reason you were happy to play second fiddle to laughing boy," said Duval, referring to me. A thoroughly objectionable man.

"You had to," Duke muttered to Duval. "You had to. You just couldn't let it alone."

"Your mother?" asked Bobbie, delighted to be at the epicentre of such revelations. "Show business royalty?"

Joe, being drunk, was more than a little pleased with himself. "Yes, my mother. Evangeline Fisher. Echo Endor. But I wanted to make it on my own. I didn't need her help."

"Of course you didn't," Bobbie said compassionately, lobbying the table for support. "Of course he didn't. He wanted to go his own way. What a brave boy!"

Joe raised his glass again and hiccuped. "She gave me George."

"Good business!" thought Ward aloud. "Echo Endor's son!"

"Could business be any better?" asked Duke. "One visit from the law and you'd be *out* of business altogether!"

"Bugger business!" said Joe, not noticing that he had just thrown the contents of his glass of red wine across the table.

"Fighting talk! They ought to enlist you to fire the first shot," said Ward with a laugh.

Two frustrated diners came to the table to remonstrate with the rowdy show folk intent on making everyone else's meal a misery. Bobbie shooed them away, hens clucking around his feet. Rebuffed, they took their complaint to the head waiter.

"I can't believe it," said Bobbie. "I wish my mother were someone fascinating. It's too good to be true."

"And that isn't all that's too good to be true," said Duval ominously.

"I don't think I can *stand* the excitement," said Bobbie, blithely ignoring the respectfully fuming waiter who stood to the side of his chair.

"No, I don't think you can," said Duval.

"Duval," sighed Duke with an air of defeat.

The head waiter was hovering so effectively that even Joe, in his befuddled state, tried to see what he wanted. But the official would not negotiate with the wine thrower himself, and everyone else was too engrossed in the escalating conflict between Bobbie and Duval to pay him the blindest bit of attention.

"Let me see . . . ," said Bobbie. "I wonder how a vicious old queen's mind works, Duval. Hmm."

"Sir," said the head waiter. Bobbie ignored him.

"What would upset Bobbie? That's what you're thinking. I wonder what it can *possibly* be." If Bobbie was in any way anxious, he was concealing it. Joe's head slumped to the table, but this had nothing to do with the conversation.

"Sir!"

Finally the head waiter had spoken loudly enough that it had reached Bobbie, who stood up and screeched, "What? What? What? What? Whaaaaaaaat?"

"Sir, your table is disturbing our other customers."

"If you insist, we'll leave." There was a murmur of approval.

"I'll get your bill, sir."

"We are being forcibly evicted. We are not paying a thing."

The head waiter fumed and said through gritted teeth, "Go. Quickly. Now."

"And never darken our napkins again!" Bobbie turned round to the table and said with total calm: "Always works. Now we leave. Pack up George and Belle. Quickly, dears, as the management suggests." Joe was attempting to sit up without success. "And you," Bobbie said. "You're in no fit state to go home. You're coming back to Bobbie's for a nice hot mug of cocoa." He addressed his next remark to Duval, though he was talking to Joe. "Can't let your wife see you in that state, can we?"

"Sorry, Bobbie," said Duval, with considerable prodding from Duke. "We were concerned. We didn't want to see you . . ."

"Concerned, my eye. Duval, you're pitiful. I didn't think about it. . . . Well, I won't lie. But not in the real world. Not in this lifetime." His mood changed entirely as he considered the glittering chandelier in the lobby. "It's very nice here. And the price was right. I'd come again. I like a prix fixe, but I'm always willing to go à la carte."

There were surprisingly few pictures of our host on the walls of Bobbie's rooms. The furniture was spotless, the antimacassar headrests perfectly symmetrical on the sofa. Joe had been sobered somewhat by a swift walk around the block and the wind gusting onto his face in the backseat of the cab. Both Belle and I, symbols of the earlier triumph, were also given some air.

"You just sit there," said Bobbie. "I'll be in the kitchen."

"I don't much want to be alone," moaned Joe.

"I'm only through here," Bobbie called from the kitchen. "I'll open this wee hatch, and you won't even have to take your eyes off me."

"I'm sorry," said Joe. At least his eyes were now open. "I don't quite know why I got so drunk."

"It was probably the alcohol, lovey," said Bobbie. His theme song drifted through the hatch: "My mother knew it from the minute I was born, / She thought it best to tell my pa, so he was duly warned . . ."

"Sorry," Joe said again when Bobbie came through.

"Don't you worry, my pet," said Bobbie. "Happens to the best of us. Drink some of this. It's the antidote."

"I don't think I can," said Joe. "I feel all right, but I want to lie down."

"Well, I'll bring it through here, then. Stay there." Bobbie turned the light on in an adjacent room. "Come on, then, Mr. Fisher." Joe moved slowly to his feet, the arm of the sofa his crutch. "Come on, then, son of Echo Endor," said Bobbie, offering a firm elbow. They made their way to the guest room. "You'll be comfy in here."

"Light," I heard Joe complain, and the light went off as Bobbie emerged. He left the door open a crack, sat down to drink his tea, and opened a book. Fifteen minutes later, he took a quick look in at Joe, shook his head in amusement, and closed the door quietly. Before he went to his own room, he turned around to Belle and me: "And you two, keep it down!"

We were lying next to each other on the dining table, our only light the single bar of an electric heater and whatever the moon shone into the second-storey window, our bottom sheet a tablecloth covered in romantic drawings of Japanese bridges and teahouses.

"Are you awake?" I heard in the darkness. Despite the long night, I was awake and alert. Up until that moment I might have been ready to do nothing, to lie there in blissful silence.

"Yes?"

"Don't be scared."

"Of what?"

"You know."

I looked out of the window. If this was all left up to me, there was no way forward. She said nothing.

"I'm not scared. I don't know what to do."

"Shh!" she said. "Lie still."

"But . . ."

"We're all the same. That's the beauty. I'm just like you."

We lay next to each other.

"Do you want to try?" I heard her ask.

"Yes."

I could see nothing of her against the light, only her shadow.

Old Boys' News

George left Upside in disgrace, a cheat and a vandal, but this went unmentioned at home. Rather, the early family reunion was celebrated as a triumph for good sense. If any Fisher felt otherwise, she did not say.

An education would now detain George no longer than necessary. He spent the spring and summer at home, in imaginary convalescence after his great escape. His strict regimen with his grandfather's books gave a scholarly appearance, and this looked like a proper education to Queenie. Frankie came home to fulfil some commitments — a weekly singing spot at a cabaret. It was like old times, at first, as if Upside had never intruded.

The next September, two months before he turned thirteen, George started at a local comprehensive, an unfortunate necessity for which Frankie could summon no enthusiasm. Hand in hand, they considered the building, a two-storey edifice entirely of huge sheets of glass, partitioned by once-white columns, window frames, and grey slate beneath a flat brown roof. Part greenhouse, part fish tank, Malcolm Collins School and Technology College was spared from resembling an experiment in monotone geometry only by children's art taped to classroom windows.

"Better go in on your own, Georgie," Frankie said considerately.

At this school of no great ambition, George had only to take care of the most basic requirements: uniform was not compulsory, tests spoken of but rarely set, attendance apparently negotiable. O levels were too far off to merit consideration. There was no chapel, no school play, no vetting of paperbacks, and no library; in fact, few amenities at all. The playing fields, accessible only by bus, had a different postal code — those who didn't care to participate in games saved the school the bother of carting them to and fro. As far as George was concerned, Malcolm Collins was perfect.

The new boy arrived to find himself in the first year. He sucked his pencil to make problems look difficult and showed his working. There was no need to cheat. His new label, *egghead,* gave him the perfect excuse for not bothering with games and not participating at break. A sense of humour saved him once or twice, and the cards were always handy.

At home, progress on his grandfather's books was slow. Since the first volumes, with their consistent tone of practical instruction, they had yielded little more of great interest and nothing at all on voice throwing. He hoped that he would turn a page to see a clear path ahead, but for the time being, they felt a little like homework.

Queenie and Reg were always off, Reg happy to chauffeur her any distance to a waiting cheque, however small. Frankie had a frustrating summer: a tour of *Exit, Pursued Bare* (Ricky Mitchell's suggestion) was a low. Farce was a genre that did not feature strong parts for women or principal boys, so Frankie spent much of act 1 waiting in a chest at the end of a bed, wearing nothing but the frilliest excuse for underwear. Her character, fully clothed, led the ensemble through the predictable close shaves and mistaken identities of act 2, but it was a far cry from *Peter Pan.* Where was the magic? George saw the show in Maidenhead in a characterless municipal theatre, a cinder-block Malcolm Collins. The poster featured a caricature of a barely covered Frankie, towel perched on an unrealistic bosom, chasing a vicar across the stage, herself pursued by a man in a bear suit. "Ribald! Hilarious! May the farce be with you!" proclaimed the *Maidenhead Gazette*. "Laugh? I nearly *did!*" said Frankie pointedly. *Exit, Pursued Bare* was an indignity she would never have suffered if Des had been alive. To his credit, however, Ricky (once he saw he could not talk her round) took her displeasure seriously and created a package around her for the following summer. His idea, in this case a good one (for which the evidence was a whirr of finger work on a calculator, then the triumphant display of a resulting total): a revival of the Fisher Fol-de-Rols.

After the war, Echo had struggled on with this heirloom. Variety was dying a slow death, heading for the coast, where it could breathe easier in the carefree sea air, and by 1950 the show took its final bow. The modern equivalent was still the rule in pier theatres, but the seasonal nature of seaside entertainment meant a show could tour only three months, and perhaps at Easter. Even in variety's prime constituency, down among the donkey rides, 99s, and mini golf, attendance was falling; the holiday camps made sure that Glamourous Granny and Knobbly Knee contests satisfied the punters' cultural needs.

It was Ricky's suggestion that the Drolls, in its pure form, was ripe for rediscovery. He would tailor a classy piece of nostalgia for old-age pensioners who knew the name Fisher to be inseparable from Fol-de-Rols: a big-hearted good class summer show, as lush as they could manage — simultaneously a "thanks for the memories" and an introduction to the stars of tomorrow (who boasted Ricky's representation). It would play Tuesday to Saturday and move on the Sunday, just like the good old days. Even without a major draw, the tour for the following summer was booked in less than a week. The calculator never lied.

In a small registry office just after Christmas, the registrar pronounced Mr. Reg Fleet and Mrs. Queenie Fisher man and wife.

When it was time to kiss the bride, Reg dipped her as far as he could and said, "I never thought I'd live to see this day," and their twenty guests cheered. At the reception, in the pub next door, Reg gave a speech. He'd asked for help with the phrasing, but the thoughts were all his own. He would have waited a thousand years for Queenie; she had kept faith in him through the darkest hour, saved his life. Evie went unmentioned, though one note of sadness was allowed to intrude: "We have a daughter, and we wanted so very, very much for her to be here today. But she ain't ready to make that step yet. *Yet!*" He repeated it with a brave smile before the toast: "To our girl — we weren't here for you, but now we're here whenever you need us."

"You're the best man," said Queenie after George's speech, "but you might as well give me the first dance." George led her around the floor at a stately pace. Reg tapped him on the shoulder, and George, at a loss how to withdraw gracefully, was cajoled into dancing with a blowsy woman who clasped him to her rippling bosom and repeatedly said he was too young for her.

A Fleet car took Frankie to her evening performance in Luton, as the menfolk lamented the loss of this coveted dancing partner.

The happy couple honeymooned on the Cornish Riviera. Though he was invited, George stayed in Cadogan Grove. He could have neglected the beginning of the spring term altogether, but a postcard arrived from Tintagel the day before he was due back: "Having a wonderful time. Remember to go to school. Back on Tuesday. Love to Frankie, Q and R."

Things changed at Cadogan Grove. He had pictured, after Evie's death, a triumvirate of his mother, his grandmother, and he, but after their honeymoon, less and less was seen of Queenie and Reg as they enjoyed their newfound freedom. Reg treated her like the queen she was, always opening doors for his "old gal," asking her what she wanted. No wonder she'd seemed so disinterested in men; she'd had one. "It's so romantic," Frankie said. "And soon you'll have a girlfriend, and maybe even I'll meet someone. Till then, we have each other."

*   *   *

The Fishers' brief flirtation with the education system came to an end after George's first year at Malcolm Collins.

"We're hoping to send him to a public school," Frankie lied when she called the headmaster in September, but public school didn't come into it. George was running away to join the circus; more specifically, the Fol-de-Rols. Frankie was prepared to pass on all her knowledge until she could send him somewhere he would be welcome: perhaps even Franca DeLay, her alma mater.

Touring was just as it had always been, with one crucial difference: George was put to work. He understudied, mixed drinks, attended prop school, sold programmes, and deputized on follow-spot. Life backstage was like it had been in Wimbledon, but the personnel had changed. Northern Bernie had been replaced by Northern Mack Wilson, the magician; Glyn, the stern dogsbody of drab SW19, was now Brenda, the colourful and unflappable touring stage manager, modelling daily from her stupendous collection of contemporary boutique-wear. And all were now in the employ of the Fishers. Frankie, Ricky, and, by extension, George were at the top of the ladder. Odd hours became normal: he ate late and slept later.

He thought the busy summer had to end, as all runs must, that reality would intervene; but it didn't. The Fol-de-Rols kept rolling, and George stayed on. It was he who reminded Frankie about Malcolm Collins, and his mother who said she couldn't spare him and would make arrangements.

Frankie and George took time off in the New Year, bidding farewell in Eastbourne with a party that was the scene of mild flirtation between George and Joanne, Wimbledon's Slave of the Lamp, recently drafted in as a cast member. Despite her figure, he thought her young. Frankie and he arrived in London as the sun came up.

Frankie fulfilled her normal commitments, accompanied by George, sometimes introduced as her son, sometimes as her bodyguard — at fourteen, he was taller than she — but most often as her manager. The Fol-de-Rols was already booking for April.

The next run was not quite as successful as expected. Various reasons were put forward — "the weather" and "the mood of the country" elicited sympathetic nods — and the Drolls ended unexpectedly early, running out of steam three months earlier than the previous year. The party, which doubled as George's fifteenth birthday celebration, was a modest affair. Of course, they'd all see one another next year.

To his relief, George was almost at the end of his project with his grandfather's books. What had begun a devotion was ending a chore.

So much work had gone into the journals — every curve of the pen, every erasure, every emphatic three-line whip — but George had come to know virtually nothing about the man: he was invisible. The only thing that mattered was technique, its perfection. Though George would never admit as much to Frankie, the books had not lived up to their initial promise: where they had started out as "how to" books (which he might have preferred, if anything, to be a little less cold and mechanical in tone), they had mutated into something, if possible, even less personal: abstruse speculation into "pure magic," with pages of diagrams for illusions too elaborate to re-create. He got used to skimming, despairing of further detailed instruction.

The seventh volume had ended with grand plans, all in the realm of Platonic speculation, about distant voice, but the eighth volume took a left turn into *theoretical escapology*, of no interest whatsoever. There was only one remaining volume, and George held out no great hopes, glad that he would be done. He liberated Echo's scrapbooks from the trunk in the sitting room and flicked through the pages, the still-glossy programmes, and the postcards of seaside towns, black ink faded brown on their reverse. He tried to imagine Joe's right hand writing the words on the pages of the notebooks. But in his photos, there was no right hand in view: it was always working his dummy.

George wondered whether he shouldn't spend his modest per diem on a modern guide. He pictured a book, more instruction manual than arcane volume of mystery, with diagrams as dull as those in *How Sound Works*. *How Magic Works* — it told him everything he needed to know in clear type.

Frankie happened to run across Brenda, the Fol-de-Rols stage manager. A fortuitous meeting, Brenda said. Her family business was two people short in their busy season, and they needed a quick learner, someone smart. She wondered whether George was free for the winter, into Christmas. There'd be cash in hand and perhaps a little education.

"You'll enjoy it. Trust me," said Frankie, who hadn't been specific as to the nature of their trade.

George liked Brenda, from whom each backstage crisis had elicited no more than a giggle and a shrug, so he set out with an address in the West End, just off D'Arblay Street. He rang the bell for Crystal Clear, wondering what sort of concern hid behind this unprepossessing exterior. Brenda herself opened the door. A little younger than Frankie, yet somehow immeasurably older, she was wearing one of her collection of gaudy dresses (part muumuu, part tent) as though it were a completely normal piece of clothing: this a psychedelic purple-and-green paisley that fell from her bosom, making infrequent contact with the rest of her body. She was a large woman without being fat, her lips exaggeratedly full, her cheekbones surprisingly well defined in her fleshy, friendly face, her hair uniquely frizzy. When she smiled, her eyes closed entirely, as if in ecstasy. She was a good person to make laugh.

"Glad you've come," whispered Brenda, and pointed downstairs. She beckoned him, treading lightly. The musty hallway led to an even danker basement. At one end sat a man at a console; most of his attention was turned to the climactic moment of a horror film in which someone was about to drive a stake into the heart of a vampire in his coffin. A red light shone above a door to their right. Brenda put her finger to her lips, smiled, pointed, and mouthed, *My father*. From the speakers above the console came the sound of crunching bone.

"Not bad," said the man at the desk. "But the timing's gone for a Burton. Once more, Tim." Brenda's father sent the film backwards. Just as the vampire hunter lifted his hammer to plunge the stake home, a sneeze exploded through the speakers. "For crying out loud! Could you do that off mic?"

"Sorry! Sorry!" broadcasted a stuffed nose over the sound system. The red light flickered and went off. A man emerged holding a large cabbage in which was embedded a hammer.

"Dad, Tim," said Brenda. "Frankie's son, George, here to help."

"Thank Christ for that!" said the man behind the desk, as Tim passed on his way to the bathroom. "Hello, lad. I'm Roger. Done anything like this before?" Roger, who had the flattened features of a pugilist, laughed when George shook his head. "It's time for a crash course. Can you do this?" He flicked a coin and grabbed it in midair. "Hand-eye coordination. You'll get nowhere in this lark without it." He flipped it at George, who caught it.

"I can do this," said George. He rolled the coin over the back of his fingers.

"You, my lad," said Roger the Boxer, "are just about to embark on a new career; a career for which you will get absolutely no credit at all, the height of your ambition for which will be *not to be noticed,* and in which if you *are* noticed, it will only be because you have made a complete cock-up."

"He always gives this speech," Brenda said to George, as Tim sneezed again on his way by. "Just applaud when you think he's finished."

"We have a hell of a backlog at the moment from Daedalus Studios. This masterpiece is *Blood from the Vampire's Tomb;* next up, *Satan's Abacus,* then *Burn Sinner Burn* and *Sebastian DeVries' Tales of Terror.* Normally we have ten days a picture, give or take. . . . Well, we have one week for this whole lot."

"And we do the sound effects?" asked George. He liked everything about the place: its seedy atmosphere of industry and its subterranean seclusion. He particularly liked the still of the expiring vampire, which flickered over the recording console.

"We're footsteppers," said Brenda.

"The Yanks call it Foley," interrupted her father. "There, we are *Foley artistes,* or *Foley walkers,* but here in dank Mother England, we are still footsteppers. But we don't just do *footsteps;* we do bloody everything. Right. Let's get cracking. Tim, you're in no fit state to be behind a microphone. You're going to show this live wire exactly what to do. Brenda, you're going to help, but first the shopping list. Tim?"

Tim produced a scribbled piece of paper from his back pocket. "OK. Erm. One-inch steaks, four, plenty of fresh onions, some sea salt, about five pounds of fresh carrots, celery, two head of lettuce, and a cabbage . . ." George was envisioning a particularly hearty stew when Tim added, "Not forgetting two packs of press-on nails, cotton wool, some marbles, and a thing of aspirin."

"Any size or shape jar?"

"They're for my cold."

"Right," said Brenda.

"Young man," said Roger, rubbing his hands ghoulishly, "step inside my laboratory."

A large screen covered one wall, showing the same gruesome flickering still. A carpet was rolled back to reveal four different surfaces: pavement, sand, gravel, and a linoleum tile. There was a large tank filled with water, an oversize fridge, an echo chamber, and enough extra junk that the room could pass for a church hall on jumble day.

"It was just one paving stone when I started," said Roger, slipping into reverie. "And they expected you to give them *Gone With the* ruddy *Wind!*"

Tim sniffed as he lit a cigarette. "Everything you see on the screen, except for the dialogue, is made in here. It's up to us to put the right sound there at the right volume."

"And in the right mix. When the film gets to us, they've only recorded the dialogue, and they probably dubbed that after. All the other noise they try to get rid of."

"And then you put it back in," said George.

"Exactly!" said Roger, and clapped him on the back. "And

that's how a movie has dominion over sound. Ready? Right, let's go back to those footsteps, that bugger we forgot in the bridge scene." George rolled aside the carpet, and Tim showed him how to judge his timing by the actor's shoulders.

"You mostly can't see their feet or they're offscreen anyway," he said. "And even if you can see them, the audience aren't much looking."

"It doesn't have to be perfect, then?" asked George.

Tim laughed. "Look, when you go to a cinema, it's not like the actors are speaking from the screen. Their voices are coming out of speakers somewhere, certainly not from their actual mouths, but you don't care. Same as this. If it's there or thereabouts, everyone's happy." He pointed to the screen. "Looks all right, doesn't it?"

Time flew by. George listened to Roger in his headphones and did whatever Tim and Brenda said: keep your eyes on the screen, stand this far from the microphone, snap celery like this. Carrots were breaking bones; an umbrella was opened and closed for the swooping of bats; and when Dracula's tomb door rolled away, they slid the top from an old toilet tank. The steaks were used for any kind of blow. Coconuts did not really sound like horses' hooves, though a sheet of metal was a good substitute for thunder.

"I'm just not buying the hammer in the cabbage for the stake," said Roger, as they considered their day's work. "It's too clean."

"How about I bite into an apple?" George suggested off the top of his head.

Roger's eyes twinkled. When they watched the final reel of *Blood from the Vampire's Tomb* again, George heard a film for the first time, and he felt a surge of pride as the stake made its appropriately gruesome plunge into the vampire's heart. When the star put out a cigarette, the smouldering was no more than a thumb pressed into an ashtray full of dirt, and when the happy couple kissed before the credits rolled, it was merely a fifteen-year-old boy sucking the underside of his wet right forearm. By eleven, they were finally done. Brenda offered George a lift home and a heavily tenderized steak. "Perks of the trade," she said. "One each."

Two teams worked around the clock, deadlines were successfully extended and met — the crisis was averted, and George was invited to stay on.

Going to work was a pleasure, and George was too tired to notice returning, which he often did with Brenda, sometimes after a quick stop at the Monkey's Head just around the corner, where he stuck to a shandy and a packet of crisps.

"These crisps might be better for that avalanche than the cotton wool, Roger. Listen."

"Sonny, you have to know when to turn it off. Or it'll drive you insane."

As he was setting off one morning for Crystal Clear, a large flat envelope arrived in the mail. He knew the postmark well. Upside had caught up with him.

His daily journey to the tube station took him by grim Malcolm Collins. His satchel made him look like any other fifteen-year-old schoolboy, but the contents were specific to his new profession: his favourite lighter, some extra-thick cardboard that would surely be useful, a tin full of ball bearings, and some old cutlery he had found lying by the side of the road: all rubbish had sound potential now.

He could barely recall anything of his year at Malcolm Collins. Of Upside, however, he remembered every moment. Three years on, it was the bucolic aspects of the school that came most readily to mind: the gardens sloping gently down towards the surrounding fields, the morning walk to the conker trees, the empty playing fields in winter. There was something he was forgetting to remember too, something out of reach.

He'd have left Upside by now. Perhaps if he'd won a scholarship he'd be at one of those tersely named and important schools that sprang from teachers' tongues — Eton, Harrow, Stowe — but if he'd failed, then he'd have ended up at long-winded Malcolm Collins School and Technology College anyway. Perhaps nothing in life made any difference, however radical a break it felt at the time. At Malcolm Collins (and probably at Eton too, for all he knew), they were just emerging for morning break. A passing boy yelled at him.

On the tube, he opened the Upside envelope with some trepidation, removed the contents, and laughed. That was all they had for him? The last four copies of *The Upsider*? Did they waste a magazine, a stamp, and an envelope on every black sheep? He glanced in the oldest: the first eleven, the second fifteen, the field trip to Arundel, the old boys, the library, the obituaries, and a review: "Androcles a Roaring Success," the headline. There was plenty of praise for Burgh's performance, the review written by an Ernest Bunbury: possibly Burgh himself? George read between the lines, behind the words — everything was a sham. But the magazines held a morbid fascination, and he returned to them at any free moment at work. That day's project involved a lot of stabbing for a particularly violent crime movie. Most of the morning was spent burying knives of all sizes into meats of every cut. Queenie and Reg would eat well tonight — almost certainly stir-fry.

At lunch, in the Monkey's Head, George nursed his half pint while the rest of Crystal Clear stood at the bar and solved the industry's problems. George had read as much of the magazines as he could bear. Hessenthal had gone on to another school, and Poole was now vice headmaster. He flicked through the old boys' news in the most recent issue: most of the names meant nothing to him, but a couple of the oldest boys from his year were already covering themselves in glory at their senior schools. Why they wanted to let Upside know about it, he had no idea. Lunch break nearly over, he cast his eye over the most recent obituaries. It was then he saw.

> Hartley, Donald (1937–1976). Pupil from 1945 to
> 1950 and sometimes groundsman at Upside; son of
> Stewart, headmaster, and Mary Hartley. A memorial
> service, to be followed by reception, will be held at
> noon on December 5th at St. Stephen's, Marylebone,
> W1, to which all O.U.s are invited.

George's eyes suddenly swam with tears. Things never happened when you predicted they would. But when a possibility was left unconsidered, fate crept through the cracks. He would never forget that.

The memorial service was in two days' time. Of course he would go, but he wouldn't tell his family. He didn't want to remind Queenie and Frankie about the Upside fiasco, about which for the first time he felt guilt, as though he had wasted a valuable opportunity; he owed everyone an apology. He tore out one page, then threw the magazines away as he headed back from the pub.

Frankie had been asked to step in at the last moment as one of three soloists on a tour for a "Best of the Musicals" show, *West End Story*. The tight budget and the unforgiving publicity schedule at local radio dictated, to Frankie's displeasure, that much of her travelling was done overnight.

On the day of the memorial service, Queenie and Reg were sitting over breakfast, chattering aimlessly, as George left for work. As usual he had his satchel, but a shirt and a tie replaced the normal clutter inside. He changed in the lavatory of the hamburger chain restaurant opposite the church, where, to avoid standing in an inch of water, he had to perch on the porcelain. Someone had attempted to mop up the flood by throwing yards of toilet roll onto it, which had disintegrated into a messy sludge.

He had intended to walk straight to the front door of St. Stephen's to pay his respects, but his nerve failed unexpectedly when he saw the Hartleys ahead, and he dodged down a side street by the graveyard until they were safely inside. He hadn't considered the congregation and he was suddenly filled with an urge not to see them or to be seen by them. He loitered around the corner until the bell rang twelve, then waited for the first hymn.

An old woman, impressed by the smartly dressed young man who had crept in so considerately, handed him an order of service and motioned him forwards, but George shook his head, turned around, and climbed to the gallery, where he could pay his respects unobserved. The stained-glass window behind him, through which no light shone, looked unfinished. At the end of the hymn, the vicar faced the congregation: "The Lord giveth and the Lord taketh away. Today we remember the life of Donald Hartley. We will begin with a reading from the Gospel of Saint John."

Hartley made his way to the pulpit, his pipe bobbling in his top pocket. George slunk back out of view as Hartley's booming voice echoed in the rafters: "From John, chapter eleven, verses twenty-one to twenty-seven. 'Then said Martha unto Jesus, Lord, if thou hadst been here, my brother had not died . . .'" George opened the order of service. Here was what his friend Donald had come to, a name and some dates on a badly printed and ill-folded photocopy. "'And Jesus saith unto her, Thy brother shall rise again. Martha saith unto him, I know that he shall rise again in the resurrection at the last day.'" How convenient: he'd heard all this from Hartley's own lips in the Upside chapel. Then it had seemed pointless; now it seemed like a good lie to tell yourself when your son had died. "'And whosoever liveth and believeth in me shall never die. Believest thou this?'" He doubted whether Donald had believed it or that he wanted to rise again.

Hartley's footsteps echoed down the pulpit stairs. George imagined his shoulders rising and falling with each step. The vicar himself read before calling another hymn number, "a great favourite of Donald's from his days at Saint Catherine's."

The congregation was about sixty strong. With their backs to him, it was hard to make identifications, though he knew Commander Poole from his naval uniform, his cap neatly tucked under his right arm, his hymnbook held as though he were presenting arms. Next to him, a pewful of Upside representatives: three or four teachers, mumbling their way through Donald's supposed favourite, "All People That on Earth Do Dwell." Towards the back, a family of four was sitting together, mother holding a baby. A woman in the front row wore a large black hat, from the back of which dangled a feather so extravagant that no one could sit directly behind her. It was a wonderfully absurd hat on such a small woman. And what a strange character she made in the church, sitting on her own in the front row — quite the oddest person at the memorial. A dotty relative, perhaps, singing loudest of all.

The organ kicked into overdrive for the last verse, encouraging the congregation to sing more jubilantly. They resisted, and the final exultant chord heralded only a round of throat clearings and the creak of pews as they sat down for the sermon. That creak was worth remembering — quite specific, but nothing you couldn't fake at Crystal Clear.

"Let's talk about Lazarus," suggested the vicar. "And then we'll talk about Donald."

The congregation settled in for the slow slog of the sermon. How long ago had Donald died? Presumably the first piece of business — the practical end of the matter: the burial, the cremation — had taken place some time ago. Since then, they'd been able to give Old Upsiders enough notice by putting the invitation in the school magazine. Had it been worth the wait? Had old boys turned up? Yes, obviously. George was there.

The impossibility of paying attention to the sermon, due partly to the enervating oboe-ish quality of the vicar's voice, led George to compose his own silent elegy. He had been so anxious about the memorial that he had forgotten the man — and now memories came flooding back: how Donald had first introduced himself, the trip to Mrs. Cakebread's, and the walkie-talkies; not to mention the Ventrilo, the ring of which, painlessly but with a little coaxing, had made a belated reappearance far too late to alert Donald. George kept it with his loose change: at least he knew where it had been. He remembered how Donald had stolen *Valentine Vox* back for him. The thought of the book coincided with the baby crying, and George imagined the mayhem Valentine could have wreaked at this service. Perhaps the baby was entirely innocent, his wails the wild talents of Vox throwing his voice from another part of the church, hiding up in the gallery next to George.

Vox would have pretended to be Donald come back to life, to show the vicar for the pompous old fool he was: "That wasn't my favourite hymn! I didn't like that one at all. Sing something I liked, you old hypocrite!" And the vicar would have got more and more annoyed as he struggled to make himself heard over the heckling spirit, until Valentine revealed himself, and everyone, including the unfortunate vicar, dissolved into gales of laughter.

Oh, Valentine! Where are you now? And you, Donald?

The gallery was the ideal hiding place for a Valentine, and this solemn event the ideal occasion, but George lived in the real world — a world where the trick would be an outrage, another atrocity perpetrated on the Hartleys and Upside by its darkest pupil. Other forms of ventriloquism were acceptable, neither noticed nor commented upon, but Valentine's was out of the question.

In the real world of St. Stephen's — if one could consider a church realistic — there was merely a baby crying, annoying some, who wondered what kind of parents brought a baby to a memorial service, and touching others, a reminder of the renewal of life. The vicar was winding down, phrasing sentences like a normal human being: all were welcome at the reception in the church hall, please sign the book, perhaps adding a cherished memory. George wouldn't go. He was there as an old boy, invited as such, but it would be unfair to confront the Hartleys with the unexpected on this of all days. He would leave and write a letter of condolence; that was the right thing to do.

A final hymn was attempted. The Hartleys were the first to leave. As they made their way down the aisle, she smiled stoically, and he nodded at people reassuringly. George hid behind a large pillar, but they didn't look up. As though the blessing had given it permission, light streamed through the stained-glass window behind him, and getting down on his hands and knees, he crawled forward for a better view.

The congregation shook hands and made for the hall. In the front row, the dotty relative in the black Ascot hat didn't move. She was crying, as she leaned on the rail in front of her. Out of kindness, one of the Upside crowd, whom he didn't recognize, offered her his arm, which she took. Before long, somewhat recovered, she was ready to leave. As she turned round, George caught sight of the woman's face for the first time.

It was Frankie.

He hid himself behind the rail of the gallery.

Frankie.

His mother, dabbing the corners of her eyes with a handkerchief, just as she did when she cried during a movie.

How could his eyes have fooled him into hallucinating Frankie as the dotty relative in the big hat?

It couldn't be her for a thousand reasons: she was on the *West End Story* tour miles away in the north, playing (he was sure) Manchester. But forget why she *couldn't* be here; why *would* she be here? She had no reason to be at Don's memorial service, to know it was happening, let alone to pay her respects to a man she had only heard of in passing. It couldn't be her.

He peered over the edge of the gallery, desperate not to be seen. Frankie stood just beneath him, talking to the Hartleys as if she knew them, as if she had ever set foot near Upside. He could just make out her smile, her beautiful smile.

Out of sight again, he lay on the clammy disinfected carpet, trying to block out the polite indistinguishable murmurings that floated upwards. He was waiting only for silence to descend, for the church to be empty besides the old lady clearing up leftover orders of service. Then he would make his escape.

He would get back into his normal clothes and return to Crystal Clear, where problems were so easily solved.

8

Tonic for the Troops

What with Belle and Bobbie, and our glorious nights at the Gala, I hadn't been paying attention to the gathering storm. I'd heard the measured tones of BBC announcers (Hitler this, Hitler that) and the bleating beneath Duval's beret, but, despite the forecast, I expected a light shower at worst. A few months ago, no one had mentioned it, but as the clouds darkened they spoke of nothing else, huddling around wirelesses, shaking their heads in resignation, tutting the latest news. Everyone just wanted to get it over with, to be at war. And soon enough we were. A car mowed down some poor old sod painting a kerb white for the blackout: the first casualty on British soil.

At first, I was indifferent. Doubtless there were similarly unconcerned little Fritzes perched on the knees of Herr Fischers. *We're just the little people,* I thought. *It isn't up to us.* We wouldn't be sent to the front; it was all beside the point, a distraction from our true purpose. But then I started to wonder what the war would mean for us. What if we were called up to fight, dispatched to a trench in some godforsaken muddy field? And what if we weren't? What should we do then? What would happen to the theatres, the smokers, and the nightclubs? Would there be any? And what about Belle? Bobbie had the best attitude: "I'll do my bit," he said. "I've always fancied myself a Florence Nightingale, entertaining the men in their beds . . ." Very Bawdy. Very British.

Without consulting his family, Joe volunteered. The first thing Echo and Queenie knew, he had failed his medical. They ascribed his impulsive act to a previously unknown heroism, but the real reason for the rush of blood was obvious: he could no longer stand Cadogan Grove. WAR was written in blinking lights above an exit door, and he saw no reason to wait for his call-up. To them, he came home a hero of sorts, but he was in fact a traitor, to his family and to me — happy to ditch me along with the women, to leave me marooned in the attic, a sitting duck for the falling bombs — a traitor whose health had failed him. Let down by his lungs! Foiled by some bronchial trouble! He cared for his life even less than I thought: not only had he volunteered, he'd chosen the air force.

War had one saving grace: evacuation. When hostilities commenced, whole schools of children would disappear to the countryside in a puff of steam, and *The King and Queenie Show* would officially be no more.

Operation Pied Piper began on September 1. We sat backstage at the Gaiety listening to a plummy broadcaster. "Here we are on the number eight platform at Charing Cross Station. The train's in and the children are just arriving now — Saint Andrew's School from Islington. And now here come the older children . . . behaving impeccably, I must say."

"Operation Pied Piper?" spluttered Bobbie in disbelief. "Do they remember what happens to the children in that story? And the moral? Always pay the entertainment. Poor little buggers."

Joe spoke finally: "Queenie's taken Frankie away." There were relatives in a village on the drab marshy border of Kent and Sussex.

"Shh!" said Bobbie, and broke into song: "Wish me luck as you wave me good-bye."

I felt as bad as if I had ordered Frankie from London myself.

*   *   *

Blackout restrictions were immediately imposed; theatres and cinemas were closed forthwith, putting almost the entire entertainment profession out of work overnight.

In their hour of darkness, people needed the camaraderie of the theatre, the laughter from favourite shows, not a stodgy diet of radio news followed by Sandy McPherson and his uninspiring organ. They needed to be uplifted. And that was where the Fishers could answer their country's call — for however much people wanted entertainment, the Fishers' need to entertain was even greater. That was where I came in. The coming conflict would provide me with the thing I least expected: increased chances for ventriloquism.

Echo had already attended tense meetings between those involved with the war effort who wanted to employ well-known artistic talent to keep morale high, and those artistes' agents who, having their clients' best interests at heart, could not accept the insultingly lower fees, war or no war. Voices were raised.

ENSA, the Entertainment National Service Association, envisioned an army of entertainers, at a salary of ten pounds per week (irrespective of billing), ready to go wherever troops were stationed. Bobbie was enthusiastic: "You know me! It's the closest I'll get to going over the top with the boys!" Besides, he was happy with a regular pay packet, however paltry — "Ten quid'll keep us in spangles" — and he instructed Duke Duval to take soundings. Within a fortnight, he had accepted ENSA's invitation. They asked him if he'd ever been abroad. "I've *always* been a broad," he told them. "ENSA: Every Night Some Adventure!" he wrote on a forces postcard. He was right at home.

Echo had other ideas. She immediately conscripted her own private militia of players, designed an ersatz military costume, and announced, within hours of the declaration, a gruelling tour of army bases throughout England. "No appeasement for Miss Endor!" trumpeted *The Herald*. She even tried to enlist a Private Joe Fisher, but he was having none of it.

Fisher's Fighting Fol-de-Rols roared into action, with Echo in her own personal coach, painted patriotic colours, the company name emblazoned proudly on both sides, "Say Her Name Once More" on the back. Joe called it the Evacuation Tour — bound as far as possible from the bombs that were sure to rain on London.

The storm had yet to break two weeks later, and the theatres reopened, allowing the stars back where they belonged. Echo's move looked a little premature, and she immediately readied herself for a triumphant and patriotic return to the West End.

Best of all, Joe and I could get back to work to take our mind off Bobbie and Belle's absence. When the sirens went off in the middle of our turn, the ushers blew short blasts on their whistles. We were to ask the audience whether they wanted to leave and, when they didn't (they never did), we improvised in front of the curtain until the all-clear. Sitting on the edge of the apron, leading the sing-along, we felt brave. We were doing our bit, ready for action anywhere. Early on, because of an air raid that never was, we found ourselves huddled in an Anderson shelter — two kids, their parents, and us. Half-buried in the ground, protected by a blast wall and steel plates at either end, I thought we'd died and gone to hell, but when Joe and I started to banter, the atmosphere changed, and time passed more happily. The worst circumstances can bring out the best in people.

With the West End reopened for business, ENSA was having more difficulty than ever finding the necessary talent, and held open auditions at their Theatre Royal, Drury Lane, headquarters. Joe and I, who were not known enough to merit an invitation, joined the queue among the comedians and the jugglers, the contortionist-xylophonists, and the unicycle acts. These were the performers hardest hit — no one was going to the seaside, except those who had followed the Pied Piper. Three in front of us, an elderly woman, enamelled, lacquered (and seventy if she was a day), sang "Land of Hope and Glory" with accompanying tap. There was an unmistakable "Oh!" of distaste from the ENSA triumvirate in row M when the old girl spat out her teeth on the climactic "made thee mightier yet." Our audition went well, and we were ushered to the far side of the stage, where a man called Ranulph

Rex, who was not wearing military uniform but wished he were, shook Joe's hand, flipped through the pages on a clipboard with a newly sharpened pencil, and promptly offered him a position in a travelling troupe. "The show will be called *Tonic for the Troops*," Rex announced, gauging Joe's reaction. "You're going to fit in nicely."

"Is there a medical?"

"Inoculations and so forth. Nothing to worry about."

"Where will we be going?"

"Classified. Expect to hear from us soon, very soon." He marched back and forth, clipboard underneath his arm. "We go where they go. We're here for their morale, to let the fighting men, however far away, know they aren't forgotten. Our work is every bit as important as theirs, as vital as food and rest." Rex saluted, the knuckles of his extended fingers to his forehead, his palm visible. In the spirit of the moment, Joe raised my hand to my forehead and poked me in the eye. "I like that!" said Rex. "Perhaps the little chap could salute. It would mean a lot to the boys." He meant the soldiers. "Think how they'd like him if he were in uniform, one of them. Have a word with this fellow." He handed us the familiar Romando business card. "He's jolly keen to do his bit, but until now I didn't honestly know how he could help."

I fancied getting into uniform, even if Joe couldn't. He might have failed his medical, but King and Country would have accepted *me* in a minute — a little chip here and there, perhaps a spot of woodworm, but all eminently treatable: nothing to stop me representing Britannia at the very highest level.

The ENSA medical was a success. Joe returned, his arm a join-the-dots of vaccinations, with a khaki canvas kit bag — the whole world was turning dull brownish green — complete with soap, towel, rations, and candles. He placed this next to his other bags by the front door, ready for his orders. My bag was packed too. The only thing yet to be put inside was me.

Joe worked at his desk as though his life depended on it. Perhaps this was common behaviour, to dot the *I*'s and cross the

T's, to close the circle, to write a will. He couldn't wait to be gone. I knew. He seemed satisfied as he filed his writing books away.

One morning, a key turned in the front door, and Frankie came darting into the kitchen, a smudge of red coat and matching scarf. Queenie struggled behind with two suitcases.

"Dada! Dada! I saw the sea!" Frankie buried her head between Joe's knees, clutching his calves so tightly that he was unable to offer Queenie any assistance.

"Hello," said Queenie coolly, surveying the house and shaking her head with amusement at the wooden shutters Echo had had installed in the front room and kitchen. "There was nothing much happening where we were, and if there's an invasion, they'll probably do it straight through Evelyn's back garden. So we decided to come back from holiday a little early."

"I saw the sea!" said Frankie, as Joe prised himself from her and scooped her into his arms, bouncing her above his head. She laughed until he put her down. "George!" she said, bouncing me up and down in the same way.

"Strange thing is . . . ," said Joe, "I joined ENSA. I'm on my way to report now." His bags were his evidence. "Echo asked me to join the Evacuation Tour, and that was my only alternative."

"Were you going to leave a note?" asked Queenie, but she was resigned to his silent comings and goings.

"I wasn't expecting you back. I was going to write."

"And where are you going?"

"I don't know. It's all, you know, hush-hush."

"Wars have ears," said Frankie.

Joe knelt so they were at eye level. "I have to go, Frankie."

"Stay!" she commanded, expecting the rewards of petulance.

"Want to say good-bye to George?"

"Joe," said Queenie, "you'll worry her. You'll be back in a week or so. She'll only have to say hello all over again then. We'll see you soon."

"Bye, George," said Frankie, and waved.

"Welcome home," said Joe as he put me away.

They talked for a few moments more, and then I felt myself lifted up and out of the house.

The cold air circulated around me. I heard the click of the door. We were free.

Tonic for the Troops, a no-name concert party, offered a nostalgic variety entertainment with a little glamour. "Tricks and tunes with a touch of tits and tinsel," whispered the director when the girls couldn't hear. The personnel numbered six: Joe, conjurer and ventriloquist; an acrobat called Phoebe; a pianist (the unforgettable Toots Lowery); a Scottish male comedian; a soubrette; and a singer who doubled as our "incomparable compere," the debonair Jack Heath.

There was great camaraderie from the first rehearsal. There had to be. We travelled in the same transport, with all our props — of which I was one — and a piano lashed to the inside of the van. Joe, despite being the most withdrawn, was well liked, as a man who mucks in without complaint will be. The others joshed him but took no offence when he kept to himself.

During rehearsals in the Methodist church hall, I received my new Romando uniform. Of course they remembered me, the Romandos had said in their reply. How could they ever forget? It was especially made by Nellie herself, with an embroidered label: *For our boys.* And what a perfect Tommy I made. We admired ourselves in the mirror of the kitchen khazi: the ventriloquist and his soldier. There I was dressed to kill, ready to fight for the cause. I had my first major operation of the war lying facedown on the draining board, as Joe calmly performed reconstructive surgery (without the use of anaesthetic) from instructions sent by Romando. I was soon up and about again, saluting at will. Ranulph Rex was right; the boys did like it a lot.

With the uniform, we finally created the character I had always wanted. I became the boy soldier who won against all odds, who loved his country as he loved his mother, and who always kept his sense of humour about him, not to mention a stiff chamois upper lip. And this is why Joe and I were always in work, why we never went home.

The beginnings of the tour were happy days, driving around from gun emplacement to barracks, endlessly lost (because the road signs had been removed to confuse German paratroopers — a good tactic because it certainly confused us), and often late. We were working to a testing schedule put together by the head office. They knew the distances but hadn't allowed for the fact that all eighty-mile van journeys are not created equal, or that directions are useless without road signs. When we arrived, and we always did, we set up wherever we were told. Sometimes we couldn't even get the piano inside the officers' mess, and more than once, Toots played al fresco while Jack sang inside. Nissen huts were good in fine weather and terrible when it rained, the clatter on the corrugated steel so intense that the audience couldn't hear a word. When the sun shone, we performed outside. Our portable stage didn't prove quite portable enough, and substitutes were as rudimentary as two tabletops secured together. Word filtered down that it was good practice for a time when mobility would be our prime concern: only the small shows could make it to the front. When we were left heaving the piano through a field after an unexpected downpour, we understood.

Careless talk costs lives, they told us. Ironic, really, that I, whose whole life was based on the kind of careless talk and casual quips that represented the antithesis of this patriotic sentiment, was now in a position to advocate its benefits. We did what we could, slipping stirring slogans into our routines as instructed: *Britain'll pull through! Keep Mum! She's not so dumb! Don't telephone when a letter or postcard will do!*

The material picked itself. I voiced what the lads were feeling; I spoke of them missing their sweethearts, their families. I helped them laugh. It was clear, too, what kind of entertainment they didn't want. A little sauciness was de rigueur, they expected it, but they didn't want to dwell on sex. Women were the embodiment of an ideal, the model of fidelity the fighting men had left behind, the perfection they fought to defend — no joke should sully this image. Lines that would have gone down a treat at the Gaiety were scratched. Self-censorship of this type became second nature: it was just a question of knowing your audience. We learned the hard way.

We played for the dashing RAF boys, their last entertainment before the Tannoy sounded. If there was a second show, you couldn't help checking whether any familiar faces were missing. And we played at the Queen Victoria Hospital in East Grinstead, and Queen Mary's in Roehampton, where the worst of the burn victims, perhaps yesterday's RAF boys, were cared for. Their faces mummified and suppurating, some were unable even to see us perform, moaning quietly throughout, smoking cigarettes through holes in their cheeks. Phoebe burst out crying and found herself on the sharp end of some harsh words from Jack. Our audiences deserved utmost professionalism at all times.

There was a hospital somewhere in the rolling fields of Wales where the patients had yet deeper wounds, ones we could not see: these were "the war weary," the shell-shocked, our quietest audience. As we ran our routines, one of them stared at me vacantly. I wondered what he was thinking and whether he could ever think normal thoughts — *Shall I make a cup of tea?* — again or whether he was stuck in his world forever, staring but not seeing. This same man was encouraged by the doctor to touch me. There was very little participation of this sort. Joe sat me on the man's knee. His fingers were soft, and though he put a gentle hand in my back, he hadn't the strength to move me, so we just sat together, in silence. He wanted to say something, but he couldn't bring himself. Tears welled in his eyes. Joe guided the man's fingers and showed him, without words, how to pull my strings. He showed him that I cried too, and the man and I cried together.

"My son," the man murmured by way of explanation, and his hand fell away from my levers. I slumped forwards, and Joe took me from the patient, who was wheeled back to his room.

"His first words since he arrived two months ago," said the doctor as we walked away. "Your troupe lives up to its name. Come and see us again."

There was a steady stream of letters from Bobbie: "Dunkirk? Talk about a humiliating withdrawal!! (I've had a few of those.) If ever there was a time to surrender on a beach in the dark, that was it!" And in every letter, a private joke from Belle to me, from Bobbie to Joe. These tided me over, kept me going.

They'd gone straight to Bengal, where Bobbie had taken his show to the forces at the end of the line, the arse-end Charlies who got little in the way of entertainment. His drag act — he always preferred "female impersonation" — had become extremely popular among the troops under the jurisdiction of BESA, the Bengal Entertainment Services Association. They appreciated his presence all the more knowing that there were no roads, that he had walked behind his mules and slept rough to get to them. This society excluded women entirely — they could go no nearer the front line than two hundred miles — and Bobbie Sheridan was the best alternative, the substitute object of desire, allowing the men to lust for women while laughing at the urge. There was nothing to be ashamed of, no infidelity involved: Bobbie was just a bloke in a frock. He was a man, the audience was men, and they were all in it together.

Gone were the costume changes, the orchestra, and the scenery, but the act retained its glamour, and the material (unlike ours) needed no adaptation. When Bobbie said, "They asked me to review the troops. I said, 'I'll only do it when they're standing to attention. And I hope for some very high marks,'" he got a cheer, whereas a normal comic would have been booed from the stage. A real woman could never have dreamed of saying such a thing.

I could hear his exact turn of phrase in every line of his letters, see his arched eyebrow in every double exclamation mark: "They love my ditties. And they should. I made them myself!! Wait till I whip out my Londonderry air!! (Think about that one!)" Somehow, despite the weather, the diet, and the constant struggle with dysentery, described in microscopic detail, Bobbie dazzled everywhere. In that part of the world, there was no bigger star.

And where was Belle, my Belle? She was with him every step of the way, in her scruffy suitcase, bouncing on the back of some beast of burden. But when would I ever see her again?

London had become unbearable, and Echo, after her belated return, had quit the city for a funk hole. She earnestly did not want to go where there were still troops to be entertained (distant places like North Africa and India, Persia and Iraq — there had been none in Europe since Dunkirk), and another bus tour of England would be thankless and arduous, so she secured herself a house in the Cotswolds, in the village of Northleach. Here she would either come up with another plan or see out the war entirely.

Queenie, however, didn't care to leave London again. The need for party entertainment hadn't dried up, and *The Auntie Queenie Show* rolled on, though she now performed purely out of the kindness of her heart: to ask for two guineas from single parents and orphanages felt like extortion, to deny them entertainment unpatriotic. Queenie had initially been rejected by ENSA, but with resources severely stretched during the blitz, she was welcomed on reapplication as an honorary member. Armed with nothing but matchsticks, magic painting, and my handsome doppelgänger, she descended to entertain the little ones. Reg, still her regular driver from Fleet, had found an old projector in a bombed-out cinema, and at her suggestion, he took it down to a shelter. She brought a sheet and some drawing pins, did some tricks, and christened the entertainment "The Magic of the Movies." (The real magic, she wrote, was where he got the movies *from*.)

One night, they nearly died. Huddled in the crowded shelter, showing the scratchy Western serial Reg had unearthed, they hadn't even heard it coming. Suddenly they were under water, spitting dust, shouting and still not being heard, looking at each other to see where they were bleeding. The Hillman that had taken them to so many parties was wrecked, but they hadn't given up. Reg rolled the projector around in a custom-made pushcart constructed from a pram and a fruit crate, steered with a skipping rope. Just the job.

Queenie wrote to Joe, but it was a one-sided conversation she was hard-pressed to keep up. His excuses were see-through: the mail was bad, he was busy, he wasn't allowed to be specific about his location. What was he meant to say? She implored him to write to his daughter, but he never could.

The blitz was nothing to Frankie. She was having the time of her life and every night was bonfire night. At the long-distance suggestion of Echo, and with her financial assistance, Queenie enrolled Frankie at the Franca DeLay stage school. This led to her being cast as a film extra, and then to her first speaking role in a patriotic Capital Studios comedy called *Heil Who?* starring Tommy Bright, "the Bright Spark" himself. At a pivotal moment, an unnamed street urchin, played by Frankie, sings the first verse of the national anthem, bringing a drunk Bright to his senses with the realization that every man must do his duty. After this, she was cast in *Britain'll Do It, Church Bells Will Chime Again,* and *The Headmaster Heads Abroad,* in which she played her whole scene in great discomfort, too embarrassed to mention that she had wet herself. Frankie wrote that she was seeing the world — she'd been to Paris, Egypt, and New York without ever having left film studios in the London suburbs. Increasingly, Frankie accompanied Queenie to her engagements too, taking her mother's part in the mesmerism act and often bringing the show to a close with her popular version of "God Save the King."

"Mummy is still smiling and loving and I am going to start being good," she dictated to Queenie, her amanuensis.

Rumour had it that *Tonic for the Troops* was going away, much farther away, and this was confirmed when they suffered their next set of inoculations, for diseases Joe hadn't even considered.

Granted two days' leave, he strapped me on the back of a

motorbike and we drove over the downs to Northleach, where Frankie was staying with Echo. He sat outside a local, fortified himself with a beer, tidied me up, took a deep breath, and headed for Echo's front door. By now, we were both in uniform: Basil dress they called his, after the leader of ENSA. We were both Tommies.

Diane opened the door. "Hail the conquering heroes!" she said with unexpected enthusiasm. And we were taken through the oak-beamed warren to a sitting room where Frankie and Echo were playing pelmanism.

"Ha!" Echo shouted in triumph the moment we entered. "She's doing all right at pelmanism, but I just can't teach this child canasta. She can't pick it up."

"She's only five," said Joe.

"Yes, but I can *play* older," said Frankie, her own agent, and, with that clear, ran towards us. She was about to throw herself around Joe's legs when she stopped in surprise. "George! You're a soldier now!"

"Yes, Private George, reporting for duty." I saluted my new salute.

"Marvellous," said Echo, with genuine admiration, betraying the fact that she wished she had thought of this for herself and would steal both the uniform and the salute for Narcissus. "You both look very dashing."

"Is the war over? Can we go home?" asked Frankie.

"I wanted to come and see you," said Joe. "We're being sent abroad."

"Where?" asked Echo with a forced air of unconcern.

"They won't tell us, but my kit bag is full of exotic items like little blue tablets, mosquito nets, hurricane lamps, powdered everything — meat, potatoes, and carrots — and a roll of lavatory paper."

"Hmm . . . ," said Echo. "Well, the Welsh still have lavatory paper, so that rules out Swansea. Can we sit outside? Do you have time?"

It was a lovely afternoon, soft, green, and daisied. Diane

brought tea as they chatted, the war far away. Joe held Frankie's hand, asking her about Capital Studios and her interactions with the Bright Spark. She was not in the least starstruck and had a most matter-of-fact attitude to her new career. In a crowd scene, she advised, it was best to blend into the background rather than try and be at the front looking at the camera. It was annoying to have to do more than one take if you got it right but the camera people, who had the least to do but made the biggest fuss, got it wrong. Most frustrating was when another actor fluffed his lines. The Hungarian director had told her she could be in all his films.

"Now, we mustn't just talk about ourselves," warned Echo, "or we'll end up with a big head." Joe, however, was keen to deflect questions, so he asked Echo her plans.

"I am to be packed off, kit and caboodle, to America," said Echo, as if Winston himself had talked her into it. "It's no secret that we need assistance." Though I allowed myself visions of Narcissus's fraught negotiation with Charlie McCarthy, persuading him to join in the struggle against the Axis, the reality was less a mission upon which rested the hopes of a nation and more a personal reconnaissance–cum–pleasure trip. (And perhaps in the back of her mind, she was hoping to find a vacancy at the top of the profession right up there next to Edgar Bergen — we knew of no great American ventriloquistes.)

"Leave politics to the politicians," I said. "The boys need you in Burma." I saluted, and Frankie giggled.

Echo held up her hand to silence us all. "I know. There is a need for foot soldiers, brave men like yourselves, Jojo and George, as never before. But we battle-weary colonels, we old Blimps, who have lived through a Great War already, we must use our hard-won experience for the good of the country."

It was confirmed then. She was running away.

The afternoon glided by on tea and thin slices of cake, as Frankie grew a little morose at the prospect of our departure.

"Are you going to see Queenie?" asked Echo.

"I can't. There isn't time. In fact, I must go." He turned to Frankie. "I've left some books upstairs at Cadogan Grove, and should the house survive, they're for you, and for your son." This was beyond her. "For the future. When you grow up, get married, and have children."

"Like you and Mummy? Well, why can't you give them to me *then?*"

"Oh, hush," said Echo. "Do stop being so morbid. You'll frighten the child."

"I have to go . . ."

". . . or they'll have you on a charge!" reprimanded Frankie, but she wouldn't meet my eye.

"Joe," said Echo in valediction, as she leaned on the back of the garden bench, "we're so proud of you, how war has shown us the real you. Feckless in peacetime you were — and heaven knows where that came from; it must have been some flaw in your father's side of the family, God rest his soul — but we're all so very proud of you, Frankie and I . . . and Queenie too. . . . And I ask you, as a mother, to be in touch with her more. She's doing wonderful things with those movies and a few silly tricks. And she needs the support of a man." Echo covered Frankie's ears with her hands and hissed urgently: "You're losing her and you don't even care. There's not much I can do from here. Write to her, for the sake of . . ." She glanced downwards as the object of pity writhed free of her clutches.

"What are you saying?" Frankie laughed.

Echo continued: "One day the lights will burn bright again, the church bells will chime, and carol singers will go from door to door in the snow on Christmas Eve. Pubs will open, and people will live together again in peace, not listening anxiously for the all-clear. And then this will all be a thing of the past, this uncertainty, this fear. And we'll be together again as families, in the way we are together now as a country."

"Grandma," Frankie piped up, "that's just what the Bright Spark said at the end of *Heil Who?!*"

"Not as well as that, he damn well didn't," said Echo, "and

don't call me Grandma. I can't stand *Grand* and . . ." Frankie joined in: "I'm going to hate *Great!*" Echo tickled Frankie under the arms. Frankie ran away, screaming, collapsing in a heap by the fishpond at the end of the garden. Joe lifted me up and we watched her. I saluted. Frankie ran towards us, crying.

"It's all right," said Joe, as he handed me carelessly over to Echo and hoisted Frankie up. She was worn out, poor thing, and he carried her inside, her head on his shoulder. Echo rummaged inside me, trying to work out the engineering that had gone into my salute. Joe laid Frankie down on the couch in the sitting room, and Echo sat beside her, stroking her hair.

"Back to Capital for you tomorrow, young lady, and we can't have big red eyes," said Echo.

Frankie sucked her thumb, looking at me as if she knew it was the last time she would ever see me.

Then we were on the move. Joe knew as little about where we were going as I did, and we weren't always able to travel together. By the time I next got another good look at the two photos pinned to the inside lid of my box — Frankie, and one of Bobbie holding Belle — we were halfway across the world.

We reached Cairo in June of 1941, as the Germans started fighting. Initially, we only saw the perimeter of the desert, and our entertainment was confined to small city theatres and various military buildings. But as the conflict grew, we ventured farther, first playing for the wounded at the rear of the action, then slowly making our way forward. There was no great bravery involved — we just went where we were told. Besides, it didn't matter where you were: machine gun fire was liable to strafe the stage at any moment.

There was no property at stake in the desert war; the purpose was purely to annihilate the enemy, and since the fighting was mobile, the entertainment followed suit. As the Eighth Army pushed west, the performers followed. At first we were in a concert party — still the nucleus of *Tonic for the Troops* — that travelled in a jeep towing a converted caravan called Cairo Cara, the side of which could be taken down to make a stage and, if folded again, create screens on either side for the wings.

The desert was something apart, and my first glimpse was unique: one hundred soldiers sat on the ground in front of the stage, and another hundred stood behind them, a happy, sand-weathered bunch separated from me by the band, which consisted of a tiny drum kit and a piano. Beyond them, nothing. Sand. Nothing. No sign of civilization. The shimmer of the horizon stunned me.

"Blimey!" I said. "This is the biggest bunker I ever saw. Must be a huge golf course!"

"This is no golf course, George."

"Nice sandpit, then. Better than the one at the playground."

"Now, George," said Joe. "You're a soldier now, not a schoolboy anymore."

To show how right he was, I tried to have a fag, but I couldn't. Standards of hygiene had fallen during the last few weeks. My home sweet home had become dingier (*home sweat home,* we called it), less of a private sanctuary and more a spare kit bag for papers and all sorts of old gubbins that Joe wanted to hang on to but didn't have a proper place for: addresses, photos, other small mementos of his travels. An extremely irritating pencil had rattled its way around my innards for the last week and somehow got lodged in my mechanism, jamming one of my levers.

"I'm gasping!" I pleaded, waiting for the fag to pop out. Joe rummaged around, got hold of the obstruction, gave a brutal yank, and removed it, tossing it into the audience.

"That'll get the lead out!" someone yelled as I lit up. We'd use that.

The blackout meant we couldn't perform at night, and the possibility of attack often prevented us from performing by day, so we pioneered Moonlight Matinées at the oases and wadis where the armies were laagered. Every now and then we would find a well-organized camp — where they'd managed to rustle up a generator and a rudimentary marquee, where the latrines were not just a large circular hole around which everyone squatted, like wise owls facing outwards — but most of the time we took our work as we found it, travelling outrageous distances to reach an audience, men dying of boredom, looking forward to a shoot-up just for a change of pace.

The whole troupe learned as they went. Props were improvised from mosquito nets and Sten gun slings, scenery dyed with tea. The girls made do without dressing rooms, holding up blankets for each other or wrapping themselves in a sheet and changing beneath. At night, they lived in Cara while the men put up hammocks under mosquito nets or shared tents as part of the bivouac. Joe swung on his hammock, strung between the back bumper of the caravan and a eucalyptus tree, writing letters by the light of the moon.

There was a special kind of desert night when it was windy but not so windy that you had to keep blinking sand out of your eyes. These nights were perfectly cool, and the heat of the day was almost forgotten. The stars were manifold and shone with a brilliance that made you feel kissed by the history of the place — these were the same stars that had shone on the pharaohs, on Jesus Christ, the same stars that shone on Belle. And there lay Joe, alone, separate from the rest of the party, reading and writing, just like always, but now so far away from home.

And the troupe became real troops, doing the things that soldiers did. They got their TAB and typhus injections without complaint. They wore their Basil dress, with shorts mostly, and learned to salute. When the natives walked out in protest during "God Save the King," they returned the compliment by singing insulting words to the Egyptian national anthem, an unassuming ditty that sounded wholly English. The ruins and wreckage of war ceased to shock, and they drove past without comment. The soldiers taught them the tricks of the desert: how to keep water cool in the heat by filling your hat and hanging it in the shade, and how to produce water out of thin air by stretching a groundsheet between two trees overnight. The cold night condensed the humid air, and there was fresh, cool water by morning. Magic.

* * *

Heaven knows how long we had been travelling when Joe got ill for the first time, and heaven knows, since conditions were so poor, how he had managed to stay healthy so long. The heat was so bad, and the water so short, that the only time anybody could wash was when it rained, and there were flies everywhere, swarms too relentless to repel, settling on rubbish, meat, excrement, flesh (dead or alive), moving promiscuously among them all.

At first, Joe was stricken with desert sores. These began with a cut, which got infected — the sand didn't help — and festered into an oozing ulcer. Some soldiers were covered in the sores, which they daubed with a blue ointment that made them look polka-dotted. The flies were to blame: their maggots ate into broken skin, causing the boils. Once the infection had found a way in, it spread, emerging wherever there was a scratch. But the sores didn't quite do enough to lay you low: everyone went about his business, spotted blue and itching. Joe wasn't only blue. He was also pale yellow, which he suspected was jaundice. What he didn't know was that he also had malaria.

We were barely into our spot one Moonlight Matinée when it became obvious that something was wrong. There was no strength in Joe's clammy fingers, and beads of sweat formed on his forehead as we struggled on. Before even a few seconds of this agony had passed (that horrible moment of silence between missed line and prompt), Joe stood up gasping for breath and lurched forwards, taking me with him off the edge of the stage. We landed just by the drum kit, surrounded by soldiers even before the flies had a chance to swarm.

We were out of it for some time, taken at first to a field sanatorium (arriving with a temperature of 105), then to a hospital in Cairo, and finally to an Australian hospital ship for long-term convalescents. I don't remember much of this, and I can't remember how long we were there. But Joe's condition was critical — his kidneys practically packed in. The hospital ship was paradise after months in the desert. He had been used to bully beef and

Machonachies M&V, an unappetizing canned meat-and-potato stew; on the *Canberra,* he ate chicken for the first time he could remember.

Time is all one to me. I'm happy sitting where it's safe. Sometimes I can drift out of my body and look at myself; other times I forget I'm there at all. But it was certainly nice to find myself floating at sea, away from the flies and the sand. And to see Joe, smiling in bed at our reunion, no longer the yellow-and-blue boy. He seemed so rested, as I hadn't seen him since before *Tonic for the Troops* began.

Once he was well enough, we amused the other patients after dinnertime. Joe wrote from his bedside, and letters arrived, which always put him in a good mood. BESA had given Bobbie the honorary title Dame Bobbie Sheridan, though he claimed it hadn't changed him at all: "No airs and graces, I'm still out here mucking in. I've got a new song, though: 'The Dame Who Was Made Wrong.' Get it? (Hint: some of the other anagrams are very saucy indeed, and far too devilish for Cecily Censor!)" But there was less mention of Belle. I pictured her far from the front line, waiting for Bobbie in a Delhi hotel, fanned by palm fronds, ordering room service on Dame Sheridan's account. And then we didn't hear from Bobbie for some time. This was to be expected: Frankie's Christmas card, containing the news that she was going to be in her first pantomime, arrived in March.

The *Canberra* was too good to last. I thought we would have to go back to Egypt before too long, but I was wrong. *Tonic for the Troops* had been posted elsewhere in Joe's absence, and Joe himself was going to a different part of the world. He was hoping for India. He got Paiforce: Persia and Iraq.

Belle, we are edging closer.

Persia is a blur.

We were issued a Matchless 350cc with a sidecar. As itinerant entertainers, we drove ourselves everywhere on that desert tiger, and we were doing more shows than I could possibly remember. Did they even count as shows? Stop the bike, out of the sidecar and then the box, say hello, a quick monologue (for example, a parody of that old chestnut "The Green Eye of the Little Yellow God"), and then a brief chat in front of a tiny audience. Then into the box, back into the sidecar, and so on. We had done well in the troupe, but this suited us even better: no stages, no set times, just improvised banter.

We played to audiences of one man and audiences of five hundred, in gun sites, olive groves, and hospitals. We rarely had any accompaniment, but who needed it when everyone was singing along? And of course, we talked together, about home, about the desert, about what we would do when the war was over.

It was while we were in Iraq that we started to make our mark, that news of us and our heroism — that's what they called it — reached home. The men of Paiforce weren't forgotten, not as a unit and not individually. And we were the proof. ENSA gave us an award we never saw. We brought a lot of happiness everywhere we went. We weren't the only ones — George Formby, Gracie Fields, for example: and come to think of it, hadn't my very initials destined me for the tip-top of our profession? — but Joe and I were on the front line if we were needed.

"He hasn't been home in years!" I heard a bloke say as we passed. "He's like Lawrence of Arabia!"

After this, I took to wearing a little Lawrencian white veil to great comic effect. But the private was right. We did what ENSA told us, although they rarely knew precisely where we were. We became a law unto ourselves. And, of course, though we couldn't record the fact anywhere, we also took the odd despatch here and there, information we could convey as easily as anyone else. It was in Iraq that Joe earned the nickname Death Wish Fisher. Our legend spread.

Something was driving us forward; there was wilful loneliness in our perpetual movement, this endless tour undertaken in perfect solitude. Yes, we were keeping up morale — but what of our own? Where was our own peace of mind? There was emptiness in the constant motion. We were always running away and never towards.

What others saw as bravery — the quality that had earned that soldierly nickname, such a privilege for a civilian — was fear, despair, and defeat.

I only found out as we were shipping out of Persia.

Bobbie was dead, his throat silently slit while he was relieving himself in the dark night of the jungle. Bobbie Sheridan, whose smiling picture was pinned just above my head, his Adam's apple hidden behind an elegant choker.

And Belle, my Belle. Where are you now? Who will look after you? Who knows how but I?

Old Boys' Reunion

The evening of the memorial service, George was relieved to find the house empty. He wanted to lose himself, to disappear into the shadows. The further his bedroom fell into darkness, however, the more his eyes fought to accustom themselves, and there he was, staring back at himself in the mirror.

A light, three floors down, announced Reg and Queenie's return. "Georgie!" sung upstairs. "Fish and chips." He had no choice.

"Reg, remember when you found that bullet in your fish?" said Queenie, offering an oily newspaper package.

"Air gun pellet, it was," said Reg, holding his fingers apart to indicate its gauge. He spoke with his mouth full, and George could see chewed but as yet unswallowed white fish lodged in the pouch between gum and cheek. "Course we were lucky to have fish at all back in the war, but they didn't have to shoot the poor buggers." George couldn't bring himself to participate. "Work all right?" asked Reg, picking at the front of his teeth with one of his ubiquitous toothpicks.

"Just tired, I suppose. Where's Frankie tonight, then?"

"Manchester tonight, Sheffield tomorrow," Queenie read from the scribbled itinerary stuck to the fridge door.

"I'd like to see the show," said George. "Maybe Sheffield."

"All the way up there? Just like that?" asked Reg.

"Tomorrow?" asked Queenie discouragingly.

He left the table soon after. There was only one thing on his mind, and he couldn't mention it. He couldn't now tell them about his sighting of Frankie. He hadn't simply forgotten to mention the school magazines, Donald's death, and the memorial service; he had deliberately kept it all from them, as he was lying to them now.

But were they lying too? Perhaps they knew Frankie had been in town; perhaps the inanities of their dinner table conversation were designed to convince him that everything was normal. Perhaps they were in on it. What an absurd idea! Reg and Queenie weren't in on anything. They were too wrapped up in their own little world, planning parties and the journeys there and back: all they cared about was the fillings of their packed sandwiches, the price of petrol, and their AA directions, before they sighed and put their legs up in front of the TV at the end of the day. He caught himself disparaging their *little* world, as though he was above it. Perhaps he was.

In bed, he opened the final volume of his grandfather's notebooks, but it was hard to concentrate on anything, let alone that. He wanted the books to be done. What could stop his mind? Frankie had to tell him, of her own accord, why she had been at the service. Even before he went to sleep, it was as if his prayers were answered.

"Frankie! On the phone!" Queenie shouted up the stairs. He traipsed down in his pyjamas.

"Hey, sleepyhead. How's tricks?"

"Tricks are sleepy." He hadn't heard the phone ring.

"It's the interval; I have a little breather before my big finale, and I just wanted to tell you that I was thinking of you and I love you." Normally this sentiment would have been rewarded with an ironic groan, but for the moment he didn't know how to react. He would have to act well. She continued as though he had groaned. "I'm your mother. It's permitted."

"Why were you thinking of me?"

"I'm always thinking of you." She did not accept this first invitation. "How's the world of Foley? Still bringing home the bacon? Queenie said you were going to come and see the show." Although there was enthusiasm in her voice, an unspoken *but* coloured the end of the sentence. Would she dissuade him?

"She told you already?" He wasn't sure how to disguise his suspicion.

"We were just chatting. . . . You know . . ."

"It's good, eh? The show?"

"A nice bunch of people, good houses," she said. "But nothing exceptional. Nothing you haven't seen before." She never belittled her work.

"I'd love to see it. I am your manager, after all."

"You *are* my manager. Why not come to Birmingham? Next Tuesday, I think." He was aware of the concentration of silence around him.

"Well, everything's pretty close to London, isn't it? Not difficult to get anywhere and back in a day." His second invitation.

"Yes, next Tuesday. We're working our way home. Will you come then, Georgie? Oh, do!" She made it sound as if she were thrilled he could come so soon, rather than relieved that she had put him off until then.

"I'll see with work."

She yelled away from the phone, her hand over the receiver, "I'll be right there!" Then to him again: "An audience awaits, darling. See you in Birmingham. Perhaps Reg and Queenie want to come too?"

"Perhaps." That was the last thing he wanted.

"Going up to Birmingham?" Queenie called through from the kitchen, but he didn't answer. There was a bad taste in his mouth.

Far from answering his prayers, the phone call had given him more to think about. There were two questions: why she had been there, and why she had not mentioned having been there. The more tired he was, the more ludicrous his theories became — she wasn't on tour at all; she had rung from a hotel in London, having arranged a sub for that night's show; at one point, it honestly occurred to him that she had a twin, or that Sylvia had dyed her chestnut hair like Frankie's and was masquerading as her. And then these theories became absurd fantasies: her hat, a giant raven, toppled from her head and swooped around the chapel, cackling and crapping on the congregation.

Sleep finally came as the night wore on, but he woke too early, his scalp tight, his body itching.

To his relief, Queenie and Reg couldn't make it to Birmingham, so he took the train alone and walked from New Street to the Abbey Theatre, where *West End Story* had its one-night stand.

He'd never seen such a futuristic dressing room. In this de-contaminated safety zone, fresh white towels hung from polished nickel racks beneath spotless mirrors. A battalion of gleaming bulbs surrounded the dressing-room mirror, and here he located Frankie, bathed in their glow.

"Georgie!" They hugged. The real her could easily displace the fictional one who had wormed her way into George's mind, the pseudo-her who did not share secrets.

"Wow!" gushed George, taking in the intercom system, a complex instrument panel beneath the sleekest hi-fi speakers, straight from the bridge of the *Enterprise* itself. He produced a box of After Eights.

"You didn't! It doesn't feel much like home," Frankie said. "Mind you, I shouldn't complain. You could eat your dinner off that counter. I arranged you a room at Joyce's — we're moving south this evening, I'm afraid. The bloody routing, excuse my French, but honestly . . . Cup of tea? Could you?"

The kettle was pristine, presented on a black tray whose perimeter marked the prescribed limits of all messy brewing activities. Everything you could possibly require was neatly sorted within this boundary. George surveyed the many options: "Milk? Carnation? This powdery stuff?"

Ricky's Bunterish face beamed up at the door. "Hello, George. . . . Just a drop of Carnation. . . . Look, pet, according to *his majesty* you're totally overpowering poor *you know who* on the duet. . . . Could you rein it in just a little? Think of it as a compliment?"

"I will not dignify that with an answer." She was curling fake eyelashes. She made a better principal boy or Peter Pan: those clothes didn't look like costumes on her.

"Tea, Ricky?" asked George.

"Keep your tea, sonny Jim. Come and have a man's drink with me. You're of age, aren't you?"

"Go on," said Frankie. "He's got your comp."

"Halftime?" asked George, expecting to breeze back.

"At the end, Georgie. Other people to consider. . . . It's not a Fisher production."

"Far from it, in fact," said Ricky, as Frankie blew a kiss. "Come on, boy. Pint'll put hairs on your chest."

They went to the downstairs bar, which, in contrast to the rest of the building, was cosily ancient in design, the walls decorated with coats of arms and facsimile Excaliburs. A fire burned medievally up a central chimney, as a rabble of peasants scrabbled for service, gesticulating with rolled-up programmes, flicking folded five-pound notes in the air. Ricky walked to the side of the bar, winked at one of the girls, and was served immediately.

"Always come in and look after the bar staff evening of the show," he advised George with a confidential wink as they sat down. Ricky was always dispensing tips, as if he assumed that you were applying to be his apprentice or, failing that, simply wanted to be like him. George had the vague feeling that Ricky was here to tell him something, even beyond the usual handy hints, but he knew that this could be the figment of an imagination already on alert. Ricky talked business, as he always did, whether people cared or not. George listened and nodded, sipping his pint. Eventually, he was saved by the bell, a strange electronic bong that dropped in pitch on each chime. Ricky said he'd rather die than sit through it again — he'd stand at the back, wielding the clicker with which he always kept a head count, independent of the theatre's — so George took his seat in the stalls. A huge geometrical chandelier hung ominously from thin metal cables directly above his head.

It wasn't a bad show. The dancing and singing were well done, the band proficient, and the audience enthusiastic. Frankie, dressed in gingham, first appeared for a medley of songs with the male lead and a chorus of farmers and cowhands. Her partner may have been the bigger name, fresh from his hit television show, but it was she who owned the stage, even under instructions to rein it in.

However, the show lacked an emotional component, and George, vaguely remembering that the MD had rejected a couple of Frankie's arrangements in favour of something "more adult," wondered whether the material was to blame. When she was giving it everything on the closing number at the end of act 1, however — a moment that would usually have brought the lump to his throat — he was reminded that the quality of the show did not usually affect his reaction: he had even teared up at *Exit, Pursued Bare.* The occupant of the seat behind his had not thought a hacking cough reason enough to miss her big night out, and when George felt a drizzle of germs spray the back of his neck for the third time, he turned his collar up conspicuously. The enormous chandelier poised above, George watched from his seat, irritated and unmoved.

For Frankie's rendition, in the second act, of a song he had never heard her sing before from a musical he didn't know, the light found her at the top of a staircase in silhouette. At first, he focused on the cigarette holder poised at her mouth and didn't notice the wide-brimmed black hat with the long feather that projected behind. But once he had seen it, he could see nothing else. The woman behind peppered him with snot once more, and feeling sick, he barged his way towards the aisle and went to stand at the back of the auditorium. Here he found Ricky.

"Voted with your feet, have you? It's a bit stiff, I know, but your mum's doing a great job. And look at 'em. They're lapping it up."

After the curtain call, they went backstage. Frankie was ravenous. "When does the coach go?" she asked.

"Too soon for haute cuisine," said Ricky. "But we'll pack up something."

"Can we go and eat quickly?" asked George. He was used to meals on the fly: the usual request to hurry the order as they sat down (clinched by the mention that they were playing the local theatre), the momentary glance at the menu, a wolfed main course, dessert or coffee always accompanied by the bill. But tonight there was no time.

"We have to go to the bar," said Ricky. "Those BBC fellows are here, and I promised we'd say hello. Time is money."

Frankie saw George's disappointment. "I'll be home next week. Let's go and have some fun now." She put her arm around him and they walked to the bar. The black hat, on its way to costume, passed in the hands of a dresser.

"Nice hat," said George. "Looks like a big raven." Frankie rolled her eyes: *I wear what I'm told.*

Ye Olde Abbey Tavern was less crowded than it had been. Frankie introduced George to everyone.

"Looks too old to be your son, Frankie," said an elderly man. "Sure he's not your younger brother?"

"Your boyfriend?" said another.

"Hey!" said Ricky, and he laughed before awkwardly catching George's eye. George had seen that one coming all night. Ricky had finally inherited everything of his uncle's.

When Ricky called Frankie into his jovial negotiation, George knew there would be no chance to talk.

"Look! There's Joyce," said Frankie, realizing he was left out. "Where we stayed with the Drolls."

"No, I have to be at work tomorrow. I can get the last train home." He hadn't bothered to check the schedule, but he felt a great urge to be back in London.

"There you go, then!" said Ricky to Frankie. "I'll give Georgie boy a ride to the station, and you can sweet-talk Mr. Light Entertainment."

Ricky walked George to his car, parked right outside the theatre. "Key space, this," said Ricky. "Look!" He gestured around him so George could admire its proximity to the back-stage door. "You don't want to be in the car park, not at a place like this. But I don't mind giving it up to do a mate a good turn. That's what it's all about."

George was so relieved to be at the station that he wouldn't have been disappointed to find he *had* missed the last train. He hadn't, but it was late. He would have to change at Coventry, which, at half past midnight, was dark, wet, and empty. There was no sign of the other train (or its potential passengers). George asked the only official.

"Not tonight," said the burly man, a cigarette stuck to his top lip. "Sorry, mate, cancelled. Next one's at four-fifteen in the morning. Sleeping rough? Kid like you? I shouldn't really, but you can lie down in that waiting room if you like." He pointed to another platform.

His accommodation smelled of pee, and George was quite relieved when the guard offered a cup of tea, saying his office was warmer.

"Homeless, eh?" he asked, as they sat in front of a two-bar electric fire. The guard had a keen interest in his living situation. George explained how he came to be there, as the guard scrutinized him through his thick pebble glasses. "Not twenty-one, are you?"

"Nowhere near."

"Not legal!" he said, as though this were a bad break for both of them. "All right, then," said the man reasonably. "Only sometimes, you know, you get lucky. And you look quite a big lad. I don't understand what all them age laws are about anyway." He told a long, sorry story of the two willing kids, nice boys, who'd gone home with him. He'd come back the next day to find the place cleared out, everything stolen, and his TV smashed on the pavement.

"Why didn't you go to the police?" said George, who knew why but wanted it said.

"They was underage," said the guard and sniffed. "Little bastards. And I'm not protected in any way. Wanna digestive?"

George started yawning regularly, saying he'd sleep in the waiting room, though he imagined he wouldn't. As George left, noticing that the man had locked the door behind him as they entered, the guard said: "Well, it was nice to chat, anyway. It can be a long lonely night here, just me and me tea. Nice to have some company." Back in the waiting room, George moved the bench so it blocked the only entrance and lay down.

He wasn't sure how to broach the memorial service with Frankie. If she didn't mention it, that was because there should be silence. Their family had always been one of noise and chatter, but silence was how you kept secrets. Silence was the thing. Silence.

He was woken up early by another guard's fierce banging on the door.

Crystal Clear emptied his mind. It was therapeutic to supply life with its proper soundtrack at the correct volume.

At home, he found solace in finishing his grandfather's books. He had been determined to get them done, but it was in the very last volume that George finally glimpsed the man. He was somehow able to put his other worries aside.

The final book began predictably enough with a lengthy encomium upon the virtues of distant-voice ventriloquism, its divine origins, the theoretical implications of its power. There was no precise instruction — George had long since given up hoping — but, unlike anywhere else in the recent volumes, there was a practical application for this knowledge: more than a practical application — an Act, an "Original Act." A prologue boasted: "The audience will not believe that only one man is behind the entire spectacle." Here, on paper, was the performance for which Joe had worked, timed to the last second, plotted to the square inch; the performance to which all his technical mastery, so minutely detailed elsewhere, had led; the performance on which he had staked his career. Here was the crying child, the retreating watchman, the midnight séance and the singing spirit in the rafters, the argument between two invisible protagonists.

It was a grand entertainment ("comic, vocalic, mimetic, multiformical, and maniloquious"), a celebration of the history of ventriloquism from the Pythian oracle to Vox Knight — and there it stopped. There was no mention of a dummy.

George had lost himself in this last volume, this Revelation, which reached a thunderous climax on page 92, as the curtain fell on Joe Fisher's imaginary triumph. This entry was dated 1931, but on the next page, scribbled in pencil, crossed out so brutally that the lead had broken halfway: "Enough! Enough! Enough! This rough magic I here abjure." The page was defaced with other random words: Technique, Personality, Charisma. All crossed out.

After this outburst, there was another coda, a postscript, dated 1940. The pen, the hand: all was different, yet clearly the same man.

> I laugh at my ideals, the dreams of a young man that
> led only to frustration. But I was wrong, I was weak,
> to give up this work as I did. I took bad advice, afraid
> to do anything else, a cowardice for which I have paid
> ever since: but I alone am to blame. Through fear,
> I allowed my*self* to be trapped, and then my voice
> *it*self was trapped. But no more. No more "Theoretical
> Escapology"! Now I escape. And for my first and final
> act, I will unchain myself — the key was passed in
> a kiss — and I am gone, to a better world, a world
> I would wish for anyone as sad as I have been. I
> unbreak my staff! Undrown my book! Through me,
> voices can appear! The dead can talk! The living can
> hear! Only *one boy* knows how and he can tell you
> *everything*. Talk to George.

And there, finally, the only mention of his dummy: the last word of the final sentence.

Why had the books stopped for nine years after the description? He asked Queenie if Joe had ever done his great act. No, she said, and nothing like. Evie had scared it out of him: a shame, though Evie was probably right. He did a bit here and there, but audiences never really took to it, and his greatest successes were with George. She read the postscript too, shaking her head. "He was a lonely soul. You just couldn't get through to him. I suppose he's in a better world now."

That "Great Act" had stayed on the page, unrealized. George's work with the books should have been done. How he had longed to file them away, put them back on the shelf where they could rest forever. But that was impossible now: these books passed a baton with their very last word, and George couldn't rest until he found the dummy. It was the sheer relief of having a quest to take his mind off more pressing business, a quest that took him away from himself, that did not require his family. In what way could a dummy tell him everything?

He couldn't even remember where the dummy was. Flicking through the scrapbooks, he saw him in his initial splendour at the Imperial War Museum — there were numerous clippings of him on display, sporting a large George Cross, saluting the various onlookers. Churchill himself had promised to visit the convalescent, reported *The Herald.* There were rather fewer clippings of the return of the dummy to the Fisher family. And then there was the dummy, still in his Tommy uniform, back behind glass again, after his sale to the Armed Forces Museum in Clapham. A brochure for this poor relation of the Imperial War proclaimed it an independently run museum dedicated to the "artefacts and memorabilia of war."

George couldn't help laughing. Could the dummy possibly be as near as Clapham?

What little information the brochure gave was years out of date: Clapham 82 looked more like a bus route than a telephone number. George was surprised to find an up-to-date one in the yellow pages. Getting through to the museum, however, was another matter. He tried for three days and gave up. The only thing to do was visit in person.

The door opened only a crack, as far as the safety chain would allow. Old eyes peered round the corner.

"Are you open today?" asked George politely.

"Well, I'm here, if that's what you mean," whistled through false teeth.

"Are you open, though, for visitors?"

"I can be."

Museum was an exaggeration; it was no more than a collection of curios in the dusty terrace house of a retired brigadier, Edwin Coffin, VC, who tore tickets, gave guided tours, sold faded postcards at the end of the visit, and lived in the basement, three floors of motley memorabilia piled above him.

"No, delighted," he said, as he shook George's hand after grappling with the safety chain. His moustache appeared stuck on, and George wondered if he had woken Coffin up. "Always a pleasure to show a youngster around. School project?"

"Personal interest."

"Well, we open just mornings three days a week now. A few visitors here and there, but quite spotty, I'm afraid, ever since the wife died. . . ." He glanced at his watch. "Oh, my lord. We should be open now anyway. Needs a younger man, I'd say." Coffin sized George up as a possible applicant. "A guided tour will be fifty of your new English pence."

It would have been mean-spirited, however specialized George's interest, not to feign curiosity about the rest of the collection. Coffin led the way, reciting the history of the museum. He unlocked the door to every room and locked it with equal care as they made their way. The floorboards creaked; even the guided tour, which Coffin hadn't been overly keen to dust off, was in need of a thorough oiling. Coffin himself could hardly be bothered with it, preferring to point out individual items of particular interest. His presentation was peppered with gloomy asides about the uncertain future of the collection.

George finally caught sight of his namesake in a rather dirty glass case in the front parlour of the second floor. He had expected Coffin to give the exhibit pride of place, but despite the centrality of the large display, it would have gone unmentioned had George not enquired.

"Oh yes, well, he really *is* interesting, actually. He was at the Imperial War Museum just after the war," said Coffin, suddenly a promoter boasting that his main draw had previously head-lined the Theatre Royal. "That's George Fisher, the ventriloquist dummy and constant companion of famous ENSA star Joe 'Death Wish' Fisher. Probably before your time," he added with a sigh.

Immediately, George was making plans. So long ago, on his trip to Romando's with Bird, the man had mentioned a room full of dummies. Perhaps he could get a substitute, a dummy dummy, make it up exactly, smuggle it into the museum on his next trip, and substitute one for the other when Coffin's back was turned.

Coffin continued: "Spent a pretty penny on him, probably over the odds, but hindsight's a wonderful thing. And besides, I had a good offer for him not so long ago, so . . ."

George was enumerating the various ways he could wrest control of the dummy, but he was overelaborating; the thing was there right in front of him. Coffin clearly needed the money. He should make an offer.

"It was at Montebianco, August '44," said Coffin, warming to his theme as he narrated a rather overegged version of Joe's death, concluding: "They were both legends by then anyway, stars throughout the theatre of war. And George Fisher here was the first and only ventriloquist dummy to be given the George Cross."

"Honorary," said George.

"Yes, honorary," confirmed Coffin, tetchy at the correction.

"Can we get him out of the case?"

"I beg your pardon?"

"I wondered if I could touch him."

Coffin bristled. "It hasn't been out of the case for years. I can't just open the case like that."

"Why not? How much do you want for him?" said George.

"Sorry?"

"Can I make an offer for him?"

"This is a museum, not a flea market!" George was surprised at the vehemence of Coffin's offence. "I can't just open it for any

Tom, Dick, or Harry as asks me. Besides," said Coffin, relenting somewhat, "I have no idea where the key is."

"Brigadier," said George respectfully, "my name is also George Fisher. Death Wish Fisher was my grandfather."

"No, he wasn't."

"My mother is Frankie Fisher. And I am named George Fisher after . . ." He gestured at the case. Coffin was having none of it. "I have spent my entire life looking at the two George Crosses framed together above our fireplace."

This domestic detail clinched it; Coffin beamed. "Well, why ever didn't you say? That's wonderful. Worth a spread in the local rag."

"Yes, I suppose so, but what I want is to hold George, to work him a little. We are related."

"He's very fragile."

"I'll be very careful."

Coffin's right eye twitched. "Only if you promise. This is my pension. I'll pop and see if I can find the key."

George circled this piece of family history: Joe's dummy that would tell him everything. What did he want to know? Three sides and the top of the case in which the dummy sat were glass; behind him was a poorly rendered backdrop of an army settlement in which nothing was to scale, complete with huge sandbags, tiny military vehicles, and a squadron of planes dwarfed by their pilots. The dummy sported his Tommy uniform, familiar from the clippings, with a pair of opera glasses, presumably meant to be binoculars, around his neck. The floor of the case had been carpeted with unconvincing fake grass.

The creaking stairs announced Coffin. George stood back, anxious not to appear too eager, though it took all his patience to watch the old man's spindly fingers fumbling with the keys and the lock. It was the back of the case that opened, but Coffin was thoughtlessly trying to work his fingers along the edge to prise off the top.

"Here," said George. He opened the back, putting his hand into the case to stop the dummy falling backwards. "Out you come."

"Easy does it," warned Coffin. "He'll have to go back exactly as we found him."

George sat down, placing the dummy on his lap. What was he expecting to find? Something physical? Or was it merely the concept that held the key? No, Joe had been a keeper of secrets, a shy, lonely man, a hoarder of fragments of poetry and arcane diagrams — the books had led to the dummy. George awaited further instructions.

"What an interesting afternoon." Coffin chuckled.

"Well, if you have anything else to do . . ."

"No, no . . . I'll stay . . . er . . ." There was no immediate prospect of a resolution to this polite standoff, so George slipped his hand inside the dummy and began a sly exploration. "Do you do any, erm, ventriloquizing yourself?" asked Coffin politely. There was silence as George groped blindly inside the torso. "How long did you have in mind?"

"I beg your pardon?"

"Out of the case . . . You know."

George didn't know whether to bore Coffin with feigned ventriloquial practice in the hope that he would leave of his own accord, or to ask him to go. The latter seemed less time consuming. "Well, I was hoping for a little privacy with my ancestor. Just a few minutes."

Coffin bowed solemnly and left, indicating that he would be right outside. The moment he was gone, George laid the dummy on the floor and opened up his back as best he could. He could feel the metal and wood of the mechanism but nothing else. Perhaps there was something written on the inside of the dummy. He could sense Coffin's presence beyond the door, desperate for admission.

He removed the dummy's jacket and rolled up the back of the shirt so he could peer inside the torso. He held the dummy up to the light, where he could make out a set of characters: a code of some kind, but nothing more than the date of manufacture (he presumed) in Roman numerals. He memorized it. Behind the nape of the neck, just below an ugly join in the papier-mâché, another code: Romando G-28/7 #3 head. This wasn't a message from the dead but an innocent reference number. George was looking for more.

Inside, he found nothing. He started to undo the boy's trousers. Thinking better of it, he rolled up the trouser legs. He had never considered the makeup of a dummy's legs: these were solid blocks of wood, joined at the knee with a beautifully crafted bracket. But nothing else. There was only one chance left.

"Everything OK?" Coffin called in.

"Yes, done in a moment."

George started to strip the dummy. He removed the musty clothes as carefully as he could. The dummy was naked before him on the floor, a mess of metal, wood, and string.

Announcing himself with the swiftest of coughs, Coffin opened the door. He stood in the doorway, quivering with indignation. "That does it. I'm calling the police." He slammed the door, locked it from the outside, and creaked down the stairs.

The police, thought George, wasn't good — escape was out of the question — but it did buy him time. He searched the dummy from head to toe, disappointed to find nothing out of the ordinary. Perhaps he was years after the fact, and whatever had been there was there no longer — of course. Satisfied that further scrutiny would yield nothing, he dressed the dummy, replaced the opera glasses round his neck, and positioned him next to the sandbags exactly as he had first seen him. He secured the back of the case and sat down to await his arrest. Everything was just as it had been when he entered the room; perhaps improved. The inside of the case had been aired and dusted for the first time in years.

After half an hour, there was a cautious knock on the door. "We're coming in." A uniformed policeman, whose amused expression put George at ease, followed him.

"Sir, this gentleman accuses you of attacking one of the exhibits."

"He claims to be the grandson of Death Wish Fisher," interrupted Coffin. "An obvious fabrication."

"Death Wish Fisher?" asked the policeman ironically.

"A war hero, my grandfather," said George.

"Name, sir?"

"*George* Fisher."

"Age and address?"

There was an explanation to be given but no charge to answer. To Coffin's disappointment, George left a free man, uncuffed; to George's disappointment, the policeman rang Queenie, informing her of George's involvement in a disturbance at a museum involving a ventriloquist dummy. He advised her that her grandson henceforth stay away from the Armed Forces Museum on Locke Lane.

George offered to make himself available for any newspaper coverage that might help the museum, but Coffin would not meet his eye.

"What on earth were you doing?" said Queenie.

"Did they file a report?" asked Reg earnestly. "Don't want a silly thing like that going on your record, messing things up for later."

"No, nothing like that. The owner was a bit of an old woman, that's all," said George. "I went to see my namesake, grandfather's dummy, George Fisher."

"And he's there?" said Reg. "In a museum?" George could just as well let Queenie give the explanation, but she was curiously silent. "And so you went to have a look at him, I get it, but why the *police?*"

"Well," said George, "I wanted to see how he worked, so I got him out and took his clothes off. . . . I couldn't resist."

"Well, you're loopy." Reg laughed, making the cuckoo sign with his index finger. "You can't go round . . ."

"Did you find out, then?" asked Queenie, breaking her silence with a nervous laugh.

"How he worked?" asked George.

"No, did you find out? You're a clever boy."

"Find out what?"

"That isn't George at all," said Queenie blithely.

"You're both dotty!" Reg sat back in his chair in exasperation. "I thought he was in the museum!"

"Well, we *sold* him to the museum," said Queenie. "But at the last moment Evie got sentimental and didn't want to see him go. And they'd be none the wiser, so we changed his clothes with my old dummy Pip Squeak's, and . . ."

George stood up without having meant to. "So that isn't George at the Armed Forces Museum?" Queenie shook her head in silence. "It's Pip Squeak?"

"In George's soldier clothes," confirmed Queenie quietly.

"So I went to the Armed Forces Museum and nearly got arrested, and it wasn't even George?" He wasn't used to raising his voice.

"Well, you didn't ask! We didn't know!" she said firmly. "It wouldn't have been a secret from you, Georgie!"

"But why are there secrets at all?" George shouted, unable to stop himself. "And if that's the other one, where is George?"

"Now, now, George," said Reg, massaging Queenie's shoulder. "This is your grandmother you're talking to."

"He's in the attic!" she shouted back, her voice trembling. "Where he's always been!"

Half an hour later, George was on his knees in his bedroom, the door locked.

In front of him lay his second victim of the day, facedown, naked but for his trousers. The rest of the uniform — cap, white shirt, striped tie, forest green blazer — was scattered across the floor.

George had found him in the attic wrapped in a tartan blanket, just as Queenie had said, hidden in a turquoise valise beneath a tower of forgotten suitcases. Despite the pungent smell of camphor, frail silken threads clung to his blazer, the cuffs and the lapel of which were partly eaten away.

This boy weighed less than the other. George turned him over.

"Speak to me."

The tattooed date was where he expected, and there were tiny silver welts around the boy's heart: on closer inspection, pieces of embedded shot. George pulled the trousers down slowly. Whereas the other boy's legs had been entirely wood, elegantly hinged, these were different. Beneath each knee, a metal tube was attached with wire to the wooden thigh above and the shoe below.

"Sorry," George said as he took his pliers to the wire beneath the right knee. A leather shoe dangled from the bottom of the newly amputated metal shin. He put the tube to his eye, telescope-style, but found his view blocked by something he couldn't shake from its hiding place. He coaxed the contents towards the opening with his little finger until he was able to pinch their top edge and pull them out. It was a rolled document, tied with string. George performed the same surgery on the left leg to find a matching manuscript, rolled tighter.

At first, he simply stared. Then he undid the string on the first, expecting the pages to spring forth in celebration of their new freedom, but the brittle paper had been too long in confinement.

He unrolled the scroll from the right leg. On the first page was written "The Memoirs of George Fisher."

9

Letters to B.

I have decided to write, though there is nowhere to send a letter. Writing is all that I have. It keeps me alive, as it always has. It is how we imagine not being lonely.

We are no longer in the desert. Our final contribution was a *Farewell to Africa* extravaganza in an antique amphitheatre where the quietest whisper reached the farthest row. And now we're on the move, waves lapping against the prow, back on the ocean but this time quite healthy. The word is Italy — and what a change that will make from the sores and the scorpions — but I'll believe it when I see it; when I see it as clearly as that shell, glowing red as it streaks across the sky.

Where are you?

I will never see you again. I must face the fact. But not yet.

SEPTEMBER 12TH, 1943

The first thing I saw was a mountain, and far beneath, an island exploding with colour: forests, orchards, vineyards, wheat fields, and olive groves. It wasn't a mountain, it was a volcano: Etna, no less.

Somewhere over the Straits of Messina, they are already making plans to take Rome. I shan't bore you with the details, but they don't want us on the mainland prematurely, so we will be left here kicking our heels, making the usual round of hospitals. Not so bad. I am on a beach, behind the Villa Leopardi — an elegant old pile requisitioned on our behalf, complete with croquet lawn and bandstand — watching the sea peter out against the shore and then tiptoe back again. Greedy Tommies feast from the fat of the land, helmets full of bulbous tomatoes, plucking grapes as they fancy from vineyards forsaken by their owners. We've landed on our feet in Sicily all right, but it's not all heaven. Signorina Mosquito is everywhere, and she likes my uniform; sits there, abdomen swollen with blood.

Food is scarce on the mainland, but in Siracusa they brought us baskets of fruit and bottles of wine. Perhaps they took us for soldiers. And what can we give them in return for their kindness? You, of all people, know the answer to that.

The kids are fascinated by this motley group of Inglesi. They went wild when they saw us perform for the first time. We sat on a dried-up well, and they crowded around, squatting on the ground in their homemade wooden sandals. I don't speak much Eyetie (Ti amo, and, erm, gottiglia di girra), but when we got going we might as well have been fluent. It was just gibberish, with *olio* added to the end of English words, and a *pasta* or *Bolognese* thrown in, but the kids couldn't stop laughing whichever one of us was speaking. It was as though they'd never seen such a thing before. My attitude to children and their parties has changed: laughter is in short supply here, and what better medicine do they have?

An older girl came to fetch her brother, the loudest and most hysterical of our audience. He stubbornly refused to notice her, so she waded into the crowd, at which he grabbed the handle of the well so she couldn't drag him away. Everyone was laughing — his reluctance, her determination, their slapstick.

Finally it fell on me to tell him, as sternly as I could, to go. He went and she smiled. Probably doesn't speak a word of English.

After this impromptu turn, we visited the hospitals. Even when you've seen it all, sometimes you've seen enough, and today was one of those days. They can't smile; they can't laugh; some of them can't see — but at least they're alive — at *least* — hanging on, or having the nurses and doctors hang on for them. They're not doing much for themselves. I'm sure they'd rather slip away, relax their fingers and float, but they can't. They're not allowed. Effort is so painful; our knuckles are white, yet we keep clinging. The alternative is suicide — and we are too fearful for that.

When it's time to give in, there is no need to say a word. I won't stop you. Don't stop me either.

SEPTEMBER 29TH, 1943

I don't sound like myself, I know. Perhaps I am a little *war weary;* perhaps I have seen enough. But on we drive, newly reunited with our precious pink Matchless, so we can go deeper, farther, faster.

The boy who clung to the well? His name is Ettore Ansalone and he came to find us at the camp. He's eight years old, an astonishing little thief, and appears to have fallen in love with us. Seriously. He is nervous, anxious not to cause offence, but he can't help himself bringing gifts, offerings from Sicily: yesterday some shrimp, and today a guinea pig those nimble little fingers of his swiped from some trap. What on earth are we going to do with a guinea pig? We manage conversations based on a little Italian and a great deal of mime. As for the guinea pig . . . Oh, dear . . . I'm afraid it's meant to be eaten.

Last night, the kid begged for a ride on the Matchless, so we drove him home, bombing down the country lanes, Ettore in the sidecar, navigating, the wind gusting through his hair. Ettore shrieked. We took corners a little too fast. Ettore shrieked louder. We drove too close to the side of the road so the unkempt branches stung our cheeks. Ettore shrieked loudest of all. It was the ride of his life.

Home was a ruin of an old farm with a circular driveway, weeds worming their way through the cracks unopposed, and lizards darting between them, in two minds about their destination. At the announcement of the engine, the whole family appeared: all women — a grandmother, Mamma; a mother; and two sisters, one of whom was the pretty girl who had tried to drag Ettore from the well. He sprinted towards them, rattling off rapid-fire dialect. The mother, a beautiful, strong-faced woman with long black hair, invited us in. The interior was in a terrible state: the main staircase had collapsed, leaving no way to the second floor, and all the banisters around the edge of the second storey had fallen away, not that there was any way to get up there. The elder sister, refusing help, walked down the hill with buckets to fetch water from a neighbouring spring.

We sat around the large kitchen table that was placed in the very centre of the house, where, every now and then, shifting plaster sprinkled us like icing sugar from a sieve. I looked up to see stars twinkling through the dilapidated roof. The mother offered a cup of coffee, and Ettore amused himself by making a little extra cup — sweet boy! — then drinking it and laughing. Whenever we spoke, he monitored the reactions of the various family members with a glint in his eye. The elder Mamma sat in her rocking chair and chuckled when we made a joke of spitting out plaster. The elder sister still hadn't said a word but seemed pleased to see her brother so happy.

Their story emerged, courtesy of the mother Annagrazia's broken English. The father had been involved in various illegal operations, one of which had involved the accidental shooting of an Italian soldier. It was possible to hide many things in Sicily, but not this, and the Mafia strong-armed Annibale into giving himself up. The worst might not happen, they had consoled him — there were ways of ensuring this — and his family would be cared for if it did. The sad state of the house was proof that they hadn't kept their word. The elder brother, Salvatore, called Turi, had stepped into his father's shoes, and now he too was dead, buried without honour in the back garden. They were still claiming his food ration.

And that left Mamma, Annibale's mother; Annagrazia; and three of his children: Chiara, eighteen; Valentina, ten; and Ettore, eight, living in a house that needed repairs they couldn't possibly afford, that might barely last another winter. Ettore and Valentina couldn't stop talking — they wanted to keep us up all night — but Chiara was a silent enigma, her serious expression always directed somewhere else, far away.

"Va bene?" I asked. She smiled her sad smile as she twirled her sun-bleached hair with her right index finger, making the softest of whistling sounds. She'd stop for a few seconds when she caught herself, and then start again without noticing, just the same, twirling it loosely through her one finger, never letting it get too tight, never letting it slip from her finger. Annagrazia smiled indulgently. Shortly after, Chiara kissed them both and left through the front door. I wondered if she could possibly be going for more water so late at night. "It was very bad for her," Annagrazia said matter-of-factly. "After Annibale die, and her elder brother, Turi, no one to protect her. Such a lovely girl. She don't speak of it now. Nothing."

Annagrazia offered a small bottle of bitter alcohol. To Ettore's delight, we produced chocolate in trade. When cigarettes followed, it was adult eyes that lit up. A few minutes later, I noticed a petal on my right leg. I thought nothing of it as Ettore rationed the chocolate equally between us, but then another floated just past my eye, a pink rose petal. Valentina had fallen asleep at the kitchen table, but Ettore immediately looked up.

"Chiara!" he said, and laughed. At that moment, a handful of petals cascaded down on us, fluttering dizzily all around. I looked too, but there was no sign of her. When I asked how she got up there, Ettore showed us a ladder outside, wedged between two paving stones. They all slept up above, he said in charades, except Grandma, who was too fat for the ladder. He was also sent up before too long, but Valentina was already fast asleep, so we carried her up the ladder and laid her on her mattress. After another gift of chocolates, we said our good nights and got back on the Matchless.

"Good-byee, Giorgio!" Ettore shouted from the top window as his mother shushed him. "Arrivederci, Giorgio mio!"

P.S. This morning, another love token on the water tank outside the barn: a dead squirrel.

OCTOBER 15TH, 1943

We have left Sicily far behind.

There was a final show on the Leopardi bandstand, coincidentally featuring a partial reunion of *Tonic for the Troops*. Recently arrived on the island, terribly well rested, tanned, and healthy, they explained the concept of leave as though we'd never heard of it. No Toots, sadly — he had succumbed to a heart attack in Delhi. Yes, the Tonics had gone to India. Malaria had condemned us to the pleasant prison of the *Canberra* while they'd been posted precisely where we had wanted to go: where you were.

But our reputation has so risen in the meanwhile that there was a change in their attitude towards us. A revue means no star, but there was little doubt who was topping the bill, and Phoebe in particular fawned all over us. Even the Ansalones, invited en masse, commented upon it, much to our embarrassment. It was good to see the troupe again; their war, they hoped, was over. Could we have packed it in and gone home too, I wondered? To what? We'll see it out until the end.

Before we left the island, Ettore pestered us as often as he could, showering us with possibly edible gifts. Between shows at the hospital, we went back to the Ansalone house to help them fix the roof, bringing gifts of corned beef, chocolate, and even some material for winter overcoats.

It was just in time; the rains started as soon as we disembarked on the mainland.

NOVEMBER 7TH, 1943

We have left everything in Sicily — good weather, food, and common sense. I have no idea where the rest of the ENSA folk are, but we are not with them, and at this point we are writing our own itinerary, if indeed we have one.

Our reputation precedes us. Yesterday we arrived at a camp and had barely turned off the engine before soldiers surrounded us. Did they want smokes? Chocolates? News from home? No, they'd heard that we were coming: Death Wish Fisher and George. Our most frequent stage now is the Matchless, and we sat on the saddle, surrounded by cross-legged soldiers (just like the scruffy Siciliani), and ran through a series of favourites — "The Siegfried Line," of course, and the comic memories of the desert. It's always the sketch where we come face-to-face with Hitler and his boy, Little Adolf, that gets the biggest cheer.

Rumour has it that we are spies: which is rather more daring than the truth — we deliver the occasional, probably rather tedious, message on the Matchless. But it adds to our mystique that the boys think us so daring — and we could hardly deny it.

NOVEMBER 20TH, 1943

Rain falls heavily from leaden skies, the countryside reduced to a quagmire by the constant to and fro of vehicles. The Matchless can handle the rain but hates mud, and the sidecar is a swimming pool: "Put me in the shallow end" always gets a good laugh at the end of the act. Oh, for the Villa Leopardi!

The Germans have fallen back slowly, destroying every bridge on the way, bombing dams, booby-trapping buildings, mining roads indiscriminately; anything to delay our inevitable advance. In the middle of our show two days ago, there was a huge explosion that sent us crashing from the piano stool and brought the show to a rapid close. We gingerly left the building (with our entire audience), tiptoeing our way to the front gate on only the most solid-looking of the stones. The house was found to be littered with devices, any of which could have gone up at any moment.

I used to worry about my number being up. That's passed. We've had the chance to die so many times that I assume we are ghosts, that we must have died once. Perhaps this eases our guilt at having thus far avoided the short straw.

And still it pours. We sleep in improvised quarters; last night, a sheet slung between font and lectern in a bombed-out church. We parked the Matchless where the altar would have been. And tomorrow night — who knows where we will be then? Perhaps nowhere.

They say we will be held south of Rome for the whole winter. But I don't think we can be held anywhere, not when there is petrol in the tank and a seat on the Matchless.

JANUARY 1ST, 1944

Happy New Year. You didn't notice I didn't write, but that doesn't stop me being ashamed. In my defence, the weather hasn't got any better, extremely wet, extremely cold, and we have been itinerant since late November. Apart from anything else, the beautiful Romando box, *the best presentation box at no extra cost to the customer,* is no more. The good news: it was empty.

We carry on regardless, sometimes sleeping in the sidecar under a piece of tarpaulin, with a sou'wester and army-issue raincoat. Pray for spring.

If there's any kind of stage, then there's a show: ceilings are surplus to requirements, luckily, since most have been blown off, walls an unnecessary luxury. The act has now become something of a communion of faith in the victory to come. We play our roles: the Honest Tommy and the Blimpish Top Brass. Plenty of laughs there, but nothing bad for morale, of course.

The show itself (rather than our frequent impromptu improvisations on the Matchless) feels important now, with all those people seeing us, so we no longer make it all up as we go along. The audiences are coming to see something they have heard about, and we mustn't disappoint. Certain routines are expected of us, and the jokes are carefully scripted: the act delivers every time. Few of them see it twice, so this works well for the theatres. These shows are not as much fun. I like when we're sat on the saddle — then we chat as we used to, free to be ourselves as we were during the air raids in London, the nights onstage with you, the happiest times of my life.

Words fail me. Writing no longer keeps me full of hope.

FEBRUARY 14TH, 1944

It's Valentine's Day. I am keeping my identity a closely guarded secret. I won't even sign my name. I think back to little Valentina Ansalone — how I wish we were being pestered by Ettore, petaled by Chiara. And to Valentine Vox. How far am I throwing my voice? Perhaps nowhere.

Here is the one thing I would never ask at one of the shows, about which I would never joke — but I sometimes want to spit it out: *what if there is nothing to go home for?* The question is rhetorical — there *is* nothing to go home for. Why else have we been blindly chasing the front lines? We are trying to forget the past and ignore the future. We only have the present. A few years ago, I would have seen the name we have made for ourselves, the fame we now enjoy, as a stepping-stone to a life after the war, something we could take back to London and use as the foundation of a solid career. But, even if the war hasn't changed everything irrevocably, even if there are theatres, even if we *win* the war, even if all the even ifs: I will not want to. After all the hard work and the setbacks, there it is: the truth. There is no way forward. The war can go on forever, for it is the only thing keeping the two of us together and, ironically, alive.

I am tired of speculating about your whereabouts. I am tired of everything. I will write no more.

APRIL 2ND, 1944

I was shot.

I was shot. Not shot, shrapnel. Of course I'm fine. It went through my uniform and lodged in my right side. I'll wear it proudly.

How did I get shot? As ever, we were looking for an audience and somehow, somehow, we found ourselves through the German lines, though we had absolutely no idea until we came under fire. We were shelled and bombed: they wasted a lot of ammunition on one man and his ventriloquist dummy. And we both got hit.

We are in harm's way.

JUNE 14TH, 1944

Banished from the front line, we have spent the last two months in comfortable and rather dull theatres. News of our injuries spread far and wide. It's all a big fuss about nothing. I'm fine.

For once we're sitting ducks for communication and, unexpectedly, there was a letter from Queenie. If I wondered whether we had anything to go home for before, I know now. Frankie won't remember me — I haven't written to her in years — and now she has a sister I won't even know: Sylvia. Why *Sylvia?* "Who is Sylvia? What is she?" I last saw Queenie five years ago. The letter read like a death warrant.

JUNE 24TH, 1944

Echo and Narcissus were playing the Bellini Opera House (Belle-ini, I thought); they're flocking over now it's safer. We went to see her, to see what she had to say about the letter. Mission unaccomplished.

Just before curtain, a bomb fell somewhere in the distance.
It was nowhere near enough to worry a full house desperate
for a laugh or two, but Echo was in her coach and back to Bari
before you could say Jack Robinson, leaving the entire audience (us among them) in the dark. The announcement that Miss
Endor was unavoidably detained was met with booing, which
gave way to foot stamping and a painfully slow hand clap. What
else could we do but cover for her? What else but stand up,
announce ourselves, and give those soldiers the show of their
lives? And of ours. Good to end on a high.

For a finale, I led a sing-along chorus of the new theme song
of the Italian campaign:

> *We landed at Salerno, a holiday with pay.*
> *The Jerries brought the bands out to greet us on the way,*
> *Showed us the sights and gave us tea.*
> *We all had girls and the beer was free.*
> *We are the D-day Dodgers in sunny Italy.*

In the tumult, as they rushed the stage, we were hoisted
on shoulders and marched around the theatre to a never-
ending chorus of "The D-day Dodgers." We ended up
at opposite sides of the ruined theatre, and as we were
bounced past each other, I remembered why we had come to
the theatre: a birth, a death.

We were passed over many an outstretched arm back to the
stage, and the chair that had earlier been meant for Echo. We
hushed the chanting and singing. "Death Wish!" turned into a
long "Shhhh!" as they struggled to hear.

"What's that, George? I didn't quite hear. Listen closer,
everyone! What's that you say, George?"

Quietly: "Berlin or Bust!"

"What? They can't hear you."

A little louder: "Berlin or Bust!"

"Louder!"

"BERLIN OR BUST!"

"Louder!"

Everyone joined in the chant:

"Berlin or Bust! Berlin or Bust! Berlin or Bust!"

JUNE 29TH, 1944

In show business terms, we have decided upon early retirement. There is no future for the act. It is better that we split up.

JULY 8TH, 1944

Our number is up. You will never hear from me again. You are dead. And I will soon be dead too. Find me in Paradise, where we shall never be parted. I know you will. Arrivederci.

In the words of the immortal Nellie Wallace:

> *A man may kiss a maid good-bye;*
> *The sun may kiss the butterfly;*
> *The morning dew may kiss the grass;*
> *And you, my friends . . .*
> *Farewell.*

Part Two

The Tip of My Tongue

We are George Fisher. We speak as one.

In fact, we don't speak at all. When we finally met, there wasn't much to say. There was much *not* to say.

Oh, we used to chatter away, never together, naturally, but with our various ventriloquists and interlocutors. We were always happiest in conversation with our family.

No longer.

One word: everything changed. Therefore, silence.

What is a child given to make him quiet? A dummy. In America, a pacifier. It shuts baby up.

I wrote that for Dr. Hill almost a year after I found George I thought I was writing about one thing; I was writing about another.

"We" was, needless to say, just I. Of a dummy and his partner, only one is doing the talking — the other might look as if he is, but this is only an illusion. The same goes for the silence. But "We" felt safer, "I" insufficient, foreign, and, after what I had read, frightening: the isolated voice, unheard and unfulfilled, self-justifying, shy and withdrawn, captured for eternity, aching for release, willing its own extinction.

And why did I end up hiding behind my namesake in silence, as Joe had? I told myself that by suppressing the diary, I was protecting those I loved: keeping my mother in blissful ignorance of her father's true character, saving Queenie the needless pain of knowing his aversion to her. Imagining myself their protector perhaps gave me the illusion of control.

It was gradual.

From the time of his attic liberation, we were inseparable. The diary was back where I'd found it — rolled into its twin tubes, secured with twists of wire — and, with George on my knee, there was no fear of the contents' getting into the wrong hands. He was a card I kept close to my chest, out of sight only when he was in his box. His old home demolished, I put a handle on my Upside tuck box (which seemed appropriate — it *literally* had his name on it) and padded the interior with foam. With a needle, thread, and some matching green felt, I patched his blazer where the moths had done their worst. He looked perfectly presentable at the dinner table.

"It's so strange having George back down again," said Queenie, clinking an imaginary wineglass with her own, pleased to humour me in what she saw as an amusing eccentricity in cherished family tradition. "The cleaners did a nice job on that blazer."

"Hope they gave you a discount," said Reg. "Hardly seems fair to charge full price."

Expressionless, I rolled my last pea back and forth across the plate. We could natter on as normal about the price of dry cleaning, but there was only one question worth asking, and I didn't know it at the time. It was on the tip of my tongue. Small talk was impossible. Words were running out.

For the first time since anyone could remember, Frankie's dance card was empty until the regular Christmas knees-up. Her engagement with *West End Story* had ended acrimoniously. A Fisher always jumped, was never pushed, but the unscheduled departure left Frankie with time on her hands while Ricky tried and failed to pull a replacement rabbit from the hat.

A celebration, which coincided with my sixteenth birthday, welcomed her home, but the reunion meal, typically the most joyful of get-togethers, seemed theatrical, phony. I thought it was perhaps the unwelcome addition of Ricky at the family table. I felt distant, having to keep myself in check, to remember my lines. Frankie accepted my namesake without question, winking at me as though his presence were primarily for her benefit. I struggled to keep up amid anecdote and gossip, but the surface volume was too loud, like the dust and scratches on a 78. They didn't seem to hear me over the crackle — so I gave up and sat motionless, staring aimlessly into space, wondering who was standing at the top of the staircase in silhouette now, wearing the black hat and veil, posing with the cigarette holder.

"What's up, Georgie?" asked Frankie, who had been enumerating the shortcomings of the *West End Story* cast. "You're not your normal smiling self."

"There's two of 'im, for a start," said Ricky with a cackle.

"And both looking so handsome! Good seeing you back downstairs on Civvy Street, George. Anyway, glad to be rid of *them*," said Frankie, polishing off the previous conversation. "And there are some quite nice opportunities out there, right, Ricky?"

"We'll rustle something up," he said, unreassuringly.

Rustle something up? I had never heard Frankie speak of *opportunities*, only firm *offers*, alternatives between which she could choose with a wave of her magic wand. *Peter Pan* again or a tour of *Seven Brides*? Ding! The lesser option disappeared in a puff of smoke. An *opportunity* was demeaning: it implied an audition that allowed the possibility of rejection. As Ricky rattled on about changing tastes, it became clear that business was not all that it might have been. I said nothing.

And then it happened.

"What are you moping around for, Georgie?" Frankie curled an eyelash in the folding side-wing mirrors of the dresser that had been her father's, as she readied herself for Ricky to drive her into town for one of the auditions. Fisher women could chat unhindered through any facial contortion, whatever the factor of its difficulty, so makeup had always been a good time for stories and secrets. "Sit on my bed, like old times."

George and I plonked down in silence. He had sat here many times before, watching Joe prepare; I'd spent hours watching Joe's daughter. Backstage, in the infinite fun-house reflections, Frankie threw on the slap with aplomb, always finishing off with a celebratory cloud of fixing powder. The real world, however, where the view from the balcony mattered less than the subtle close-up, was more demanding. She mouthed instructions to herself — tweeze, conceal, brush, powder, blush, and line.

"Look at you two," she said, without moving her lips, as she bared her teeth to eradicate rogue lipstick with a determined little finger. "I remember sitting next to him with my dad: me on one knee, him on the other. They used to read me Beatrix Potter together in this very room. . . ." She gave a snippet in their two voices and fell into reminiscence about her childhood. I found myself avoiding eye contact at any mention of the war hero, an acrid taste at the back of my mouth. I fiddled around in George's hollow. ". . . And then I only saw him once more, when he came down to the Northleach house where I was staying the weekend with Evie. I was already in a few parts here and there, I think . . . '40, '41, yes. In fact, they've asked me to talk about Tommy Bright at a tribute, but I don't recall him liking children at all, and I shall probably have to make something up. . . . And that was the last time I saw my dad and George, both in their uniforms, heading off to be heroes. I can't remember much besides that and the noise of his motorbike. It's funny what you forget."

I wanted to tell her every detail: they had been playing pelmanism when her father came to the door; they drank tea and made daisy chains in the garden; she had told stories about the Bright Spark then too. The bleakness of my situation, the loneliness of the secret-bearer, took me by surprise: tell her any of that and she would have to know everything.

"That was the last time I saw Dad. I still have his letters, of course. . . ." She opened a drawer and took out the familiar box in which she kept the bundle of her father's letters. She read at random: "Don't imagine that the scene on the front has any connection with our present whereabouts, little miss — that's just to fool the enemy!" "Good luck in your next part, my darling girl. We'll hope they send a print out here for us." "Give my love to your mother; be good to her." Taking one look, and remembering what he had said in the diary, I saw what Frankie could never have suspected: none were from her father. They were forgeries, either Evie's or Queenie's, or at their behest. These were all the memories she had of him. And I could crush them in a second. I had to protect her.

Seeing my tears in the mirror, she stopped, tweezers poised uncertainly, smile disappearing with the dimming of her eyes. She took me in her arms, stroking my hair, without asking what was wrong. I could have stayed forever in her silence. Finally: "Georgie?" I shook my head. She started to cry too, laughing at herself in recognition of the fact that, though it was selfish to worry, her makeup remained a concern. She checked the time, a practicality neither of us could ignore. "What is it, darling? Is there anything wrong? Is it serious? You must tell me." She was perplexed that her mothering hadn't made the difference. I thought hard before I answered, too long for her. "In trouble? Ill? A girl? Something you want to talk to Reg about?" I shook my head. She considered a quick reapplication, tilting her head back to avoid further misfortune. "Good," she said, giving the word the full weight of conclusion. She shook her face out, testing the elasticity of her cheek with a disappointed harrumph, and decided where the damage limitation should begin. She marshaled her arms into a small purse for last-minute cosmetic manoeuvres, and presented herself to the mirror again, then to me. "How's the repointing?" She looked perfect. The doorbell rang, and she whispered the mildest profanity as she gathered accessories. "We'll talk about it later."

We wouldn't. She blew a kiss, to avoid unnecessary messing, and left us sitting on her bed.

"Knock 'em dead" were the last words I said.

*   *   *

It was just like the war: *careless talk costs lives*. The secrets felt safer that way: my eyes open, my mouth closed. And I felt better too — protecting them with my silence.

At first, it wasn't mentioned, as if I were avoiding exacerbating a sore throat. Frankie treated it as an elaborate joke between inverted commas for everyone's amusement. There was the occasional remark, but no one threw me against a wall and ordered me to make conversation. When it could no longer go undiscussed, the family was all sympathy.

"It was a big change leaving Malcolm Collins," Reg theorized. "Perhaps he'd rather go to another school."

"School!" Frankie thought the problem (assuming it could even be labelled a problem) would politely go away if ignored. "He's perfectly happy working with Brenda's lot, aren't you, Georgie?"

"Perhaps he's a little depressed," said Queenie. Would food be my cure?

Only Ricky hit the wrong note on a couple of occasions ("Still in Coventry, are we?"), for which he received Queenie's withering stare.

"I've been down in the dumps myself," Reg said considerately. "There's nothing wrong with being down in the dumps."

"Of course there isn't," said Frankie. "That's one thing, but not *depressed*."

And round, and round.

Work at Crystal Clear, however, went on unaffected. Frankie was right. I trusted Brenda, and the work suited me. I'd taken George in as soon as I'd found him.

"Creepy" was Brenda's verdict.

"A real antique!" said Tim. "But think about it: not much good to us down here, old son."

"Don't you believe it," said Roger, shaking his head as though he'd just been set up on *Candid Camera*. "I got our new selection from Daedalus, and the first movie is . . ." He flicked through a few sheets of paper. "*The Dummies of Doctor Diabolicus.* You couldn't make it up."

"Sounds *diabolical*," said George. It was unspoken policy not to comment on the quality of the movies to which we lent our expertise, but the remark was allowed, given the source.

My withdrawal made little difference as I stood beneath the screen and poured fizzy lemonade on the patch of tarmac to accompany the silent rippling of the sea on the shore. I'd never said much down there anyway, except to Brenda. Roger nicknamed me Harpo, and that was about it.

Work commenced on *Doctor Diabolicus,* a low-budget rip-off of the recently popular *Magic* with Anthony Hopkins, which had featured a mentally unbalanced ventriloquist whose astonishingly unattractive dummy, Fats, "talks him into" murdering his agent (and probably his girlfriend, Ann-Margret, too, though I slept through the end).

If George had now been able to write the second volume of his diary — *The Comeback Years,* a sequel no one could have predicted — he would have been horrified with the current state of ventriloquism. It had gone to hell.

A glorious Indian summer in the 1950s (when ventriloquism was so fashionable that Peter Brough's dummy Archie Andrews was voted "Most Popular Radio Personality") had eluded George entirely. TV had been bad news for the radio vents, their poor technique brutally exposed by a remorseless camera. The illusion was better in the audience's imagination, and Joe had been far ahead of his time in his quest for perfection. But no technique could help George now. He looked as old-fashioned as Narcissus had once seemed to him. He was lucky anyone wanted him out of the box at all. People no longer wanted to see a little schoolboy sitting on a grown man's knee.

The contemporary dummy of choice was an anthropomorphized cuddly toy — a huge yellow ostrich or a small white sheep, a massive crow or a cheeky monkey: theirs was a neon menagerie of Emus, Orvilles, and Nookies. Even Queenie had Mikey, her green astrakhan alien, a floppy mass of fur through which were discernible only two eyes, a mouth, and a dangling nose in technicolor orange. As Joe had predicted, the dummy had taken over in spectacular fashion.

The movies were responsible. Ever since *Dead of Night*, they had added spice to a tired idea by bringing centre stage the dynamic between ventriloquist and dummy, emphasizing the schizophrenic nature of the act, the violence latent in the frantic verbal sparring. When the audience could no longer suspend its disbelief, it was left with a man on stage, frustrated by, arguing with, committing violence on, himself. George, the chirpy Cockney schoolboy, became a malign midget, a devil doll, the ventriloquist's id. Perhaps the furry, flopsy friends made it all seem fun and harmless again. Once a religious mystery, Joe's sacred art, ventriloquism was now a creepy nostalgia act, a party trick on a par with juggling. Rarely seen on television, it survived only on the pier and at the children's party, those last refuges of old hat. It had been a very Eden, but now there was no return. Paradise was lost. No wonder people looked at us funny.

"Oi, Harpo!" Roger shouted when we were getting nowhere with *The Dummies of Doctor Diabolicus*, which featured (inevitably) a schoolboy not unlike George as one of the satanic ventriloquist's malevolent mannequins. "Stick him out here. We need some inspiration." George became our mascot.

I took my daily tube in to Crystal Clear, often returning in Brenda's car. She even encouraged me to let her give me some recreational, and illegal, driving lessons so, conversation now at a premium, we could occupy ourselves on the way home. She was unflappable, long-suffering: she taught driving as she stage-managed.

As the months went by, the central debate became whether I needed *help*. *Help*, however, required a clear admission that it was required (tantamount to a plea of guilty), and this would not yet willingly be given. Fishers had little truck with doctors and dentists, their instruments, invoices, and appointment books; rather Madame Arcati with her crystal ball and tea leaves than a psychiatrist. My retreat wasn't normal, yet I went to work, came home, watched TV, washed dishes, and generally remained a regular, if not vocal, member of the household. I hadn't ceased communication entirely. I hummed, I pointed, nudged, and tapped, all of which was incorporated into the daily routine. I just didn't chat.

"You don't mind going to see someone, do you?" asked Reg finally. The voice of reason spoke directly to me. He saw no stigma at all.

"He doesn't *need* to," said Frankie firmly. The very fact that it had been mentioned showed how worried they were, how changed I was.

"Perhaps he *wants* to. Unless he's planning to be the world's first silent ventriloquist act. . . ."

"A mime!" suggested Frankie in my cheerful defence.

"Look at him! It's time to *see* someone," said Reg. Frankie got up, thrust her chair under the table, and walked to the kitchen, but Reg was firm. "This has gone on too long."

As years before, I found myself unexpectedly moved by his concern, his unsentimental masculine common sense. I shrugged and nodded.

"All right, then, me old cock!" said Reg and clapped me on the shoulder.

Frankie popped back in with a look of relief, as though she had been complicit, hers a necessary role in his plan to bring me to my senses. I smiled, which she took to be thanks.

I had told myself I would be humouring them: *help* was useless. I knew full well why I wasn't talking; I didn't need someone to shuck me for the truth.

But when I shrugged and nodded, it was an elbow in my ribs. Whatever the reason, I was a shadow of the boy they knew. Sullen, sad, sluggish, silent: I needed help.

As I sat in a waiting room decorated with educational posters and children's storybooks. I tried not to speculate about Dr. Hill's other patients: the redheaded, harelipped eight-year-old whose appointment always preceded mine; the pretty ten-year-old who quietly read while her father listened to a tiny lisping portable radio through an earplug; the Indian boy whose mother talked at him only in his native language. And what on earth did they make of the sixteen-year-old perched on the small chair, with the ventriloquist dummy and the tin of rolling tobacco?

"Yes," said the doctor apologetically, surveying the scale model chairs in her empty waiting room as she saw me in. "There's a lack of reading material for grown-ups. I normally work with younger people." I was an anomaly, a case study.

A physical exam revealed nothing, despite my bad stomach and occasional nausea, both possible symptoms of the family of disorders that was Dr. Hill's area of expertise. To my family's surprise, she had encouraged me to bring George — Reg in particular had thought she would wrest him from me as soon as possible. George was rather larger than the dummies she generally liked to use in therapy, but since he was already implicated, she saw no reason to throw him out of the act. She liked to watch us together, and when, during the first session, she asked him directly, "How can I help you, George?" I answered through him, "Don't like to talk." I had never wanted to talk through him, only to have him about me, but it felt comfortable in her office.

She smiled and thanked him. "I knew you were here for a reason. Now, his grandmother tells me he gradually stopped talking after he found you, George?" George nodded. "Was there anything about you that upset him? Did you remind him of anything?" Her formal white technical coat was at odds with her sympathetic brown eyes. George shook his head. "Was there a particular reason that he stopped when he found you?" I didn't want to commit myself. I wondered for a moment whether to show her the diary, but I worried that word might leave the confessional. I nodded. "Good," she said. "Good."

At first, our conversations were one-sided, but she was used to that: she spoke, I answered with nods, shakes, and the odd word.

There was no emphasis whatsoever on *getting* me to talk. She allowed me to fall into silence whenever I wanted, while I tried to work out how she maintained her room at such a constantly comfortable temperature and looked at my tiny reflection darting in her fishbowl glasses. She asked me how ventriloquism worked, and George showed her the techniques for substitution, a D for a B and so on. She didn't push it, and that was that.

She asked me to keep a journal, full of praise even when I barely covered two pages. I hated the journal, hated even the word *I* on the page, but its effect on her was so startling that I made myself. I started using *we* with limited success. And so the weeks passed.

She asked me what I really enjoyed: I showed her my tobacco tin.

"I don't approve, and don't think I'm going to let you smoke in here, but you have to occupy your mouth with something, I suppose," she said. "Why did you start?" I showed her Don's old pewter ashtray, how its curve fitted my back pocket. Everyone around me smoked — Reg, the whole of Crystal Clear, even George — so I thought I'd give it a try. I laid my smoking kit out on the table: the ashtray, the tin, the lighter that fitted perfectly inside, and the dependably solid colour of the Rizla package. "You seem more addicted to the paraphernalia than the nicotine," she observed, but best of all was the patient ritual: the separation of the strands of tobacco, the allotment of the precise amount in the fold of the paper, the persuasive roll between thumb and index finger, and the tender lick along the top. From urge to ash, I could make a cigarette last an age.

"The difference between you and most of my patients is that you're in control of when you speak," she said. "It's as though, instead of hunger strike, you're on speech strike. Or should that be silence strike?" She caught me looking at her and smiled. "Have you given your family your demands?"

I saw how it appeared: me sitting there, holding on to my schooldays, having a schoolboy speak for me. She asked me to tell her when I was last happy, and to my own surprise, over the next weeks, I told her the story of Upside. Her encouragement was a kind persuader in that peaceful room, shelves lined with academic books, walls covered with children's drawings, a cassette recorder always running, but I certainly wasn't yet ready to take the act outside.

At the end of the Upside story, she handed me the shoe box of tapes, each marked only with my name and a number.

"Your dummy is good for you, George. You have to be careful about what you say. He slows the process down for you. Write these up for me," she said. "In the third person, like you're writing about someone else, or writing lines for an actor. Perhaps you'll remember other things too."

I liked the idea of my past written by someone else. I was starting from scratch and I couldn't cheat: there was no essay waiting in a desk elsewhere.

When she asked me about home, I wouldn't answer. Things had changed even since my first appointment. Reg and Queenie had given up on the parties; they were quite as happy to put their feet up. For mainly recreational reasons, Reg kept a fruit stall for a friend at the local market. Sometimes we coordinated the spoils of work: he'd contribute the veg. Queenie felt quite special.

Frankie found herself in forced retirement. It became clear that she was no longer considered a bankable lead, but that producers could imagine her in no other role. It was hard to say what had changed. Perhaps I had closed my eyes to a gathering recession. Ricky was rather too candid about it: peerless though she was in her favourite roles, she was still best remembered as a child star in those Bright Spark movies, an image she had not yet managed to shake. I hadn't thought of her career in this light. She wasn't a Hollywood star, of course, but I had always assumed she was exactly where she wanted to be. She had certainly never complained. But even in panto, until so recently her undisputed personal showcase, she wasn't inviolate — there was a new breed of principal boy, younger, better known, on TV, in the charts. When it was announced that next Christmas, she would

play not the *titular hero* (as Bernie would have said) but the good
fairy, the trend seemed irreversible. She had to tell the public a
new story, Ricky said, make a new *marketplace impression,* bring
herself up to date.

Queenie shuffled the blame in his direction: the alternatives
were too painful. Perhaps he didn't have his uncle's connections.
After all, he had rather fallen into the job. Everything was complicated by the fact that he was still *squiring* Frankie. Everyone
trod carefully around this awkward detail, a dog mess that might
not smell unless it was disturbed.

Finally, Frankie's lean spell came to an end. She was unexpectedly offered a part in a new sitcom, *Fish Out of Water,* playing one of the denizens of a seafront hotel run by an eccentric
spinster. This being TV, the alchemist's stone that transmuted
base careers, Ricky was insufferably pleased with himself. The
exteriors took her away on location to glamourous Leigh-on-Sea,
leaving me with Queenie and Reg for the first extended period
in months.

At dinner the night she left, we sat over Reg's fricassee, George
at my side as usual. I could hardly bear to look at my food. It was
time to speak. I wasn't ready to get back into the world of idle
chat immediately, but I couldn't ask with pen and paper.

"Queenie?" said George. Reg was startled by this guest-
speaking role, but Queenie didn't take her eyes from her plate.
"Did you write Frankie letters from her father in the war?" I
asked through my deputy. Even I was a little surprised — I was
using a voice only slightly different to my own. She was happy to
hear me talk, but her sad smile told me everything.

"Oh, Georgie. Is that it? Evie arranged for them," she said.
"Letters home from the war hero. Sad, isn't it? Her father could
never have managed them himself. How did you know?"

"It was obvious. She doesn't know, does she?"

"It's really all she has of him. It would be hard to tell her, particularly for me. Evie could have, perhaps, but not me. It would
seem a kind of revenge."

"Don't, love," said Reg. "Don't."

We sat in the tentative silence of a shared secret. Queenie finally reached out for my hand. "Welcome back, Georgie."

When Frankie rang later that night, Queenie announced a breakthrough. She held the receiver at arm's length as Frankie shrieked.

With George, I could ask questions, and I was unlikely to be asked many in return: he was my act.

Dr. Hill was delighted. Outside her office, I may have been talking only in the third person, and through an antiquated automaton, but I was talking.

"What did he ask?"

I told her.

"And were they forged?"

"Yes." I saw my next step. I was safe in her confidence. I had invited her question.

"Is this something that he found out through you, George?"

"Yes," I said.

And, placing him on the floor, I removed the two manuscripts and handed them over.

The interiors for Frankie's sitcom, *Fish Out of Water,* brought her back to town. She insisted we come to the first studio taping, securing a car to drive us to Shepherd's Bush and, once inside, pink clip-on passes that gave us carte blanche.

Though the episode was only thirty minutes, the taping itself, counting from the warm-up man, took four and a half hours. "Energy!" he shouted between his jokes, pumping his fist like a victorious boxer. "You're having a *good time!*" Our party avoided one another's gaze. It was one thing to boo and hiss with the kids at Christmas, quite another to be berated into laughter by a sweaty club comedian in ill-fitting black tie; but we were there for Frankie.

I had seen her in good and bad, but never coarse. Much of the leering blue was aimed at Frankie, the divorcée with the seafront room ("I'd like to see down *her* front") and no punch lines of her own, although she had been provided with what seemed to be a catchphrase, used twice: "Very salty!" Her departure put its own wiggling full stop on the last scene as the camera zoomed in. I could imagine the accompanying music — piccolos and tympani. The scarcity of arm squeezing and sideways glances told me Queenie was similarly underwhelmed.

Pink passes were herded into an antiseptic cubicle, where curls of crisp paper-thin ham protruded from white crusted sandwiches set in wreaths of withered lettuce, to be washed down with flat champagne. Frankie made straight for us, fielding compliments as she fought her way through. "Well? Think it'll be a hit?"

Queenie and Reg made enthusiastic noises. It was a pity I had George with me, since his absence might have spared me an opinion. "Very salty!" said George, and everyone laughed.

Our party mingled, and I saw this as an excuse to test the power of my pink pass. A red glow drew me round the corner and down a corridor to some double doors at which a uniformed guard, lost in the magpie-like admiration of an extravagant silver wristwatch at odds with his BBC-issue attire, stood next to a sign that announced, STAR'S ON SATURDAY WITH BRUCE STAR and a large red warning: TRANSMISSION. The guard, who was considering the watch's many functions at various distances as it glittered in the fluorescent strip lighting, snapped from his trance as though I had caught him stealing. Eyeing George suspiciously, he snarled, "What do you want?" I said nothing. "I'm not a guard, I'm an actor. So, no offence, but unless you want to make an unscheduled appearance on TV, you might want to bugger off."

At a signal from his walkie-talkie, the guard barked at me to keep my distance, and assumed a pose of watchful attention. He seemed to be counting down to himself, taking a calming breath in preparation for whatever lifted off at zero. One side of the double door was flung open, revealing a man's silhouette against the bright lights within, a camera hot on his heels; beyond, the shimmer, heat, and buzz of the studio. I stood back from the glare, not wanting to ruin the actor-guard's moment of glory.

The silhouette saluted the guard, who returned the greeting, his sleeve sliding up his arm to reveal the silver watch. With a triumphant gesture, the silhouette, dressed dashingly in entertainer's old-fashioned formal, his magnificent rich burgundy-lined cape unfurling around him, brandished the guard's wrist towards the camera, which had ventured on its tracks to the very edge of the studio. The house band played a climactic chord, and the audience burst into a prolonged round of applause. Removing the watch from the guard with a private wink of apology, the silhouette turned to close the doors. I saw his face for the first time.

He was in his early forties, his hair slicked down and parted to the left, his neatly cropped black beard hiding a face creased with character, his makeup glistening from the heat beyond. While hidden from the cameras, he took a moment to dab his forehead with a voluminous white handkerchief he produced from somewhere inside his jacket.

It was then he saw us.

The applause continued relentlessly behind him, and the voice of Bruce Star announced his name, Tower, inviting him back into the studio. Not knowing what else to do, I smiled, throwing in a wink from George, expecting this to be the end of a short and meaningless interaction. But still the man stared, first at George, then at me.

The guard, at another short blast on his walkie-talkie, pushed the right door closed. The bearded man, as if waking from a dream to realize he was in the middle of a performance, lurched around to acknowledge his applause, dropping the white handkerchief. Bowing, he strode back inside, and the guard closed the left door behind him. The whole incident had taken no more than twenty seconds. George and I were left staring at the fallen handkerchief, lost for words.

The actor sniffed, rubbing his wrist where the timepiece had so recently been. It was all in a day's work, he implied, and the handkerchief was beneath his consideration — such treasures fell his way the whole time — though it was mine if I wanted a souvenir. I stuffed the handkerchief into George's top pocket and made my way back to the party, where Reg and Queenie were waiting for Frankie, who struggled back in laden with wardrobe, juggling bags. "All aboard. Should we take some of those sandwiches? They don't look terribly good. How were they?"

"Very salty" got us another laugh.

I examined the handkerchief at home. In detective stories from Holmes to Marlowe, handkerchiefs were invariably monogrammed, hats could be identified by the manufacturer's mark, and matchbooks always had addresses: criminals could be condemned on such scanty evidence. In real life, a clean white handkerchief was more than likely a blank slate that told you nothing. But not this one. I thought I had felt something, and on further inspection, I found a small triangular pocket in one corner, from which I pulled out a neatly folded playing card: the eight of clubs. From this I could deduce one thing, the one thing that I already knew: it wasn't a handkerchief. It was a magician's silk.

Dr. Hill's reaction to the diaries surprised me. I had expected sympathy in reward for my trust.

"I thank you very much for sharing this with me. I know you feel you need to keep it private . . . and it's always a great thrill to meet an author," she added, referring to my namesake with a smile. "It's a very sad record, but I'm not sure I see why you feel such a strong need to protect your family from this diary." She dismissed the papers with a careless flick. "I think your reaction might be disproportionate to the contents."

I gave her a quizzical look.

"Well, your grandmother seems to have moved on successfully from her relationship with your grandfather. She's happily married again, right? Would she be worried about what Joe said about her in his diary all those years ago?"

She paused and eyed me. I had a mental image of an onion being peeled.

"I imagine Joe projected onto your grandmother certain negative attributes that were in fact associated with his mother. It would have made their relationship impossible. Queenie could have been anybody, behaved any way, and it would have made no difference: he had to run. But Queenie obviously wasn't so distraught that she couldn't find happiness elsewhere."

Quite the reverse, I thought.

"Do you really think she'd be upset now?"

I thought about this.

"And though it would be sad for your mother in some ways, I would think the diary might well give her some longed-for insight into the father she never knew."

"But Frankie's letters!" I said.

She didn't even look up when I spoke. "Ah, yes, the letters. It might be disappointing for her to know they weren't really from him, but she's no longer the fragile child they were addressed to. She's a grown woman who has survived a long time with the loss of her father. That's her burden, not yours."

Queenie and Frankie certainly had survived, even thrived without Joe. So what was I protecting? I felt empty, as though I hadn't eaten for a week.

"And I think deep down you know that your silence isn't really necessary to protect them. But the diary was illuminating. I was particularly struck by some similarities between you and your grandfather. Would you say you and Joe have anything in common?"

I hadn't been expecting this. I shrugged and waggled George.

"Absolutely. You have in common the author of this diary. It's interesting that you chose to reenact Joe's method of talking through him. Perhaps, like your grandfather, you felt that no one was listening to you and you had to disguise your voice in order to be heard. My worry is that you will repeat some of his other patterns of behaviour. By his own account, Joe appears to have been a solitary and melancholy man, and I'd like to guard against you becoming the same."

I felt like the redhead with the harelip.

"My guess is that Joe wasn't able to trust his mother, and so he wasn't able to form a loving, trusting relationship with another woman. Do you think this is true of you?"

I shook my head.

"Do you have a girlfriend?"

I shook my head again.

"If Joe did mistrust women, it's possible that men would have seemed safer and more nurturing in comparison. And yet where is Joe's father? Barely mentioned in this diary: 'little more than a presence.' With no male role model and an overbearing mother, Joe must have been ambivalent: perhaps he tried to love this man who claimed, however humourously, to have modelled himself on Joe's mother. But what's relevant here is that Joe wasn't able to be an attentive, loving father because he didn't have one himself. Do you see why that's important?"

The world paused. Acid rose in the back of my throat. I swallowed, but it wouldn't go away.

"Tell me about your father."

"He's dead."

"Yes, but tell me about him."

I shook my head. I remembered when I had imagined him an astronaut, a politician, an explorer; the Father of a Thousand Faces; a twisted wreck at the Abbey Curve.

"Will you tell me anything about him?"

I wouldn't answer. I wouldn't speak at all.

"In your own time," she said.

Saturdays found me on my knees in our local library, where silence was requested and always welcome, researching names from the diary in the modest Nostalgia subsection of the Entertainment holdings. A selection of very old pensioners tutted as they hobbled towards me. They represented the right target readership, but their interest lay in the large-print novels beyond.

Echo Endor was easily found (as was her son), Bobbie Sheridan all but forgotten. I finally located him as I scanned the forbidding columns of close type in a directory of entertainment war casualties. The cursory reference "Female Impersonator and Ventriloquist," with dates, perhaps his only gravestone. Even his theme song had proved unfaithful to his memory, posthumously attaching itself to another performer.

Bobbie was privileged to be a footnote. Most of the other acts had gone forever, bowed and not returned for an encore, tap-danced into eternity and left no footprints. For their final trick, the magicians had made themselves disappear. The index to the random memoirs of a retired comedian occasionally took me by surprise: "Tubby Jeans, that irrepressible dresser and bon viveur, died in Costa Rica in 1962, having made his fortune in coffee." I searched in vain for obscurer names, but these books had nothing to tell me of Toots Lowery or Jack Heath. They had thrived only forty years ago, galvanized the nation through a war, yet now their whole world of entertainment was dead, done away by Mr. Television in the lounge with a microphone. Variety had lingered before being put out of its misery by the game show — the only vehicle left for an all-rounder. All that remained were the yearly panto, the odd TV show (like Bruce Star's), the seaside summer season, and the forgotten corner of a branch library that was forever Music Hall. If I'd found anyone alive, I'd have written; perhaps they'd have been cheered by a reunion with their old comrade George. But there was nothing for me here. I was just joining the dots, purely for my own satisfaction, to pass the time, to keep myself occupied, to avoid taking the necessary steps.

When I had exhausted the local library's sparse selection, Brenda, who had watched the parade of memoirs, biographies, and photo histories that accompanied me with increasing amusement, suggested the British Television and Film Library on Charing Cross Road. Here I felt more scholarly as I dialled my way across sheets of microfiche. Bobbie Sheridan, real name Robert Plissey: three contemporary articles, a number of mentions in brochures ("the Fairy Godmother of Innuendo!") and handbills (available in copy form only), and an essay in a university press publication called *Homosexuality in British Pre-War Entertainment,* a book so dry that the title was followed by a colon and *Five Case Studies.* Toots Lowery, yes; Duke Edwardes, yes; Max Large, yes. I looked for my family, as you will, and amid the expected columns of articles on Vox, Echo, Joe, Frankie, even Sylvia (Sylvia! I'd never managed to send her that postcard, though I had it written so perfectly in my head . . .), I was shocked to find *me*. Of course, it was my namesake.

You could find anyone in the BTFL. So: why not him?

I remembered the first time I'd seen that front page of *The Express:* the barrier rope, the oil drums and straw bales. The librarian, thinking it a treat for the curious nine-year-old, had taken me into a cavernous basement, where he showed me how the newspapers were filed, demonstrating how easy it was to find the specific date I had requested.

At the BTFL, ten years of *The Express* careened in front of my eyes on microfiche. And there was the picture again: still no evidence of a human. Last time, I'd left the library and, ashamed, told no one. Now I felt nothing.

It was nothing to do with me at all.

Continual conflicts, none unwelcome, meant I was able to keep deferring my next trip to Dr. Hill.

Three weeks after my trip to the library, Reg, Queenie, and I settled down in front of the television to catch my possible guest appearance on *Star's on Saturday.*

"Right," said Star after the first break, smirking as he clapped to signal a change of mood. "Illusionist, ventriloquist, magician, mesmerist — he's got the lot, and if he doesn't have it, he will by the end of the show; so check your pockets! He had my watch at rehearsal!" (He regretfully showed us his bare wrist.) "And I have to get it back somehow, so here we present to you, Tower!"

Joe's books had never considered magic on TV, where, since camera trickery can fake anything, it was the magician's extra burden to reassure the audience at home that he would not stoop so low. The new breed of conjurers exploited the humour of this irony in their patter — "This seems impossible, but it isn't, and I'll show you how I do it" — and much conjuring had gone the way of comedy. Elegance had disappeared with the arrival of the cheeky chap. Evidently, no one had told Tower.

Dry ice crawled across a stage dimmed moody purple as atmospheric electronic music piped in. On strode the bearded Tower, a gaunt vampire against the stark background, the black bat wings of his cape flapping above the dense wreath of fog. He eased into a stylish, if predictable, routine, circa 1940; first, rings, chained, then effortlessly freed. From a hat, he produced a dove, which just as quickly became white silks, like the one I had in my pocket, bundling from his sleeves. These silks transformed into a white parachute, floating elegantly to the floor. He paused only for applause, saying nothing.

"'Struth! Smooth, isn't he?" enthused Reg.

"Very nice. Very old-fashioned," said Queenie approvingly. It was just her cup of tea: the same kind of tricks Joe had done, performed by a man roughly the same age he had been, in the same clothes. Tower picked out a particular audience member, whom he beckoned to the stage, firmly grabbing his wrist and depositing him on Star's sofa. *Plant*, I thought.

"Hello!" said Star, with the scripted panic of the calm showman. "Welcome to my show. Well, I *say* that. It *was* my show; I'm not sure whose show it is anymore!" There followed much business about whether the guest was Peter from Bilborough or Bill from Peterborough, the innocently awkward comedy of which caused me to revise my cynical opinion of his status.

Out came a fresh pack of playing cards, for the trick that I felt sure was meant to climax with the eight of clubs. And perhaps it would — the man was a magician, after all. The gist was: Tower would telepathically communicate the identity of Peter/Bill's chosen (and replaced) card to Star, who, despite the fact that neither he nor the magician had seen this card, would identify it on a piece of paper.

Midway through Tower's studied impression of thought transference, as he drummed the fingers of one hand dramatically on his forehead (his other hand posed Napoleonically between waistcoat and jacket, up to no good), the magician interrupted his own card trick (*misdirection,* it was clear) to reveal the reappearance of Star's watch on the host's wrist. To everyone's surprise (even, apparently, Tower's) this watch belonged to Peter, who was dumbfounded to have it returned before he had known it was gone. Star seemed genuinely excited: "Where's *my* watch? Has it been stolen?"

Tower, seemingly on an inspiration, marched over to the double doors, threw them open, saluted the fake guard, and retrieved Star's watch, to the audience's massive approval. But the magician did not linger in the doorway as he had in real life. Thanks to the magic of the cutting room, he immediately returned the watch to Star with a bow of apology. He was back at the table without the eight of clubs, as I fingered the corner of the missing card in my pocket guiltily.

"Confident, Peter? I'm not," said Star.

Tower pointed at Star with both index fingers, as if to say, *Now!* The host did as he was told and put the piece of paper into the envelope that Tower had provided.

"Eight of clubs!" I had George say.

"Go on!" said Reg. "You'll be lucky."

I shrugged.

Tower picked up the envelope and handed it to the guest. "Eight of clubs!" said Peter, nodding in wonder as he led the audience in mad applause.

"Eight of clubs!" squawked Reg, as though I had turned water into wine. I considered the casual production of the card from my pocket. "Eight of bleedin' clubs! Queenie!" He needed impartial confirmation.

"He was at the filming, Reg," said his independent observer.

"Oh yeah, course you were," said Reg, deflated. "That's cheating, that."

"It's all cheating," she confirmed.

"Incredible," said Star as the applause died down. "But where *is* the eight of clubs?"

In my pocket.

But a good magician always has a Plan B.

"I've got it!" shouted a voice somewhere in the television studio. Tower immediately focused attention to the left of the audience by the double doors, as the camera made a halting search in that direction for the culprit.

"Hold on," said Star, thrilled with this dramatic turn of events. "Live television as it happens! Maybe it's that thieving security guard!"

"Over here!" shouted the voice. "It's here!" Star and Tower followed a movement with their eyes. My heart started to beat faster: it was as though Tower had thrown his voice into me. It was, after all, I who had the card, I who knew how he did it. There was a commotion by the side of the stage, and Tower strode over, confident he had cornered his prey. With his back to the audience, he lifted the wings of his cape as though trapping someone in his net.

He turned around, raised himself to his full height, facing the camera, mouth shut. "I've got it!" said a voice that seemed to come from somewhere inside his mouth. It spoke again, more quietly: "I've got it!" Tower swallowed, smiled, and looked down at his stomach, from which there was a tiny final pianissimo peep: "I've got it."

He conducted the orchestra in a climactic chord, as Star announced him: "Tower! Illusionist supreme! And he's appearing at the Magic Castle every Saturday and Sunday this month. Ladies and gentlemen, the Mysterious Mr. Tower!" The audience roared its approval.

"That bloke was good!" said Reg, as the volume doubled for the adverts. "Couldn't see *you*, George. Lucky, mind. Everyone would have thought it was you heckling. What did you think, love?"

"Bit like seeing a ghost!" Queenie laughed. "Just like the old days. I know how he signalled that eight of clubs; same way we used to."

That was basic mesmerism from my grandfather's books — but I knew how Tower had done practically everything. There was no wonder it reminded her of the old days.

What left its mark, however, was not the tricks, their failure and victorious rescue, nor the silent presentation that had been in such perfect harmony with his sophisticated old-fashioned charm. It was the unintended coup de théâtre: when he threw his voice, no one was expecting him to speak at all, so no one suspected him. The camera, and the audience, looked where his eyes looked: the illusion had worked. In no more than fifteen minutes, the audience had been given a history lesson in twentieth-century conjuring, climaxing in a remarkable piece of reanimation that had caught everyone, including me, by surprise: for one tiny moment, to the wonder of all, ventriloquism had lived again. We had heard the distant voice. It was we who had seen a ghost.

And that was when I knew, though I couldn't work out how it was possible. I knew.

One thing was certain: I would return Tower's handkerchief at the Magic Castle.

Things had gone quiet at Crystal Clear after the back lot guignol of *Doctor Diabolicus.* Horror season passed, and the next autumn presented a dull series of cold war thrillers: footsteps on gravel, gunshot, the squeal of tires, and sharp blows with blunt instruments. Lunches were spent in the pub as normal. Perhaps it looked funny, me reading with my pint, my rollies, and George — but I minded my own business, and no one bothered me.

"Need a lift, George?" asked Brenda at the end of our Saturday, peering out at the shroud of grey drizzle. She sat idling the engine until I gave in, putting my box on the backseat. "Home?" I shook my head. "Well, where shall I take you? You'll have to tell me."

I pointed straight ahead with both index fingers, just as Tower had denoted the card to his host. She drove. "Hope that new show works out well for your mum. Be nice to see her back where she belongs." There was silence, as there was apt to be, and I gesticulated second right. "This isn't really my way home, you know. Sir, wher*ever* are you taking me?" We inched up Tottenham Court Road as she nattered on. Finally, one more right, and I made the sound of brakes. She stopped outside the Magic Castle and peered up at the awning. "Here? Doing your audition?"

I wanted to thank her, so I leaned over to give her a kiss on the cheek. As she turned, I foresaw an awkward exchange where we now had to avoid each other's lips, but this didn't happen. She stayed where she was, moved a fraction towards me, and I found myself kissing her. Her lips were pillowy and wet: I didn't pull back. Closing her eyes (I was far too surprised to close mine), she kissed around the perimeter of my lower lip, until second thoughts made her sit back.

"Sorry," she said, a chastened schoolgirl giggling at herself. Everything about her was generous — her laugh, her smile, even her age. I shook my head to dispel any worries, pleased that I hadn't unwittingly offended her, surprised that my first kiss had come from this unexpected source, a woman I had known since I was fourteen. I leaned over and kissed her again, once, briefly, finally. She sighed as though she could fall asleep there and then, gave me a rather sad look as I got out, and put the car back in gear. It had started to pour.

I looked down at my side and panicked. I wanted to shout at the top of my voice, but I felt momentarily seasick. As she pulled away, I stepped into the road and banged on the boot of her car. She slammed on the brakes and wound down the window. There was a polite toot of the horn from the car behind. I pointed at George's case in the backseat.

"Forget something?" The car behind honked again, and she had to shout to be heard over the traffic and rain, which made it sound less teasing than she had intended. "Oh, shut up!" she shouted over her shoulder. "Go round!" I stood in the rain with the box in my hand, signalling to the driver, whose horn now brayed continually, to pass. "That would have made a short audition. See you Tuesday."

I was getting soaked to the skin as I waved her off. I could still feel the weight of her lips on mine, the vegetable taste of her lipstick. The rest of the evening could hold no surprises.

I made for the backstage door.

The moment you walk in the front of a theatre, you sign an

agreement to be a part of the herd — backstage access will be strictly limited, monitored; permission will be required. Tonight of all nights, that wasn't a precedent I wanted to set. If Fisher genes had taught me anything, it was how to pass through a stage door unnoticed, or rather, to be perfectly well noticed but to be admitted. I stood a little taller, lifted George's box in a rather arrogant gesture ("You know I'm important and you can see I'm in a rush"), and suddenly found myself beyond the limited security at the Magic Castle. I casually walked the length of the deserted corridor and found Tower's dressing room at the far end nearest the stage. Taking stock of my bedraggled appearance in the mirror outside his door (my soaking hair, my just-kissed lips), I scribbled on a scrap of paper that I slipped into George's top pocket. Too wet to wait, I knocked.

"Avanti!" came the invitation. It was just like when the interrogators slap the suspect in one of those espionage movies — would he give himself away with some Bolshevik expletive?

Mr. Tower was sitting in an armchair, reading a newspaper. "Ciao?" he said. "Posso aiutarla? Can I help? Do I know?" I made a little bow, but he couldn't place me. "Ah, you are surprised I am Italian?" I wasn't at all surprised. He sipped on a whiskey, not yet convinced there was reason to rise. "Meester Tower, they call me here. The Eengleesh no like, eh, foreign magi, magician." He laughed urbanely. "Neither the French. So in England, Meester Tower; in France, Monsieur LaTour; in Germany, Herr Turm. You understand. Tower, at your service." I hadn't even considered the coincidence of the name. He bowed the same fraction he had on television. Even offstage, his behaviour suited his clothes. "An autograph?"

There was nothing else for it but to play my trump card. I opened the box, and as I produced George, Tower nodded. "Sì, in the studio at Shepherd's Bush!"

"Yes," said George. "We came to return the silk." Again, the illusionist, smiling in silent amusement, could not take his eyes from us. "And the eight of clubs. Hope it didn't ruin the act." Tower made the uniquely Italian gesture that said it did not matter. "You dropped it on the floor in your . . . surprise. After all, it was the first time you'd seen me in some while."

This he ignored, walking towards us so he could look closer, a prospective buyer examining the goods. "Yes. Marvellous. Romando, certo. I might be interested in buying; this is why you are here, yes? I can make a generous offer." He walked to a desk and sat down. From his case he removed a chequebook.

"No, no," said George. "I'm not for sale! I'm not a present. I'm a way of life!" There was a moment's silence. "Guess my name."

"How can I know?"

"You know! Do a little mezzermerism."

"You tease me, Meester . . . er . . ."

"Guess my name!" I didn't want to put his ability on the spot, but I felt he was in a strong position to hazard a guess. "Look. I've written it down on a bit of paper. You guess it. It's in the top pocket of my blazer."

"George?" he said.

George and I looked at each other as though completely dumbfounded. "You're a genius, Herr, Monsieur, Mister, Signore! Look in my top pocket."

"Very amusing," said Tower, though he was evidently not enjoying floundering after the motive for our visit.

"Aren't you going to look?"

"I don't need to. I'm sure you are right."

"But it's disappointing if you don't look. Like the end of your trick on TV the other night. Anyway, how did you know?" He didn't answer. "Did you ever know a boy called George?"

He thought hard about this. "No."

"No?" Only a very proud man would deny it. I knew it was him: his bizarre reaction when he had first seen us loitering in the corridor, coupled with the silent mystery of his act, and the specific shuffles and tricks identical to those in my grandfather's books; now the Italian, the name, his age. There could be no doubt.

"No." He had recovered himself and was firm in his denial. "No. It was obvious, the name George. For the first, Romando made many beautiful dummies, and many were called George. Any scholar can know this. For the second," he added with a self-deprecating shrug, "I am mesmerist, mind reader."

"So, you are saying you don't know me?" George and I were a little upset. It wasn't how I had envisioned this reunion. "Would you recognize me better in uniform?"

"Your Romando is very beautiful. You know I am collector and I make my offer to buy. You are not for sale. You talk only through your dummy. I don't know you." He sat down and opened the newspaper again.

"You don't know me?" George asked again.

"No. No."

"I'm going to have to ask three times for obvious reasons."

"I must ask you to leave this private dressing room. Thank you, sir. I didn't know your name."

"My name, as you well know, is George. You can find me here." I handed him his silk, into the small pouch of which I had folded an official Crystal Clear business card with our name scrawled instead of Roger's. With an imitation of his curt bow, I made for the door. "Good-bye, Signore Ettore Ansalone." I'm sure his name was commonly available, so this shouldn't have shocked him. "Thanks for the dead squirrel and the guinea pig."

The surprise I saw at that moment was something Ansalone would have seen many times in the eyes of those he *mesmerized*. He knew it was a trick — it was all cheating — but he didn't know how it was done. This couldn't be the real George, could it? And how could we know these stories? In a second, he recovered himself, but he spoke with an air of apology. "I do not understand. I say good-bye."

But he did understand. George winked one last time. Tower had already returned to *Corriere Della Sera*.

The rain convinced me to stay for the early show. This time I bought a ticket at the box office and was ushered in the front door. Offered a stage-side table, I demurred, opting instead for one at the back, out of the lights, where he would never offer me a card, never even know I was there.

*   *   *

The first episode of *Fish Out of Water* aired on the holiday Monday. Frankie's offhand description of the job as "a paycheque" was a first. This epithet had only previously been used to disparage underachieving costars.

Unexpectedly, the show wasn't the fiasco we had feared. The gags flew by, leaving barely a moment for your groan, as Frankie hammed and wiggled, occasionally proclaiming, "Very salty!" to canned laughter amped to a volume that bore no relation to our exhausted studio response. Ricky celebrated with a tedious running commentary and toasted the moment in self-congratulation. The relief that Frankie was emerging unscathed, combined with the bubbles, left us all light-headed.

For the pursuant promotional chat show appearances, Ricky stipulated that she re-present herself, in elegant evening wear, as an attractive mature actress. The pinnacle was a celebrity game-show appearance, where she covered herself in glory, winning a host of prizes for her civilian partner. The public didn't know it — none of these spots had yet aired — but Frankie was back.

This return to the public eye was not on her terms, however. Recast in a certain light by *Fish Out of Water,* she had been offered a movie that she wouldn't want us to see, an "upmarket adult sex comedy." The project had Ricky's full endorsement. He had put all his eggs in Frankie's basket — their personal relationship had alienated other clients — and the sure way of making his percentage was to keep her in work.

Though Frankie asked George and my opinion, she was defensive when it was given and abruptly changed the subject with a disparaging remark about Dr. Hill. Ricky later took me aside, accusing me of making her life difficult. He knew we thought him a poor replacement for his uncle, a situation further muddled by their relationship: dinners were frosty. When her career had run itself, there had been no real need for any greater force than Good Old Desmond, calling his pals to fill her calendar, booking her two years in advance, ferrying her around, checking arrangements, writing the cheques, and doling out pocket money. But she had been in a bubble of Des's making too long, and without his old-school influence, things had gone wrong.

No one was looking after Frankie now. Ricky didn't have her best interests at heart; Queenie and Reg were too happy in their nest. Evie had done it once, at the expense of Sylvia. But now it was up to me.

Sylvia. I had never managed to write to her. In my head, I'd had it phrased perfectly, but on paper my sympathy looked flimsy. And I had a question for her: a question I couldn't ask Frankie, that Queenie couldn't answer. It was on the tip of my tongue.

After some debate, Reg gave me the address they had.

I wanted her to know that I knew. I would have wanted her to do the same for me.

Crystal Clear was boisterous in its praise for *Fish*, congratulating me on Frankie's behalf. "Harpo!" Roger kept calling through the headphones without the least excuse. "Very salty!"

If I had been expecting any awkwardness from Brenda after our kiss, I misjudged her. What I had previously taken to be friendliness and sympathy — her open smile, her attention to my reading matter, the driving lessons, the lifts — was now revealed as a flirtation of which I had been quite ignorant. Her first look told me that she had, like me, let the memory linger over the weekend. After a day of self-conscious propriety, she offered me my usual ride home, casually asking if I wanted a quick drink. The moment we were in the car, we kissed. Her breasts pushed against my chest, our only obstacle the hand brake. "We're not going to your place, are we?" she asked, the drink forgotten. "Mine, then?"

I was a mess of thoughts, excited, nervous.

"Everything OK? Just say if there's a problem." She reached over for my hand, and I realized that she was nervous too. I started to worry about practicalities: how stupid I would look, contraceptives (if, when, how), what time was too late to come home.

"Don't forget George," she said as we parked. "Not going to get much out of you without him, am I?"

Her apartment was done in the same colourful, bold designs she wore, patterns (I regretted) that had once been a little joke between Frankie and me. A bottle of wine appeared from the fridge, and she deliberately placed George next to me on the sofa.

"*Someone's* going to have to whisper in my ear." I liked the way she teased, but I waved her away, picked him up unceremoniously (with a muffled "Help! Help!"), and let the lid fall. I couldn't stop myself thinking of the last time George had been confronted with this situation and felt bad for all of us, particularly Queenie.

"No three-way? Very cosy." She sat beside me, knees together. At the same awkward moment, we sipped from our wineglasses. "George, I know this is a little strange . . ." She left a brief pause before adding, ". . . because of work and everything. But I'm not after anything big. I'm happy to be friends."

I let my body fall towards her. If I had been expecting resistance, there was none, and I found myself horizontal on top of her, my face sliding on her dress. This was how we stayed, communicating only through minute finger movements. She stroked my hair, and I traced the patterned surface of her bra. I was too gingerly to take the plunge, to explore the depths; due to the nature of the ensemble, the only possible access was from below.

After a few minutes of pleasant impasse and limbo, a lull I had no idea how to convert into frenzy, she extricated herself by silent mutual consent, going to the kitchen, where she arranged an irrelevant tray of crackers. A familiar Polaroid camera from Crystal Clear, one of the ones we used to record "sonic continuity," sat on the kitchen table. She smiled. "Want to take a picture? Document the setup?" she asked. I nodded and had her stand in front of the closed curtains. "Shall I smile?" We watched intently as the picture developed, crackers sitting ignored before us, disco revolving on the crackly stereo.

"Oh, I look awful," she said and tried to grab it, but I held fast. She didn't at all. She looked as though she were just about to take her clothes off. "Let's throw that one away, take another."

I shook my head as she tried to snatch it again. "It's not leaving here, that's for sure." She lunged. I shook my head and ran away as she screamed. She thought she had me cornered behind the sofa, but I leaped over it, bouncing once on the cushions, and sought sanctuary in the only room available: her bedroom.

"Isn't he bold?" She stood at the doorway in a parody of seduction. "What do I have to do to get that photo off you, George?" I lay on the bed. "Want to take another?" she said. I shook my head. "Are you sure?"

In one movement, she pulled the dress over her head. Problems evaporated: her dress could be either entirely on or entirely off, and it was now lying lifeless on the floor, as though the wicked witch had just melted from it. Brenda bit her bottom lip and threw a defensive arm over her bra; then, looking away for a moment, she let her arm fall. Her eyes met mine. Even without her dress, underwear covered much of her body. With the light of the sitting room behind her, she was a painting in the National Gallery, luxurious in the extreme, lavishly upholstered, her breasts cradled by a mauve-and-pink bra, her white Rubenesque tummy puffing out above her knickers, her waist with the lazy curve of a guitar. Who would have dared imagine what lay beneath her clothes? Who would have thought her so beautiful? Her manner in no way advertised this perfection.

"No more photos?" she asked, smiling. I shook my head and started to get out of my trousers. "Hey," she said. "Stop." I sat back down on the bed. "Don't do as I do; do as I say." Just before she joined me, she asked, "Light on or off?"

I could think of nothing worse than not being able to see her.

"Yes, on," she said. "What have we got to hide?"

I woke continually throughout the night, unable to get over the novelty of the situation, but sleep finally came. In the morning I opened my eyes to find Brenda on her way out. She kissed my head and whispered: "I know you're not coming in today. Let yourself out. See you Thursday."

I slept a little longer and rose to find everything neatly tidied away. On the kitchen table was the Polaroid, beneath which she had written: "It's the quiet ones you have to watch out for . . . Love, Brenda." I looked through her zigzag dress as though it weren't there.

I took the tube to Victoria, where I got the train south, a strange ride that shunted one way into Eastbourne and then reversed out again, which made the last part of the journey feel like a long ignominious retreat. I was in a daze, lost in the uncertain chronology of the previous night. From time to time I pinched myself by surreptitiously checking the photo, as though its public display would be offensive, as though anyone else could see what I saw. Opposite me, a man read *The Sun*. He turned his page, and I was confronted with the bland toothy smile of a Page Three girl.

Hastings Station smelled of piss, and mocking seagulls swooped above before settling in the rafters. I walked down an alley at the side of the station past a telephone box with every pane smashed out, receiver dangling limp, paper shredded all over the floor. It seemed rude to ignore the sea, so I walked along the front, beyond the closed amusement arcades, before a tiring walk uphill to the park. I began to regret George's weight, and stopped at a playground to roll myself a loose cigarette that burned out quicker than I had intended. Two children played on the swings, screaming and laughing, laughing and screaming.

Number 14, Park Terrace was an imposing Victorian house converted into apartments. I looked at the three bells; none said Fisher. The basement flat had a separate mailbox, and there I found her. After a cold delay, a woman opened the door.

It was Sylvia, barely. Her features were careworn, her skin rough, hands bruised and torn like a bare-knuckle boxer. Her hair, the lustre and length of which I had allowed myself to file in my palace of memories as the archetype of all female beauty, was cropped short and the wrong colour. She looked at me blankly, not seeming to recognize me. Was this how I would have aged in eight years? Possibly.

"What do *you* want?" It was worse than her not recognizing me; she recognized me and wasn't happy to see me. "Come in, then," she sighed, angry at having to apologize. "Could have told me you were coming." We walked down a bare corridor, past an uninviting and unlit sitting room, past the stairs to the parlour floor, which were blocked off. "Have they sent you for something?" I shook my head. She led the way into the farthest room, a kitchen where a plastic radio hissed sibilantly into the gloom. Dirty windows, too small for the room, looked out on a back garden she couldn't use. "Sit down, then. Coffee?" I nodded. "Jesus, well, you didn't come for the fucking conversation. Cat got your tongue?"

I didn't recognize her. It was hard to imagine the sequence of photographs tracing her decline. I had expected a Fisher, a home, *a life of her own*. That's what they'd always implied: not this.

"What's in the box, then?"

I got George out. At last, she smiled. Then she laughed, but the laughter was as hollow as her eyes. "*I* don't fucking want it. I'm the last person who should get it."

I sat him on my knee. "Hello, Sylvia."

Her look mingled disgust and disbelief.

"Oh, don't you start. What a fucking circus." She turned her back and put the kettle on. "I see they worked their magic on you too, didn't they?" Talking away from me, she fussed unnecessarily with the kettle flex. "It's instant," she said, flicking the coffee jar, her voice quivering with uncertainty.

"They didn't send us," said George.

She slammed her mug against the kitchen sink. "You can leave right now. I won't talk to you like that. I don't fucking need it."

"They didn't send me," I said. I was still holding my prop, doing fingering exercises inside him, but I didn't move his mouth. What secrets did we have to hide from Sylvia? None. "I came because I wanted to see you. I wanted to ask you something. I kept meaning to write, but I never did. They told me about Reg being your father."

Sylvia sneered. "Finally told you, did she? Well, there, you know. Thanks for that. You can go now." She put two cups of coffee on the table, without the offer of milk or sugar. A scum of unstirred granules floated on the surface froth.

"This is real, *right?*" I asked — her catchphrase-that-never-was.

"Oh, shut up, George." She stared resolutely at the side of the fridge. Her first sip made her relent somewhat. "I'm sorry. I'm sorry. It's not you." The pipes filled the ensuing silence with a screech and grumble. "How are you?"

"Getting better," I said.

"I mean, are you in the *family business* or are you . . . ?" She didn't know how to put it.

"I haven't been talking a lot recently," I said in explanation.

She laughed without pleasure and shook her head. "You and me, George. Living proof."

I let this identification hang in the air. The coffee was still too hot, but she was gulping hers.

"Family?" I asked.

"Couple of boyfriends, not that it's any of your business. And don't tell them anything about me, not about this house, not what I do, not how I live, all right?" I nodded. "And how's little Miss Perfect?"

"*Fish Out of Water.*"

"Don't watch TV," she said, though I hadn't mentioned TV.

"She's doing well." It was hard to look at her as I talked.

"Of course."

"She had a rough patch," I said, thinking it might help. "But she's back now."

"Yeah, well, so did I, and I still am, and I'm not fucking back yet." The expletives she sprayed had a particular viciousness; there was no greater symbol of her estrangement from the family where a sotto voce "Bugger!" was the strongest possible expression of anger.

"How did you find out about Reg?" I asked.

"Evie. We were having an argument about Frankie, who was getting all the parts and always had done. I was being stupid, complaining that she had all the talent. And Evie says: '*Of course* she has all the talent.' *Of course!* And we started a slanging match, and she told me. Just like that. '*Where do you think your mother is right now?*' I can just hear her.

"We were all under her thumb. Vindictive old bitch, she was, punishing me for Mum's sins. And I just decided I'd had enough. Cinderella did all right out of her, but the Ugly Sisters were fucked." She switched the kettle on again. I pulled out my tin and rolled a cigarette.

"Give us one," she said. Her fingers shook, and I took the papers back so I could roll one for her. She lit her cigarette and inhaled desperately. It made me want to quit immediately. "Swept it all under the carpet, they did. Quite happy to forget me, so they could go on as if nothing happened. Trade me in so they could live as they always had, just so Frankie could keep milking the golden cow."

"Evie's gone now," I said. "Queenie and Reg are married, living in the old house. Frankie knows. I know."

"You've just got it all worked out, haven't you? It's all very pretty where you live." She spat tobacco from the tip of her tongue. "Couldn't stand the shame of an illegitimate child who could only see her father on visiting days. Better a perfect dead war hero than a shameful live criminal. What does he care anyway? I've never even met the man."

"Reg thinks Evie shopped him." I couldn't help but smile at how reasonable this ludicrous sentence sounded.

"Which time?" She rolled her eyes. "All of them?"

"It destroyed him." I wanted to tell her about Reg — his advice, the pack of cards he gave me my second term at school, how he asked me to be his best man, how he was the one person to insist I got help — but there didn't seem any point just now. And I knew from my own experience: there were times when you didn't want to be cheered up.

There was a knock on the door. She yelled, "Hold on!" and walked down the corridor. I heard mumbling through a door partly opened. She was telling someone she couldn't do whatever it was they expected. The door closed. She sighed as she returned.

The quiet was disturbed only by the radio's harsh metallic crackle. "As for perfect dead war hero . . . ," I said, "I think you had the pick of the fathers." She narrowed her eyes, as though I was patronizing her. "I mean it, Sylvia. I found stuff Joe wrote in the war. He hated his mother, his marriage; he was only too happy to ditch his family and escape to war; he found out about you in a letter from Queenie; he wasn't a war hero at all. He was in love with somebody else, who died, and he was pleased to die himself. . . . Look, you're the only person I can tell. They don't know any of this, so you can't tell anyone."

"Does it fucking look like I'm going to tell anyone?" Sylvia stubbed out her cigarette. There didn't seem much more to say, and she surprised me with a question: "And when did they tell *you?*"

"After they got engaged. They just thought it was better out in the open. They rang you that Christmas."

"No, not about me. When did they tell you about you?"

I didn't answer her immediately. *About me.*

"I don't know much," she said, "but I know families are happy to repeat the same mistakes over and over again. And you and me are the same. You know about *your* father, right?"

Oh, that. Now I knew what she was talking about. She knew I knew.

"Yes, of course. Car-racing accident at Silverstone. Handsome married bloke. They met at the Clarendon. Queenie's told me everything." The radio was still spitting out tinny hits punctuated by the unctuous tones of the early-afternoon DJ. Now it was her turn to be silent. "Can you turn that radio off?"

"Yeah." She sat back down. There were children playing in a nearby playground, screaming and laughing, laughing and screaming.

"Look what's happened to you, George. You were such a lovely little kid, so happy, so outgoing."

"Like before you cut your hair," I said, ashamed that in her eyes, my fall was somehow as great as hers.

"You and me, George; we're what playing happy families does." She shook her head. Unexpectedly, she reached out to hold my hand. I was still smoking, so I let go of George. Her hands were rough, like the edges of my bitten nails. "Listen to me: the racing bloke wasn't your dad. . . . Queenie thought so, 'cos Frankie wanted her to, and apparently she still thinks so. I didn't mean to tell you. I thought you knew." I closed my eyes as she dug her nails into my hand. "I don't know who he was: her and Evie always kept that to themselves. But I remember Evie telling her: 'He'll hold you back! He doesn't deserve you! He's not a strong man!' and Frankie crying her eyes out in her room. And it was never to be mentioned after that. Nothing was allowed to get in the way of her precious career — not him, not you, not me. But I never knew who he was. Only Frankie and Evie knew."

I let her massage my hand as the dark shadows of her eyes filled with reflective tears. Without my assistance, George flopped back on my chest and tumbled to the floor.

We were the same after all, me and my forgotten Auntie Sylvia.

"I know who," I said.

The silence was broken by another knock at the front door, which she tried to ignore, though she whispered when she spoke. "I'm so glad, Georgie. I didn't want to break that to you. I don't want you to think of me like I think about Evie. I want it all to be over, done."

I nodded. There was another knock.

"Fucking fuck off!" she muttered. I stood up and bundled George back into his box. I had tried to put it to the back of my mind, scared to think of it, to hope it was true. "Don't go now," said Sylvia as I threw my rollies into my coat pocket and did up the catches on the box. "Not right now," she pleaded, but I could make her feel better another day. She clung to my sleeve. "No!" she whispered through her clenched teeth. "Please. At least, not till he's gone." She thrust a thumb in the direction of the front door: hers was a pragmatic request. We stood like musical statues. I slowly extricated myself, letting her know I would wait. "Just five minutes, till the coast's clear," she said, and closed the kitchen door gently. "It's not how it looks, George. It's the landlord, that's all."

We stood in silence. She put her arms around me and held on as though only extreme concentration would send him from the door.

"Sorry, George. Sorry," she murmured, partly in apology, partly in sympathy.

"I miss you," I said. "I miss you singing in the kitchen. I miss your laugh. Queenie does too."

"You wanted to ask a question?"

"You answered it." My eyes stung. "This is real, *right?*"

"Yes, Georgie. It's real." Her head fell on my chest, and I put my fingers through the scrub of her hair. We stayed there longer than we had to, she needing the warmth of another human, I thinking of what I now had to do.

"I have to go," I said. She pulled away from me.

"Thanks," we both said at the same moment. She opened the front door cautiously. When nothing pushed by, she let me pass.

"George, don't send the cavalry." I shook my head. She pointed at George's box. "And I don't want to see that fucking thing ever again. Or hear it." She pulled my head towards her and kissed my forehead. "Good luck, boy."

The weather on my return to London was dismal, the slow train empty except for the occasional shoal of sheltering children who left puddles when their journeys ended two stops later. That morning's news carelessly decorated the floor, temporary doormats for those bothered to wipe their feet. Another herd traipsed in, blue and grey, blazer and tied. A stolen cap was hurled around on a dare. They were only four or five years younger than I was.

I moved into the corridor, where I sat down on George's box. Rain spat across my face as the white noise of passing countryside mixed with the rhythm of the train. The two carriages shifted backwards and forwards at my feet like miniature tectonic plates. I stood up and put my head out of the window, a dog in the passenger seat. Stung by the rain, I remembered a cold, windy trip to the seaside where

Frankie, clutching her fedora, watched me from the safety of the deck chairs while I stood on the stony beach and let the waves crash over me. Des called me in, but I felt invincible. Afterwards, I took her to tea at a pier café for her birthday. I was seven.

Unable to open my eyes against the rain, I let the world rush by, imagining the rolling fields and ragged hedges, the bottles of beer thrown down the embankments, and now the houses, their fenced back gardens, their families whose dreams were full of trains. It was getting dark.

The noise gathered in intensity, like takeoff, as we smacked into another tunnel. I shouted into the echo chamber, my voice lost in the churning roar of the engine and wheels. And then we were through, slowing down to make another stop. School-children got off, and the car park was slowly emptying. Mothers, waiting for fathers on the next commuter train, read by interior lights: not a care in the world.

An endless procession of suburbs announced the city, and I turned my attention to the tracks themselves, glinting beneath the early-evening moon and the lights of the wet metropolis. I fixed on one and let it take me away, away, and then back, as it converged with another line. An empty train also heading for the city seemed about to career into us but gracefully steered itself parallel in a polite race.

London didn't notice or bother me, until I went underground and emerged into the echoing greenhouse of Charing Cross. With time to kill, I went to the station pub, a grim sanctuary for a congregation of solitary pilgrims and lost souls, with an unused fruit machine that kept burbling noisily, suggesting it was going to spew cash at any moment. A woman with glass red lips, her breasts frothing above the V-neck of a white sweater obscured in the cloud of its own fluffiness, asked me what was in the box. I didn't answer, and she turned her attention elsewhere.

The train west was full of commuters, doing the same crosswords, reading the same sports news. I fell back into the corner, lulled by the noise and the motion, the box safe under my knees. I thought of

Brenda's bed and wondered where I would sleep tonight. Fishers were used to strange beds, but I couldn't remember two nights where I hadn't *known* where I'd be sleeping. Last night's soft pillows and firm mattress had become this evening's headrest and cold window-pane: what would they be tonight? In sleepy panic, I couldn't find the Polaroid. By the time I checked my inside top pocket and felt its sharp corners, I was asleep.

I woke with a parched throat. It was 8:45 and dark when I bundled myself out. I walked down the meagre main street, past the barber's and the newsagent, past the toy store where boys bought their records. There were no taxis, no buses, no cars. Only the pub, the Duke of Athole, showed signs of life. I had little money, but at least enough for a pint of beer.

Some of the Upside staff favoured the saloon bar, so I went into the public bar, a dissolute and smoky Olympics of bar billiards, darts, shove ha'penny, and competitive drinking. I peered into the saloon beyond, where business, tweed, and Barbour mingled. At the far right, as if my imagination had placed him there, stood Mr. Morris, deep in the reception of a joke. He took the head off his beer, wiping his top lip with finger and thumb. Patrick would be thinking about university.

My pint, and my money with it, was gone before I noticed I was drinking, and I set out for Upside, the country lanes glistening in the moonlight. Occasionally a car passed, announcing itself throughout the countryside, bare trees slicing through the glow of its headlights, and gave me a wide berth. George was heavy in his box.

Finally, I was at the end of the driveway, thinking about the last time I had made this trip. I checked for cars, ready to duck into the undergrowth. An unknown young man holding a small wooden tuck box and walking the Upside driveway in the middle of the night was suspicious. The hour obviated my only good excuse: "I'm an old boy. Just having a walk down memory lane." Beyond the conker trees, I caught sight of the school for the first time. I took a left turn past the unused cricket pitch, cordoned off for the winter as usual, to the rear of the pavilion, where Donald had kept his tools. The smell took me back.

Dropping the makeshift curtain, I turned the light on. The supply room, where Donald and I had spent so many hours chatting, looked like a bomb site. I had half thought of spending the night here, but there was no chance of that. The armchair was covered in traffic cones, and the two chairs around the table were occupied by tubs of congealed white marker. I rolled a cigarette and put the pewter ashtray down, pleased to reunite it, however momentarily, with the table where it had sat so often, but I could barely find room for George's box.

It'll never do was the phrase that went through my head, over and over, as I looked at the mess. So I set George on the windowsill to keep guard and started to tidy up, a task complicated by the fact that I didn't want anyone to be alerted by the light. This meant a great deal of circular shuffling of the contents, Rubik's cube–style, before I opened the door to make some space. Hidden in a drawer, I found the current groundsman's guilty secret — a half-drunk bottle of scotch. I sniffed it to make sure it wasn't turpentine, meths, or petrol and, reassured, took a sip. Now I was getting somewhere. Emboldened, I sifted out the junk — antique lawn mower parts, splintered wickets and smashed hurdles, rotten pads, handleless shovels, slats of a broken cricket cradle — and turned the light off: out it all went. I also wheeled out the marker machine and the two mowers to give myself more elbow room.

Back inside, light on, I was left with the salvageable, the cricket score numbers, the cones, the creosote, the petrol cans and bottles of turpentine, the balls of yarn and odd lengths of rope, the usable tools, and the various forlorn items that had never received the required repairs: the broken weather vane, goals of net, trampled boundary flags. I cleared off what had once been a work space and hung the tools back on the nails in sensible order. I had no idea how long I had been working: the scotch made it a pleasure.

We admired my handiwork. I wasn't tired and I had a sudden craving for the smell of the marker paint. I merrily mixed the powder with a little water from the rusty tap above the trough, as

I had been taught, first making a smooth paste before diluting it further and stirring well. This done, there wasn't anything for it but to pour it into the ancient machine, apparently the same one I had trundled around the hockey fields. Armed with the bottle, I took the marker outside.

I sat George against a tree, took a stake that I drove into the ground in the centre circle, and unraveled a ball of yarn. Then I started to practise: straight lines weren't easy, but the circles represented a huge challenge, and there was barely any moonlight to guide me as I found a way of leaning into the curve, which seemed to smooth my progress. It was all feel: I could barely see the ground beneath my feet. Time to get to work.

When I could no longer hear the mixture slopping against the sides of the bucket, I finished — my supply of both scotch and mixture ran out simultaneously, and unexpectedly quickly, while I was marking one of the centre spots. I regretted that I was not allowed the satisfaction of leaning on my shovel and gazing across the new boundaries of my kingdom. That would wait till tomorrow.

I'd worked up a sweat and found myself shivering in the darkness. Though I now had the choice of a usable deck chair or a nearly cleared table, the pavilion was too cold for a bedroom — where was that little fan heater when you needed it? — and it was surely the alcohol that persuaded me that it was a shame to shiver in silence when there was a schoolful of beds so near, one of which had to be unoccupied.

I hid George's box behind the chair, put him on my arm, and walked towards the school, seeing few lights except those left on in empty classrooms and deserted corridors. I passed the new assembly hall (long finished, though it still had the air of a recent development) and looked into the murk of the copse behind, unable to see from which perch I had enjoyed my bird's-eye view of the Vox-inspired mayhem.

The back gate was unlocked, and I walked along the gravel path, past the headmaster's study. The griffin door closed itself politely behind me. No one would come running at the click of a door. My only goal was to avoid being seen.

Inside, nothing had changed. It could have been a hundred years either side. I half-expected *The Daily Mail* on top of the billiard table cover to be dated the day I left. I had imagined that Upside would seem diminished, Lilliputian, but the school was actually somewhat larger than I remembered. Perhaps I felt small; I was certainly tired. I walked past the tuck box room, past the kitchen, and past the changing rooms, where my footsteps echoed louder and the disks dangled in formation. I walked up the back stairs and past the elder boys' dormitory. It was too late for the Blackout Society, too late for reading under the covers, too late even for Matron to be making her rounds. It was even too late for me.

One final set of stairs, just past the deputy headmaster's rooms, and I was on the top floor. Nothing stirred, beyond the infrequent squeaking of metal bed frame and the creak of floorboard under-foot. Swift, Dryden, Johnson, Pope. All present and correct. My eyes accustomed to the gloom, I looked in each in turn. I walked down the rows of beds, between the bodies, slowly. A dreamer murmured from the other end of the room. "You'll have to . . ." The rest of his sentence drifted back into his sleep.

I could have happily slipped between some sheets, regard-less of the consequences, but there wasn't a spare bed, so, in the humming darkness, I tiptoed to the location of my old bed, though nothing was wedged in as mine had been. I sat on the end of the nearest bed; the slumbering occupant generously rolled away from me to give me more room. In his dreams, perhaps I was his father, the under-matron, his dog. I sat there, exhausted.

George whispered: "'There's a one-eyed yellow idol to the north of Khatmandu, / There's a little marble cross below the town. . . .'"

The moan of a dreamily murmured question was met with a satisfied purr of reassurance from elsewhere. I was conducting their dreams. And there I stayed, pulling their sleepy strings, until I was too tired to do anything but sleep myself.

Walking past the dispensary, I remembered the sick bay, a legendary (and perennially unoccupied) Eden of warm milk and kindness, comics and cough drops. Past the washbasins on parade, I opened the door that led to this Shangri-la: few had been there, and those who had were never able to find their way back once they'd been discharged. It turned out to be another dull corridor, from which came three rooms. I could just make out two beds in the first and I opted for the nearest one. Closing the door behind me, I sat George down on the bedside chair, took off my jacket, and slipped under the top cover. Lying in bed, I thought of Brenda, into whom I was just disappearing when a timid voice materialized in the darkness.

"Excuse me?"

I sat bolt upright but said nothing.

"Excuse me?" the fearful whisperer asked again, even more surprised than I. "Does Matron know you're here?"

"Go back to sleep," I hissed. There was silence. I pictured us both lying there with our sheets pulled up to our necks.

"I'm Smith-Price," he said, confident that I offered no great threat. "I had chicken pox, but I'm not contagious anymore. I'm out tomorrow morning."

"Good. Go to sleep." I was a grown-up and should be obeyed. I certainly didn't owe him an explanation. I could hear him thinking, preparing for a midnight chat.

"What are you doing here?"

"I'm the new groundsman. I got lost."

"What happened to Mr. Murdoch?"

"I took over. What time does Matron come round in the morning?"

"She comes here first, about six forty-five a.m."

"Look," I said, "it's kind of embarrassing that I got lost. I don't want you to mention it to anyone, and it's important that I don't see Matron tomorrow."

"I can set the alarm on my digital watch if you like, for six-fifteen."

"Thank you, Smith-Price. Don't tell a soul."

"Mum's the word. It's nice in here. They have a whole pile of comics."

"Did you read the adverts in the back?"

"Yeah, but my dad says they're all rip-offs. We bought some sea monkeys, and they were a dead loss."

"It's good just to imagine the possibility."

There was a long silence, during which each knew the other was wide-awake. It was Smith-Price who spoke first. "Can you tell me a story?"

"Promise not to scream?"

Smith-Price was still dead to the world when I woke. It was time for breakfast. Making the bed with a minimum of fuss, I picked up George and walked down the corridor. Seeing no one, I went back downstairs. If someone called out to me, I would keep walking. If someone approached me, I would dart down the nearest corridor.

The family in charge of the kitchen was already hard at work: 200 eggs, 200 pieces of fried bread, 15 huge teapots. This was their cherished hour before the bell clanged and the inconvenience began. They were easy to avoid as they scuttled back and forth to the dining room with vats of milk and plastic containers of cutlery. I stuck my hand in the back door and stole a loaf of bread and two hard-boiled eggs.

Heads down, we sauntered from the school towards the new assembly hall, where I found a comfortable corner upstairs in the balcony, leaving a mess of crumbs and shell that I swept under a radiator, hiding what I hadn't eaten. Beneath me, the hall was a giant romper room of wall bars, basketball hoops, and competing courts — badminton, five-a-side, indoor hockey — each marked with different coloured tape on the ground. The boys ambled down to the conker trees, exchanging the time-honoured diurnal greeting with Hartley before they settled in for breakfast, after which there was a march towards the hall. I was quite safe in the balcony. The boys filed in first, standing in rows, largest at the back like chess pieces; then the masters (Poole, tick; Bird, present; Morris, tick; Hessenthal, yes, sir; but no sign of Potter or Wilding) in front of the wall bars. Last to come in was Hartley, looking not a day older behind his beard. He gave a brief address and announced that the first eleven were playing St. Anselm's in the Cup that afternoon: support was *always* appreciated and in this case compulsory.

With everyone safely in class, I took George back to the pavilion. The room looked much better: tools in order, junk outside, neatly piled, awaiting removal. I sat George in his box and talked to myself as I went about my work. There was a lot to do: the spongy buffers on the rugby posts, the swimming-pool cover. Nobody had bothered to replace the weather vane on top of the pavilion, and I made this my first job. After hammering its feet out on the concrete, I found a way to jimmy the north-south arrow so it didn't need welding. I propped the ladder against the back of the pavilion, and within a few minutes the weather vane was in its rightful place, turning acceptably. In the distance, a member of staff, seeing nothing amiss, offered me a friendly wave, which I returned.

Back in the pavilion, I inspected and mended the nets, and set about getting the cricket cradle ready for next summer. I was making improvements. The morning went quickly. Heaven knows what this Mr. Murdoch was up to.

By lunchtime, I was hungry and climbed my favourite tree to plan my next forage. From this perch, I was able to take in my previous night's handiwork for the first time.

What had I been thinking?

The finger of suspicion pointed directly to the pavilion, the origin of a crazy, mazy white line that finally terminated in a comically large centre blob, the size but not the shape of the Rank gong, where much of the marker paint had either leaked or spilled. I winced when I realized that I had neglected one of Don's first lessons: a wheelie was necessary to ensure you marked only where you needed lines. Nor could I tell where my supposed practice ended and my work began: some of the "circles" were better than others, but none was in the right place. The first-eleven football pitch was now an unplayable nightmare of irregular shapes, like the floor of the new assembly hall done in white, resembling a controversial new piece at the Tate. I had meant to help, but under the influence of the darkness and Murdoch's single malt, I had got carried away. On top of the pavilion, the weather vane, which had seemed so sturdy only an hour or two ago, had fallen to one side, one of the arrows — it had been *north-south,* now it was *up-down* — spinning helplessly.

I had nearly made it to the back of the pavilion through the copse when I saw an elderly red-faced man in denim dungarees, Mr. Murdoch, I presumed, roll up for his day's work. Murdoch, scratching his head with amusement, called over an assistant as he looked at the junk piled outside the back room. The young man indicated the telltale white trail, and Murdoch scurried off on his paper chase, leaving his sidekick to poke through the bric-a-brac like a bargain hunter at the church fête. I could do nothing, so I went back into the assembly hall and retrieved the rest of my breakfast from beneath the radiator.

After lunch, a surprise assembly effectively penned me upstairs. The awed murmur among the pupils, not to mention the exemplary muster of staff, established the curiosity and gravity of the event. Poole took a mental roll call, eyeing his charges beadily as he counted them in.

"The Vandals were an East Germanic tribe who captured Rome in 455 AD," said Hartley, speaking at speed as he walked in, shadowed by a disgruntled Murdoch. "Their name is proverbial for barbaric plunder and destruction." He ground to a halt at his lectern, his eyes firmly planted where his text would have been. "Why am I telling you this? I am telling you this because today, the spirit of the Vandals lives on at Upside. The first-eleven pitch has been *vandalized.* We'll do it the easy way." He looked up for the first time. "Anybody?" I surveyed the assembly from my crow's nest: Poole's dandruff-specked shoulders, Bird's tiny head. "Or perhaps I do you wrong . . . ," Hartley continued when no one volunteered. "Perhaps I misjudge you. Perhaps none of you is the trickster in question, the jolly scamp, *the wag* responsible for this *jape.*" A nervous murmur of laughter hung about the rafters. "But if one of you knows who, how, or why this happened, then I advise you to come forward immediately. I will ask one more time."

A timid voice piped up. "Sir?" Boys turned towards the speaker and then backed away as if Smith-Price were still contagious.

"Fresh from sick bay, we welcome a boy not previously celebrated for his criminal genius, Edward Smith-Price," said Hartley, momentarily a game-show host. "Smith-Price, shoot!" Silence. "Or would you rather speak to me alone?"

"I think it might have something to do with the new groundsman, sir."

Hartley flinched. Murdoch bristled. Poole rocked on his heels.

"The new groundsman?"

"The new groundsman who took over from Mr. Murdoch. He got lost last night and slept in my room in the sick bay."

Hartley spluttered. I didn't hold it against Smith-Price. I'd have done the same.

"The new groundsman, you say, who took over from Mr. Murdoch, who got lost last night and slept in your room in the sick bay. Does anybody else know anything about the new groundsman who took over from Mr. Murdoch, who got lost last night and slept in Smith-Price's room in the sick bay?"

Hartley made private speculations on the previous night's sleeping arrangements, saw how this might read in letters home, and dismissed the assembly, which parted before him, dissolving into chatter as lesser members of staff turned usher.

"Do what you can, Mr. Murdoch, whatever you can," called Hartley. "Perhaps the under-eleven pitch?" His voice echoed around the empty hall. "Now, Smith-Price." Only the two of them remained. "What on earth happened and why didn't you tell anyone?" Hartley quickly discounted any darker nighttime crimes, relieved by Smith-Price's blithe explanation.

"Can you describe this rogue groundsman?"

"Well, it was dark, sir, and he didn't turn the light on. He was very nice. We talked about comics and he told me a bedtime story. One thing, though, sir. He had a little person with him."

"A what?"

"I saw him on the chair next to the bed. A little person."

"A dwarf? A homunculus? Tiny Tim?" Smith-Price shook his head. "Toulouse-Lautrec? Thumbelina? The monkey from the Rue Morgue?"

"Not a real person and not an animal."

"What on earth are you *blithering* about?"

Just then, Murdoch's assistant arrived back at the open door, out of breath, his boss following just behind.

"Come 'n' see, Mr. Hartley," he said. "Come 'n' see. I've found something." Hartley looked up, displeased with everything around him. "The pavilion's been completely cleared out. And there's something that wasn't in the pavilion before. A ventriloquist dummy."

Fuck. George.

"A vent . . ." Hartley was just about to express complete bafflement when he smiled. "Ah! The fog lifts." He put his palm on Smith-Price's head and, swivelling him bodily 180 degrees, pushed him towards the door. "And there we have your mysterious midnight mini-creature. Well done, Smith-Price. You may go. Mr. Murdoch, all is revealed. A criminal signature left by a nocturnal groundsman. Show me this ventriloquist dummy," said Hartley. "The game is afoot."

Caught red-handed in the pavilion.

My hands were clammy as I watched George surrendered. Hartley held him in as dignified a manner as possible, while daring schoolboys pointed in amusement as George and his unlikeliest partner disappeared towards Upside. Murdoch made comical attempts to ready the pitch for the game as the St. Anselm's minibus parked by the Green Court. Soon twenty-two boys were limbering up on the touchline, while the groundsmen screwed hooks into the crossbars and posts of the under-eleven goals, shortly to be graced with nets for the first time.

Interest in the match was at an all-time high. The rumour of the phantom groundsman (vastly preferable to Murdoch) and his act of wanton vandalism had captured the student imagination. A stream of pupils, shooed away by teachers stationed for this specific purpose, was unable to resist the urge to wonder at the mysterious white crop circles. Hartley emerged to mollify his visiting counterpart, who swung a shooting stick disdainfully over the surface of the new field.

When the game finally kicked off, I made my way down, across the Green Court and back into the school. It was time to get George. Keep walking straight ahead, I told myself. If you see a child, bark an order or ask the way to the games fields — he'll assume you're a visiting member of the St. Anselm's staff. If you see Poole or Bird, walk very slowly in the opposite direction.

Hartley's lair was my starting point. The door was open, his study even more heavily smoked with the passing of time. I saw the same chair, the same cane among the bouquet of umbrellas, the same books on the same shelves. Hartley was cheerleading, Mrs. Hartley preparing the postmatch tea: there was no chance of seeing either, but I tiptoed through the sitting room and up the back stairs, past the same telephone where the same picture of the Hartleys stood in its seashell frame.

Had they hidden George or was he bait? The room where I had slept throughout that odd half-term was more of a storeroom than previously, but the bed was still there, hemmed in by neatly packed boxes. I lay down.

The bedside clock ticked over slowly. Distant chants trickled from the field, and my eyes were drawn to the towers of folders and the fat spines of the books lying flat on the shelves at the foot of the bed. The first was marked *School Pictures (Chronological)*. I remembered the day ours was taken on the Green Court, 1973. Out of curiosity, I got the book down: our year was the first immortalized in colour. The photo revolved around the Emperor Hartley in his purple gown (alone worth the upgrade from black and white), his great bear grin sparkling above a selection of trophies. Either side of him, his generals, ready for battle, sat in the row to which every Upside adult was admitted, though their importance diminished towards each end: matrons and under-matrons, menials, kitchen staff, music teachers, groundsmen. There was Donald, in an unusually smart jacket, looking away from the camera, eyes down. Above were the regular troops, the rank and file of Upside, but beneath them the cannon fodder, the poor little boys, unarmed, not even issued long trousers, amongst whom I had been made to sit. And there was I, smiling at the camera, thinking of my last view of Frankie waving on the platform, unaware that Donald was gazing at me.

I flicked back through for the photographs when Donald himself was a schoolboy. There he was, easily found — happy, confident, smiling as I had been. What had happened to him since? What, come to that, had happened to me? This remarkable year was also the last year of Hartley's prebeard days: there he was, a junior master, to the right of the headmaster, looking ahead, planning his whiskers. By the sound of the cheering outside, the home team had scored. Inexplicably, I felt proud.

Several of the other photo albums were catalogued: *Marcia, Paris 1970, Outward Bound, Donald*. I had no choice.

The order of the service for the funeral was neatly photo-cornered to the inside front cover, but on the first page the photos went back to the beginning: faded black and whites of a baby in his crib; one of the three kings, in a red dressing gown, bearing gifts at Christmas; a three-year-old football player, one foot on an oversize leather ball; his period parents pointing out the Eiffel Tower as he gazed at an ice-cream stand; and next, the ice cream smeared over his smiling face, dripping from his fingers. And later, growing up as a junior master's son at Upside, playing for the team, handsome in creased whites; his newly bearded father tossing down a long hop to him in the nets that Donald would later end up mending; picking up a book on prize-giving day. And beyond, in front of a large archway on his first day at college; a heavily panting cross-country runner taking a final corner, *St Catherine's 72* safety-pinned to his chest, cheered on by one lone damp spectator. And summers at home, the facilities of Upside at his disposal, not abandoned as I had been, but free to use its swimming pool and slide, the heir to his father's kingdom, he and his younger sister its only citizens.

There were no more of his school, no more sport, no graduation, no mortarboards, no shaking hands with the teachers. Time has passed, and there he is again, sitting with a blanket across his lap in a garden, but not at school. Everyone around him is older. Someone points the camera out to him, and Donald smiles reluctantly. I fill in the gaps: a breakdown, his first, a year of rest. Above me, the titles of the same books that surrounded me that half-term so long ago now tell me a story: *Depression and Its Causes, The Tao of Mental Health, Answers to Suicide.*

And then, a recovery, a second chance — he looks older, gaunt but unexpectedly handsome, a student teacher perhaps at a comprehensive, where he is overseeing some kind of gym class: no, of course — those books in the corner again — a drama class, where his students are apparently under instruction to be trees. And another, where he is showing someone how to walk with a crutch, as though he is missing a leg.

Amongst the last of these drama photos, he is onstage, drawn but happy, alive, on an empty stage in front of rudimentary scenery; and there is a woman with him in rehearsal, with whom he studies a play script — he is biting the skin on the knuckle of his thumb as he listens to her point of view, seeming to ask her, with his index finger, what she is recommending. And she is beautiful and blond, a little boyish, her hair cut in a smart bob that cannot hide her charming smile.

And she is my mother. And I am theirs.

And the page swims before me, my tears heavy like honey. And I cannot bring myself to look away or close my eyes, because I fear that if I do, this knowledge — that I could not admit to myself, that I lied to myself about, but that I now, for this very moment, *know* — may be lost to me forever; that I will be back at square one with the Father of a Thousand Faces, anything I wanted him to be, rather than the Father of Only One, my own. Finally, my eyes close of their own accord. I keep them tight shut, and when I open them, the photo is still there.

I flick forwards, keeping my finger marking the page. On the next is the only picture I was sure would be there: me declaiming at the school concert, witnessed by a proud father, a grandfather. And there are more: Donald with a pint of beer; Donald pushing the roller across the field, the familiar school tie around his waist; Donald receiving a Christmas present. But he is rarely in company, nor does he ever smile. His soul is withdrawn, giving nothing away. He is growing invisible. Finally, a picture of him smiling: the one I took of him on top of the pavilion.

I got up, a ghost who could move unhindered, unseen, who could walk through walls, and floated through the apartment. Children were screaming and distant doors were banging, like the ones in the haunted house, which opened and closed, opened and closed. I came to rest in Hartley's office on the large armchair, clutching the album, thinking of Sylvia's bruised knuckles. I had watched my mother on television in this very room, sitting cross-legged on the floor, leaning back against this very armchair. That was before I met my father.

Perhaps I was asleep. Perhaps I woke as Hartley walked in. He opened the curtain to check on the last of the bedraggled, dripping into the showers. Without turning round, he spoke my name.

"We should thank you, I suppose: we won. That substandard pitch rather favoured our long-ball game." *There'll always be an Upside.* "Your library system survives to this day. Now you want to be groundsman?"

"Sorry."

He sat down, dismissing my apology with a shake of the head. "I shan't be interviewing you. Given the *overwhelmingly* negative evidence before us, I'd say you're not *cut out* to be a groundsman."

"Nor was Donald."

"Perhaps not, perhaps not. But he was a particularly *good* groundsman. We had high hopes originally, of course. A director of theatre, we thought, or, failing all else" — he smiled — "a teacher . . ." Hartley ran his finger along the stems in his pipe rack. He dismissed the thought. "And we do what we can. There are better ways to be close to him, George. You're not a groundsman. You're a Fisher."

I'm a Hartley, I thought. It was as if I had spoken aloud.

"I'm sorry, George. It was your mother's decision. We agreed because we thought that it would be good for you, that it was a way he could help you — an education your family couldn't afford — and good for him, that it was his chance. But he was in no fit state to be a father. You mustn't hold that against him."

"I don't." I thought of walkie-talkies, teas, afternoons together on the games fields. "He was a good father."

Hartley got up awkwardly from behind his desk. Looming over me, he sat down on the arm of the chair. There was a knock on the door, to which Hartley gave a firm "No!" Then, with his previous tone of voice: "He wanted to be."

"He was." So much suddenly seemed comical about the situation: this unapproachable hulk of a man so close I could taste the perfumed tobacco on his jacket as we spoke about the strange sham of my schooldays; the person on the other side of the door, perhaps a visiting dignitary, refused entrance to the inner sanctum.

"He had little opportunity, and I'm sure he would be very proud," said Hartley. "Though not of your groundsmanship. And now . . ." He paused, weighing up the relative merits of the alternative. ". . . though it may be the *booby prize* . . . you have us." Indicating that I should stay where I was, he went to the door for a muttered conference that lasted only a few seconds. When he returned, he did not offer the same intimacy, sitting behind his desk and tamping down the tobacco in his meerschaum. I rolled a cigarette, and we admired our mutual smoke as it fingered its way around the chandelier.

"Did your mother tell you?"

"No," I said. "She wouldn't tell me. I had to find out for myself."

"May I give you some advice, George?" Smoking, he was a more satisfied man. "Your mother did what she thought best. And there were certainly times — the years Donald was not . . . with us — when it was the best thing. And just as she was to tell you, things got very much worse for him; having you here was too much, and the only thing was to get the help he needed else-where. But he'd been through it all before, countless times, and he couldn't bring himself to go through it again. Don't hold that against him. Or her."

"She should have told the truth."

"The truth is not always the best thing."

"*Vincit Veritas?*"

He smiled, considering the school motto. "In this very Eden, we offer certainties, for there will be no more. You're not a school-boy, George. The truth can be selfish. Life, as you know, is com-plicated. One day you will have the opportunity to tell the truth, and, for whatever reason — because you think it best, because you don't want to hurt someone, because you do want to hurt someone, because you want to get reelected — you will lie. And then you will understand." I put my cigarette out in the ashtray on his desk. "And that is the pep talk that I never had the chance to give you before. I'm afraid there is the small matter of tea as we commiserate with the vanquished semifinalists, but if you'd like to wait here . . ."

"May I make a phone call?"

"Treat the place as your own, but *don't* scare my wife, *don't* frighten any more infirm schoolchildren, and *don't* smoke my tobacco."

"*Do* call you Grandfather?"

"*Don't* push your luck, Fisher."

"Two things: I'd like this photo album and George."

"George?"

"My dummy."

"Ah. The photo album? A loan, no problem. The dummy? There we *do* have a problem. I'm afraid *George* was shanghaied by Smith-Price on behalf of the junior third, who are currently honing their skills on him under the careful supervision of ab-solutely no one at all. . . . I thought it might help the little fellow with any residual trauma from last night, but I will get him back. Be here when I return."

"Yes."

"Apologies, apologies," I heard him call into the world beyond as the door closed behind him.

I picked up the phone and dialled Crystal Clear.

"Six four three five?"

"Brenda?"

"Who's that, please?"

"George."

"George? George? Oh, thank God."

"What?"

"Your family's been in touch; they're worried sick. They haven't seen you in two days. They rang here and they were going to call the police. I had to say you'd stayed at my place. I thought you were going straight back. . . ." There was dead air. "Nice to hear your voice, by the way. Literally."

"I need a driving lesson."

It was dark when she arrived. When I introduced her to Hartley, she described herself as a work colleague.

"Don't be a stranger," said Hartley, offering me his hand. "After all, you're not. Far from it."

"I won't. Thank you."

I pointed to the pavilion as Brenda and I drove away. "That's where I first saw my father. And where I last spoke to him."

"Tell me," she said, squeezing my knee.

"I'll show you some pictures when we're back in London."

It was the middle of the night. Staying awake was no longer an option.

"Say my name," she said.

"Brenda."

"I like to hear you speak every now and then so I know you haven't relapsed." She was sitting on my back, rubbing my shoulders.

"Brenda," I murmured. "Brenda. Brenda."

"Not a very pretty name, but it sounds nice when you say it. It means fiery hill, according to Dad. . . ." She carried on this little monologue quite happily, not caring if I was listening. "Oh, I forgot, there was a letter at work for you. I've got it here somewhere. From Italy, I think."

Beyond my grasp on the floor, there was a bottle of red wine. The label swam in and out of focus, something Italian. It had sent me a letter. It tasted like the glue on the back of a stamp.

As I turned the key to our front door late the next afternoon, the house itself seemed to take a deep breath. Supposing the silence to mean nobody was home, I flicked on the hall light and went into the kitchen. All the energies of the house were concentrated here.

At first, they didn't notice me. Reg leaned against the fridge with his hands behind him. Queenie sat with Frankie at the kitchen table. Frankie's eyes were bloodshot, a handkerchief clutched in her right hand, knuckles white. Normally, I'd have rushed up and wrapped my arms around her, found out what was wrong. But I didn't. The many possible causes held me back: the first that came to mind, selfishly, was my disappearance.

"Georgie," said Queenie with a puff of her cheeks, letting me know that I had interrupted a crisis.

It was nothing to do with me at all. I had come home, armed with the photo album, ready to talk. I had not considered that there would be an issue of timing.

"Cup of tea for the prodigal?" asked Reg, anxious for a little respite.

I drew up a chair, feeling somewhat irrelevant.

"Frankie's had a bit of an upset," said Queenie.

"What's up, Frankie?" I asked her. She lifted her chin on hearing my voice — it was the first time they'd heard me ask a question in some while — but, as she was about to speak, she bowed her head once more, overcome with tears. I reached out and she clutched at my hand. "What is it?" I asked again.

"She's had a bit of an upset," Queenie repeated, as though this were all that needed to be said.

"Tea," said Reg, as he placed a mug in front of me. He caught my eye and, when no one else could see, mouthed *Ricky*, making the slit throat sign across his neck with his index finger.

"Is it Ricky?" I asked her.

"They've had a big argument," said Queenie.

"I didn't want to be in it," gulped Frankie, speaking in staccato bursts. "Not when I saw the script."

"Did you lose the part in that film?"

"She *resigned* her part," said Queenie, her spokeswoman. "It was unsuitable." Thank goodness for small mercies.

"What was wrong?"

The synchronization of their stares told me it was something unmentionable, something beyond consideration. Reg rolled his eyes.

"And I . . . said . . . I wouldn't . . . ," said Frankie, but she was sniffing too much to speak. Queenie came to her assistance.

"And they had a big row about it. . . ."

"And we broke up." I held one hand and Queenie the other. "And I've got nothing now. No agent. No work. I'm too old for the parts I love. I'm starting again. And I don't know what to do." With this, she dissolved once more.

Reg smiled mirthlessly and moved random pans fractional distances around the sideboard as quietly as he could.

"Frankie, you've got everything," I said. She looked pitiful, eyelids puffy, mascara smeared; but her decision had been brave. "You're not starting again."

"I'm not?" She was slowly focusing through the blur. Of course she wasn't, the three of us agreed. "You were right about the movie," she added, somewhat recovered.

"What was the problem?"

Frankie shook her hands in disgust like little claws, making the face that accompanies a gulp of sour milk. "I can't."

"No, she really can't," confirmed Queenie.

"Did you have to . . . ?" I didn't finish the sentence, not knowing how to ask.

"Yes, she did," said Queenie, "and we'll leave it at that."

I warmed my hands on the mug of tea, though I wasn't cold. "You're not starting again, Frankie. There's no disgrace. You're ditching a bad agent on a point of principle." I avoided Queenie's glance that told me it wasn't time for *I told you so.*

Frankie smiled and rubbed my hand. "You should be my agent, Georgie." Sadly, she wasn't joking. "And I've got my family, haven't I?"

We agreed she had. And I had mine, though news of it had to wait. I thought of Dr. Hill, of Brenda, of Sylvia. I felt the happiest I could remember: cheering Frankie up, helping her forwards. Besides, I had other news, substitute news, for which the timing was perfect.

There was nothing to say in the minutes that followed, but Frankie showed no sign of letting go her grip. A Morse of tuts and sighs let us know she was recovered. Reg boiled a kettle as he emptied the pot: the possibility of another cup of tea provided a suitable distraction.

"Shall I be mother?" asked Queenie. Four brown mugs sat expectantly in front of her. It was a moment to honour ritual: the swirling of the not-quite-boiling water round the pot, the spooning of the loose tea (four and one more for the unexpected guest), the slow pouring of the water when it reached a galloping boil. No one spoke while the tea brewed — four minutes, she always left it — and this interval she filled with the pouring of milk into the mugs and the delivery of a plateful of biscuits. She placed the strainer over the first mug and poured. She always had been mother. We'd skipped generations. Evie had been Frankie's, and Queenie had been mine.

We spoke of Sylvia. I told them of my visit, though I said nothing she wouldn't have wanted. *In her own time,* I told them. *In her own time.* ". . . And since we're all sitting comfortably, I have an announcement of my own."

"Not more revelations," said Reg, clutching his heart with a mock groan. "Oh, my God! I can't stand the strain. Can't we get the food on?"

I fetched George, returning seconds later to the aftermath of a hastily whispered conference. Eyes were brighter; smiles had returned.

"It's lovely to hear you again, Georgie," said Frankie, delivering their conclusion. "Here's to Dr. What's Her Name."

"Hear, hear," said Reg, toasting me with his mug. "As it were."

"I didn't want to talk until I knew what to say."

"And you do, darling?" asked Queenie.

"Yes, I do."

Candles gave dinner a celebratory feel. I set George up on a chair, explaining that it might be the last meal he would attend for some time.

"Brenda gave me this. It arrived at work." I tossed the envelope onto the table, where it lay conspicuous in its anonymity.

"Inland Revenue, is it?" asked Reg.

"I'll read it. It's from Signore Ettore Ansalone."

"Who's 'e when 'e's at 'ome?" asked Frankie, the Artful Dodger.

"He's an illusionist, and the long and the short of it is that he wants to buy George. He saw us at the television studio."

"Your mate Tower!" exclaimed Reg. "Mr. Eight of Clubs!"

"That's the one. He's made an extremely generous offer."

"To buy George," Frankie said in confirmation.

"Well, we've sold him once already," said Queenie, "to that Armed Forces Museum. They think *they've* got him."

"The point is," I said, "does anyone have any objection?"

"Good price?" asked Reg innocently.

"It's up to you, Georgie," said Queenie. "The books were meant for you, and I'm sure George was too. It's up to him, right, Frankie?"

"Yes. George is yours," agreed Frankie.

"And I have no need for him anymore."

"Is it a *fair price?*" insisted Reg.

"Listen: 'Dear Mr. Fisher, Following serious consideration, and consultation with my family, we have decided that we would

like to buy your ventriloquist manikin. As you know, I am a serious and passionate collector of the ephemera of ventriloquism; to
me is not imaginable a more perfect example of a manikin, type
Romando 1930, and so I am disposed to make you a very considerate offer for the dummy and its effects.'"

"Considerate? Does he mean considerable?" said Reg, lick-
ing his lips.

"Effects?" queried Queenie.

"Clothes?" I said. "Scripts? Box? Fleas? He just wants to
make sure he's getting the lot, I suppose."

"Medal too?" asked Queenie.

"He doesn't ask for it, but a family really only needs one
George Cross, so I'd consider it. And then he makes the offer,
blah blah blah, before he continues: 'Please excuse my recent
behaviour backstage. I have now left for my home in Italy, where
pressing family reasons will keep me for the coming months.
Distinct greetings and all best wishes, Ettore Ansalone.' And he
gives his address."

Each of them tried to envision the amount.

"Well?" Reg had tired of speculation.

"It's a lot of money," I said.

Reg rubbed his hands together. "What number does it start
with?"

"Five."

"Five hundred," said Reg, nodding approval around the table.
"Probably about right."

I pointed up.

"Five hundred and fifty?"

"It's like an auction," said Queenie. I indicated higher.

"Five ninety-nine?" That was the highest Reg could reasonably conceive. Any higher was:

"Five thousand?" asked Frankie.

"Five. Thousand. Pounds," I confirmed.

"For a lump of wood?" spluttered Reg. "No disrespect, course,
but five . . ." Reg could get no further, and whistled in exhalation.

A reverential hush hovered around us, broken only by Reg, who said in his most reasonable voice, as though the sum in question were fifty pence, "Take the money."

"There must be some mistake," said Queenie, reappraising George as he basked in a new, glorious light.

"No mistake." I put the letter down on the table and underscored the figure with my thumbnail.

"It's lira!" said Reg in exasperation. "He must mean bloody lira!"

"No." I shook my head. "Pounds. Five thousand lira is forty quid or something."

"Yes, that doesn't seem quite fair," said Queenie, removing the cellophane from a packet of After Eights.

"Well," said Reg. "If he's offering *silly* money . . . don't look a gift horse in the mouth."

"I'm not going to," I said. "George was stuck up in that attic doing us no good at all."

"Package him up and send him . . . ," said Queenie.

"Post bloody haste!" said her husband.

"I'm going to do better than that," I said. "Since it's such a very reasonable offer, I'm going to hand-deliver the goods. I'm going to take George back to Italy, scene of his greatest glory."

"Can you afford that?" asked Queenie, before chuckling. "I suppose you can. What if it's a joke?"

"It isn't. And if it is, then we're going to get a holiday out of it."

"We?" asked Queenie.

"I'm going to take Frankie. We're going to relax by a swimming pool far away and draw up a plan for her next career move."

"You're taking me to Italy?" asked Frankie. "Wouldn't you rather take your . . . er . . . Brenda?"

"I want to take you."

She smiled her most dazzling smile. "I knew having you was going to pay off."

It was my hope that the Ansalones would tell her wonderful stories that I could never tell her without revealing the diary: of her father driving in on his motorbike, putting on shows in the town square, giving them chocolate, helping mend the roof. It would be a gift Frankie would love. The diaries, which told so many horrible truths, needn't come into it. The Ansalones would remember another side of Joe, the Joe that Frankie wanted to remember: the father she knew from another man's letters.

Reg placed a bottle of whiskey ceremoniously in the middle of the table, standing back with folded arms to consider it for a second before he poured four glasses. Frankie turned to fretting about passports, hotels, bathing suits, and plane travel.

"Don't worry," I said. "We'll work everything out. We'll go when we're ready."

"And whatever are you going to do with the money, Georgie?" asked Reg as he poured.

"Put it somewhere safe until I decide. More school, perhaps."

Reg pushed the glasses towards the four points of the compass. "To George," he said, and lifted his to the Romando. "Couldn't happen to a nicer boy."

"To George," we said, toasting my inheritance.

"Good luck to you . . . both of you," said Reg.

It was the bandstand that did it, and the views of the sea lapping lazily at the house beneath a grand veranda where guests sipped elegant cocktails. The most adventurous of their companions enjoyed an idle game of croquet in the cool of early evening. The waiters, dressed in burgundy, their place of business a striped Venetian marquee, moved through the clientele as if invisible. A small ensemble played on the bandstand where Joe had once performed; a stately pleasure boat made one of its occasional paddling excursions into the sea.

The moment I showed the travel agent the Ansalone address, he tapped the globe on his desk with a pencil and produced a vast array of pamphlets from distant drawers. Of these, one name caught my eye: the Villa Leopardi. "'A break at this magnificent villa, nestling in the protective shadow of Mount Etna, with its splendid views of the Mediterranean, will ravish the senses and replenish the soul . . . ,'" I read aloud.

"And break the bank . . . ," discouraged the travel agent, appraising my price bracket by my age and clothes. He produced a pricing guide for local hotels, their relative costliness denoted by an increasing number of pound signs: the villa was not listed.

"What kind of hotel is it?" Frankie asked later.

"It's nice," I said.

"Like that one we stayed at in Blackpool that time?"

"Nicer."

Two weeks later, Reg dropped us off at Gatwick with a chirpy *arrivederci*. Frankie cried as though we were fleeing a war zone, giving Reg and Queenie up to certain death. The biggest good-bye, however, was for George; I even opened the box. "I remember the first time I ever saw you," said Queenie. Reg had advised I keep him on me as hand luggage: "Don't let that little beauty out of your sight."

Frankie had brought nothing to read, and after flicking through a catalogue jettisoned by a previous passenger, she treated herself to a glass of champagne, which made her chatty. When sea had dissolved into cloud and the journey had settled into a horizontal lull, a tensely uniformed stewardess approached and asked if Miss Fisher would by any chance mind signing a picture for the pilot. Miss Fisher was delighted to be recognized.

"Can we go in the cockpit?" she asked, quick as you like, as though this were the standard bargain. The stewardess wiggled away to ask. "I've heard this works."

"Do you even *want* to go in the cockpit?"

"Not really. But fair's fair. Don't you?"

As we walked beyond first class, we felt very special. Show business: the ticket money can't buy. With a bow, the copilot vacated the cockpit to make room for the VIP.

"Perhaps a glass of champagne, Miss Fisher?" asked an identical stewardess as we ducked. And there we were, in the nose of the plane, my mother sitting next to the pilot and I standing behind her.

"A Fisher out of water! What a pleasure," said the pilot from behind his sunglasses and svelte moustache, as he paid the sky ahead no attention whatsoever. "Have you ever been in a cockpit before, Miss Fisher?"

"I've never been in a *plane* before," she said, as he gasped with excitement. "But I've always *believed* I could fly. All you have to do, children, is think nice thoughts." Riding above the fleecy mattress of clouds, Frankie was ready to deliver a star turn. The reference, however, was lost on the pilot. "Like Peter Pan," said Frankie in explanation.

"Peter Pan?"

"One of my favourite parts. Watch out for that cloud, Cap'n!"

"Well, we all know you from *Fish Out of Water,* of course," he said unapologetically. She obliged him with her catchphrase. I imagined him running his eyes up and down the passenger list for his next victim.

As the channel passed far beneath, Frankie chatted away as though she were interested: a master class in undivided admiration for her hero of the skies. As far as she was concerned, it was all for my benefit, but I could drum up no interest in the cockpit, its incomprehensible dials and its suntanned regent on his great leather throne. I stared over their shoulders at the empty sky. I was here only because she would have been disappointed if I had gone back to my seat, only to make sure that she was safe. I put my hand on her shoulder, and she looked up at me. *Isn't this great?* she asked silently. Somehow, she was in her element, up in the air, lost in the clouds, in Neverland.

At the door of the Villa Leopardi a woman, who introduced herself as Muria, curtsied and gave Frankie a posy. Frankie rewarded her with the delighted appreciation that was to accompany every one of the many occurrences of good service at the Leopardi. I was expecting some kind of registration process, but we were merely relieved of our cases and passports.

"A bottle of Prosecco?" Muria suggested in perfect English, generously offering us the run of the veranda with an understated sweep of her arm.

"Thank you," I said, as our feet crunched gravel, causing skeletal lizards to scuttle for shelter. We sat down at a table behind the house at the top of the steps that led down to the shore. An inconspicuous hotel employee immediately came to our aid, opening the umbrella to shield our eyes from the sun. Within moments, our bottle arrived, presented on a tray, which also contained glasses, an ashtray, three kinds of nut, and serviettes. I fumbled for my wallet, but the waiter brushed away my concerns; it was the last time I thought of money until the moment we left.

"This is the life, eh?" asked Frankie, letting her head fall back so the sun was full on her, glinting on her black sunglasses. "Can we really afford this?"

"Don't worry," I said. "Toast George."

By our second glass, I had ceased to consider the whereabouts of our bags or worry when we would be shown our room.

"Signore and Signorina Feesher," said a man with a Germanic accent, whose body's natural state was a deferential bow. "May I welcome you personally. I am Alberto Dilucca, the manager of the Villa Leopardi."

The three of us wasted no time looking at one another, gazing instead at the twinkling sea, as Dilucca politely enquired about our flight. I pictured the soldiers lying on the stony shore, waiting for orders, thinking of ways to kill time. Frankie asked for the ladies' room. Dilucca lifted a finger, at which another tall elegant burgundy ghost escorted her away. There was a silence that did not require breaking, but Dilucca did not leave, maintaining his half bow, staring at the sea, until my mother had disappeared into the house.

"Just one question, signore, to be quite certain. Your reservation; it says one room, two beds. We would hate to make a mistake."

"Yes, precisely. My mother . . ."

He lifted his hand in apology, requiring no explanation. "Perfetto," he said. "Mi scusi. Therefore, your room is ready."

So we settled into our week at the Villa Leopardi, where the outside world was easily forgotten. Every morning, we watched the removal of leaves that had had the temerity to fall during the night, then the raking of the gravel that they might possibly have disturbed. Our room itself was a mystery of artful, effortless perfection, from the seemingly self-replenishing supply of Prosecco and almond biscuits to the petals (which we had no alternative but to guiltily flush away) sprinkled daily in our toilet. Any loose clothing laid aside or absentmindedly dropped was cleaned and pressed by the evening, then returned to our wardrobe, in some cases in a better state than it had originally been bought. Messages from the hotel were left on the pillow, handwritten on elegant monogrammed notepaper adorned with a little ribbon fastened to the top corner with a pin.

It was as if this were all free — and much of it came with the price of the room. Everything else was on account, and there would be a healthy reckoning on the judgement day of departure, but the villa provided an atmosphere in which it felt unnecessarily strenuous to keep up with one's expenditure. And at night, the orchestra played from the bandstand, melodies shared by accordion and violin, accompanied only by the waves lapping at our feet as the stars shimmered above.

There was a little debate as to whether we should get our business out of the way early or leave it until the end. I knew the distance to the Ansalone house, and with much concerned help from the concierge — such as there was a concierge; the place was so elegant that there was barely even a front desk — I planned our route and even our mode of transport. The villa had apparently never before fielded a request for a motorbike with a sidecar, but it was the staff's avowed intent to create the illusion that everything was at their fingertips, so, although I saw a momentary cloud of concern pass over Fabrizio's face, I saw no more, and by the end of the third day, a splendidly old-fashioned dark green motorbike, complete with sidecar, was parked at our disposal in front of the villa. I didn't even think to wonder whether or how much it cost. The place did that to you.

Because the Ansalones were not expecting us, and when no phone number could be found for them in the local directory, we decided to interrupt our leisure right in the middle of the week. If they weren't there, we could leave them our address at the hotel, where they would still have three days to contact us. And as we waited, we whiled away the time by the swimming pool, where only the slow pan of the sun, and the irregular interruptions of hand-delivered gelato and ginger drinks, told us time was passing. Topless was the way to go, but Frankie was not seduced: "I'm not showing them on TV and I'm not showing them here either."

"Ricky wants to get back together," she murmured idly into the warm balsam air, as though she had been thinking about it for hours. "Says I'm right to trust my instincts." I didn't say anything. "But he should have known that all along, shouldn't he? Besides, my instincts should be his instincts, shouldn't they?"

She wanted to be in musicals, in pantomime, not situation comedies and sex romps — and we made a plan: no more family friends, no more agencies where Echo's name was still a valuable entrée. We would research who represented everyone Frankie admired, and Frankie, who still had a name and could, would meet with these agents one by one until she found the perfect candidate.

That evening, the timing was right. There was still more of the holiday remaining than we had already enjoyed. We had made our decisions about her work and were to transact our main business, including what I hoped would be a treat for Frankie, the next day.

When the sun finally exhausted itself, we waited for the abundant assortment of petit fours and candied fruits — *dainties*, Frankie always called them — that accompanied any order of tea or coffee, obviating the need for dessert. I excused myself, went up to the room, and fetched the photo album.

At the table, I reached for her hand; her eyes reflected the torches flickering around us. She had acquired a warm glow in the sun, her hair blonder than ever. When I put the photo album on the table between us, her moment's frown turned quickly into impish curiosity: more than anything else, she loved a surprise. I could think of nothing else to say. "My grandfather lent this to me."

She smiled at the mention of *grandfather,* but when she saw the name on the spine, her eyes closed; she subconsciously withdrew her hand from mine and inhaled asthmatically. When we touched again, she flinched as though there were static. Opening her eyes, she couldn't look at me and in her disorientation didn't know what to do. I shifted my chair over to hers and put my arm around her. Her head rested on my shoulder.

"Oh, Georgie, Georgie. We never found the right moment. It was always too late," she said, as she put her arms around me. "You've only me now."

"I know." I turned the album page by page, stroking her back, soothing her. The nightmare was over. She couldn't speak for some time, though she didn't cry.

In a pouch at the back of the album, there were some clippings. "Actors Drawn to School Charity Event," whispered a modest headline, above a photo of five people: a headmaster; Frankie, showing her dimples; Donald, the drama teacher; and two smiling children. "Had the boys been nervous working with seasoned professionals?" the paper asked of teacher "Donald Hartly." "They put us all at our ease. The kids listened to everything they said, and it was a real privilege for all of us." "It's a very worthy cause," said Frankie, who would be appearing in *Mother Goose* at Worthing.

She didn't need to read the piece. She remembered it quite well. She had loved his quiet way with the children, his calm, gentle authority. In some ways, it reminded her of her own father. She had been in no way prepared for her first experience of his depression. Whether it was brought on by their affair or its collapse, she couldn't remember: the whole thing was over before it began.

By the time she found out she was pregnant, she had realized that she was alone, that Donald, who was on permanent sick leave from his job, could offer no support. She had turned to Evie, of

course, as she did for everything. Evie had always encouraged
Frankie to come to her, to think of her first. And in return for this
loyalty, she fought tooth and nail for Frankie; most particularly,
for her career, the sum of Frankie's parts.

Evie, surveying the evidence at hand, had declared him, and
his entire sex, useless. That was what you got for straying outside
the theatre. He was a weak man, unworthy of her; it was Evie who
suggested that Des save the day. All Frankie's dreams played
second fiddle to her career. They could manage perfectly well
without Donald's help, and the baby would lack for nothing. They
all did what Evie said. She had never made any bones about
what Queenie was being punished for, why Sylvia was not the star
package Frankie was.

Frankie had never seen Donald again, though she had written,
care of his parents. Queenie had known nothing of Donald and was
allowed to draw her own conclusion about the pregnancy — the
charming theatrical entrepreneur, with the racing cars and centre
court tickets, who had taken such an interest in Frankie's career
and who indeed had charmed the girl on occasion. Nothing was
done to disabuse Queenie. No wonder Frankie had only shrugged
when told of his death. She had barely known the man, and she'd
never been in control of what Queenie told me. And suddenly,
there it was: the fiction became fact, something everyone knew,
though Frankie had never even commented upon it. Evie just
laughed. It was her and Frankie's secret. Queenie presumed that
the Upside fees had been donated by some similarly extravagant
benefactor.

Frankie murmured apologies, telling me what she remembered of my father, his illness, his hospitalization, the decisions
they had had to take about me. I told her about Donald, as I had
known him.

"Do you wish I'd told you?"

"I saw you at the funeral," I said. "You told me by not telling
me. But I didn't dare know. It was too lonely."

She didn't seem to hear me. "I wish I'd told you too," she
continued. "We were always waiting for a better moment: when

he was better, when Des was better, when Evie was better, when I was better." I had never heard her use the word *we* to mean, rather than the Fisher matriarchy, two parents who made mutual decisions they thought best for their son, for me. "It was never the right time, and then, when he was gone, I couldn't see the point. I just wanted everything to be as it had always been. I was afraid everything would change."

"I had to know."

"I know. And I'm glad you do. But . . ." She stared out at the sea, divided in half by a shimmering moon. Thoughts glimmered on her lips. "But I don't have to know. I don't want to know anything more than I already do. . . . In such a night, eh?" She looked at the twinkling stars, the faltering Christmas-tree lights strung above our heads, and, lost in the immeasurable, stroked her arm. She remembered what she was saying. "Dad . . . Donald . . . Des . . . Evie . . ." She paused at length between each name, telling me their stories in the silence — the father she never had; the invalid who couldn't look after us; the older man she didn't love who could; the woman who had delivered her a career and taught her secrecy, as if life, the whole play, could be manipulated from backstage, plotted and blocked. Frankie had known little else. "And then I thought we were losing you too, and I cursed him all over again for your inheritance; but you came back, and here we are. This is the beginning of a new life for me, a new career, a new family, a second chance. And I don't want to know anything more. I just want things to be like they are right now."

"Are you sure?"

"Yes."

"Nothing will change any more."

"Promise?"

"I promise."

The waiter approached almost apologetically with the tower of diminutive desserts.

"Fancy a dainty?" She laughed. "We'll tell Queenie. That was another thing the time was never right for. Poor Donald."

That night, we lay next to each other in our single beds. I remembered a conversation.

"Donald asked me about you once. It surprised me."

"What did you say?"

"I said you were like a character in a fairy story."

"Which one?" She smiled.

"That's what he asked too."

"Cinderella? I can't do housework; my feet are too big. Sleeping Beauty? Insomnia. Jack? I hate cows."

"Peter Pan, I said."

"What did he say?"

"He said, *I bet*."

After a few minutes, she asked sadly, "Have I outgrown Peter Pan, do you think?"

She needed Neverland. I pretended I was asleep.

"Good night, Georgie."

The next day, the day of our excursion, a lazy morning passed in a haze that threatened rain it did not deliver. At noon the clouds vanished and the irrepressible sun shone again. As we came downstairs, Muria dangled matching pairs of goggles in our direction. I showed her the contents of George's box, which she was considering in light of its relative size and the stowage options offered by our transportation.

"Ah, *pupazzo*," she said with politely suppressed distaste.

"Have no fear," I said. "He won't return. He'll have a new home here in Sicily."

Misinterpreting our feelings, she shook her head in disbelief, as if to say, *What pervert would want that hateful little incubus?* When the box was closed and strapped to the back of the bike with two bungee cords, Muria (convinced that she was now safe from the dummy's evil influence) stepped forward and, with a curtsy, offered us a paper bag containing two packed lunches lovingly wrapped in wax paper. We thanked her; "Nothing!" was her cheerful response.

The motorbike gave a throaty roar of approval as we left the grounds for the first time since our arrival, wreaking havoc on the recently raked gravel. Only three days into our stay, it was surprising to find a world beyond.

Frankie navigated, relying heavily on her own personal semaphore, though I could hear her perfectly well. It seemed appropriate to use old-fashioned hand signals, though I also had an indicator. "Young man," she shouted into the wind, in tribute to one of Queenie's oldest jokes, the one about the old woman on her first taxi ride through London, perplexed by the driver's hand signals, "you concentrate on the driving; I'll tell you whether it's raining or not."

The roads were exactly as I had imagined, wriggling hairpin turns, overhung with uncontrollable foliage. Every direction was uphill. We met few cars but found ourselves stuck behind a slow farm vehicle whose apologetic driver looked unhurriedly for somewhere we could pass. Free of him, I took the corners fast, as if making up for lost time. Frankie's captivation with the Villa Leopardi and its many luxuries had taken precedence over this, the excuse for our holiday, but she was having the time of her life behind her fighter ace goggles.

"Where did you learn to drive like this?" she shouted.

"Brenda!" I shouted back.

"Three cheers for Brenda!" she yelled, surrendering to the onrushing wind. It was magical mystery tour and switchback combined.

Three quarters of an hour later, after a few wrong turns, and a brief hiatus for an impromptu picnic when the view finally overwhelmed us, we turned through the Ansalone gate and found ourselves in low gear on a long steep driveway where the rays of the sun couldn't pierce the tunnel of soaring cypresses. This finally opened onto the circular driveway I recalled from the diary. At the top stood the house, looking a good deal newer than I had imagined it. Etna rose up behind a citrus orchard dotted with decrepit farm buildings; a dense arrangement of trees and rock obscured any view of the sea from the front of the house.

An old man was seated in a chair by a scullery door, peeling potatoes. As we came to a stop, he rose, leaning heavily on a stick, to alert those within that they had company.

"Lovely!" said Frankie in admiration, turning her goggles into a necklace. "How often does Vesuvius go off?" she asked, pointing. I had never seen her so relaxed and playful, except onstage with the child volunteers.

There was none of the dilapidation that Joe had described. The roof was newly tiled in neat parallel lines; beneath, each window frame fitted snugly into its surrounding stone. I tried to picture the house when a ladder had been the only access to the upper floor, and wondered through which of the windows Joe had hoisted the sleeping Valentina.

A woman with long grey hair opened the top of a Dutch door and called out to us in Italian. Her tone told us that unexpected visitors were rare. I walked towards her.

"Scusa. Non parlo Italiano. Signore Ettore Ansalone?"

"Ah! Un attimo, per favore!" she said, miming that she would go and find him. It was that simple. Here he was and here we were. The transaction was almost complete. She noticed the unfinished potatoes, slinging the peelings onto a small compost heap and taking the saucepan inside. I pinged the straps on George's box.

The familiar figure of Ansalone emerged, blinking in the sun as he stooped to get through the door, wiping his hands on a tea towel. The older woman stood behind him, peering over his shoulder, unsure whether to accompany him or not, presumably deterred by her lack of English.

"Ah!" he said, and turned to her and explained. She scuttled back into the kitchen, and he approached, slinging the tea towel over his shoulder. "Mr. Fisher," he said in welcome, but with the guarded smile of a gentleman who does not like to be taken by surprise. "My apologies. Did I miss a letter from you? Should we be expecting you?" His eyes fluttered around, settling not on Frankie or the bike, but on George's box.

"No, I should be the one to apologize for the intrusion." I spoke formally and slowly, so there was no miscommunication.

"We are on holiday, and having considered your generous offer, I thought I could take the opportunity to deliver by hand."

He cast his eyes over our mode of transport, before giving it his cautious seal of approval. "Very . . . *intrepid*, I think is the word? But on such a lovely day, why not? And this is?" He held out his hand in greeting.

"My mother. Frankie."

"Surely not *mother*," he said as though the word had only negative connotations, taking Frankie's hand and kissing it. "But, Signore Fisher, there is a difficulty, a problem." He furrowed his brow, shrugged in apology, and gestured to the box. "I am delighted to know your acceptance of my offer, but . . ." He showed us his empty palms and then pulled the linings from his pockets. "I am afraid that not even I can produce such money out of thin air. We were not expecting you."

"Nothing up your sleeve?" Frankie asked him with a smile.

"Nothing, dear lady, I assure you."

"Of course; I understand," I said. "We are staying at the Villa Leopardi until Sunday. . . ."

"Leopardi!" said Ansalone in admiration, as if the word itself were a delicious homemade sauce.

". . . and you can find us there, or perhaps draft the money directly to England through your bank."

"Yes, yes. What am I thinking? You wait. You have come all this way, and I would like to invite you . . . We are in the middle of . . ." He whipped the tea towel from his shoulder as though this explained everything. "Un attimo, per favore."

"Charming man," whispered Frankie, as he walked back into the scullery, closing the door behind him.

"He seemed to like you."

"George! Anyway, lost to womankind, I'm afraid," she said, twanging her goggles. "I came third, after the dummy and the bike! Will you leave George here?"

"I think Ansalone's good for it."

Ansalone reemerged, this time through the portico of the front door, and ushered us within. The interior was perfectly restored. We sat at a large circular kitchen table, a huge slab of highly polished wood. Frankie leaned back in wonder to see the arched ceiling through the ruff of banisters two storeys above.

"Ah, yes," he said, stamping on the floor to demonstrate the durability of the house. "Many, many years of restoration. The house was practically destroyed in the second war." Ansalone opened a bottle of white wine as the grey-haired woman prepared a small plate of food. "This is my sister," he said. Frankie caught my eye surreptitiously, confirming her previous analysis — unmarried man, living with sister — as the sister smiled in greeting and placed a bowl of olives before us. "Chiara. I'm afraid she doesn't speak English." Chiara sat down, although her folded arms told us that this was only a momentary respite from other tasks. As we exchanged pleasantries, she let her hair fall through her fingers, twirling it gently. What was she seeing, this once silent girl whose cascade of petals from the floors above had taken Joe by surprise, when she looked at us, his family? It was as though, despite the renovation of the house, I was going back in time.

"May I?" asked Ettore with a gleam in his eyes, once the wine was poured.

"Of course. Consider him yours now."

He rubbed his hands together, with a suggestive smile for our benefit, and pulled George from his box, nodding as he did. He sat him on his knee. What was at first a look of boyish enthusiasm slowly gave way to the ruthless eye of appraisal. "Excuse me," he said, as he bent George forwards, pulled aside his clothes, and shone a small torch into his back. Quite satisfied with whatever he saw, he continued his medical with the manipulation of each separate piece of the mechanism: the salute pleased him particularly. As this went on, Chiara drifted away from the table and, picking up the rest of the unfinished potatoes, disappeared into the farther reaches of the house as we sat in silent observation. Ettore indicated George's blazer indifferently.

"The clothes?" he said.

"The original Romando clothes. Restored, of course, like your house."

"We had thought he was in the museum."

"A long story," I said apologetically.

"Not the uniform?" asked Ansalone, without criticism.

"A long story. Not in our possession, but we know where it is. Does that change . . . ?"

"Niente, niente," said Ansalone dismissively. He smoothed George's trousers, feeling the replacement metal legs, the wire joints. "Sì, sì." He smiled in approval. "Perfetto." I was surprised that the prosthetic additions, which seemed a potential draw-back, since they were clearly not the Romando originals, didn't bring out the haggler in him. But it was the faces these experts wanted.

"We have a deal," he concluded. "A wonderful deal."

"It's an awful lot of money," said Frankie, the voice of reason.

"For a very remarkable *ragazzo* . . . boy," said Ansalone, as though she needed to be persuaded to let him pay it all. Perhaps he suspected her of cold feet.

"A boy!" said Frankie. "That's what my family has always called them. How did you become interested in ventriloquism?"

I saw my moment.

"My mother doesn't know," I interjected quickly. "I think she'd like to hear the story."

Ansalone glanced at me, chewing the inside of his cheek.

"What don't I know?" she asked, willingly teased.

"Yes." He laughed. "What doesn't your mother know?"

"About how your interest began."

"Va bene . . ." He gave a laugh from which I inferred that I had put him in an awkward position, though I couldn't see why. "The story of ventriloquism and me is quite well known. . . ." And he told a bland but charming tale, aimed specifically at Frankie, about his life in wartime Sicily, how his skill at ventrilo-quism and magic had helped his family survive: first the Italians and the Germans, then the Allies, and through it all the Mafia themselves — where there was laughter, there was hope.

Why, when I had specifically asked him, did he feel he had to lie? Why did he think that he could make no mention of her father, the ENSA performer who had sat where we were sitting now, who had a dummy on whom Ettore had showered a series of bizarre gifts? His caginess made me ill at ease; there were two Ettore Ansalones, and this one was as strange as the one in the dressing room.

"What a lovely idea," said Frankie. "My father entertained the troops in Italy too. He was decorated for it."

"I know. As of course was George," said Ansalone matter-of-factly. "Don't think that my offer is made naively. I am not an amateur. I know everything about this little boy, even his serial number. I am surprised only that you will sell him to me, though of course I do not discourage you. I will show where he is going to live. Come with me. Come."

Following Ansalone up the elegant curve of the staircase, my hand on the cool of the marble rail, I caught sight of a terrace through the large window that faced the volcano. There I saw Chiara talking to the man who had been peeling the potatoes. Light glinted on them from a clear blue swimming pool.

"Here," he said, as he reached for a key to the door of the room directly above the kitchen, "is where George will rest. It is, how you say, my life's work."

He flicked on a row of switches; first the room was bathed in the glow of indirect museum light. Then bulbs shone with search-light precision on the various display cases and show posters that surrounded us.

"Welcome to my lair, Mr. Bond," said Frankie with a wink. "How unexpected. You're quite the collector. Very much our family history too. I wish Queenie were here."

"Some men like skiing; others, if you will forgive me, keep mistresses. This is my vice. May I show you? For example, this" — he turned on one final light — "is where I will put George. I think you particularly will like this, Mr. Fisher." In this central case, there was only one dummy, but there was room for two. "This beautiful girl, in her delightful riding gear, is Belle. American. Kember of Chicago, 1934. Absolutely unique."

"Yes, she is lovely," said Frankie. "Isn't she, Georgie?"

She was. I had never seen her before and I felt like George in Duke Duval's waiting room the moment he laid eyes on her: his dream, his able equestrienne. I caught sight of a small accompanying framed portrait of Bobbie with Belle, on a London stage, happy, alive.

George (Joe) had written that he knew he would see her again: "You are dead. And I will soon be dead too. Find me in Paradise, where we shall never be parted. I know you will. Arrivederci." George's story was done. Somehow he had known that they would be reunited. And here they would be, finally: an appropriately bizarre double grave for such impossible lovers. George and Belle next to each other for eternity: were we in Paradise? Sicily had seemed a paradise from the Villa Leopardi — and given all I had read in the diary, this was a kind of happy ending, yet it left me distinctly uncomfortable. Had Ansalone gone to the ends of the earth to find Belle? How had he known to? How had he known where to go?

"Georgie?"

I couldn't answer, and I felt the indigestive nausea that had occasionally accompanied my failed attempts to speak. Ansalone, who noticed the change in me, began to explain something for Frankie's benefit, as if diverting her attention. I couldn't communicate to her the shock of seeing Belle. I submitted to a nagging chain of thoughts, what ifs — the presence of Belle in pride of place in this museum, the sum of money Tower had offered, the familiar nature of his stage act, his behaviour in the dressing room, his reluctance to tell Frankie his memories of her father, even his lack of complaint about the prosthetic legs. What was it all telling me? One thing was certain: I hadn't even bothered to consider that Ansalone might know about the diaries, that he was prepared to pay so much for George because he wanted them. How could he possibly have known? Would Joe have told the

Ansalone family? It was absurd. And, come to that, what would
Ansalone do when he found the diary was missing?

There was only one conclusion that made sense of everything.
I needed time.

"Georgie?"

Small talk was out of the question. I couldn't summon the so-
cially correct response, and my reaction, dragged from me, was
inappropriately dismissive. I wanted to be alone, to think things
through. Above all, there was Frankie. I hadn't meant to drag her
into this, thinking only that she would be charmed by happy tales
of a wartime friendship with her father. And if I was right about
the conclusion to which the facts pointed, how could everything
stay the same for beautiful Frankie, as she had asked, as I had
promised?

"And this is where we shall put George, of course," said Ansalone. "Next to Belle."

"I'll go and get him," I said.

"No, no, not yet. Certainly not until the transaction is complete, and, of course, George will have an appointment in my
workshop before any such ceremony can take place." Ansalone
led my mother persuasively by the arm to the far corner of the
room. "Now, this, signorina, you really will be interested in. . . ."

My heart was beating faster, unbearably faster, until I calmed
myself by repeating my conclusion slowly, over and over. I wanted
to eliminate it on the grounds of being impossible. But it wasn't.
It was just horrible. And it was the only answer.

Ansalone was showing off a wall full of historic photographs
of various ventriloquists and conjurers. Amongst them, I spotted
a black-and-white picture of a young Joe, sitting on a well in the
marketplace, smoking a cigarette; next to him was a young boy
working a dummy too big for him. Frankie, charmed by everything
she saw around her, was oblivious to this needle in the haystack:
she wasn't looking for evidence of her father, as I was. Ansalone
insisted on bringing it to her attention. It was as though the wine
had gone to my head.

"And you know this one, I think," he said, pointing to the photograph.

"Georgie!" said Frankie with delight. "It's Dad."

"Yes," said Ansalone. He pulled out a portfolio and flicked idly through some ENSA handbills. "Very famous in Italy in the war. Here you see, Joe Fisher and George, in Bari. Also on the bill, the night before, Echo Endor. A little piece of family history, I think. I give this to you."

"Thank you," she said, humbled.

There was silence as we looked at Joe.

I was convinced. There was one thing left to find out.

"Is he forgotten in Italy now?" I asked with care.

"Oh, yes," said Ansalone. "I'm afraid so, quite forgotten. As with many of the war entertainers, forgotten by the whole world."

"Yet still alive in *this* house," I said as casually as I could, aware of a constriction in my throat that I had to cough away.

"Yes, as you see." He told me what I feared. "And in yours?"

"Gone but not forgotten," Frankie said.

Ansalone considered this, looked at me, and turned his attention back to the photo. "And if you know him, then you know this one," he said, pointing to George as Frankie smiled. "And then perhaps you can guess this one here?" He pointed, with the edge of the nail of his little finger, to the boy. I stood back and watched like a hawk, considering the best course of action. "This piccolo Ettore." They had met. He'd lied about this before, but now he seemed ready to reveal everything.

"It can't be — yes, yes, I can see!" said Frankie. "Well, of course you want George. I understand everything."

Ansalone took the rest of the tour exquisitely slowly, unlocking cases and cooing over treasures, demanding a response Frankie was in the mood to provide. I stood off. It was taking far longer than it needed. The air was close, and I wished I had an ornate silver wristwatch I could glance at and insist that we had to be getting along.

"It is a rare pleasure to have an appreciative audience," said

Ansalone in conclusion as he adjusted the dial on the humidifier and turned off the lights. "It is so sad not to share it more often." He locked the door behind him. We went back downstairs, where George was waiting for us at the kitchen table.

"I wonder where is Chiara," he said, and excused himself.

"He's an obsessive," whispered Frankie with enthusiasm. "Take the money and run." I couldn't answer. "Are you all right, Georgie?" I smiled but could say nothing. "Sad to see him go?" I nodded.

Ansalone returned momentarily with some sheets of paper and a pen. "Before you go, two things: we need to make a receipt for George, acknowledging that you agree to pass ownership to me, after the payment, naturally. I would like also, if I may, to ask you to write out an invoice for me for his sale, for Italian-tax purposes; perhaps you could give as many details of the . . . provenienza . . ."

"Provenance?" suggested Frankie.

"The provenance, as you know. Perhaps Signorina Fisher would like to take a walk through the front gardens while you do this. I can show her some most beautiful fruits." He offered her his arm graciously.

"How could I resist some fruit?" said Frankie.

Still unsure of Ansalone's motives, I hesitated, not knowing what to do. I didn't want the two of them together, but it was clear that he was leaving me alone on purpose.

"Mr. Fisher," said Ansalone seriously. "I can assure you that Miss Fisher is quite safe with me. In my protection." Frankie raised an arch eyebrow in recognition of this overly courteous proclamation, putting it down to imperfect English. He bowed to me and took her through the front door.

I knew where to go. The moment the door closed, I walked to the terrace at the back of the house. Stepping outside, I saw the profile of the man who had been peeling potatoes, his saucepan now set down next to a colander of peelings. His hand was on a walking stick propped against his chair, his other holding an un-opened book. A deep scar, partly lost in the folds of age, marked the left side of his face, stretching as far down as his neck, as permanent as the fissures on the face of the mountain at which he was staring. Chiara sat next to him, twirling her hair, stroking his arm.

"Joe," I said. He didn't answer, eyes obscured behind sunglasses. He swallowed too often.

"No," said Chiara firmly. "Salvatore. *Turi*."

He took his hand from his stick and firmly clasped her upturned wrist. Turi. I'd only ever seen the name once before — the dead brother they had buried in the back garden so they could still collect his food rations.

"I'm Frankie's son, your grandson," I said, disbelieving my own calm, as though I were dreaming, as though I had somehow stepped back into the pages of the diary that only I had read, as though I were finishing it. "Named after George. I read your books: card tricks, escapology, disappearing acts, voice throwing. I found George's memoir."

He nodded, without turning to me, and said nothing. A smile crept across his lips, a remorseful smile not meant for me. Still there were no words. I filled the silence with his imagined thoughts: the life lost to him, the family he had fled, the lie in which he had taken refuge, the ghost he had become, the grandson he had imagined and to whom he had spoken across decades. Here I was by his side, his sole reader.

He gestured with his right hand. Chiara scampered off and returned with a pen and paper: she couldn't be insisting on the transfer of ownership and the receipt? That had surely been Ansalone's diversion so he could remove my mother.

"Non parla," she said, and put her hand over her mouth. The old man reached out for the pen and paper and looked for something to lean on. He didn't talk? Since when? Since the war, the war in which he hadn't died? Since illness, cancer, old age? He was younger than Queenie but seemed twice her age, his skin spotted and wrinkled by the sun. Chiara handed him a magazine.

"My mother is here. She knows nothing." I saw my face reflected in his sunglasses.

Four or five different thoughts danced on the end of his pen, but he could commit to none of them. I wouldn't have recognized him from the old pictures. It was not just the scar and the deep clefts: he was changed, wrung out, a faint echo. Was this what he had always wanted, to be emptied out, everything exterior to him? He had won. He had escaped. But now he couldn't project at all — he was dying, unburdening himself of his dying words. Even his own daughter, who knew the same photos, wouldn't have known him. Nor would she have the chance.

He hushed Chiara, who was trying to speak. Because I couldn't say it out loud, even in front of his uncomprehending wife, I snatched the pen and paper from his hand and wrote: "You have been dead for many years. You can't speak through me. We have been happy without you."

I put the pen and paper back in his hand.

He had been a dead grandfather, a missing father, a cowardly husband, a spineless son, an AWOL entertainer. He couldn't exist now.

He handed me a piece of paper, written on it: "Tell them I'm sorry."

How could I when he was dead? I shook my head and walked away.

The empty house was murky, echoing like a tomb. The sunlight beyond was a relief, and when I saw my mother and Ansalone walking arm in arm down the drive on their way back, I ran towards them.

"Georgie!" shouted Frankie, who was holding a basket of fresh fruit. "You should see Ettore juggle oranges!" She unhooked herself from her companion. "Thank you so much, Ettore. A lovely walk."

"It's all done," I said. "Time to go."

"Do you know the way home?" asked Ansalone. "Downhill diretto," he said, slicing the air with his hand. "Always straight. Always down."

I saw Frankie into the sidecar, allowing her a fond good-bye with our host and indicating that I had some final business with him.

"Thank you," he said, walking me off to a safe distance. "One final thing: I think you are a magician yourself, practising a little sleight of hand. Some *papers* are missing."

"I removed them myself, not knowing they were of interest to you. But now I see that they belong with George. I will send them to you with some books for . . ."

". . . my brother? If so, God, and *il dottore,* advise speed. May I visit you at the hotel before you leave to complete the transaction?"

"No, you will never see us again." I couldn't rid myself of the image of the old man's hand crawling across the page. His writing had been childish, spidery, like his mother's when she had arthritis. "Go to the hotel on Sunday evening after our departure and pay our bill. That's all I want."

"You are sure?"

"That's more than he's worth. My family is happy to be rid of him."

"But you speak in haste. If you have second thoughts, you know where we live. We are in your debt."

I got on the motorbike and revved the engine. Frankie squealed as we took the first corner downhill.

As the last sorbet melted away into a puddle of mint and lime, I wrote Sylvia the note I had been composing for years, and Brenda the postcard that would arrive long after I saw her. I ordered a final bottle of Prosecco from a gliding burgundy coat.

"There's one free in the fridge in the room, you know," tutted Frankie. I had thought she was asleep.

"I'm down here, though."

"Very swish." She hadn't opened her eyes.

"Anyway, Ansalone is paying for the hotel," I said. "I drive a hard bargain."

"He was such a nice man."

I thought about this for a moment.

"Yes, he was. Actually, he's *just* paying for the hotel: that's the deal I gave him."

"What about the five thousand pounds?" she asked without great concern.

"I told him this was all we wanted. He said I could reconsider."

"You haggled him *down?*" She didn't care either way. It had always been ridiculous: Fishers knew that money didn't grow on trees. "*Ice*-cold negotiation," she said, balancing her glass on the flattest piece of grass available. "Reg'll be disappointed, though," she added and laughed.

"Anyway," I thought aloud, "if the money was going anywhere, it should really go to that poor old git who runs the Armed Forces Museum. He's the one who thinks he bought George."

Frankie wasn't listening. "Easy come, easy go. We had this lovely holiday. I could get used to this. I feel invigorated. Something's going to pop up — I just know it." Around us, the staff efficiently closed large sunshades, securing them with velvet sashes. Places were set for dinner beneath the striped marquee. "How about you, Georgie?"

I sat up. They were lighting candles to keep the early-evening mosquitoes at bay. "I'm going to go and see my grandfather. I need career advice."

"It's nice you finally having a grandfather, isn't it? Two, in fact. Can't wait to see Queenie and Reg. Let's buy them something nice from the hotel shop."

"Put it on the room."

"Anything else you'd like, sir?" enquired a previously inconspicuous employee.

"Mum?"

"No," she said. "Everything is perfect. Simply heaven."

The sun was sinking. By this time tomorrow, we'd be home.

Acknowledgements

Particular thanks to Jennifer Rudolph Walsh, Judy Clain, Olivia de Dieuleveult, Dan Franklin, Christopher Stace, Nigel Hinton, Mark Linington, Lid Paris, Edoardo Brugnatelli, Anik LaPointe, Rachel Cugnoni, Nick Hornby, Amanda Posey, David Grand, Melanie Stace, and Molly Townson. Thanks also to Tracy Fisher, Eugenie Furniss, Alicia Gordon, Caroline Michel, and everyone at William Morris; Michael Pietsch, Sophie Cottrell, Amanda Erickson, Betsy Uhrig, and everyone at Little, Brown; Patrice Hoffmann, Camille Germain, Charlotte Ajame, Gilles Haeri, and everyone at Flammarion; and everyone at Jonathan Cape and Vintage.

My grandfather Clifford King Townson died in 1954. He was a ventriloquist and a member of ENSA; his dummy (who survives and is pictured on the front cover) was called George; there the similarities with Joe Fisher end. My mother provided me with clippings about my grandfather's life, his various copies of *Magical Digest*, *The Demon Telegraph*, and *Goodliffe's Abracadabra*, as well as a journal that contained some of his scripts and performance notes. The Longfellow quotation was printed on his brochure.

Of the books mentioned in *by George,* the following are real: *The Life and Adventures of Valentine Vox the Ventriloquist* by Henry Cockton, first published in 1840 and a massive bestseller; *Bunter the Ventriloquist* by Frank Richards, a late flowering of the same tradition. All mention of Charles Brockden Brown's *Wieland* has been edited out, but the influence of this bizarre ventriloquial text remains, all the more bizarre for being "the first published novel by the first native-born American author to make a profession of, and a living by, writing" (from Jay Fliegelman's introduction to the Penguin paperback, which pairs it with *Memoirs of Carwin the Biloquist*). The Ventrilo ad appeared about five times (in various guises) in a 625-page Johnson Smith & Co. catalogue. All other books mentioned are fictional.

The literature of ventriloquism is a mixed bag. Particularly useful were *Dumbstruck* by Steven Connor, *I Can See Your Lips Moving* by Valentine Vox (no relation), and Stanley Burns's beautifully illustrated but catastrophically copyedited *Other Voices: Ventriloquism from B.C. to T.V.* Ventriloquial advice, mostly to do with the upkeep of George himself (who turns out to be a Quisto, rather than an Insull, on whom the character of Romando was very loosely based), was kindly given by Alan Semok and Lisa Sweasy (curator of the Vent Haven Museum, Fort Mitchell, Kentucky).

It's Behind You by Peter Lathan and *Oh Yes It Is!* by Gerald Frow were both helpful as references for Frankie's pantomimes; a selection of my sister's e-mails was best of all. For Vox and Echo's world, I turned to the sturdy literature of the music hall, including *Music Hall Parade* by M. Willson Disher, *Working the Halls* by Peter Honri, and *A Hard Act to Follow* by Peter Leslie. For the Drolls and variety beyond, all I needed were the collected works of Bill Pertwee: *Promenades and Pierrots, Beside the Seaside,* and his autobiography, *A Funny Way to Make a Living.* Of particular use for Joe's World War II were *Fighting for a Laugh* by Richard Fawkes, *As You Were* by Douglas Byng, *Stars in Battledress,* also by Bill Pertwee, and the reminiscences and letters of Joyce Grenfell: *The Time of My Life, Darling Ma,* and *Joyce Grenfell Requests the Pleasure.*

Thanks, most of all, to Abbey and Tilda Stace.

BACK BAY · READERS' PICK

Reading Group Guide

by
George

A Novel by

Wesley Stace

Res Ipsa Loquitur

Wesley Stace on the origins of *by George*

I should admit that ventriloquism runs in my family.

I never met my grandfather, Cliff Townson — he died when my mother was twelve — but I knew his dummy. George (his name, by no coincidence) was a constant feature of my childhood, often perched on my grandmother's knee. He now sits on the piano in my front room in Brooklyn. I thought my baby daughter would be scared of him — his glazed eyes, his lead-paint skin, his fright wig — but quite the opposite: she seemed to spot a kindred spirit, or at least someone her own size.

Between then and now, however, George went missing. My grandfather's magical effects were scattered among the family, a rather complicated family it turned out, and so I started writing letters. It was during my search that I came up with the story for *by George*. What if, when I found him, George had something to tell me: about my family, its history, its secrets and lies? What if, basically, he could talk? And if he had a story to tell, who'd be doing the talking? Would it be a magical realist world where wood talks — anything is possible in fiction — or would someone else be speaking for him? And, in a family, who ever speaks for himself?

Of course, the truth was all rather mundane: he turned up, money changed hands, and now he's propped on my piano, a conversation (or apology) waiting to happen. But he rarely goes unmentioned. "I hadn't noticed that dummy till this morning," read an e-mail from a houseguest who was staying in our absence, "and if you say, 'What dummy?' you'll really freak me out."

Why, besides nostalgia, was I looking for George in the first place?

I read a review — a famous review, endlessly quoted — of Peter Carey's novel *The True Story of the Kelly Gang* describing it as "a dazzling act of literary ventriloquism." The phrase stuck: it was such a good way to think of writing. If all novels are ventriloquism, Dickens was clearly the greatest ventriloquist of all: you never see his lips moving.

But where therefore was the novel that took the metaphor at face value? Nothing sprang to mind — surprising for such fertile subject matter. (In fact, the very first novel written by a professional American writer, *Wieland,* by Charles Brockden Brown [1798], hinges on the unlikely talents of the sinister Carwin, even though Brown himself didn't quite seem to understand what ventriloquism was, let alone explain how it was done. But he had other fish to fry: the novel, with its companion piece *Memoirs of Carwin the Biloquist,* asks the very novelish question: "Where does the authorial voice come from, and whence does it derive its authority?" It was described by Steven Connor, in his excellent ventriloquistry, *Dumbstruck,* as "the first and last examples of this minority genre." No longer the last. . . .)

I started learning about ventriloquism's origins in religious mystery, in the divination of communication with the dead; and the Pythian Oracle at Delphi, who, amid a lot of smoke and mirrors, uttered the god's words in an incomprehensible frenzy — she wasn't a very good ventriloquist. These necromancers, Edgar Bergen before Charlie McCarthy, were called engastrimyths — literally, *in-belly-speakers*: the only way to explain the voice that seemed not to come from the mouth. Over the years, the meaning of ventriloquism changed from "the state of being possessed by a voice" to "the production of a voice that is 'thrown' elsewhere." In the mid-nineteenth century, the art was at its zenith, its powerful, anarchic best, a huge crowd-puller: with only the power of his voice, a ventriloquist had dominion over unbounded space.

And then came the dummy: the perfect portable visual aid. The character of the boy captured the ventriloquist's voice and the audience's attention. Ventriloquism became a slick portable double act, the drama of which depended on the ventriloquist's natural voice versus his assumed voice, and the psychological interplay between the two. As the prop took over, the ventriloquist became the straight man: the boy killed his father.

So recently a crowd-pleaser — think of Bergen's fame on the radio in America, Charlie's verbal sparring with W. C. Fields, Great Britain's own Archie Andrews, voted the top radio personality of 1959: and think about *that* for a second — ventriloquism's stock is now at an all-time low, a quaint, even slightly seedy parlor trick, in constant need of a reinvention that no one can quite pull off.

Freud's to blame. Ventriloquism was damaged irreparably by the arrival of the evil dummy. My interest lay beyond this cliché, popularized by the movies, of the ventriloquist's id: Hugo (*Dead of Night*), Fats (*Magic*), Billy (the recent *Dead Silence*), and Chucky (*Child's Play 1, 2, 3*, etc., not to mention *Bride*, and then, *Seed of Chucky* . . .).

The themes and structure of a novel were clear enough — there was even a murder (though I didn't go there) — but I had no characters; nothing that makes a novel worth reading or writing.

And that's when I decided to track down the family heirloom, my old friend George. If he was sitting in the room, encouraging me with his antique, scruffy, roguish charm, he might inspire the novel where ventriloquism got to speak for itself. All I needed was the quest to find him. By the time he made his belated appearance, I had the plot and its people — a family spanning one hundred years of entertainment via vaudeville, music hall, ENSA [Britain's version of the USO] in World War II, summer seasons, pantomime, the birth of television, and the death of the variety show. It's a family of constant chatter and song, where silence is interpreted as unhappiness, where the women rule and the men are boys, just like George himself.

And so *by George,* written by two Georges, each trying to be heard above the din of their family: one a very chatty dummy in the 1930s — he could only ever be called George — recounting the ups and downs of his career, from papier-mâché mix to

unlikely war hero; the other a withdrawn and eccentric schoolboy in the 1970s who, in the search for a voice of his own, finds a
paper trail leading straight to the dummy, now on mute display in
a dusty museum, still holding the key to the family secrets, just
waiting to be asked.

Questions and topics for discussion

1. Wesley Stace's *by George* is narrated by two boys named George Fisher: one is made of wood, one of flesh. How do they echo each other? Why do you think they part at the end?

2. The book follows a motley cast of characters across generations of the entertainment industry, from vaudeville to television. Which characters and settings did you most identify with?

3. The first epigraph of the novel is from Henry Wadsworth Longfellow:

   Imaginations, fantasies, illusions,
   In which the things that cannot be take shape,
   And seem to be, and for the moment are.

   In what ways can these lines apply both to the tricks of a magician and the techniques of a novelist?

4. George grows up in a household ruled by women. How do you suppose this environment affected George in his upbringing? What are the different female archetypes that appear in *by George*? Where else do gender dynamics crop up in the novel?

5. Like his grandson George, Joe Fisher grew up without a father. In what ways does this common feature make these two Fishers similar, and how do they remain essentially different? How do George's feelings about his grandfather change, and what do you make of George's opinion of him at the end of the book?

6. Did you think at any point that you, as a reader, were meant to know things about George that he himself hadn't realized or that he knew but couldn't admit to himself?

7. Family secrets play a large role in the novel — to George, they seem to be everywhere. When, if ever, were the characters best served by maintaining a family secret? Which secrets were most damaging? In what sorts of situations is maintaining a lie defensible or necessary? Do you consider the novel's ending a "happy" one?

8. Magic works when an audience is convinced by a magician's technique — something impossible seems to occur on the stage. Can this book be said ever to venture into magical realism, or does the author keep us firmly within the limits of ordinary reality? What would you have thought if the author of the "wooden" George's story were never revealed?

9. Frankie Fisher often takes roles in the Pantomime, "a mysterious upside-down world" where old men play ugly women and beautiful women play handsome young men. Why is Frankie particularly suited to the role of Principal Boy, and where else does role reversal occur in the novel?

10. In the essay at the beginning of this reading group guide, Stace hypothesizes that in some ways all writing is ventriloquism. To what extent do you agree, and why or why not? What are some examples of books where one can "see the author's lips moving," so to speak, and what sorts of books most successfully pull off the illusion?

Also by Wesley Stace
Misfortune

"*Misfortune* reads like some inspired collaboration between Charles Dickens and Pedro Almodóvar: full of orphans, decadence, flouncy skirts, greed, deception, amnesia, incest, murder, religious and social intolerance, ballads, books, letters, wild farce, and all manner of meditation on sexual identity."
— Rodney Welch, *Washington Post*

"Sparkling . . . loopily Dickensian . . . poignantly and mordantly funny. . . . Stace has written a very jolly picaresque. . . . A most auspicious debut." — Alexis Soloski, *Village Voice*

"I laughed, I cried, I swooned — I even got the hiccups, though I don't think those were caused by *Misfortune*. I loved this book very much. Do try it."
— Audrey Niffenegger, author of *The Time Traveler's Wife*

"Gloriously funny. . . . *Misfortune* is near perfect, a bold and memorable tale of buried secrets and haunting dreams, and a story that is never less than fantastically readable."
— Christopher Schobert, *Buffalo News*

"At last, an out-of-the-box, truly original storyteller promises to soar above the literary horizon, all because he wrote the kind of book he liked reading." — Skye K. Moody, *Seattle Times*

Back Bay Books
Available wherever paperbacks are sold